WHAT IS TO BE DONE?

LIFE

LYOF N. TOLSTOÏ

WHAT IS TO BE DONE?

LIFE

WILDSIDE PRESS

PREFACE TO "WHAT IS TO BE DONE?"

THE misery and sufferings of the very poor, in the so-called "slums," have a family resemblance in all the great cities of the world. The special feature which characterizes the old capital of Russia over and above the general features of that problem in our great American cities, or in London for example, is, that the poor are, almost exclusively, Russians, instead of a conglomeration of foreigners whom the law, ill-calculated ambition, or the spirit of restlessness, have driven out of their native lands.

These poor Russians, of whom the great Russian novelist and philanthropist writes in the pages of "What is to be Done?" are, in a great measure, the victims of the Emancipation of the Serfs. The Emancipation was, beyond question, not only righteous and beneficent, but a profoundly wise administrative measure. Nevertheless, the conditions were such that the owners of estates have suffered severely, though cheerfully, in company with their former serfs, in consequence of that measure. Some of the problems on the parts of both masters and serfs have gradually solved themselves, to a greater or less degree, in the generation which has elapsed since the Emancipation. Other problems have only become more complicated — notably the one herein dealt with. The peasant is still bound to the soil by the very real fetter of taxes for the current expenses of government, and, in many cases also, for the instalments of payment for the land which he received with his freedom. This communal burden he can neither escape nor evade; yet, at the same time, the allotments of communal land grow constantly smaller through periodical subdivision to comply with the rights of the rapidly increasing population. Thus the peasant's dues often increase, while his means of meeting them decrease through no fault of his or of the authorities. The efforts of the government to extend educational facilities, and the earnest desire of the peasants themselves for more and higher education, impose still further burdens. In order to meet all these obligations, the peasants with insufficient land swarm to the capitals and join the already congested ranks of the landless peasants, handicraftsmen, and others in search of work.

Moscow probably receives a larger number of such involuntary wanderers than St. Petersburg, simply because it is nearer the agricultural region than the latter. Therefore the picture which Count Tolstoy presents may be regarded as setting forth the Russian situation at its very worst. There are, it is true, many factories in and around Moscow, and in a multitude of other places in the empire. But they are far from sufficient in number to meet the exigencies of the case. Indeed, in what country do they meet the exigencies of the case? Emigration to the rich mining regions of Siberia will do much to relieve the peasants, but, even there, there have arisen fresh problems; and, even now, with the railway and vastly increased facilities of every description, Siberia is not the place for penniless immigrants, because of natural difficulties connected with distances, and the primary requisites of wood, water, and the like.

At the time when this book was written (1886) even this outlet did not exist in such a degree as to justify its being taken into consideration; and for other reasons there can hardly be much change in the Moscow slums for many a day to come.

One must have seen and talked with the poor of Moscow in order fully to realize the pictures which wrung Count Tolstoy's heart, and which he offers to us as the Russian contribution to the World's Exposition of Wretchedness. Wealthy Russians of all classes are pitiful and extremely generous with their money for all good works. They are equally generous with their personal labors. It is the custom for wealthy merchants (who, more than the nobility, keep up certain ancient traditions) to bequeath large sums to free soup-kitchens and night lodging-houses. The recipient of the bounty murmurs a prayer for the soul of his benefactor as he eats the generous portion of savory cabbage-soup and hulled boiled buckwheat (kasha), and sour, black rye bread, which is provided. That is one form of relief — only temporary of course; and also, of course, in Russia, as elsewhere, there are people who prefer a wretched, precarious existence to systematic labor.

One of the many more vigorous and extensive efforts to cope with the misery of Moscow, which I might cite, is a free, permanent lodging-house for widows and their children, with the most approved and modern arrangements for cooking and washing enjoyed in common by all the inhabitants. There is even a private church, with its priest, in the house. This princely gift to his town by a Moscow merchant-prince is only one of many noble deeds of men who do their good deeds with absolute modesty. But the problem of misery still remains unsolved, except in tiny oases.

The history of this present translation is interesting. The publication of Count Tolstoy's Manuscript in its entirety was not permitted in Russia. A firm in Switzerland, which makes a business of printing forbidden books and pamphlets, issued the first half, and I made my translation from that Swiss pamphlet. After long and vain endeavors to obtain the second half from the same source, I was briefly informed, without explanations, that the firm had decided not to publish it. I then had recourse to the Russian edition, authorized by the censor, for the second half. In that edition the censor's omissions of words, phrases, and entire paragraphs, were sometimes indicated thus: . . . Sometimes (as I found by comparison) no indication was given. The original publication in English, therefore (1887), consisted of a perfect first half and of a mangled second half, as I explained in a foot-note.

Shortly after my arrival in St. Petersburg, in the

autumn of 1887, one friend of Count Tolstoy offered me, on the author's behalf, the unabridged Manuscript; another friend offered me the present complete translation, and it seemed wiser to substitute it in the Complete Works of Count Tolstoy, for the imperfect version. I was requested to correct and rewrite certain parts (*i.e.* make a new translation of them), which I did. Perhaps the most curious and interesting point connected with the affair is the explanation which was given to me of the Swiss firm's real reason for not publishing Part II. That firm is revolutionary, anarchistic in politics, and it published Part I. because it regarded the sentiments therein contained as suited to the aims of that faction. (This judgment evidently coincides with the judgment of the Russian censor!) But Part II. would not have made a good "campaign document," so it was practically suppressed, exactly as the censor would have suppressed undesirable matter. Of a truth, extremes do meet! It is difficult for an outsider, an impartial judge, to perceive in what particular this procedure on the part of the revolutionists differs from the procedure of the censor's office to which they so strongly object, unless it be that the revolutionists are more sweeping in their condemnations, that they "out-Herod Herod," to use a phrase which ought to meet even their views of the case.

It may add to the reader's interest if he will try to read the last half, with one eye on the censor and one on the revolutionists, after the good old Russian fashion mentioned in the "Byliny" (Epic Songs) as the peculiarity of Nightingale the Robber, who kept "one eye on Kieff, one on Tchernigoff."

ISABEL F. HAPGOOD.

CONTENTS

CONTENTS

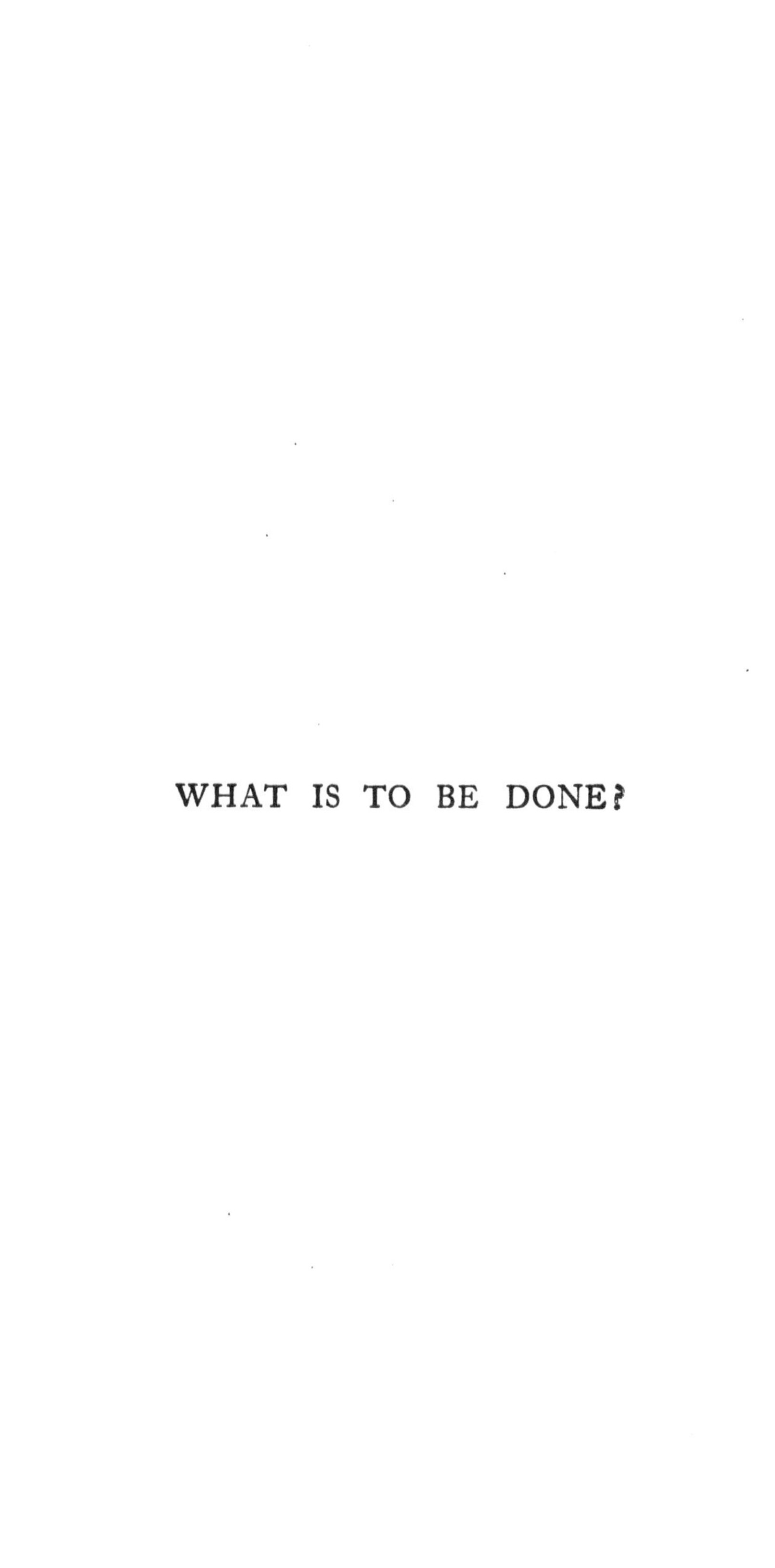

WHAT IS TO BE DONE?

WHAT IS TO BE DONE?

"*And the people asked him, saying, What shall we do then?*

He answereth and saith unto them, He that hath two coats, let him impart to him that hath none; and he that hath meat, let him do likewise." — LUKE iii. 10, 11.

"*Lay not up for yourselves treasures upon earth, where moth and rust doth corrupt, and where thieves break through and steal:*

But lay up for yourselves treasures in heaven, where neither moth nor rust doth corrupt, and where thieves do not break through nor steal:

For where your treasure is, there will your heart be also.

The light of the body is the eye: if therefore thine eye be single, thy whole body shall be full of light.

But if thine eye be evil, thy whole body shall be full of darkness. If therefore the light that is in thee be darkness, how great is that darkness!

No man can serve two masters: for either he will hate the one, and love the other; or else he will hold to the one, and despise the other. Ye cannot serve God and mammon.

Therefore I say unto you, Take no thought for your life, what ye shall eat, or what ye shall drink; nor yet for your body, what ye shall put on. Is not the life more than meat, and the body than raiment?" — MATT. vi. 19–25.

"*Therefore take no thought, saying, What shall we eat? or, What shall we drink? or, Wherewithal shall we be clothed?*

(For after all these things do the Gentiles seek:) for your heavenly Father knoweth that ye have need of all these things.

But seek ye first the kingdom of God, and his righteousness; and all these things shall be added unto you." — MATT. vi. 31–33.

"*For it is easier for a camel to go through a needle's eye, than for a rich man to enter into the kingdom of God.*" — LUKE xviii. 25.

CHAPTER I

HAVING passed the greater part of my life in the country, I came at length, in the year 1881, to reside in Moscow, where I was immediately struck with the extreme state of pauperism in that city. Though well acquainted with the privations of the poor in rural districts, I had not the faintest conception of their actual condition in towns.

In Moscow it is impossible to pass a street without meeting beggars of a peculiar kind quite unlike those in the country, who go about there, as the saying is, "with a bag and the name of Christ."

In Moscow beggars neither carry a bag nor ask for alms. In most cases, when they meet you, they only try to catch your eye, and act according to the expression of your face.

I know of one such, a bankrupt gentleman. He is an old man, who advances slowly, limping painfully on each leg. When he meets you, he limps, and makes a bow. If you stop, he takes off his cap, furnished with a cockade, bows again, and begs. If you do not stop, he pretends only to be lame, and continues limping along.

That is a specimen of a genuine Moscow beggar, and an experienced one.

At first I did not know why such mendicants did not ask openly; but afterward I learned why, without understanding the reason.

One day I saw a policeman push a ragged peasant, all swollen from dropsy, into a cab. I asked what he had been doing, and the policeman replied: —

"Begging."

"Is begging, then, forbidden?"

"So it seems," he answered. As the man was being driven away, I took another cab, and followed. I wished to find out whether mendicancy was really forbidden, and if so, why it was. I could not at all understand how it was possible to forbid one man asking something from another; and, moreover, I had my doubts whether it was illegal in a city where it flourished to such an extent.

I entered the police station where the pauper had been taken, and asked an official armed with sword and pistol, and seated at a table, what he had been arrested for.

The man looked up at me sharply, and said, "What business is that of yours?"

However, feeling the necessity of some explanation,

he added, "The authorities order such fellows to be arrested, so I suppose it is necessary."

I went away. The policeman who had brought the man was sitting in the window of the anteroom, studying his note-book. I said to him:—

"Is it really true that poor people are not allowed to ask for alms in Christ's name?"

The man started, as if waking up from a sleep, stared at me, then relapsed again into a state of stolid indifference, and reseating himself on the window-sill said:—

"The authorities require it, so you see it is necessary."

And as he became again absorbed in his note-book, I went down the steps toward my cab.

"Well! have they locked him up?" asked the cabman. He had evidently become interested in the matter.

"They have," I answered. He shook his head.

"Is begging, then, forbidden here in Moscow?" I asked.

"I can't tell you," he said.

"How," I said, "can a man be locked up, for begging in the name of Christ?"

"Nowadays things have changed, and you see it is forbidden," he answered.

Since that time, I have seen policemen several times taking paupers to the police station, and thence to the workhouse: indeed, I once met a whole crowd of these poor creatures, about thirty, escorted before and behind by policemen. I asked what they had been doing.

"Begging," was the reply.

It appears that, according to law, mendicancy is forbidden in Moscow, notwithstanding the great number of beggars one meets there in every street, whole rows of them near the churches during service-time, and most of all at funerals. But why are some caught and locked up, while others are let alone? This I have not been able to solve. Either there are lawful and unlawful beggars amongst them, or else there are so many that it is impossible to catch them all; or, perhaps, though some are taken up, others fill their places.

There are a great variety of such mendicants in Moscow. There are those that make a living by begging. There are also honestly destitute people, such as have somehow chanced to reach Moscow, and are really in extreme need.

Amongst these last are men and women evidently from the country. I have often met such. Some of them who had fallen ill, and afterward recovered and left the hospital, could now find no means either of feeding themselves or of getting away from Moscow; some of them, besides, had taken to drink (such probably was the case of the man with dropsy whom I met); some were in good health, but had been burned out of house and home, or else were very old, or were widowed or deserted women with children; some others were sound as to health, and quite capable of working.

These robust fellows especially interested me, — the more so because, since my arrival in Moscow, I had, for the sake of exercise, contracted the habit of going to the Sparrow Hills, and working there with two peasants, who sawed wood. These men were exactly like the beggars whom I often met in the streets. One was called Peter, and was an ex-soldier from Kaluga; the other, Simon, from Vladimir. They possessed nothing save the clothes on their backs: and they earned, by working very hard, from forty to forty-five kopeks a day; out of this they both put a little aside, — the Kaluga soldier, in order to buy a fur coat; the Vladimir peasant, in order to get money enough to return to his home in the country.

Meeting, therefore, in the streets similar individuals, I was particularly interested in them, and failed to understand why some begged while others worked.

Whenever I met a beggar of this description, I used to ask him how it was that he had come to such a state. Once I met a strong, healthy-looking peasant: he asked alms. I questioned him as to who he was, and whence he had come.

He told me he had come from Kaluga, in search of work. He had at first found some, such as sawing old timber into firewood; but after he and his companion had finished the job, though they had continually looked for more work, they had not found any; his companion had left him, and he himself had passed a fortnight in the utmost need, and, having sold all he possessed to obtain food, had not now enough even to buy the tools necessary for sawing.

I gave him the money for a saw, and told him where to go for work. I had previously arranged with Peter and Simon that they should accept a new fellow-worker, and find him a companion.

"Be sure you come! There is plenty of work to be done," I said on parting.

"You may depend on me," he answered. "Do you think there can be any pleasure in knocking about, begging, if I could work?"

The man solemnly promised that he would come; and he seemed to be honest, and really meaning to work.

Next day, on coming to my friends, Peter and Simon, I asked them whether the man had arrived. They said he had not; nor, indeed, did he come at all: and in this way I was frequently deceived.

I have also been deceived by those who stated that they only wanted a little money to buy a ticket, in order to return home, and whom I again met in the streets a few days later. Many of them I came to know well, and they knew me; though occasionally, having forgotten me, they would repeat the same false tale; but sometimes they would turn away on recognizing me.

In this way I discovered that, even in this class of men, there are many rogues.

But still, these poor rogues were also very much to be pitied; they were all of them ragged, hungry paupers; they are of the sort who die of cold in the streets, or hang themselves to escape living, as the papers frequently tell us.

CHAPTER II

WHEN I talked to my town friends about this pauperism which surrounded them, they always replied, "Oh! you have seen nothing yet! You should go to the Khitrof Market, and visit the lodging-houses there, if you want to see the genuine 'Golden Company.'"

One jovial friend of mine added that the number of these paupers had so increased, that they already formed not a "Golden Company," but a "Golden Regiment."

My lively friend was right; but he would have been yet nearer the truth had he said that these men formed, in Moscow, not a company, nor a regiment, but a whole army, — an army, I should judge, of about fifty thousand.

The regular townspeople, when they spoke to me about the pauperism of the city, always seemed to feel a certain pleasure or pride in being able to give me such precise information.

I remember I noticed, when visiting London, that the citizens there seemed also to find a certain satisfaction in telling me about London destitution, as though it were something to be proud of.

However, wishing to inspect this poverty about which I had heard so much, I turned my steps very often toward the Khitrof Market; but, on each occasion, I felt a sensation of pain and shame. "Why should you go to look at the suffering of human beings whom you cannot help?" said one voice within me. "If you live here, and see all that is pleasant in town life, go and see also what is wretched," replied another.

And so, one cold, windy day in December, two years ago, I went to the Khitrof Market, the center of the town pauperism.

It was on a week-day, about four in the afternoon. While still a good distance off, I noticed greater and greater numbers of men in strange garb, evidently not originally meant for them; and in yet stranger footapparel, men of a peculiar unhealthy complexion, and all apparently showing a remarkable indifference to all that surrounded them.

Men in the strangest, most incongruous costumes sauntered along, evidently without the least thought as to how they might look in the eyes of others. They were all going in the same direction. Without asking the way, which was unknown to me, I followed them, and came to the Khitrof Market.

There I found women likewise in ragged capes, rough-looking cloaks, jackets, boots, and galoshes. Perfectly free and easy in their manner, notwithstanding the grotesque monstrosity of their attire, these women, old and young, were sitting, bargaining, strolling about, and abusing one another.

Market-time having evidently passed, there were not many people there; and, as most of them were going uphill, through the market-place, and all in the same direction, I followed them.

The farther I went, the greater became the stream of people flowing into the one road. Having passed the market, and gone up the street, I found that I was following two women, one old, the other young. Both were clothed in some gray ragged stuff. They were talking, as they walked, about some kind of business.

Every expression was unfailingly accompanied by some obscene word. They were neither of them drunk, but were absorbed with their own affairs; and the men passing, and those about them, paid not the slightest attention to their language, which sounded so strange to me. It appeared to be the generally accepted manner of speech in those parts. On the left we passed some private night lodging-houses, and some of the crowd entered them; others continued to ascend the hill toward a large corner house. The majority of the people walking along with me went into this house. In front of it, people, all of the same sort, were standing and sitting on the sidewalk and in the snow.

At the right of the entrance were women; at the left, men. I passed by the men; I passed by the women (there were several hundreds in all), and stopped where the crowd ceased.

This building was the "Liapin free night lodging-house." The crowd was composed of night lodgers, waiting to be let in. At five o'clock in the evening this house is opened and the crowd admitted. Hither came almost all the people whom I followed.

I remained standing where the file of men ended. Those nearest to me stared at me till I had to look at them. The remnants of garments covering their bodies were very various; but the one expression of the eyes of all alike seemed to be: "Why have you, a man from another world, stopped here with us? Who are you? Are you a self-satisfied man of wealth, desiring to be gladdened by the sight of our need, to divert yourself in your idleness, and to mock at us? or are you that which does not and cannot exist, — a man who pities us?"

On all their faces the same question was written. Each would look at me, meet my eyes, and turn away again.

I wanted to speak to some one of them, but for a long time I could not summon up courage. However, eventually our mutual exchange of glances introduced us to each other; and we felt that, however widely separated were our social positions in life, after all we were fellow-men, and so ceased to be afraid of one another.

Next to me stood a peasant with a swollen face and red beard, in a ragged jacket, and worn-out galoshes on his naked feet, though there were eight degrees of frost.[1] For the third or fourth time our eyes met; and I felt so drawn to him that I was no longer ashamed to address him (to have refrained from doing so would have been the only real shame), and asked him where he came from.

He answered eagerly, while a crowd began to collect round us, that he had come from Smolensk in search of work, in order to be able to buy bread and pay his taxes.

[1] Réaumur.

"There is no work to be had nowadays," he said; "the soldiers have got hold of it all. So here am I knocking about; and God is my witness, I have not had anything to eat for two days."

He said this shyly, with an attempt at a smile. A seller of warm drinks,[1] an old soldier, was standing near. I called him, and made him pour out a glass for him. The peasant took the warm vessel in his hands, and, before drinking, warmed them against the glass, trying not to lose any of the precious heat; and whilst doing this he related to me his story.

The adventures of these people, or at least the stories which they tell, are almost always the same. He had had a little work; then it had ceased: and here, in the night lodging-house, his purse, containing his money and passport, had been stolen from him. Now he could not leave Moscow.

He told me that during the day he warmed himself in public houses, eating any stale crust of bread which might be given him. His night's lodging here in Liapin's house cost him nothing.

He was only waiting for the round of the police-sergeant to lock him up for being without his passport, when he would be sent on foot, with a party of men similarly situated, to the place of his birth.

"They say the inspection will take place on Thursday, when I shall be taken up; so I must try and keep on until then." (The prison and his compulsory journey appeared to him as the "promised land.") While he was speaking, two or three men in the crowd said they were also in exactly the same situation.

A thin, pale youth, with a long nose, only a shirt upon his back, and that torn about the shoulders, and a tattered cap on his head, edged his way to me through the crowd. He was shivering violently all the time, but tried, as he caught my eye, to smile scornfully at the peasant's talk, thinking thus to show his superiority.

I offered him some drink.

[1] A sbiten-seller; *sbiten* is a hot drink made of herbs or spices and molasses.

He warmed his hands on the tumbler as the other had done; but just as he began to speak, he was shouldered aside by a big, black, hook-nosed, bare-headed fellow, in a thin shirt and waistcoat, who also asked for some drink.

Then a tall old man, with a thin beard, in an overcoat fastened round the waist with a cord, and in matting shoes, had some. He was drunk.

Then came a little man, with a swollen face and teary eyes, in a coarse brown jacket, and with knees protruding through his torn trousers, and knocking against each other with cold. He shivered so that he could not hold the glass, and spilled the contents over his clothes; the others took to abusing him, but he only grinned miserably, and shivered.

After him came an ugly, deformed man in rags, and with bare feet. Then an individual of the officer type; another belonging to the church class; then a strange-looking being without a nose, — and all of them hungry, cold, suppliant, and humble, — crowded round me, and stretched out their hands for the glass; but the drink was exhausted. Then one man asked for money; I gave him some. A second and a third followed, till the whole crowd pressed on me. In the general confusion the gatekeeper of the neighboring house shouted to the crowd to clear the pavement before his house, and the people submissively obeyed.

Some of them undertook to control the tumult, and took me under their protection. They attempted to drag me out of the crush. But the crowd that formerly had lined the pavement in a long file, now had become condensed about me. Every one looked at me and begged; and it seemed as if each face were more pitiful, harassed, and degraded than the other. I distributed all the money I had, — only about twenty rubles, — and entered the lodging-house with the crowd. The house was enormous, and consisted of four parts. In the upper stories were the men's rooms; on the ground floor the women's. I went first into the women's dormitory, — a large room, filled with beds resembling the berths in a third-class railway-carriage. They were arranged in two tiers, one above the other.

Strange-looking women in ragged dresses, without jackets, old and young, kept coming in and occupying places, some below, others climbing above. Some of the elder ones crossed themselves, pronouncing the name of the founder of the refuge. Some laughed and swore.

I went up-stairs. There, in a similar way, the men had taken their places. Amongst them I recognized one of those to whom I had given money. On seeing him I suddenly felt horribly ashamed, and made haste to leave.

And with a sense of having committed some crime, I returned home. There I entered along the carpeted steps into the rug-covered hall, and, having taken off my fur coat, sat down to a meal of five courses, served by two footmen in livery, with white ties and white gloves. And a scene of the past came suddenly before me. Thirty years ago I saw a man's head cut off under the guillotine in Paris before a crowd of thousands of spectators. I was aware that the man had been a great criminal; I was acquainted with all the arguments in justification of capital punishment for such offenses. I saw this execution carried out deliberately; but at the moment that the head and body were severed from each other by the keen blade, I gasped, and realized in every fiber of my being, that all the arguments which I had hitherto heard upon capital punishment were wickedly false; that, no matter how many might agree as to its being a lawful act, it was literally murder; whatever other title men might give it, they thus had virtually committed murder, that worst of all crimes: and there was I, both by my silence and my non-interference, an aider, abetter, and participator in the sin.

Similar convictions were now again forced upon me when I beheld the misery, cold, hunger, and humiliation of thousands of my fellow-men. I realized not only with my brain, but in every pulse of my soul, that, whilst there were thousands of such sufferers in Moscow, I, with tens of thousands of others, filled myself daily to repletion with luxurious dainties of every description, took the tenderest care of my horses, and clothed my very floors with velvet carpets!

Whatever the wise and learned of the world might say about it, however unalterable the course of life might seem to be, the same evil was continually being enacted, and I, by my own personal habits of luxury, was a promoter of that evil.

The difference between the two cases was only this: that in the first, all I could have done would have been to shout out to the murderers standing near the guillotine, who were accomplishing the deed, that they were committing a murder, though of course knowing that my interference would have been in vain. Whereas, in this second case, I might have given away, not only the drink and the small sum of money I had with me, but also the coat from off my shoulders, and all that I possessed at home. Yet I had not done so, and therefore felt, and feel, and can never cease to feel, myself a partaker in a crime which is continually being committed, so long as I have superfluous food whilst others have none, so long as I have two coats whilst there exists one man without any.

CHAPTER III

On the same evening that I returned from Liapin's house, I imparted my impressions to a friend, and he, a resident of the town, began to explain to me, not without a certain satisfaction, that this was the most natural state of things in a town; that it was only owing to my provincialism that I found anything remarkable in it; and that it had ever been, and ever would be, so, such being one of the inevitable conditions of civilization. In London it was yet worse, . . . therefore there could be nothing wrong about it, and there was nothing to be disturbed and troubled about.

I began to argue with my friend, but with such warmth and so angrily, that my wife rushed in from the adjoining room to ask what had happened. It appeared that I had, without being aware of it, shouted out in an agonized voice, gesticulating wildly, "We should not go on living in this way! we must not live so! we have no right!" I was rebuked for my unnecessary excitement; I was told that I could not talk quietly upon any question; that I was irritable; and it was pointed out to me that the existence of such misery as I had witnessed should in no way be a reason for embittering the life of my home circle.

I felt that this was perfectly just, and held my tongue; but in the depth of my soul I knew that I was right, and I could not quiet my conscience.

The town life, which had previously seemed alien and strange to me, became now so hateful that all the indulgences of a luxurious existence, in which I had formerly delighted, now served to torment me.

However much I tried to find some kind of excuse for my mode of life, I could not contemplate without irritation either my own or other people's drawing-rooms, nor a clean, richly served dinner-table, nor a carriage with well-fed coachman and horses, nor the shops, theaters, and entertainments. I could not help seeing, in contrast with all this, those hungry, shivering, and degraded inhabitants of the night lodging-house. And I could never free myself from the thought that these two conditions were inseparable — that the one proceeded from the other. I remember that the sense of culpability which I had felt from the first moment never left me; but with this feeling another soon became mingled, which lessened the first.

When I talked to my intimate friends and acquaintances about my impressions on Liapin's house, they all answered in the same way, and expressed besides their appreciation of my kindness and tender-heartedness, and gave me to understand that the sight had so impressed me because I, Leo Tolstoï, was kind-hearted and good. And I willingly allowed myself to believe it.

The natural consequence of this was that the first keen sense of self-reproach and shame was blunted, and was replaced by a sense of satisfaction at my own virtue, and a desire to make it known to others. "It is in truth," I said to myself, "probably not my connection with a luxurious life which is at fault, but the unavoidable circumstances of life. And thus a change in my particular life cannot alter the evil which I have seen."

In changing my own life, I should only render myself and those nearest and dearest to me miserable, whilst that other misery would remain the same; and therefore my object should be, not to alter my own way of living, as I had at first imagined, but to try as much as was in my power to ameliorate the position of those unfortunate ones who had excited my compassion.

The whole matter, I reasoned, lies in the fact that I, being an extremely kind and good man, wish to do good to my fellow-men. And I began to arrange a plan of philanthropic activity in which I might exhibit all my virtues. I must, however, here remark that, while planning this charitable effort, in the depth of my heart I felt that I was not doing the right thing; but, as too often happens, reason and imagination were stifling the voice of conscience. About this time the census was being taken, and it seemed to me a good opportunity for instituting that charitable organization in which I wanted to shine.

I was acquainted with many philanthropic institutions and societies already existing in Moscow, but all their activity seemed to me both wrongly directed and insignificant in comparison with what I myself wished to do. And this was what I invented to excite sympathy amongst the rich people for the poor: I began to collect money, and enlist men who wished to help in the work, and who would, in company with the census officers, visit all the nests of pauperism, entering into relations with the poor, finding out the details of their needs, helping them with money and work, sending them out of Moscow, placing their children in schools, and their old men and women in homes and houses of refuge.

I thought, moreover, that, from those who undertook this work, there could be formed a permanent society, which, dividing between its members the various districts of Moscow, would take care that new cases of want and misery should be avoided, and so by degrees stifle pauperism at its very birth, accomplishing their task, not so much by cure, as by prevention.

I already saw, in the future, begging and poverty entirely disappearing, I having been the means of its accomplishment. Then all of us who were rich could go on living in all our luxury as before, dwelling in fine houses, eating dinners of five courses, driving in our carriages to theaters and entertainments, and no longer being harassed by such sights as I had witnessed at Liapin's house.

Having invented this plan, I wrote an article about it; and, before even giving it to be printed, I went to those acquaintances from whom I hoped to obtain coöperation, and expounded to all whom I visited that day (chiefly the rich) the ideas I afterward published in my article.

I proposed to profit by the census in order to study the state of pauperism in Moscow, and to help to exterminate it by personal effort and money, after which we might all with a quiet conscience enjoy our usual pleasures. All listened to me attentively and seriously; but, in every case, I remarked that the moment my hearers came to understand what I was driving at, they seemed to become uncomfortable and somewhat embarrassed. But it was principally, I feel sure, on my account; because they considered all that I said to be folly. It seemed as though some other motive compelled my listeners to agree for the moment with my foolishness. "Oh, yes! Certainly. It would be delightful," they said. "Of course it is impossible not to sympathize with you. Your idea is splendid. I myself have had the same; but .... people here are so indifferent, that it is hardly reasonable to expect a great success. However, as far as I am concerned, I am, of course, ready to share in the enterprise."

Similar answers I received from all. They consented, as it appeared to me, not because they were persuaded by my arguments, nor in compliance with my request, but because of some exterior reason, which rendered it impossible for them to refuse.

I remarked this partly because none of those who promised me their help in the form of money, defined the sum they meant to give; so that I had to name the amount by asking, "May I count upon you for twenty-five, or one hundred, or two hundred, or three hundred, rubles?" And not one of them paid the money. I draw attention to this fact, because, when people are going to pay for what they are anxious to have, they are generally in haste to give it. Suppose it were to secure a box to see Sarah Bernhardt, the money is immediately produced. Here, however, of all who agreed to give, and expressed their sympathy, no one immediately produced the amount, but merely silently acquiesced in the sum I happened to name.

In the last house I visited that day, there was a large party. The mistress of the house had for some years been employed in works of charity. Several carriages were waiting at the door of the house. Footmen in expensive liveries were seated in the hall. In the spacious drawing-room, ladies, old and young, wearing rich dresses and ornaments, were talking to some young men, and dressing up small dolls, destined for a lottery in aid of the poor.

The sight of this drawing-room, and of the people assembled there, struck me very painfully. For not only was their property worth several million rubles; not only could the interest on the capital spent here on dresses, laces, bronzes, jewels, carriages, horses, liveries, footmen, exceed a hundred times the value of these ladies' work; not only was this the case, — but even the expenses caused by this very party of ladies and gentlemen, the gloves, linen, candles, tea, sugar, cakes, all this represented a sum a hundred times exceeding the value of the work done.

I saw all this, and therefore might have understood that here, at all events, I should not find sympathy for my plan; but I had come in order to give an invitation, and, however painful it was to me, I said what I wished to say, repeating almost the words of my article.

One lady present offered me some money, adding that, owing to her sensibilities, she did not feel strong enough to visit the poor herself, but that she would give help in this form. How much money, and when she would give it, she did not say. Another lady and a young man offered their services in visiting the poor, but I did not profit by their offer. The principal person I addressed told me that it would be impossible to do much, because the means were not forthcoming. And the means were scarce, because all the rich men in Moscow who were known, and could be counted upon, had given all it was possible to get from them; their charities having already been rewarded with titles, medals, and other distinctions, this being the only effectual method of insuring success in the collection of money,—namely, to obtain new honors from the authorities, and that being very difficult.

Having returned home, I went to bed, not only with a presentiment that nothing would result from my idea, but also with the shameful consciousness of having, during the whole day, been doing something vile and contemptible. However, I did not desist.

First, the work had been begun, and false shame would have prevented my giving it up; secondly, not only the success of the enterprise itself, but even my occupation in it, afforded me the possibility of continuing to live in my usual way; whereas, the failure of this enterprise would have put me under the constraint of giving up my present mode of life, and of seeking another. Of this I was unconsciously afraid; therefore, I refused to listen to my inner voice, and continued what I had begun.

Having sent my article to be printed, I read a proof-copy at a census meeting in the town hall, hesitatingly and blushing till my cheeks burned again, so uncomfortable did I feel.

I saw that all my hearers felt equally uncomfortable.

Upon my question whether the managers of the cen

sus would accept my proposal that they should remain at their posts in order to form a link between society and those in need, an awkward silence ensued.

Then two of those present made speeches, which seemed to mend the awkwardness of my suggestion; sympathy for me was expressed along with their general approbation. They, however, pointed out the impracticability of my scheme. Every one seemed more at ease; but afterward, when, still wishing to succeed, I asked each district manager separately, whether he was willing during the census to investigate the needs of the poor, and afterward remain at his post in order to form this link between the poor and the rich, all again were confounded; it seemed as though their looks said, "Why, out of personal regard for you, we have listened to your silly proposition; but here you come out with it again!" Such was the expression of their faces, but in words they told me that they consented; and two of them, separately, but as though they had agreed together, said in the same words, "We regard it as our moral duty to do so." The same impression was produced by my words upon the students who had volunteered to act as clerks during the census, when I told them that they might then, besides their scientific pursuits, accomplish also a charitable work.

When we talked the matter over, I noticed that they were shy of looking me straight in the face, as one often hesitates to look into the face of a good-natured man who is talking nonsense. The same impression was produced by my article upon the editor of the paper when I handed it to him; also upon my son, my wife, and various other people. Every one seemed embarrassed, but all found it necessary to approve of the idea itself; and all, immediately after this approbation, began to express their doubts as to the success of the plan, and, for some reason or other (all without exception), took to condemning the indifference and coldness of society and of the world, though evidently excluding themselves.

In the depth of my soul, I continued to feel that all

this was not the right thing, that nothing would come of it; but the article had been printed, and I had agreed to take part in the census. I had put a plan into action, and now the plan itself drew me along.

CHAPTER IV

In accordance with my request, the part of the town was assigned to me for the census which contained the houses generally known under the name of the Rzhanoff lodgings. I had long before heard that they were considered to be the lowest circle of poverty and vice, and that was the reason that I asked the officers of the census to assign me this district.

My desire was gratified.

Having received the appointment from the town council, I went, a few days before the census, alone, to inspect my district. With the help of the plan I was furnished with, I soon found the Rzhanoff Houses, — approached by a street which terminated on the left-hand side of a gloomy building without any apparent entrance. From the aspect of this house, I guessed it was the one I was in search of. On descending the street, I had come across some boys, from ten to fourteen years old, in short coats, sliding down the frozen gutter, some on their feet, others upon a single skate.

The boys were ragged, and, like all town boys, sharp and bold. I stopped to look at them. An old woman in torn clothes, with hanging yellow cheeks, came round the corner. She was going uphill, and, like a horse out of wind, gasped painfully at every step; and, when abreast of me, she stopped with hoarse, choking breath. In any other place, this old woman would have asked alms of me, but here she only began to talk.

"Just look at them!" she said, pointing to the sliding boys; "always at mischief! They will become the same Rzhanoff good-for-nothings as their fathers." One boy, in an overcoat and vizorless cap, overhearing her words, stopped. "You shut up!" he shouted. "You're only an old Rzhanoff goat yourself!"

I asked the boy if he lived here. "Yes, and so does she. She stole some boots," he called out, and, pushing himself off, slid on.

The woman gave vent to a torrent of abuse, interrupted by her cough. During this squabble an old, white-haired man, all in rags, came down the middle of the street, brandishing his arms, and carrying in one hand a bundle of small loaves. He seemed to have just fortified himself with a glass of liquor. He had evidently heard the old woman's abuse, and took her side.

"I'll give it you, you little devils, you!" he cried out, pretending to rush after them; and, having passed behind me, he stepped upon the pavement. If you saw this old man in a fashionable street, you would be struck with his air of decrepitude, feebleness, and poverty. Here he appeared in the character of a merry workman, returning from his day's labor.

I followed him. He turned round the corner to the left into an alley; and, having passed the front of the house and the gate, he disappeared through the door of an inn. Into this alley the doors of the latter, a public house, and several small eating-houses, opened. It was the Rzhanoff Houses. Everything was gray, dirty, and foul-smelling, — buildings, lodgings, courts, and people. Most of those I met here were in tattered clothes, half-naked. Some were passing along, others were running from one door to another. Two were bargaining about some rags. I went round the whole building, down another lane and a court, and, having returned, stopped at the archway of the Rzhanoff Houses.

I wanted to go in and see what was going on inside, but the idea made me feel painfully awkward. What should I say if they asked me what I had come for?

However, after a little hesitation, I went in. The moment I entered the court, I was conscious of a most revolting odor. The court was dreadfully dirty. I turned round the corner, and at the same instant heard the steps of people running along the boards of the gallery, and thence down the stairs.

First a gaunt-looking woman, with tucked-up sleeves, faded pink dress, and shoes on her stockingless feet, rushed out; after her, a rough-haired man in a red shirt and extremely wide trousers, like a petticoat, and with galoshes on his feet. The man caught her under the stairs: "You shan't escape me," he said, laughing.

"Just listen to the squint-eyed devil!" began the woman, who was evidently not averse to his attentions; but, having caught sight of me, she exclaimed angrily, "Who are you looking for?" As I did not want any one in particular, I felt somewhat confused, and went away.

This little incident, though by no means remarkable in itself, suddenly showed to me the work I was about to undertake in an entirely new light, especially after what I had seen on the other side of the courtyard, — the scolding old woman, the light-hearted old man, and the sliding boys. I had meditated doing good to these people by the help of the rich men of Moscow. I now realized for the first time, that all these poor unfortunates, whom I had been wishing to help, had, besides the time they spent suffering from cold and hunger, in waiting to get a lodging, several hours daily to get through, and that they must somehow fill up the rest of the twenty-four hours of every day, — a whole life, of which I had never thought before. I realized now, for the first time, that all these people, besides the mere effort to find food and shelter from the cold, must live through the rest of every day of their life as other people have to do, must get angry at times, and be dull, and try to appear light-hearted, and be sad or merry. And now, for the first time (however strange the confession may sound), I was fully aware that the task which I was undertaking could not simply consist in feeding and clothing a thousand people (just as one might feed a thousand head of sheep, and drive them into shelter), but must develop some more essential help. And when I considered that each one of these individuals was just another man as myself, possessing also a past history, with the same passions, temptations, and errors, the same thoughts, the same questions to be answered, then suddenly the work before me appeared stupendous, and I felt my own utter helplessness; — but it had been begun, and I was resolved to continue it.

CHAPTER V

On the appointed day, the students who were to assist me started early in the morning; while I, the instigator, only joined them at twelve o'clock. I could not come earlier, as I did not get up till ten, after which I had to take some coffee, and then smoke for the sake of my digestion. Twelve o'clock then found me at the door of the Rzhanoff Houses. A policeman showed me a public house, to which the census-clerks referred all those who wished to inquire for them. I entered, and found it very dirty and unsavory. Here, right in front of me, was a counter; to the left a small room, furnished with tables covered with soiled napkins; to the right a large room on pillars, containing similar little tables placed in the windows and along the walls; and men here and there having tea, some very ragged, others well dressed, apparently workmen or small shopkeepers. There were also several women. In spite of the dirt, it was easy to see by the business air of the man in charge, and the ready, obliging manners of the waiter, that the eating-house was driving a good trade. I had no sooner entered than one of the waiters was already preparing to assist me in getting off my overcoat, and anxious to take my orders, showing that evidently the people here were in the habit of doing their work quickly and readily.

My inquiry for the census-clerks was answered by a call for "Vanya" from a little man dressed in foreign fashion, who was arranging something in a cupboard behind the counter. This was the proprietor of the public house, a peasant from Kaluga, Ivan Fedotitch by name, who also rented half of the other houses, sub-letting the rooms to lodgers. In answer to his call, a thin, sallow-faced, hook-nosed lad, of some eighteen years, came forward hastily; and the landlord said, "Take this gentleman to the clerks; they have gone to the main body of the building over the well."

The lad put down his napkin, pulled a coat on over his white shirt and trousers, picked up a large cap; then, with quick, short steps, he led the way by a back door through the buildings. At the entrance of a greasy, malodorous kitchen we met an old woman, who was carefully carrying in a rag some putrid tripe. We descended into a court, built up all round with wooden buildings on stone foundations. The smell was most offensive, and seemed to be concentrated in a privy, to which numbers of people were constantly resorting. This awful cesspool forced itself upon one's notice by the pestilential atmosphere around it.

The boy, taking care not to soil his white trousers, led me cautiously across frozen and unfrozen filth, and approached one of the buildings. The people crossing the yard and the galleries all stopped to gaze at me. It was evident that a cleanly dressed man was an unusual sight in the place.

The boy asked a woman whom we met, whether she had seen where the census officials had entered, and three people at once answered his question: some said that they were over the well; others said that they had been there, but had now gone to Nikita Ivanovitch's.

An old man in the middle of the court, who had only a shirt on, said that they were at No. 30. The boy concluded that this information was the most probable, and led me to No. 30, into the basement, where darkness and a bad smell, different from that which filled the court, prevailed.

We continued to descend along a dark passage. As we were traversing it, a door was suddenly opened; and out of it came a drunken old man in a shirt, evidently not of the peasant class. A shrieking washerwoman, with tucked-up sleeves and soapy arms, was pushing him out of the room. "Vanya" (my guide) shoved him aside, saying, "It won't do to kick up such a row here—and you an officer too!"

When we arrived at No. 30, Vanya pulled the door, which opened with the sound of a wet slap; and we felt a gush of soapy steam, and an odor of bad food and tobacco, and entered into complete darkness. The windows were on the other side; and we were in a crooked corridor, that went right and left, and with doors leading, at different angles, into rooms separated from it by a partition of unevenly laid boards, roughly whitewashed.

In a dark room to the left we could see a women washing at a trough. Another old woman was looking out of a door at the right. Near an open door was a hairy, red-skinned peasant in bark shoes, sitting on a couch. His hands rested upon his knees; and he was swinging his feet, and looking sadly at his shoes.

At the end of the passage was a small door leading into the room where the census officers were assembled. This was the room of the landlady of the whole of No. 30. She rented the apartment from Ivan Fedotitch, and sublet the rooms to ordinary or night lodgers.

In this tiny room a student sat under an image glittering with gilt paper, and, with the air of a magistrate, was putting questions to a man dressed in shirt and vest. This last was a friend of the landlady's, who was answering the questions in her stead. The landlady herself,—an old woman,—and two inquisitive lodgers were also present.

When I entered, the room was quite filled up. I pushed through to the table, shook hands with the student, and he went on extracting his information; while I studied the inhabitants, and put questions to them for my own ends.

It appeared, however, I could find no one here upon whom to bestow my benevolence. The landlady of the rooms, notwithstanding their wretchedness and filth (which especially struck me in comparison with the mansion in which I lived), was well off, even from the point of view of town poverty; and, compared with the country destitution, with which I was well acquainted, she lived luxuriously. She had a feather-bed, a quilted blanket, a samovar, a fur cloak, a cupboard, with dishes, plates, etc. The landlady's friend had the same well-to-do appearance, and boasted even a watch and chain. The lodgers were poor, but among them there was no one requiring immediate help.

Three only applied for aid, — the woman washing linen, who said she had been abandoned by her husband; an old widowed woman, without means of livelihood; and the peasant in the ragged shoes, who told me he had not had anything to eat that day. But, upon gathering more precise information, it became evident that all these people were not in extreme want, and that, in order really to help, it would be necessary to become more intimately acquainted with them.

When I offered the washerwoman to place her children in a "home," she became confused, thought over it some time, then thanked me much, but evidently did not desire it; she wished rather to be given some money. Her eldest daughter helped her in the washing, and the second acted as nurse to the little boy.

The old woman asked to be put into a refuge; but, upon examining her corner, I saw that she was not in dire distress. She had a box containing her property; she had a teapot, two cups, and old bonbon boxes with tea and sugar. She knitted stockings and gloves, and received a monthly allowance from a lady benefactress.

The peasant was evidently more desirous of wetting his throat after his last day's drunkenness than of food, and anything given him would have gone to the public house. In these rooms, therefore, there was no one whom I could have rendered in any respect happier by helping them with money.

There were only paupers there, — and paupers, it seemed to me, of a questionable kind.

I put down the names of the old woman, the laundress, and the peasant, and settled in my mind that it would be necessary to do something for them, but that first I should aid those other especially unfortunate ones whom I expected to come across in this house. I made up my mind that some system was necessary in distributing the aid which we had to give: first, we should find the most needy, and then come to such as these.

But in the next lodging, and in the next again, I found only similar cases, which would have to be looked into more closely before being helped. Of those whom pecuniary aid alone would have rendered happy, I found none.

However ashamed I feel in confessing it, I began to experience a certain disappointment at not finding in these houses anything resembling what I had expected. I thought to find very exceptional people; but, when I had gone over all the lodgings, I became convinced that their inhabitants were in no way extremely peculiar, but much like those amongst whom I lived.

As with us, so also with them, there were some more or less good, and others more or less bad; there were some more or less happy, and others more or less unhappy. Those who were unhappy amongst them would have been equally wretched with us, their misery being within themselves, — a misery not to be mended by any kind of bank-note.

CHAPTER VI

THE inhabitants of these houses belonged to the lowest population of the town, which in Moscow amounts to perhaps more than a hundred thousand. In this house, there were representative men of all kinds, — petty employers and journeymen, shoemakers, brushmakers, joiners, hackney coachmen, jobbers carrying on business on their own account, washerwomen, second-hand dealers, money-lenders, day-laborers, and others without any definite occupation; here also lodged beggars and women of the town.

Many like those whom I had seen waiting in front of Liapin's house lived here, but they were mixed up with the working-people; and, besides, those whom I then saw were in a most wretched condition, when, having eaten and drunk all they had, they were turned out of the public house, and, cold and hungry, were waiting, as for heavenly manna, to be admitted into the free night lodging-house,—day by day longing to be taken to prison, in order to be sent back to their respective homes. Here I saw the same men among a greater number of working-people, and at a time when, by some means or other, they had got a few farthings to pay for their night's lodging, and perhaps a ruble or two for food and drink.

However strange it may sound, I had no such feelings here as I experienced in Liapin's house; but on the contrary, during my first visiting round, I and the students had a sensation which was rather agreeable than otherwise. I might even say it was entirely agreeable.

My first impression was that the majority of those lodging here were working-men, and very kindly disposed. We found most of the lodgers at work,— the washerwomen at their tubs, the joiners by their benches, the bootmakers at their lasts. The tiny rooms were full of people, and the work was going on cheerfully and with energy. There was a smell of perspiration among the workmen, of leather at the bootmaker's, of chips in the carpenter's shop. We often heard songs, and saw bare, sinewy arms working briskly and skilfully.

Everywhere we were received kindly and cheerfully. Nearly everywhere our intrusion into the daily life of these people excited in them no desire to show us their importance, or to rate us soundly, as happens when such visits are paid to the lodgings of well-to-do people. On the contrary, all our questions were answered respectfully without any particular importance being attached to them,— served, indeed, only as an excuse for them to be merry, and to joke as to how they were to be enrolled on the list; how such a one was as good as two, and how two others ought to be reckoned as one.

Many we found at dinner or at tea; and each time, in answer to our greeting, "Bread and salt," or, "Tea and sugar," they said, "You are welcome;" and some even made room for us to sit down. Instead of the place being the resort of an ever shifting population, such as we expected to find here, it turned out that in this house were many rooms which had been tenanted by the same people for long periods.

One carpenter, with his workmen, and a bootmaker, with his journeymen, had been living here for ten years. The bootmaker's shop was very dirty and quite choked up, but all his men were working very cheerily. I tried to talk with one of the workmen, wishing to sound him about the miseries of his lot, what he owed to the master, and so forth; but he did not understand me, and spoke of his master and of his life from a very favorable point of view.

In one lodging there lived an old man with his old wife. They dealt in apples. Their room was warm, clean, and filled with their belongings. The floor was covered with matting made of apple sacks. There were chests, a cupboard, a samovar, and crockery. In the corner were many holy images, before which two lamps were burning; on the wall hung fur cloaks wrapped up in a sheet. The old woman, with wrinkled face, kind and talkative, was apparently herself delighted with her quiet, respectable life.

Ivan Fedotitch, the owner of the inn and of the lodgings, came out and walked with us. He joked kindly with many of the lodgers, calling them all by their names, and giving us short sketches of their characters. They were as other men, did not consider themselves unhappy, but believed they were like every one else, as in reality they were. We were prepared to see only dreadful things, and we met instead objects, not only not repulsive, but estimable. And there were so many of them, compared with the ragged, ruined, unoccupied people we met now and then among them, that the latter did not in the least destroy a general impression. To the students it did not appear so remarkable as it did to me. They were merely performing an act, as they thought, useful to science, and, in passing, made casual observations: but I was a benefactor; my object in going there was to help the unhappy, ruined, depraved men and women whom I had expected to meet in this house. And suddenly, instead of unhappy, ruined, depraved beings, I found the majority to be working-men, quiet, satisfied, cheerful, kind, and very good.

I was still more strongly impressed when I found that in these lodgings the crying want I wished to relieve had already been relieved before I came. But by whom? By these same unhappy, depraved beings whom I was prepared to save; and this help was given in a way not open to me.

In one cellar lay a lonely old man suffering from typhus fever. He had no connections in the world; yet a woman, — a widow with a little girl, — quite a stranger to him, but living in the corner next to him, nursed him, and gave him tea, and bought him medicine with her own money.

In another lodging lay a woman in puerperal fever. A woman of the town was nursing her child, and had prepared a sucking-bottle for him, and had not gone out to ply her sad trade for two days.

An orphan girl was taken into the family of a tailor, who had three children of his own. Thus, there remained only such miserable unoccupied men as retired officials, clerks, men-servants out of situations, beggars, tipsy people, prostitutes, children, whom it was not possible to help all at once by means of money, but whose cases it was necessary to consider carefully before assisting them. I had been seeking for men suffering from want of means, whom one might be able to help by sharing one's superfluities with them. I had not found them. All those I had seen it would have been very difficult to assist materially without devoting time and care to them.

CHAPTER VII

These unfortunate people ranged themselves in my mind under three heads: first, those who had lost former advantageous positions, and who were waiting to return to them (such men belong to the lowest as well as to the highest classes of society); secondly, women of the town, who are very numerous in these houses; and thirdly, children.

The majority of those I found, and noted down, were men who had lost former places, and were desirous of returning to them. Such men were also numerous, being chiefly of the better class, and government officials. In almost all the lodgings we entered with the landlord, we were told, "Here we need not trouble to fill up the residential card ourselves; there is a man here who is able to do it, provided he is not tipsy."

And Ivan Fedotitch would call by name some such individual, who always belonged to this class of ruined people of a higher grade. When thus summoned, the man, if he were not tipsy, was always willing to undertake the task; he kept nodding his head with a sense of importance, knitted his brows, inserted now and then learned terms in his remarks, and, carefully holding in his dirty, trembling hands the neat pink card, looked round at his fellow-lodgers with pride and contempt, as if he were now, by the superiority of his education, triumphing over those who had been continually humbling him.

He was evidently pleased with having intercourse with the world which used pink cards, with a world of which he himself had once been a member.

To my questions about his life, this kind of man not only replied willingly, but with enthusiasm, — beginning to tell a story, fixed in his mind like a prayer, about all kinds of misfortunes which had happened to him, and chiefly about his former position, in which, considering his education, he ought to have remained.

Many such people are scattered about in all the tenements of the Rzhanoff Houses. One lodging-house was tenanted exclusively by them, women and men. As we approached them, Ivan Fedotitch said, "Now, here 's where the nobility live."

The lodging was full; almost all the lodgers — about forty persons — were at home. In the whole house, there were no faces so ruined and degraded-looking as these, — if old, flabby; if young, pale and haggard.

I talked with several of them. Almost always the same story was told, only in different degrees of development. One and all had been once rich, or had still a rich father or brother or uncle; or either his father or the unfortunate himself had held a high office. Then came some misfortune caused by envious enemies or his own imprudent kindness, or some out-of-the-way occurrence; and, having lost everything, he was obliged to descend to these strange and hateful surroundings, among lice and rags, in company with drunkards and loose characters, feeding upon bread and liver, and subsisting by beggary.

All the thoughts, desires, and recollections of these men are turned toward the past. The present appears to them as something unnatural, hideous, and unworthy of attention. The present does not exist for them. They have only recollections of the past, and expectations of the future, which may be realized at any moment, and for the attainment of which but very little is needed; but, unfortunately, this little is out of their reach; it cannot be got anywhere; and so they perish needlessly, one sooner, another later.

One needs only to be dressed respectably, in order to call on a well-known person who is kindly disposed toward him; another requires only to be dressed, have his debts paid, and go to some town or other; a third wants to take his effects out of pawn, and get a small sum to carry on a lawsuit, which must be decided in his favor, and then all will be well again. All say that they have need of some external circumstance in order to regain that position which they think natural and happy for them.

If I had not been blinded by my pride in being a benefactor, I should have needed only to look a little closer into their faces, young and old, which were generally weak, sensual, but kind, in order to understand that their misfortunes could not be met by exterior means; that they could be happy in no situation while their present conception of life remained the same, that they were by no means peculiar people in peculiarly unhappy circumstances, but that they were like all other men, ourselves included.

I remember well how my intercourse with men of this class was particularly trying to me. I now understand why it was so. In them I saw my own self as in a mirror. If I had considered carefully my own life, and the lives of people of my own class, I should have seen that, between us and these unfortunate men, there existed no essential difference.

Those who live around me in expensive suites of apartments, and houses of their own in the best streets of the city, eating something better, too, than liver or herring with their bread, are none the less unhappy. They also are discontented with their lot, regret the past, and desire a happier future, precisely as did the wretched tenants of the Rzhanoff Houses. Both wish to work less, and to be worked for more, the difference between them being only in degrees of idleness.

Unfortunately, I did not see this at first, nor did I understand that such people needed to be relieved, not by my charity, but of their own false views of the world; and that, to change a man's estimate of life, he must be given one more accurate than his own, which unhappily, not possessing myself, I could not communicate to others.

These men were unhappy, not because, to use an illustration, they had not nourishing food, but because their stomachs were spoiled; and they required, not nourishment, but a tonic. I did not see that in order to help them it was not necessary to give them food, but to teach them how to eat. Though I am anticipating, I must say that, of all these people whose names I put down, I did not in reality help one, notwithstanding that all some of them had desired was done in order to relieve them. Of these I became acquainted with three men in particular. All three, after many failures and much assistance, are now just in the same position in which they were three years ago.

CHAPTER VIII

The second class of unfortunates, whom I hoped afterward to be able to help, were women of the town. Such women were very numerous in the Rzhanoff Houses; and they were of every kind, from young girls still bearing some likeness to women, to old and fearful-looking creatures without a vestige of humanity. The hope of helping these women, whom I had not at first in view, was aroused by the following circumstances.

When we had just finished half our visiting tour, we had already acquired a somewhat mechanical method. On entering a new lodging, we at once asked for the landlord. One of us sat down, clearing a space to write; and the other went from one to another, questioning each man and woman in the room, and reporting the information obtained to the one who was writing.

On our entering one of the basement lodgings, the student went to look for the landlord; and I began to question all who were in the place. This place was thus divided: In the middle of the room, which was four yards square, there stood a stove. From the stove radiated four partitions or screens, making a similar number of small compartments. In the first of these, which had two doors in it opposite each other, and four pallets, were an old man and a woman. Next to it was a rather long but narrow room, in which was the landlord, a young, pale, good-looking man, dressed in a gray woolen coat. To the left of the first division there was a third small room, where a man was sleeping, seemingly tipsy, and a woman in a pink dressing-gown. The fourth compartment was behind a partition, access to it being through the landlord's room.

The student entered the latter, while I remained in the first, questioning the old man and the woman. The former had been a type-setter, but had now no means of livelihood whatever.

The woman was a cook's wife.

I went into the third compartment, and asked the

woman in the dressing-gown about the man who was asleep.

She answered that he was a visitor.

I asked her who she was.

She replied that she was a peasant girl from the county of Moscow.

"What is your occupation?" She laughed, and made no answer.

"What do you do for your living?" I repeated, thinking she had not understood the question.

"I sit in the inn," she said.

I did not understand her, and asked again:—

"What are your means of living?"

She gave me no answer, but continued to giggle. In the fourth room, where we had not yet been, I heard the voices of women also giggling.

The landlord came out of his room, and approached us. He had evidently heard my questions and the woman's answers. He glanced sternly at her, and, turning to me, said, "She is a prostitute;" and it was evident that he was pleased that he knew this word, which is the one used in official circles, and at having pronounced it correctly. And having said this with a respectful smile of satisfaction toward me, he turned to the woman. As he did so, the expression of his face changed. In a peculiarly contemptuous manner, and with rapid utterance as one would speak to a dog, he said without looking at her, "Don't be a fool! Instead of saying you sit in the inn, speak plainly and say you are a prostitute. — She does not even yet know her proper name," he said, turning to me.

This manner of speaking shocked me.

"It is not for us to shame her," I said. "If we were all living according to God's commandment, there would be no such persons."

"Yes, yes; of course you are right," said the landlord, with a forced smile.

"Therefore we must pity them, and not reproach them as if it were their own fault entirely."

I do not remember exactly what I said. I remember

only that I was disgusted by the disdainful tone of this young landlord, in a lodging filled with females whom he termed prostitutes; and I pitied the woman, and expressed both feelings.

No sooner had I said this, than I heard from the small compartment where the giggling had been, the noise of creaking bed-boards; and over the partition, which did not reach to the ceiling, appeared the disheveled curly head of a female with small swollen eyes and a shining red face; a second and then a third head followed. They were evidently standing on their beds; and all three were stretching their necks and holding their breath, and looking silently at me with strained attention.

A painful silence followed.

The student, who had been smiling before this happened, now became grave; the landlord became confused, and cast down his eyes; and the women continued to look at me in expectation.

I felt more disconcerted than all the rest. I had certainly not expected that a casual word would produce such an effect. It was like the field of battle covered with dead bones seen by the prophet Ezekiel, on which, trembling from contact with the spirit, the dead bones began to move. I had casually uttered a word of love and pity, which produced upon all such an effect that it seemed as if they had been only waiting for it, to cease to be corpses, and to become alive again.

They continued to look at me, as if wondering what would come next, as if waiting for me to say those words and do those acts by which these dry bones would begin to come together, — be covered with flesh and receive life.

But I felt, alas! that I had no such words or deeds to give, or to continue as I had begun. In the depth of my soul I felt that I had told a lie, that I myself was like them, that I had nothing more to say; and I began to write down on the domiciliary card the names and the occupations of all the lodgers there.

This occurrence led me into a new kind of error. I

began to think that these unhappy ones also could be helped. This, in my self-deception, it seemed to me would be very easily done. I said to myself, "Now we shall put down the names of these women too; and afterward, when we (though it never occurred to me to ask who were the *we*) have written everything down, we can occupy ourselves with their affairs." I imagined that *we*, the very persons who, during many generations, have been leading such women into such a condition, and still continue to do so, could one fine morning wake, and remedy it all. And yet, if I could have recollected my conversation with the lost woman who was nursing the baby for the sick mother, I should have understood all the folly of such an idea.

When we first saw this woman nursing the child, we thought that it was hers; but upon our asking her what she was, she answered us plainly that she was unmarried. She did not say "prostitute." It was left for the rude proprietor of the lodgings to make use of that terrible word. The supposition that she had a child gave me the idea of helping her out of her present position.

"Is this child yours?" I asked.

"No; it is that woman's there."

"Why do you nurse him?"

"She asked me to; she is dying."

Though my surmise turned out to be wrong, I continued to speak with her in the same spirit. I began to question her as to who she was, and how she came to be in such a position. She told me her story willingly, and very plainly. She belonged to the lower ranks of Moscow society, the daughter of a factory workman. She was left an orphan, and adopted by her aunt, from whose house she began to visit the inns. The aunt was now dead.

When I asked her whether she wished to change her course of life, my question did not even interest her. How can a supposition about something quite impossible awaken an interest in any one? She smiled, and said:—

"Who would take me with a yellow ticket?"

"But," said I, "if it were possible to find you a situation as a cook or something else?" I said this because she looked like a strong woman, with a kind, dull, round face, not unlike many cooks I had seen.

Evidently my words did not please her. She repeated, "Cook! but I do not understand how to bake bread."

She spoke jestingly; but, by the expression of her face, I saw that she was unwilling; that she even considered the position and rank of a cook beneath her.

This woman, who, in the most simple manner, like the widow in the gospel, had sacrificed all that she had for a sick person, at the same time, like other women of the same profession, considered the position of a workman or working-woman low and despicable. She had been educated in order to live without work, — a life which all her friends considered quite natural. This was her misfortune. And by this she came into her present position, and is kept in it. This brought her to the inns. Who of us men and women will cure her of this false view of life? Are there among us men convinced that a laborious life is more respectable than an idle one, and who are living according to this conviction, and who make this the test of their esteem and respect?

If I had thought about it, I should have understood that neither I nor anybody else I know was able to cure a person of this disease.

I should have understood that those wondering and awakened faces that looked over the partition expressed merely astonishment at the pity shown to them, but no wish to reform their lives. They did not see the immorality of them. They knew that they were despised and condemned, but the reason for it they could not understand. They had lived in this manner from their infancy among women like themselves, who, they know very well, have always existed, do exist, and are so necessary to society, that there are officials deputed by government to see that they conform to regulations.

Besides, they know that they have power over men, and subdue them, and often influence them more than any other women. They see that their position in society, notwithstanding the fact that they are always blamed, is recognized by men as well as by women and by the government; and therefore they cannot even understand of what they have to repent, and wherein they should reform.

During one of our visiting tours the student told me that, in one of the lodgings, there was a woman about to sell her daughter, thirteen years old. Wishing to save this little girl, I went on purpose to their lodging.

Mother and daughter were living in great poverty. The mother, a small, dark-complexioned prostitute of forty years of age, was not simply ugly, but disagreeably ugly. The daughter also was bad-looking. To all my indirect questions about their mode of life, the mother replied curtly, with a look of suspicion and animosity, apparently feeling that I was an enemy with bad intentions; the daughter said nothing without looking first at the mother, in whom she evidently had entire confidence.

They did not awaken pity in my heart, but rather disgust. But I decided that it was necessary, to save the daughter, to awaken an interest in ladies who might sympathize with the miserable condition of these women, and might so be brought here.

But if I had thought about the antecedents of the mother, how she had given birth to her daughter, how she had fed and educated her, certainly without any outside help, and with great sacrifices to herself; if I had thought of the view of life which had formed itself in her mind, — I should have understood that, in the mother's conduct, there was nothing at all bad or immoral, seeing she had been doing for her daughter all she could; *i.e.* what she considered best for herself.

It was possible to take this girl away from her mother by force; but to convince her that she was doing wrong in selling her daughter was not possible. It would first be necessary to save this woman — this mother — from a condition of life approved by every one, and according to which a woman may live without marrying and without working, serving exclusively as a gratification to the passions. If I had thought about this, I should have understood that the majority of those ladies whom I wished to send here for the saving of this girl were not only themselves avoiding family duties, and leading idle and sensual lives, but were consciously educating their daughters for this very same mode of existence. One mother leads her daughter to the inn, and another to court and to balls. But the views of the world held by both mothers are the same; viz., that a woman must gratify the lusts of men, and for that she must be fed, dressed, and taken care of.

How, then, are our ladies to reform this woman and her daughter?

CHAPTER IX

Still more strange were my dealings with the children. In my *rôle* as a benefactor, I paid attention to the children, too, wishing to save innocent beings from going to ruin in this den; and I wrote down their names in order to attend to them myself *afterward*.

Among these children, my attention was particularly drawn to Serozha, a boy twelve years old. I sincerely pitied this clever, intelligent lad, who had been living with a bootmaker, and who was left without any place of refuge when his master was put into prison. I wished to do something for him.

I will now give the result of my benevolence in his case, because this boy's story will show my false position as a benefactor better than anything else.

I took the boy into my house, and lodged him in the kitchen. Could I possibly bring a lousy boy out of a den of depravity to my children? I considered that I had been very kind in having put him where he was, amongst my servants. I thought myself a great benefactor for having given him some of my old clothes and fed him, though it was properly my cook who did it, not I. The boy remained in my house about a week.

During this week I saw him twice, and, passing by him, spoke some words to him, and, when out walking, called on a bootmaker whom I knew, and proposed the boy as an apprentice. A peasant who was on a visit at my house invited him to go to his village and work in a family. The boy refused to accept it, and disappeared within a week.

I went to Rzhanoff's house to inquire after him. He had returned there, but when I called he was not at home. He had already been two days to the zoölogical gardens, where he hired himself for thirty kopeks a day to appear in a procession of savages in costume, leading an elephant. There was some public show on at the time.

I went to see him again, but he evidently avoided me. Had I reflected upon the life of this boy, and on my own, I should have understood that the boy had been spoiled by the fact of his having tasted the sweets of a merry and idle life, and that he had lost the habit of working. And I, in order to confer a benefit on him and reform him, took him into my own house; and what did he see there? He saw my children, some older than he, some younger, and some of the same age, who not only never did anything for themselves, but gave as much work to others as they could. They dirtied and spoiled everything about them, surfeited themselves with all sorts of dainties, broke the china, upset and threw to the dogs food which would have been a treat to him. If I took him out of a den and brought him to a respectable place, he could not but assimilate those views of life which existed there; and, according to these views, he understood that, in a respectable position, one must live without working, eat and drink well, and lead a merry life.

True, he did not know that my children had much labor in learning the exceptions in Latin and Greek grammars; and he would not have been able to understand the object of such work. But one cannot help seeing that, had he even understood it, the influence upon him of the example of my children would have been still stronger. He would have then understood that they were being educated in such a way that, not working now, they might hereafter also work as little as possible, and enjoy the good things of life by virtue of their diplomas.

But what he did understand of it made him go, not, to the peasant to take care of cattle and feed on potatoes and kvas, but to the zoölogical gardens in the costume of a savage to lead an elephant for thirty kopeks a day. I ought to have understood how foolish it was of one who was educating his own children in complete idleness and luxury, to try to reform other men and their children, and save them from going to ruin and idleness in what I called the *dens* in Rzhanoff's house; where, however, three-fourths of the men were working for themselves and for others. But then I understood nothing of all this.

In Rzhanoff's house, there were a great many children in the most miserable condition. There were children of prostitutes, orphans, and children carried about the streets by beggars. They were all very wretched. But my experience with Serozha showed me that, so long as I continued living the life which I did, I was not able to help them.

While the latter was living with us, I remember that I took pains to hide from him our way of life, particularly that of my children. I felt that all my endeavors to lead him to a good and laborious life were frustrated by my example and that of my children. It is very easy to take away a child from a prostitute or a beggar. It is very easy, when one has money, to wash him, dress him in new clothes, feed him well, and even teach him different accomplishments; but to teach him how to earn his living is, for us who have not been earning ours, but have been doing just the contrary, not only difficult, but quite impossible, because by our example, and by the very improvements of his mode of life effected by us, without any cost on our part, we teach him the very opposite.

You may take a puppy, pet him, feed him, teach him to carry things after you, and be pleased with looking at him; but it is not enough to feed a man, dress him, and teach him Greek; you must teach him how to live; *i.e.* how to take less from others, and give them more in return: and yet we cannot help teaching him the very opposite, through our own mode of life, whether we take him into our own house, or put him into a home to bring up.

CHAPTER X

I HAVE never since experienced such a feeling of compassion toward men, and of aversion toward myself, as I felt in Liapin's house. I was now filled with the desire to carry out the scheme which I had already begun, and to do good to those men whom I met with.

And, strange to say, though it might seem that to do good and to give money to those in want of it was a good deed, and ought to dispose men to universal love, it turned out quite the reverse; calling up in me bitter feeling, and a disposition to censure them. Even during our first visiting tour, a scene occurred similar to that in Liapin's house; but it failed to produce again the same effect, and created a very different impression.

It began with my finding in one of the lodgings a miserable person who required immediate help, — a woman who had not eaten food for two days.

It happened thus: In one very large and almost empty night lodging, I asked an old woman whether there were any poor people who had nothing to eat. She hesitated a moment, and then named two; then suddenly, as if recollecting herself, she said, "Yes, there lies one of them," pointing to a pallet. "This one," she added, "indeed, has nothing to eat."

"You don't say so! Who is she?"

"She has been a lost woman; but, as nobody takes her now, she can't earn anything. The landlady has had pity on her, but now she wants to turn her out.— Agafia! I say, Agafia!" cried the old woman.

We went a little nearer, and saw something rise from the pallet. This was a gray-haired, disheveled woman, thin as a skeleton, in a dirty, torn chemise, and with peculiarly glittering, immovable eyes. She looked fixedly beyond us, tried to snatch up her jacket behind her in order to cover her bony chest, and growled out like a dog, "What? what?"

I asked her how she managed to live. For some time she was unable to see the drift of my words, and said, "I do not know myself; they are going to turn me out."

I asked again; and oh, how ashamed of myself I feel! my hand can scarcely write it! I asked her whether it was true that she was starving. She replied in the same feverish, excited manner, "I had nothing to eat yesterday; I have had nothing to eat to-day."

The miserable aspect of this woman impressed me deeply, but quite differently, from what those had in Liapin's house; there, out of pity for them, I felt embarrassed and ashamed of myself; but here, I rejoiced that I had, at last, found what I had been looking for,— a hungry being.

I gave her a ruble, and I remember how glad I felt that the others had seen it.

The old woman forthwith asked me also for money. It was so pleasant to me to give, that I handed her some also, without thinking whether it was necessary or not. She accompanied me to the door, and those who were in the corridor heard how she thanked me. Probably my questions about the poor provoked expectations, for some of the inmates began to follow us wherever we went.

Among those that begged, there were evidently drunkards, who gave me a most disagreeable impression; but, having once given to the old woman, I thought I had no right to refuse them, and I began to give away more. This only increased the number of applicants, and there was a stir throughout the whole lodging-house.

On the stairs and in the galleries, people appeared

dogging my steps. When I came out of the yard, a boy ran quickly down the stairs, pushing through the people. He did not notice me, and said hurriedly: —

"He gave a ruble to Agafia!"

Having reached the ground, he, too, joined the crowd that was following me. I came out into the street. All sorts of people crowded round me, begging for money. Having given away all I had in coppers, I entered a shop and asked the proprietor to give me change for ten rubles.

And here a scene similar to that which took place in Liapin's house occurred. A dreadful confusion ensued. Old women, seedy gentlefolk, peasants, children, all crowded about the shop, stretching out their hands; I gave, and asked some of them about their position and means, and entered all in my note-book. The shop-keeper, having turned up the fur collar of his greatcoat, was sitting like a statue, glancing now and then at the crowd, and again staring beyond it. He apparently felt, like every one else, that all this was very foolish, but he dared not say so.

In Liapin's house the misery and humiliation of the people had overwhelmed me; and I felt myself to blame for it, and also felt the desire and the possibility of becoming a better man. But though the scene here was similar, it produced a quite different effect. In the first place, I felt angry with many of those who assailed me, and then I felt anxious as to what the shopmen and the dvorniks might think of me. I returned home that day with a weight on my mind. I knew that what I had done was foolish and inconsistent; but, as usual, when my conscience was troubled, I talked the more about my projected plan, as if I had no doubt whatever as to its success.

The next day I went alone to those whom I had noted down, and who seemed the most miserable, thinking they could be more easily helped than others.

As I have already mentioned, I was not really able to help any of these people. It turned out that to do so was more difficult than I had imagined; either I did not understand how to do it, or else it was indeed impossible.

I went several times before the last visiting tour to Rzhanoff's house, and each time the same thing occurred: I was assailed by a crowd of men and women, in the midst of whom I utterly lost my presence of mind.

I felt the impossibility of doing anything because there were so many of them, and I was angry with them because they were so many; besides, each of them, taken separately, did not awaken any sympathy in me. I felt that each one of them lied, or at least prevaricated, and regarded me only as a purse out of which money could be abstracted. It often seemed to me that the very money which was extorted from me did not improve their position, but only made it worse.

The oftener I went to these houses, the closer the intercourse which I had with the inmates, the more apparent became the impossibility of doing anything; but, notwithstanding this, I did not give up my plan until after the last night tour with the census-takers.

I feel more ashamed of this visit than of any other. Formerly I had gone alone, but now twenty of us went together. At seven o'clock all those who wished to take part in this last tour began to assemble in my house. They were almost all strangers to me. Some students, an officer, and two of my fashionable acquaintances, who, after having repeated the usual phrase, "C'est très intéressant!" asked me to put them into the number of the census-takers.

These fashionable friends of mine had dressed themselves in shooting-jackets and high traveling-boots, which they thought more suited to the visit than their ordinary attire. They carried with them peculiar pocket-books and extraordinary-looking pencils. They were in that agitated state of mind which one experiences just before going to a hunt, or to a duel, or into a battle. The falseness and foolishness of our enterprise was now more apparent to me when looking at them; but were we not all in the same ridiculous position?

Before starting we had a conference, somewhat like a

council of war, as to what we should begin with, how to divide ourselves, and so on. This conference was just like all other official councils, meetings, and committees: each spoke, not because he had anything to say, or to ask, but because every one tried to find something to say in order not to be behind the rest. But during this conversation no one alluded to the acts of benevolence to which I had so many times referred; and however much ashamed I felt, I found it was needful to remind them that we must carry out our charitable intentions by writing down, during the visiting tour, the names of all whom we should find in a destitute condition.

I had always felt ashamed to speak about these matters; but here, in the midst of our hurried preparations for the expedition, I could scarcely utter a word about them. All listened to me and seemed touched, all agreed with me in words; but it was evident that each of them knew that it was folly, and that it would lead to nothing, so they began at once to talk about other subjects, and continued doing so until it was time for us to start.

We came to the dark tavern, aroused the waiters, and began to sort our papers. When we were told that the people, having heard about this visiting tour, had begun to leave their lodgings, we asked the landlord to shut the gate, and we ourselves went to the yard to persuade those to remain who wanted to escape, assuring them that no one would ask to see their tickets.

I remember the strange and painful impression produced upon me by these frightened night lodgers. Ragged and half-dressed, they all appeared tall to me by the light of the lantern in the dark courtyard. Frightened and horrible in their terror, they stood in a small knot round the pestilential outhouse, listening to our persuasions, but not believing us, and evidently, like hunted animals, were prepared to do anything to escape from us.

Gentlemen of all kinds, town and country policemen, public prosecutors and judges, had all their lives long been hunting them in towns and villages, on the roads and in the streets, in the taverns and in the lodging-houses; and suddenly these gentlemen had come at night and shut the gate, only, forsooth, in order to count them: they found it as difficult to believe this as it would be for hares to believe that the dogs are come out not to catch but to count them.

But the gates were shut, and the frightened night lodgers returned to their respective places; and we, having separated into groups, began our visit. With me were my fashionable acquaintances and two students. Vanya, with a lantern, went before us in a greatcoat and white trousers, and we followed. We entered lodgings well known to me. The place was familiar, some of the persons also; but the majority were new to me, and the spectacle was also a new and dreadful one, — still more dreadful than that which I had seen at Liapin's house. All the lodgings were filled, all the pallets occupied, and not only by one, but often by two persons. The sight was dreadful, because of the closeness with which these people were huddled together, and because of the indiscriminate commingling of men and women. Such of the latter as were not dead drunk were sleeping with men. Many women with children slept with strange men on narrow beds.

The spectacle was dreadful, owing to the misery, dirt, raggedness, and terror of these people; and chiefly so because there were so many of them. One lodging, then another, then a third, a tenth, a twentieth, and so on, without end. And everywhere the same fearful stench, the same suffocating exhalation, the same confusion of sexes, men and women, drunk, or in a state of insensibility; the same terror, submissiveness, and guilt stamped on all faces, so that I felt deeply ashamed and grieved, as I had before at Liapin's. At last I understood that what I was about to do was disgusting, foolish, and therefore impossible; so I left off writing down their names and questioning them, knowing now that nothing would come of it.

At Liapin's I had been like a man who sees a horrible wound on the body of another. He feels sorry for the man, ashamed of not having relieved him before, yet he can still hope to help the sufferer; but now I was like a doctor who comes with his own medicines to the patient, uncovers his wound only to mangle it, and to confess to himself that all he has done has been in vain, and that his remedy is ineffectual.

CHAPTER XI

THIS visit gave the last blow to my self-deception. It became very evident to me that my aim was not only foolish, but also productive of evil. And yet, though I knew this, it seemed to be my duty to continue my project a little longer: first, because by the article which I had written, and my visits, I had raised the expectations of the poor; secondly, because what I had said and written had awakened the sympathy of some benefactors, many of whom had promised to assist me personally and with money. And I was expecting to be applied to by both, and hoped to satisfy them as well as I was able.

As regards the applications made to me by those who were in need, the following details may be given. I received more than a hundred letters, which came exclusively from the "rich poor," if I may so express myself. Some of them I visited and some I left unanswered. In no instance did I succeed in doing any good. All the applications made to me were from persons who were once in a privileged position (I call such persons privileged who receive more from others than they give in return), had lost that position, and were desirous of regaining it. One wanted two hundred rubles in order to keep his business from going to ruin, and to enable him to finish the education of his children; another wanted to have a photographic establishment; a third wanted money to pay his debts, and take his best clothes out of pawn; a fourth was in need of a piano, in order to perfect himself, and earn money to support his family by giving lessons. The majority did not name any particular sum of money, they simply asked for help; but when I began to investigate what was necessary, it turned out that their wants increased in proportion to the help offered, and nothing satisfactory resulted. I repeat again, the fault may have been in my want of understanding; but in any case I helped no one, notwithstanding the fact that I made every effort to do so.

As for the philanthropists who were to coöperate with me, something very strange and quite unexpected occurred: of all who promised to assist with money, and even stated the amount they would give, not one contributed anything for distribution among the poor.

The promises of pecuniary assistance amounted to about three thousand rubles; but of all these people, not one recollected his agreement, or gave me a single kopek. The students alone gave the money which they received as payment for visiting, about twelve rubles; so that my scheme, which was to have collected tens of thousands of rubles from the rich, and to have saved hundreds and thousands of people from misery and vice, ended in my distributing at random some few rubles among those who came begging; and there remained on my hands the twelve rubles offered by the students, with twenty-five more sent me by the town-council for my labor as manager, which I positively did not know what to do with.

And so ended the affair.

Then, before leaving Moscow for the country, on the Sunday before the carnival I went to the Rzhanoff house in the morning in order to distribute the thirty-seven rubles among the poor. I visited all whom I knew in the lodgings, but found only one invalid, to whom I gave something, — I think five rubles. There was nobody else to give to. Of course many began to beg; but, as I did not know them, I made up my mind to take the advice of Ivan Fedotitch, the tavern-keeper, respecting the distribution of the remaining thirty-two rubles.

It was the first day of the carnival. Everybody was smartly dressed, all had had food, and many were drunk.

In the yard near the corner of the house stood an old-clothes man, dressed in a ragged peasant's coat and bark shoes. He was still hale and hearty. Sorting his purchases, he was putting them into different heaps,—leather, iron, and other things,—and was singing a merry song at the top of his voice.

I began to talk with him. He was seventy years of age; had no relatives; earned his living by dealing in old clothes, and not only did not complain, but said he had enough to eat, drink, and to spare. I asked him who in the place were particularly in want. He became cross, and said plainly that there was no one in want but drunkards and idlers; but on learning my object in asking, he begged of me five kopeks for drink, and ran to the tavern for it.

I also went to the tavern to see Ivan Fedotitch, in order to ask him to distribute the money for me. It was full; gayly dressed tipsy prostitutes were walking to and fro; all the tables were occupied; many people were already drunk; and in the small room some one was playing a harmonium, and two people were dancing. Ivan Fedotitch, out of respect for me, ordered them to leave off, and sat down next me at a vacant table. I asked him, as he knew his lodgers well, to point out those most in want, as I was intrusted with a little money for distribution, and wished him to direct me. The kind-hearted man (he died a year after), although he had to wait on his customers, gave me his attention for a time in order to oblige me. He began to think over it, and was evidently puzzled. One old waiter had overheard us, and took his part in the conference.

They began to go over his lodgers, some of whom were known to me, but they could not agree. "Paramonovna," suggested the waiter.

"Well, yes, she does go hungry sometimes; but she drinks."

"What difference does that make?"

"Well, Spiridon Ivanovitch, he has children; that 's the man for you."

But Ivan Fedotitch had doubts about Spiridon too.

"Akulina; but she has a pension. Ah, but there is the blind man!"

To him I myself objected; I had just seen him. This was an old man of eighty years of age, without any relatives. One could scarcely imagine any condition to be worse; and yet I had just seen him lying drunk on a feather-bed, cursing at his comparatively young mistress in the most filthy language.

They then named a one-armed boy and his mother. I saw that Ivan Fedotitch was in great difficulty, owing to his conscientiousness, for he knew that everything given away by me would be spent at his tavern. But as I had to get rid of my thirty-two rubles, I insisted, and we managed somehow or other to distribute the money. Those who received it were mostly well-dressed, and we had not far to go to find them; they were all in the tavern.

Thus ended all my benevolent enterprises; and I left for the country, vexed with every one, as it always happens when one does something foolish and harmful. Nothing came of it all, except the train of thoughts and feelings which it called forth in me, which not only did not cease, but doubly agitated my mind.

CHAPTER XII

WHAT did it all mean?

I had lived in the country, and had entered into relations with the country poor. It is not out of false modesty, but in order to state the truth, which is necessary in order to understand the run of all my thoughts and feelings, that I must say that in the country I had done perhaps but little for the poor, the help which had been required of me was so small; but even the little I had done had been useful, and had formed round me an atmosphere of love and sympathy with my fellow-creatures, in the midst of whom it might yet be possible for me to quiet the gnawing of my conscience as to the unlawfulness of my life of luxury.

On going to the city I had hoped for the same happy relations with the poor, but there things were upon quite another footing. In the city, poverty was at once less truthful, more exacting, and more bitter than in the country. It was chiefly because there was so much more of it accumulated together, that it produced upon me a most harrowing impression. What I experienced at Liapin's house made my own luxurious life seem monstrously evil. I could not doubt the sincerity and the strength of this conviction; yet, notwithstanding this, I was quite incapable of carrying out that revolution which demanded an entire change in my mode of life: I was frightened at the prospect, and so I resorted to compromises. I accepted what I was told by every one, and what has been said by everybody since the world began, — that riches and luxury contain in themselves no evil, that they are given by God, and that it is possible to help those in need whilst continuing to live luxuriously. I believed this, and wanted to do so. And I wrote an article in which I called upon all rich people to help. These all admitted themselves morally obliged to agree with me, but evidently did not wish to, or could not, either do or give anything for the poor.

I then began visiting, and discovered what I had in no way expected to see. On the one hand, I saw in these dens (as I had at first called them) men whom it was impossible for me to help, because they were working-men, accustomed to labor and privation, and therefore having a much firmer hold on life than I had. On the other hand, I saw miserable men whom I could not aid because they were just such as I was myself. The majority of the poor whom I saw were wretched, merely because they had lost the capacity, desire, and habit of earning their bread; in other words, their misery consisted in the fact that they were just like myself. Whereas, of poor people, to whom it was possible to give immediate assistance, — those suffering from illness, cold, and hunger, — I found none, except the starving Agafia; and I became persuaded that, being so far removed from the life of those whom I wished to succor, it was almost impossible to find such need as I sought, because all real need was attended to by those amongst whom these unhappy creatures lived: and my principal conviction now was that, with money, I could never reform that life of misery which these people led.

I was persuaded of this: yet a feeling of shame to leave off all I had begun, and self-deception as to my own virtues, made me continue my plan for some time longer, till it died a natural death; thus, only with great difficulty and the help of Ivan Fedotitch, I managed to distribute in the tavern at Rzhanoff's house the thirty-seven rubles which I considered were not my own.

Of course I might have continued this style of thing and have transformed it into a kind of charity, and, by importuning those who promised to give me money, I might have obtained and distributed more, thus comforting myself with the idea of my own excellence; but I became convinced on the one hand, that we rich people do not wish, and are also unable, to distribute to the poor a portion of our superfluities (we have so many wants ourselves), and that money should not be given to any one if we really wished to do good, and not merely to distribute it at random as I had done in the Rzhanoff tavern; so I dropped the affair entirely, and quitted Moscow, in despair, for my own village.

I intended on returning home to write a pamphlet on my experience, and to state why my project had not succeeded. I wanted to justify myself from the imputations which resulted from my article on the census; I wanted also to denounce society and its heartless indifference; and I desired to point out the causes of this town misery, and the necessity for endeavoring to remedy it, as well as those means which I thought were requisite for this purpose. I began even then to write, and fancied I had many very important facts to communicate. But in vain did I rack my brain: I could not manage it, notwithstanding the superabundance of material at my command, because of the irritation under which I wrote, and because I had not yet learned by experience what was necessary to grasp the question rightly; still more because I had not become fully conscious of the cause of it all, — a very simple cause, which was deep-rooted in myself; so the pamphlet was not finished at the commencement of the present year (1884–1885). In the matter of moral law we witness a strange phenomenon to which men pay too little attention. If I speak to an unlearned man about geology, astronomy, history, natural philosophy, or mathematics, he receives the information as quite new to him, and never says to me, "There is nothing new in what you tell me; every one knows it, and I have known it for a long time."

But tell a man one of the highest moral truths in the simplest manner, in such a way as it has never been before formulated, and every ordinary man, particularly one who does not take any interest in moral questions, and, above all, one who dislikes them, is sure to say: "Who does not know that? It has been always known and expressed." And he really believes this. Only those who can appreciate moral truths know how to value their elucidation and simplification by a long and laborious process, or can prize the transition from a first vaguely understood proposition or desire to a firm and determined expression calling for a corresponding change of conduct.

We are all accustomed to consider moral doctrine to be a very insipid and dull affair, in which there cannot be anything new or interesting; whereas, in reality, human life, with all its complicated and varied actions, which seem to have no connection with morals, — political activity, activity in the sciences, in the arts, and in commerce, — has no other object than to elucidate moral truths more and more, and to confirm, simplify, and make them accessible to all.

I recollect once while walking in a street in Moscow I saw a man come out and examine the flagstones attentively; then, choosing one of them, he sat down by it and began to scrape or rub it vigorously.

"What is he doing with the pavement?" I wondered; and, having come up close to him, I discovered he was a young man from a butcher's shop, and was sharpening his knife on the flagstone. He was not thinking about the stones when examining them, and still less while doing his work: he was merely sharpening his knife. It was necessary for him to do so in order to cut the meat, but to me it seemed that he was doing something to the pavement.

In the same way mankind seems to be occupied with commerce, treaties, wars, sciences, arts; and yet for them one thing only is important, and they do only that, — they are elucidating those moral laws by which they live.

Moral laws are already in existence, and mankind has been merely rediscovering them: this elucidation appears to be unimportant and imperceptible to one who has no need of moral law, and who does not desire to live by it. Yet this is not only the chief, but ought to be the sole, business of all men. This elucidation is imperceptible in the same way as the difference between a sharp knife and a blunt one is imperceptible. A knife remains a knife; and one who has not got to cut anything with it will not notice its edge; but for one who understands that all his life depends more or less upon whether his knife is blunt or sharp, every improvement in sharpening it is important; and such a man knows that there must be no limit to this improvement, and that the knife is only really a knife when it is sharp, and when it cuts what it has to cut.

The conviction of this truth flashed upon me when I began to write my pamphlet. Previously it seemed to me that I knew everything about my subject, that I had a thorough understanding of everything connected with those questions which had been awakened in me by the impressions made in Liapin's house during the census; but when I tried to sum them up, and to put them on paper, it turned out that the knife would not cut, and had to be sharpened; so it is only now after three years that I feel my knife is sharp enough for me to cut out what I want. It is not that I have learned new things: my thoughts are still the same; but they were blunt formerly; they kept scattering in every direction; there was no edge to them; nor was anything brought, as it is now, to one central point, to one most simple and plain conclusion.

CHAPTER XIII

I RECOLLECT that during the whole time of my unsuccessful endeavors to help the unfortunate inhabitants of Moscow, I felt that I was like a man trying to help others out of a morass, who was himself all the time stuck fast in it. Every effort made me feel the instability of that ground upon which I was standing. I was conscious that I myself was in this same morass; but this acknowledgment did not help me to look more closely under my feet in order to ascertain the nature of the ground upon which I stood; I kept looking for some exterior means to remedy the existing evil.

I felt then that my life was a bad one, and that people ought not to live so; yet I did not come to the most natural and obvious conclusion that I must first reform my own mode of life before I should have any conception of how to reform that of others. And so I began, as it were, at the wrong end. I was living in town and I desired to improve the lives of the men there; but I was soon convinced that I had no power to do so, and I began to ponder over the nature of town life and town misery.

I said to myself over and over: "What is this town life and town misery? And why, while living in town, am I unable to help the town poor?" The only reply I found was that I was powerless to do anything for them: first, because there were too many collected together in one place; secondly, because none of them was at all like those in the country. And again I asked myself, "Why are there so many here, and in what do they differ from the country poor?"

To both these questions the answer was one and the same. There are many poor people in towns because there all those who have nothing to subsist on in the country are collected round the rich, and their peculiarity consists only in that they have all come into the towns from the country in order to get a living. (If there are any town poor born there, whose fathers and grandfathers were town born, these in their turn originally came there to get a living.) But what are we to understand by the expression, "getting a living in town"? There is something strange in the expression, it sounds like a joke when we reflect on its meaning. How is it that from the country — *i.e.* from places where there are woods, meadows, corn, and cattle, where the earth yields the treasures of fertility — men come away in order to get a living in a place where there are none of these advantages, but only stones and dust? What then do these words signify, to "get a living in town"?

Such a phrase is constantly used both by the employed and their employers, and that as if it were quite clear and intelligible. I remember now all the hundreds and thousands of town people living well or in want with whom I had spoken about their object in coming here; and all of them, without exception, told me they had quitted their villages in order to get a living; that, according to the proverb, "Moscow neither sows nor reaps, yet lives in wealth;" that in Moscow there is abundance of everything; and that, therefore, in Moscow one may get the money which is needed in the country for getting corn, cottages, horses, and the other essentials of life.

But, in fact, the source of all wealth is the country; there only are real riches, — corn, woods, horses, and everything necessary. Why then go to towns in order to get what is to be had in the country? And why should people carry away from the country into the towns such things as are necessary for country people, flour, oats, horses, and cattle?

Hundreds of times have I spoken thus with peasants who live in towns; and from my talks with them, and from my own observations, it became clear to me that the accumulation of country people in our cities is partly necessary, because they could not otherwise earn their livelihood, and partly voluntary, because they are attracted by the temptations of a town life. It is true that the circumstances of a peasant are such that, in order to satisfy the pecuniary demands made on him in his village, he cannot do it otherwise than by selling that corn and cattle which he very well knows will be necessary for himself; and he is compelled, whether he will or not, to go to town in order to earn back that which was his own. But it is also true that he is attracted to town by the charms of a comparatively easy way of getting money and by the luxury of life there; and, under the pretext of thus earning his living, he goes there in order to have easier work and better eating, to drink tea three times a day, to dress himself smartly, and even to get drunk and lead a dissolute life.

The cause is a simple one, for property passing from the hands of the agriculturist into those of non-agriculturists thus accumulates in towns. Observe toward autumn how much wealth is gathered together in villages. Then come the demands of taxes, rents, recruiting; then the temptations of vodka, marriages, feasts, peddlers, and all sorts of other snares; so that in one way or other, this property, in all its various forms (sheep, calves, cows, horses, pigs, poultry, eggs, butter, hemp, flax, rye, oats, buckwheat, pease, hemp-seed, and flaxseed), passes into the hands of strangers, and is taken first to provincial towns and from them to the capitals. A villager is compelled to dispose of all these in order to satisfy the demands made upon him, and the temptations offered him, and, having thus dispensed his goods, he is left in want, and must follow where his wealth has been taken; and there he tries to earn back the money necessary for his most urgent needs at home; and so, being partly carried away by these temptations, he himself, along with others, makes use of the accumulated wealth.

Everywhere throughout Russia, and I think not only in Russia but all over the world, the same thing happens. The wealth of country producers passes into the hands of tradespeople, landowners, government functionaries, manufacturers; the men who receive this wealth want to enjoy it, and to enjoy it fully they must be in town. In the village, in the first place, owing to the inhabitants being scattered, it is difficult for the rich to gratify all their desires; you do not find there all sorts of shops, banks, restaurants, theaters, and various kinds of public amusements.

Secondly, another of the chief pleasures procured by wealth,—vanity, the desire to astonish, to make a display before others,—cannot be gratified in the country for the same reason, its inhabitants being too scattered. There is no one in the country to appreciate luxury; there is no one to astonish. There you may have what you like to embellish your dwelling,—pictures, bronze statues, all sorts of carriages, fine toilets,—but there is nobody to look at them or to envy you; the peasants do not understand the value of all this, and cannot make head or tail of it. Thirdly, luxury in the country is even disagreeable to a man who has a conscience, and is an anxiety to a timid person. One feels uneasy or ashamed at taking a milk bath, or in feeding puppies with milk, when there are children close by needing it; one feels the same in building pavilions and gardens among a people who live in cottages covered with stable litter, and who have no wood to burn. There is no one in the village to prevent the stupid, uneducated peasants from spoiling our comforts.

And, therefore, rich people gather together in towns, and settle near those who, in similar positions, have similar desires. In towns, the enjoyment of all sorts of luxuries is carefully protected by a numerous police. The chief inhabitants of the town are government functionaries, round whom all sorts of master workmen, artisans, and all the rich people have settled. There, a rich man has only to think about anything in order to get it. It is also more agreeable for him to live there, because he can gratify his vanity; there are people with whom he may try to compete in luxury, whom he may astonish or eclipse. But it is especially pleasant for a wealthy man to live in town, because, where his country life was uncomfortable, and somewhat incongruous on account of his luxury, in town, on the contrary, it would be uncomfortable for him not to live splendidly, and as his equals in wealth do.

What seemed out of place there appears indispensable here. Rich people collect together in towns, and, under the protection of the authorities, peacefully enjoy all that has been brought there by the villagers. A countryman often cannot help going to town, where a ceaseless round of feasting is going on, where what has been procured from the peasants is being spent; he comes into the town in order to feed upon those crumbs which fall from the tables of the rich; and partly by observing the careless, luxurious, and universally approved mode of living of these men, he begins to desire to order his own affairs in such a manner that he, too, may be able to work less, and avail himself more of the labor of others. And at last he decides to settle down in the neighborhood of the wealthy, trying by every means in his power to get back from them what is necessary for him, and submitting to all the conditions which the rich enforce. These country people assist in gratifying all the fancies of the wealthy: they serve them in public baths, in taverns, as coachmen, and as prostitutes. They manufacture carriages, make toys and dresses, and little by little learn from their wealthy neighbors how to live like them, not by real labor, but by all sorts of tricks, squeezing out from others the money they have collected, and so become depraved, and are ruined. It is, then, this same population, depraved by the wealth of towns, which forms that city misery which I wished to relieve but could not.

And, indeed, if one only reflects upon the condition of these country folk, coming to town in order to earn money to buy bread or to pay taxes, seeing everywhere thousands of rubles foolishly squandered, and hundreds very easily earned, while they have to earn their pence by the hardest labor, one cannot but be astonished that there are still many of such people at work, and that they do not all of them have recourse to a more easy way of getting money, — by trade, begging, vice, cheating, and even robbery.

But it is only we who join in the ceaseless orgy going on in the towns who can get so accustomed to our own mode of life that it seems quite natural to us for one fine gentleman to occupy five large rooms which are heated with such a quantity of firewood as would be enough for twenty families to warm their homes and cook their food with. To drive a short distance, we employ two thoroughbreds and two men; we cover our inlaid floors with carpets, and spend five or ten thousand rubles on a ball, or even twenty-five for a Christmas tree, and so on. Yet a man who needs ten rubles in order to buy bread for his family, or from whom his last sheep is taken to meet a tax of seven rubles which he cannot save by the hardest labor, cannot get accustomed to all this, which we imagine must seem quite natural to the poor; there are even such naïve people as say that the poor are thankful to us because we feed them by living so luxuriously.

But poor people do not lose their reasoning powers because they are poor: they reason quite in the same manner as we do. When we have heard that some one has lost a fortune at cards, or squandered ten or twenty thousand rubles, the first thought that comes into our minds is: How stupid and bad this man must be to have parted with such a large sum without any equivalent; and how well I could have employed this money for some building I have long wanted to get done, or for the improvement of my estate, and so on.

So also do the poor reason on seeing how foolishly we waste our wealth; all the more forcibly, because this money is needed, not to satisfy their whims, but for the chief necessaries of life, of which they are in want. We are greatly mistaken in thinking that the poor, while able to reason thus, still look on unconcernedly at the luxury around them.

They have never acknowledged, and never will, that

it is right for one man to be always idling, and for another to be continually working. At first they are astonished at it and offended; then, looking closer into the question, they see that this order of things is acknowledged to be lawful, and they try themselves to get rid of working, and to take part in the feasting. Some succeed in so doing, and acquire similar wanton habits; others, little by little, approach such a condition; others break down before they reach their object, and, having lost the habit of working, fill the night houses and the haunts of vice.

The year before last we took from the village a young peasant to be our butler's assistant. He could not agree with the footman, and was sent away; he entered the service of a merchant, pleased his masters, and now wears a watch and chain, and has smart boots.

In his place we took another peasant, a married man. He turned out a drunkard, and lost money. We took a third; he began to drink, and, having drunk up all he had, was for a long time in distress in a night lodging-house. Our old cook took to drinking in the town, and fell ill. Last year a footman who used formerly to have fits of drunkenness, and who when in the village kept himself from it for five years, when living in Moscow without his wife, who used to keep him in order, began again to drink, and ruined himself. A young boy of our village is living as butler's assistant at my brother's. His grandfather, a blind old man, came to me while I was living in the country, and asked me to persuade this grandson to send ten rubles for taxes, because, unless this were done, the cow would have to be sold.

"He keeps telling me that he has to dress himself respectably," said the old man. "He got himself boots, and that ought to be enough; but I actually believe he would like to buy a watch!"

In these words the grandfather expressed the utmost degree of extravagance. And this was really so; for the old man could not afford a drop of oil for his food during the whole of Lent, and his wood was spoilt because he had not the ruble and a quarter necessary for cutting it up. But the old man's irony turned out to be a reality.

His grandson came to me dressed in a fine black overcoat, and in boots for which he had paid eight rubles. Lately he got ten rubles from my brother, and spent them on his boots. And my children, who have known the boy from his infancy, told me that he really considers it necessary to buy a watch. He is a very good boy, but he considers that he will be laughed at for not having one.

This year a housemaid, eighteen years of age, formed an intimacy with the coachman, and was sent away. Our old nurse, to whom I related the case, reminded me of a girl whom I had quite forgotten. Ten years ago, during our short stay in Moscow, she formed an intimacy with a footman. She was also sent away, and drifted at last into a house of ill fame, and died in a hospital before she was twenty years of age.

We have only to look around us in order to become terrified by that infection which (to say nothing of manufactories and workshops existing only to gratify our luxury) we directly, by our luxurious town life, spread among those very people whom we desire afterward to help.

Thus, having got at the root of that town misery which I was not able to alleviate, I saw that its first cause is in our taking from the villagers their necessaries and carrying them to town. The second cause is that in those towns we avail ourselves of what we have gathered from the country, and, by our foolish luxury, tempt and deprave those peasants who follow us there in order to get back something of what we have taken from them in the country.

CHAPTER XIV

FROM an opposite point of view to that previously stated, I again came to the same conclusion. Recollecting all my connection with the town poor during this period, I saw that one reason why I was not able to help them was their insincerity and falseness. They all considered me, not as an individual, but merely as a means to an end. I felt I could not become intimate with them, I thought I did not perhaps understand how to do so; but without truthfulness no help was possible. How can one help a man who does not tell all his circumstances? Formerly I accused the poor of this, — it is so natural to accuse others; but one word spoken by a remarkable man, namely, Sutaief, who was then on a visit at my house, cleared up the difficulty, and showed me wherein lay the cause of my non-success.

I remember that even then what he said made a deep impression upon me; but I did not understand its full meaning until afterward. It happened that, while in the full ardor of my self-deception, I was at my sister's house, Sutaief being also there; and my sister was questioning me about my work.

I was relating it to her; and, as is often the case when one does not fully believe in one's own enterprises, I related with great enthusiasm, ardor, and at full length, all I had been doing, and all the possible results. I was telling her how we should keep our eyes open to what went on in Moscow; how we should take care of orphans and old people; how we should afford means to impoverished villagers to return to their homes, and pave the way to reform the depraved. I explained that, if we succeeded in our undertaking, there would not be in Moscow a single poor man who could not find help.

My sister sympathized with me; and while speaking I kept looking now and then at Sutaief, knowing his Christian life, and the importance attached by him to works of charity. I expected sympathy from him, and I spoke so that he might understand me; for, though I was addressing my sister, yet my conversation was really more directed to him.

He sat immovable, dressed in his black-tanned sheepskin coat, which he, like other peasants, wore indoors as well as out. It seemed that he was not listening to us, but was thinking about something else. His small eyes gave no responding gleam, but seemed to be turned inward. Having spoken out to my own satisfaction, I turned to him and asked him what he thought about it.

"The whole thing is superficial," he replied.

"Why?"

"The plan is an empty one, and no good will come of it," he repeated with conviction.

"How is it that nothing will come of it? Why is it a useless business, if we help thousands, or even hundreds, of unhappy ones? Is it a bad thing, according to the gospel, to clothe the naked, or to feed the hungry?"

"I know, I know; but what you are doing is not that. Is it possible to help thus? You are walking in the street; somebody asks you for a few kopeks; you give it him. Is that charity? Do him some spiritual good: teach him..... What you gave him merely says, 'Leave me alone.'"

"No; but that is not what we were speaking of: we wish to become acquainted with the wants, and then help by money and by deeds. We will try to find for the poor people some work to do."

"That would be no way of helping them."

"How then? must they be left to die of starvation and cold?"

"Why left to die? How many are there of them?"

"How many?" said I, thinking that he took the matter so lightly from not knowing the great number of these men.

"You are not aware, I dare say, that there are in Moscow about twenty thousand cold and hungry. And then, think of those in St. Petersburg and other towns!"

He smiled.

"Twenty thousand! And how many families are there in Russia alone? Would they amount to a million?"

"Well, but what of that?"

"What of that?" said he, with animation, and his eyes sparkled. "Let us unite them with ourselves; I am not rich myself, but will at once take two of them. You take a young fellow into your kitchen; I invite him into my family. If there were ten times as many, we should take them all into our families. You one, I another. We shall work together; those I take to live with me will see how I work; I will teach them to reap, and we shall eat out of one bowl, at one table; and they will hear a good word from me, and from you also. This is charity; but all this plan of yours is no good."

These plain words made an impression upon me. I could not help recognizing that this was true; but it seemed to me then that, notwithstanding the justice of what he said, my proposed plan might, perhaps, also be useful.

But the longer I was occupied with this affair, and the closer my intercourse with the poor, the oftener I recollected these words, and the greater meaning I found in them.

I, indeed, go in an expensive fur coat, or drive in my own carriage, to a man who is in want of boots: he sees my house which costs two hundred rubles a month, or he notices that I give away, without thinking, five rubles, only because such is my fancy; he is then aware that, if I give away rubles in such a manner, it is because I have accumulated so many of them that I have a lot to spare, which I not only am never in the habit of giving to any one, but which I have, without compunction, taken away from others. What can he see in me but one of those persons who have become possessed of what should belong to him? And what other feeling can he have toward me but the desire to get back as many as possible of these rubles which were taken by me from him and from others?

I should like to become intimate with him, and I complain that he is not sincere; but I am afraid to sit down upon his bed for fear of lice or some infectious disease; I am also afraid to let him come into my room; and when he comes to me half-dressed, he has to wait, — if fortunate, in the entrance-hall, but oftener in the cold porch. And then I say that it is all his fault that I cannot become intimate with him, and that he is not sincere.

Let the most hard-hearted man sit down to dine upon five courses among hungry people who have little or nothing to eat except black bread, and no one could have the heart to eat while hungry people are around him licking their lips.

Therefore, in order to eat well, when living among half-starving men, the first thing necessary is to hide ourselves from them, and to eat so that they may not see us. This is the very thing we do at present.

Without predjudice I looked into our own mode of life, and became aware that it was not by chance that closer intercourse with the poor is difficult for us, but that we ourselves are intentionally ordering our lives in such a way as to make this intercourse impossible. And not only this; but, on looking at our lives, or at the lives of rich people, from without, I saw that all that is considered as the *summum bonum* of these lives consists in being separated as much as possible from the poor, or is in some way or other connected with this desired separation.

In fact, all the aim of our lives, beginning with food, dress, dwelling, cleanliness, and ending with our education, consists in placing a gulf between us and them. And in order to establish this distinction and separation we spend nine-tenths of our wealth in erecting impassable barriers.

The first thing a man does who has grown rich is to leave off eating with others out of one bowl. He arranges plates for himself and his family, and separates himself from the kitchen and the servants. He feeds his servants well, in order that their mouths may not water, and he dines alone. But eating alone is dull. He invents whatever he can to improve his food, embellish his table; and the very manner of taking food, as at dinner-parties, becomes for him a matter of vanity, of pride. His manner of eating his food is a means of separating himself from other people. For a rich man it is out of the question to invite a poor person to his table. One must know how to hand a lady to table, how to bow, how to sit, to eat, to use a finger bowl, all of which the rich alone know how to do.

The same holds good with dress.

If a rich man, in order to cover his body and protect it from cold, wore ordinary dress — a jacket, a fur coat, felt shoes, leather boots, an undercoat, trousers, a shirt, — he would require very little; and, having two fur coats, he could not help giving one away to somebody who had none. But the wealthy man begins with wearing clothes which consist of many separate parts, and can be of use only on particular occasions, and therefore are of no use for a poor man. The man of fashion must have evening dress-coats, waistcoats, frock-coats, patent-leather shoes; his wife, bodices and dresses (which, according to fashion, are made of many parts), high-heeled shoes, hunting and traveling jackets, and so on. All these articles can be of use only to people in a condition far removed from poverty.

And thus dressing also becomes a means of isolation. Fashions make their appearance, and are among the chief things which separate the rich man from the poor one.

The same thing shows itself more plainly still in our dwellings. In order for one person to occupy ten rooms, we must manage so that he may not be seen by people who are living by tens in one room.

The richer a man is, the more difficult it is to get at him; the more footmen there are between him and people not rich, the more impossible it is for him to receive a poor guest, to let him walk on carpets, and sit on satin-covered chairs.

The same thing happens in traveling. A peasant who drives in a cart or on a carrier's sledge must be very hard-hearted if he refuses to give a pedestrian a lift; he has enough room, and can do it. But the richer the carriage is, the more impossible it is to put any one in it besides the owner of it. Some of the most elegant carriages are so narrow as to be termed "*egotists*."

The same thing applies to all the modes of living expressed by the word "cleanliness." Cleanliness! Who does not know human beings, especially women, who make a great virtue of cleanliness? Who does not know the various phases of this cleanliness, which have no limit whatever when it is procured by the labor of others? Who among self-made men has not experienced in his own person with what pains he carefully accustomed himself to this cleanliness, which illustrates the saying, "White hands are fond of another's labor"?

To-day cleanliness consists in changing one's shirt daily, and to-morrow it will be changed twice a day. At first, one has to wash one's hands and neck every day, then one will have to wash one's feet every day, and afterward it will be the whole body, and in peculiar methods. A clean table-cloth serves for two days, then it is changed every day, and afterward two tablecloths a day are used. To-day the footman is required to have clean hands; to-morrow he must wear gloves, and clean gloves, and he must hand the letters on a clean tray.

And there are no limits to this cleanliness, which is of no other use to any one except to separate us from others, and to make our intercourse with them impossible, while cleanliness is obtained through the labor of others.

Not only so; but when I had deeply reflected upon this, I came to the conclusion that what we term education is a similar thing. Language cannot deceive; it gives the right appellation to everything. The common people call education fashionable dress, smart conversation, white hands, and a certain degree of cleanliness. Of such a man they say, when distinguishing him from others, that he is an educated man.

In a little higher circle, men by education denote the same things, but add playing on the piano, the knowledge of French, good Russian spelling, and still greater cleanliness.

In the still higher circle, education consists of all this, with the addition of English, and a diploma from a high government establishment, and a still greater degree of cleanliness. But in all these shades education is in substance quite the same.

It consists in those forms and various kinds of infor

mation which separate a man from his fellow-creatures Its object is the same as that of cleanliness: to separate us from the crowd, in order that they, hungry and cold, may not see how we feast. But it is impossible to hide ourselves, and our efforts are seen through.

And so I became aware that the cause of the impossibility for us rich men to help the town poor was nothing more or less than the impossibility of our having closer intercourse with them, and that this we ourselves create by our whole life, and by all the uses we make of our wealth. I became persuaded that between us rich men and the poor there stood, erected by ourselves, a barrier of cleanliness and education which arose out of our wealth, and that, in order to be able to help them, we have first to break down this barrier, and render possible the realization of the means suggested by Sutaief, to take the poor into our respective homes. And so, as I have already said at the beginning of this chapter, I came to the same conclusion from a different point of view from that to which the train of thought about town misery had led me; viz., the cause of it all lay in our wealth.

CHAPTER XV

I BEGAN to analyze the matter from a third and purely personal point of view. Among the phenomena which particularly impressed me during my benevolent activity, there was one, — a very strange one, — which I could not understand for a long time.

Whenever I happened, in the street or at home, to give a poor person a trifling sum without entering into conversation with him, I saw, or imagined I saw, on his face an expression of pleasure and gratitude; and I myself experienced an agreeable feeling at this form of charity. I saw that I had done what was expected of me. But when I stopped and began to question the man about his past and present life, entering more or less into particulars, I felt it was impossible to give him anything; and I always began to finger the money in my purse, and, not knowing how much to give, I always gave more under these circumstances; but, nevertheless, I saw that the poor man went away from me dissatisfied. When I entered into still closer intercourse with him, my doubts as to how much I should give increased; and, no matter what I gave, the recipient seemed more and more gloomy and dissatisfied.

As a general rule, it almost always happened that if, upon nearer acquaintance with the poor man, I gave him three rubles or more, I always saw gloominess, dissatisfaction, and even anger depicted on his face; and sometimes, after having received from me ten rubles, he has left me without even thanking me, as if I had offended him.

In such cases I was always uncomfortable and ashamed, and felt myself guilty. When I watched the poor person during weeks, months, or years, helped him, and expressed my views, and became intimate with him, then our intercourse became a torment, and I saw that the man despised me. And I felt that he was right in doing so. When in the street a beggar asks me, along with other passers-by, for three kopeks, and I give it him, then, in his estimation, I am a kind and good man who gives "one of the threads which go to make the shirt of a naked one;" he expects nothing more than a thread, and, if I give it, he sincerely blesses me.

But if I stop and speak to him as man to man, show him that I wish to be more than a mere passer-by, and, as it often happened, he sheds tears in relating his misfortune, then he sees in me not merely a chance helper, but that which I wish him to see, — a kind man. If I am a kind man, then my kindness cannot stop at twenty kopeks, or at ten rubles, or ten thousand. One cannot be a second-rate kind man. Let us suppose that I give him much: that I put him straight, dress him, set him on his legs so that he can help himself, but, from some reason or other, either from an accident or his own weakness, he again loses the greatcoat and clothing and money I gave him, he is again hungry and cold, and he again comes to me, why should I refuse him assistance? For if the end of my benevolent activity was merely the attainment of some definite, material object, such as giving him so many rubles, or a certain greatcoat, having given them I could be easy in my mind: but the end I have in view is to be a benevolent man; that is, to put myself in the position of every other man. All understand kindness thus, and not otherwise.

And therefore, if such a man should spend in drink all you gave him twenty times over, and be again hungry and cold, then, if you are a benevolent man, you cannot help giving him more money, you can never leave off doing so while you have more than he has; but if you draw back, you show that all you have done before was done by you not because you are benevolent, but because you wish to appear so to others and to him. And it was from my having to back out of such cases, and by ceasing to give, by seeming to put a limit to my kindness, that I felt a painful sense of shame.

What was this feeling, then? I had experienced it in Liapin's house and in the country, and when I happened to give money or anything else to the poor, and in my adventures among the town people. One case which occurred to me lately reminded me of it forcibly, and led me to discover its cause.

It happened in the country. I wanted twenty kopeks to give to a pilgrim. I sent my son to borrow it from somebody. He brought it to the man, and told me that he had borrowed it from the cook. Some days after other pilgrims came, and I was again in need of twenty kopeks. I had a ruble. I recollected what I owed the cook, went into the kitchen, hoping that he would have some more coppers. I said:—

"I owe you twenty kopeks; here is a ruble."

I had not yet done speaking when the cook called his wife from the adjoining room: "Parasha, take it," he said.

I, thinking she had understood what I wanted, gave her the ruble. I must tell you that the cook had been living at our house about a week, and I had seen his wife, but had never spoken to her. I just wished to tell her to give me the change, when she briskly bowed herself over my hand, and was about to kiss it, evidently thinking I was giving her the ruble. I stammered out something, and left the kitchen. I felt ashamed, painfully ashamed, as I had not felt for a long time. I actually trembled, and felt that I was making a wry face; and, groaning with shame, I ran away from the kitchen.

This feeling, which I fancied I had not deserved, and which came over me quite unexpectedly, impressed me particularly, because it was so long since I had felt anything like it, and also because I fancied that I had been living in a way there was no reason for me to be ashamed of.

This surprised me greatly. I related the case to my family, to my acquaintances, and they all agreed that they also would have experienced the same. And I began to reflect; why is it that I felt so?

The answer came from a case which had formerly occurred to me in Moscow. I reflected upon it, and understood this shame which I have always experienced when I happen to give anything besides a trifling alms to beggars and pilgrims, which I am accustomed to give, and which I consider not as charity, but politeness.

If a man asks you for a light, you must light a match if you have it. If a man begs for three or twenty kopeks, or a few rubles, you must give if you have them. It is a question of politeness, not of charity.

The following is the case I referred to. I have already spoken about two peasants with whom I sawed wood three years ago. One Saturday evening, in the twilight, I was walking with them back to town. They were going to their master to receive their wages. On crossing a bridge we met an old man. He begged, and I gave him twenty kopeks. I gave, thinking what a good impression my alms would make upon Semyon, with whom I had been speaking on religious questions.

Semyon, a peasant from the province of Vladimir, who had a wife and two children in Moscow, also turned up the lappet of his kaftan, and took out his purse; and, after having looked over his money, he picked out a three-kopek piece, gave it to the old man, and asked for two kopeks back. The old man showed him in his hand two three-kopek pieces and a single kopek. Semyon looked at it, was about to take one kopek, but, changing his mind, took off his cap, crossed himself, and went away, leaving the old man the three-kopek piece.

I was acquainted with all Semyon's pecuniary circumstances. He had neither house nor other property. When he gave the old man the three kopeks he possessed six rubles and fifty kopeks, which he had been saving up, and this was all the capital he had.

My property amounted to about six hundred thousand rubles. I had a wife and children, so also had Semyon. He was younger than I, and had not so many children; but his children were young, and two of mine were grown-up men, old enough to work, so that our circumstances, independently of our property, were alike, though I was in this respect even better off than he.

He gave three kopeks, I gave twenty. What was, then, the difference in our gifts? What should I have given in order to do as he had done? He had six hundred kopeks; out of these he gave one, and then another two. I had six hundred thousand rubles. In order to give as much as Semyon gave, I ought to have given three thousand rubles, and asked the man to give me back two thousand; and, in the event of his not having change, to leave him these two thousand also, cross myself, and go away calmly, conversing about how people live in the manufactories, and what is the price of liver at the Smolensk market.

I thought about this at the time, but it was long before I was able to draw from this case the conclusion which inevitably follows from it. This conclusion seems to be so uncommon and strange, notwithstanding its mathematical accuracy, that it requires time in order to get accustomed to it. I could not help thinking there was some mistake in it, but there is none. It is only the dreadful darkness of prejudice in which we live.

This, when I arrived at it and recognized its inevitableness, explained to me the nature of my feelings of shame in the presence of the cook's wife, and before all the poor to whom I gave, and still give, money. Indeed, what is that money which I give to the poor, and which the cook's wife thought I was giving her? In the majority of cases it forms such a minute part of my income that it cannot be expressed in a fraction comprehensible to Semyon or to a cook's wife, — it is in most cases a millionth part or thereabout. I give so little that my gift is not, and cannot be, a sacrifice to me; it is only a something with which I amuse myself when and how it pleases me. And this was indeed how my cook's wife had understood me. If I gave a stranger in the street a ruble or twenty kopeks, why should I not give her also a ruble? For her, such a distribution of money was the same thing as a gentleman throwing gingerbread nuts into a crowd. It is the amusement of people who possess much "fool's money." I was ashamed, because the mistake of the cook's wife showed me plainly what ideas she and all poor people must have of me. "He is throwing away a 'fool's money';" that is, money not earned by him.

And, indeed, what is my money, and how did I come by it? One part of it I collected in the shape of rent for my land, which I had inherited from my father. The peasant sold his last sheep or cow in order to pay it to me.

Another part of my money I received for the books I had written. If my books are harmful, and yet sell, they can only do so by some seductive attraction, and the money which I receive for them is badly earned money; but if my books are useful, the thing is still worse. I do not give them to people, but say, "Give me so many rubles, and I will sell them to you."

And as in the former case a peasant sells his last sheep, here a poor student or a teacher does it; each poor person who buys denies himself some necessary thing in order to give me this money. And now I have gathered much of such money, and what am I doing with it? I take it to town, give it to the poor only when they satisfy all my fancies, and come to town to clean pavements, lamps, or boots, to work for me in the factories, and so on. And with this money I draw from them all I can. I try to give them as little as I can, and take from them as much as possible.

And now, quite unexpectedly, I begin to share all this said money with these same poor persons for nothing, but not indiscriminately, only as fancy prompts me.

Why should not every poor man expect that his turn might come to-day to be one of such with whom I amuse myself by giving them my "fool's money"?

Thus every one regards me as did the cook's wife. And I had gone astray with the notion that this was charity, — this taking away thousands with one hand, and throwing kopeks with the other to those I select.

No wonder I was ashamed. But, before beginning to do good, I must leave off the evil, and put myself in a position in which I should cease to cause it. But all my course of life is evil. If I were to give away a hundred thousand, I have not yet put myself in a condition in which I could do good, because I have still five hundred thousand left.

It is only when I possess nothing at all that I shall be able to do a little good; such as, for instance, the poor prostitute did who nursed a sick woman and her child for three days. Yet this seemed to me to be but so little! And *I* ventured to think of doing good! One thing only was true, which I at first felt on seeing the hungry and cold people outside Liapin's house, — that I was guilty of that; and that to live as I did was impossible, utterly impossible. This alone was true. But what was to be done? This question, for any one interested, I will answer with full particulars, if God permit me, in the following chapters.

CHAPTER XVI

It was difficult for me at last to own this; but when I did get thus far, I was terrified at the delusion in which I had been living. I had been head over ears in the mud, and I had been trying to drag others out of it.

What is it that I really want? I want to do good; I want to so contrive that no human beings should be hungry and cold, and that men may live as it is proper for them to live. I desire this; and I see that in consequence of all sorts of violence, extortions, and various expedients in which I too took part, the working-people are deprived of the necessary things, and the non-working community, to whom I also belong, monopolize the labor of others. I see that this use of other people's labor is distributed thus: that the more cunning and complicated the tricks employed by the man himself (or by those from whom he has inherited his property), the more largely he employs the labors of other people, and the less he works himself.

First come the millionaires; then the wealthy bankers, merchants, landowners, government functionaries; then the smaller bankers, merchants, government functionaries, landowners, to whom I belong; then shopmen, publicans, usurers, police sergeants and inspectors, teachers, sacristans, clerks; then, again, house-porters, footmen, coachmen, water-carters, cabmen, peddlers; and then, last of all, the workmen, factory hands and peasants, the number of this class in proportion to the former being as ten to one.

I see that the lives of nine-tenths of the working-people essentially require exertion and labor like every other natural mode of living; but that, in consequence of the tricks by which the necessaries of life are taken away from these people, their lives become every year more difficult, and more beset with privations; and our lives, the lives of the non-laboring community, owing to the coöperation of sciences and arts, which have this very end in view, become every year more sumptuous, more attractive and secure.

I see that in our days the life of a laboring-man, and especially the lives of old people, women, and children, of the working-classes, are quite worn away by increased labor, not in proportion to their nourishment, and that even the very first necessaries of life are not secured to them. I see that side by side with these the lives of the non-laboring class, to which I belong, are each year more and more filled up with superfluities and luxury, and are becoming continually more secure; the lives of the wealthy have attained to that degree of security of which in olden times men dreamed only in fairy tales, — to the condition of the owner of the magic purse with an "inexhaustible ruble"; to such a state when a man not only is entirely free from the law of labor for the sustenance of his life, but has the possibility of enjoying without working all the goods of this life, and of bequeathing to his children, or to any he chooses, this purse with the "inexhaustible ruble."

I see that the productions of the labor of men pass over more than ever from the masses of laborers to those of non-laborers; that the pyramid of the social structure is, as it were, being rebuilt, so that the stones of the foundation pass to the top, and the rapidity of this passage increases in a kind of geometric progression.

I see that there is going on something like that which would have taken place in an ant-hill, if the society of ants should have lost the sense of the general law, and some of the ants were to take the productions of labor out of the foundations and carry them to the top of the hill, making the foundation narrower and narrower, thus enlarging the top, and by that means making their fellows pass also from the foundation to the top.

I see that, instead of an ideal, as exemplified in a laborious life, men have created the ideal of a purse with an "inexhaustible ruble." The rich, I among their number, arrange this ruble for ourselves by various artifices; and, in order to enjoy it, we locate ourselves in towns, in a place where nothing is produced, but everything is swallowed up.

The poor laboring-man, swindled in order that the rich may have this magic ruble, follows them to town; and there he also has recourse to artifices, either arranging matters so that he may work little and enjoy much, thus making the condition of working-men still more heavy, or, not having attained to this state, he ruins himself, and drifts into the continually and rapidly increasing number of hungry and cold tenants of night houses.

I belong to the category of those men who, by the means of these various devices, take away from the working-people the necessaries of life, and who thus create, as it were, for themselves the inexhaustible fairy ruble, which tempts in turn these unfortunate ones.

I wish to help men; and therefore it is clear that, first of all, I ought on the one side to cease to plunder them as I am doing now, and, on the other, I must leave off tempting them. But I, by means of most complicated, cunning, and wicked contrivances practised for centuries, have made myself the owner of this said ruble; that is, have got into such a condition that I may, while never doing anything myself, compel hundreds and thousands of people to work for me, and am really availing myself of this privileged monopoly, notwithstanding that all the time I imagine I pity these men, and wish to help them.

It is as if I were sitting on the neck of a man, and, having quite crushed him down, I compel him to carry me, and will not alight from off his shoulders, while I assure myself and others that I am very sorry for him, and wish to ease his condition by every means in my power except by getting off his back.

Surely this is plain. If I wish to help the poor, that is, to make the poor cease to be poor, I ought not to create these same poor. Yet I give money according to my fancy to those who have gone astray, and take away tens of rubles from men who have not yet done so, thereby making them poor, and at the same time making them depraved.

This is very clear; but at first it was for me exceedingly difficult to understand, without any modification or reserve which would justify my position. However, as soon as I came to see my own error, all that formerly appeared strange, complicated, clouded, and inexplicable, became quite simple and intelligible to me; and the line of conduct which ensued became both clear and satisfactory to my conscience by the following considerations.

Who am I that I desire to better men's condition? I desire it; and yet I get up at noon, after having played at cards in a brilliantly lighted saloon during all the previous night, I, an enfeebled and effeminate man, who thus require the help and services of hundreds of people, I come to help them! — these men who rise at five, sleep on boards, feed upon cabbage and bread, understand how to plow, to reap, to put a handle to an ax, to write, to harness horses, to sew; men who, by their strength and perseverance and self-restraint, are a hundred times stronger than I who come to help them.

What could I have experienced in my intercourse with these people but shame? The weakest of them — a drunkard, an inhabitant of Rzhanoff's house, he whom they call "the sluggard" — is a hundred times more laborious than I — his balance, so to say, — in other words, the relation between what he takes from men and what he gives them, — is a thousand times more to his credit than mine when I count what I receive from others, and what I give them in return. And to such men I go in order to assist them.

I go to help the poor. But of the two, who is the poorer? No one is poorer than myself. I am a weak, good-for-nothing parasite, who can only exist in very peculiar conditions, who can live only when thousands of people labor to support this life which is not useful to any one. And I, this very caterpillar which eats up the leaves of a tree, wish to help the growth and the health of the tree, and to cure it.

All my life is thus spent: I eat, talk and listen; then I eat, write, or read, which are only talking and listening in another form; I eat again, and play; then eat, talk, and listen, and finally eat and go to sleep; and thus every day is spent; I neither do anything else, nor understand how to do it. And in order that I may enjoy this life, it is necessary that from morning till night house-porters, dvorniks, cooks, male and female, footmen, coachmen, and laundresses should work, to say nothing of the manual labor necessary in order that the coachmen, cooks, footmen, and others may have the instruments and the articles by which, and upon which, they work for me, — axes, casks, brushes, dishes, furniture, glasses, wax, shoe-black, kerosene, hay, wood, and food. And all these men and women work hard all the day, and every day, in order that I may talk, eat, and sleep.

And I, this useless man, imagined that I was able to benefit others, they being the very same people who were serving me. That I did not benefit any one, and that I was ashamed of myself, is not so astonishing as the fact that such a foolish idea ever came into my mind.

The woman who nursed the sick old man helped him; the peasant's wife, who cut a slice of her bread, earned by her from the very sowing of the corn that made it, helped the hungry one; Semyon, who gave three kopeks which he had earned, assisted the pilgrim, because these three kopeks really represented his labor; but I had served nobody, worked for no one, and knew very well that my money did not represent my labor. And so I felt that in money, or in money's worth, and in the possession of it, there was something wrong and evil; that the money itself, and the fact of my having it, was one of the chief causes of those evils which I had seen before me, and I asked myself, What is money?

CHAPTER XVII

Money! What, then, is money?

It is answered, money represents labor. I meet educated people who even assert that money represents labor performed by those who possess it. I confess that I myself formerly shared this opinion, although I did not very clearly understand it. But now it became necessary for me to learn thoroughly what money was.

In order to do so, I addressed myself to science. Science says that money in itself is neither unjust nor pernicious; that money is the natural result of the conditions of social life, and is indispensable, first, for convenience of exchange; secondly, as a measure of value; thirdly, for saving; and fourthly, for payments.

The evident fact is that when I have in my pocket three rubles to spare, which I am not in need of, I have only to whistle, and in every civilized town I obtain a hundred people ready, for these three rubles, to do the worst, most disgusting, and humiliating act I require; and this comes not from money, but from the very complicated conditions of the economical life of nations.

The dominion of one man over others comes not from money, but from the circumstance that a working-man does not receive the full value of his labor; and the fact that he does not get the full value of his labor depends upon the nature of capital, rent, and wages, and upon complicated connections between them and production itself, and between the distribution and consumption of wealth.

In plain language, it means that people who have money may twist around their finger those who have none. But science says this is an illusion; that in every kind of production three factors take part, — land, savings of labor (capital), and labor; and that the dominion of the few over the many proceeds from the various connections between these factors of production, — because the two first factors, land and capital, are not in the hands of working-people: from this fact, and from the various combinations resulting therefrom, proceeds this domination.

Whence comes the great power of money which strikes us all with a sense of its injustice and cruelty? Why is one man by the means of money to have dominion over others? Science says, It comes from the division of the agents of production, and from the consequent complicated combinations which oppress the working-man.

This answer has always appeared to me to be strange, not only because it leaves one part of the question unnoticed, namely, the signification of money, but also because of the division of the factors of production, which to an uninformed man will always appear artificial, and not in accordance with reality. It is asserted that in every production three agents come into operation,—land, capital, and labor; and along with this division it is understood that property (or its value in money) is naturally divided among those who possess one of these agents; thus, rent — the value of the ground — belongs to the landowner; interest to the capitalist; and labor to the working-man.

Is it really so?

First, is it true that in every production three agencies operate? Now, while I am writing this, around me proceeds the production of hay. Of what is this production composed? I am told of the land which produces the grass, of capital, — scythes, rakes, pitchforks, carts, — which is necessary for the housing of hay, and of labor. But I see that this is not true. Besides the land, there is the sun and rain; besides social order, which has been keeping these meadows from damage caused by letting stray cattle graze upon them, the prudence of workmen, their knowledge of language, and many other agencies of production, which, for some unknown reason, are not taken into consideration by political economy.

The power of the sun is as necessary as the land. I may instance the position of men in which (as, for instance, in a town) some of them assume the right to keep out the sun from others by means of walls or trees. Why, then, is this sun not included among the agents of production?

Rain is another means as necessary as the ground itself. The air too. I can picture to myself the position of men without water and pure air, because other men assume to themselves the right to monopolize these, which are essentially necessary to all. Public security is likewise a necessary element; food and dress for workmen are similar means in production; this last is even recognized by some economists. Education, the knowledge of language which creates the possibility of reasonable work, is likewise an agent. I could fill a volume by enumerating such combinations, unnoticed by science.

Why, then, are three only to be chosen and laid as a foundation for the science of political economy? Why are the rays of the sun, rain, food, knowledge, not equally recognized? Why only the land, the instruments of labor, and the labor itself? Simply because the right of men to enjoy the rays of the sun, rain, food, speech, and audience are challenged only on rare occasions; but the use of land, and of the instruments of labor, are constantly challenged in society.

This is the true foundation for it; and the division of these agents for production, into three, is quite arbitrary and is not involved in the nature of things. But it may perhaps be urged that this division is so suitable to man, that, whenever economical relationships form themselves, there these appear at once and alone.

Let us see whether it is really so. First of all, I look at what is around me, — at Russian colonists, of whom millions have for long existed. They come to a land, settle themselves on it, and begin to labor; and it does not enter into the mind of any one of them that a man who does not use the land could have any claim to it, and the land does not assert any rights of its own; on the contrary, the colonists conscientiously recognize the communism of the land, and that it is right for every one of them to plow and to mow wherever he likes.

For cultivation, for gardening, for building houses, the colonists obtain various implements of labor; nor does it enter the mind of any one of them that these instruments of labor may bring profit in themselves, and the capital does not assert any rights of its own; but on the contrary, the colonists conscientiously recognize that all interest for tools, or borrowed corn or capital, is unjust.

They work upon a free land, labor with their own

tools, or with those borrowed without interest, each for himself, or all together for common business; and in such a community, it is impossible to prove either the existence of rent or interest accruing from capital, or remuneration for labor.

Speaking of such a community, I am not indulging my fancy, but am describing what has always taken place not only among primitive Russian colonists, but among so-called intellectual men, who are not few, and who have settled in Russia and in America.

I am describing what appears to every one to be natural and reasonable. Men settle on land, and each undertakes to do such business as suits him; and each, having earned what is necessary, does his own work.

And when these men find it more convenient to labor together, they form a workmen's association; but neither in separate households, nor in associations, will there appear separate agents of production, till men artificially and forcibly divide them. But there will be labor, and the necessary conditions of labor, — the sun which warms all, the air which men breathe, water which they drink, land on which they labor, clothes on the body, food in the stomach, stakes, shovels, plows, machines, with which men work; and it is evident that neither the rays of the sun, nor the clothes on the body, nor the stakes with which the man labors, nor the spade, nor the plow, nor the machine with which he works in the workmen's association, can belong to any one else but to those who enjoy the rays of the sun, breathe the air, drink the water, eat the bread, clothe their bodies, and labor with the spade or with the machine, because all this is necessary only for those who make use of it. And when men act thus, we see that they act reasonably.

Therefore, observing the economical conditions which are created among men, I do not see that the division into three is natural. I see, on the contrary, that it is neither natural nor reasonable. But perhaps the setting apart of these three does not take place in primitive societies of men, but that when the population increases, and cultivation begins to develop, it is unavoidable; and we cannot but recognize the fact that this division has taken place in European society. Let us see whether it is really so.

We are told that in European society this division of agencies has taken place; that is, that one man possesses land, another possesses instruments of labor, and the third is without land and instruments. We have grown so accustomed to this assertion that we are no longer struck by the strangeness of it.

If we will but reflect upon this expression, we cannot help seeing, not only the injustice, but even the absurdity, of it. Under the idea of a laboring-man are included the land upon which he lives, and the tools with which he works. If he were not living on the land, and had no tools, he would not be a laboring-man. There has never been, and can never be, such a man without land and without tools, without scythe, cart, and horse; there cannot be a bootmaker without a house for his work standing upon ground, without water, air, and tools with which he works.

If a laborer has no land, horse, or scythe, and a bootmaker is without a house, water, or awl, then it means that some one has driven him from the ground, or taken it away from him, or cheated him out of his scythe, cart, horse, or awl; but it does not at all mean that there can be a country laborer without a scythe, or a bootmaker without tools.

So you cannot imagine a fisherman remaining on dry land without fishing implements, unless he has been driven away from the water by some one who has taken away from him his necessary implements for fishing; so also we cannot picture to ourselves a workman without the ground upon which he lives, and without tools for his trade, unless somebody has driven him from the former, or robbed him of the latter.

There may be such men, hunted from one place to another, and such who, having been robbed, are compelled perforce to work for another man, and do things unnecessary for themselves: but this does not mean that such is the nature of production, and therefore the land and the tools cannot be considered as separate agents in the work.

But if we are to consider as the agents of production all that is claimed by other people, and what a working-man may be deprived of by the violence of others, why not count among them the claim upon the person of a slave? Why not count claims on the rain and the rays of the sun? We might meet with a man who would build a wall and thus keep the sun from his neighbor; another may come who will turn the course of a river into his own pond, and by that means contaminate its water; or an individual who would claim a fellow-man as his own property; but none of these claims, although they may be enforced by violence, can be recognized as a foundation for calculating the agents of production; and therefore it is as equally unjust to consider the exclusive enjoyment of the rays of the sun, or of the air or water, or the persons of others, as separate agents in production.

There may be men who will assert their rights to the land and to the tools of a working-man, as there were men who asserted their rights to the persons of others, and as there may be men who would assert their rights to the exclusive use of the rays of the sun, or to the use of water and air; there may be men who would drive away a working-man from place to place, taking from him by force the products of his labor as they are produced, and the very instruments for its production, who might compel him to work, not for himself, but for his master, as occurs in the factories, — all this is possible; but a working-man without land and tools is still an impossibility, just as there does not exist a man who would willingly become the property of another, notwithstanding that men have asserted their right to him for many generations.

Just as a claim on the person of another man could not deprive a slave of his innate right to seek his own welfare, and not that of his master; so, too, the claim for the exclusive possession of the land and tools of others cannot deprive the working-man of his right, like that of every man, to live upon the land, and to work with his own tools, or those of his community, as he considers most useful for himself.

All that science can say, in examining the present economical question, is this: that in Europe there exist claims of some men to the land and the tools of working-men, in consequence of which, for some of these working-men (but by no means for all of them), the proper conditions of production are violated, so that they are deprived of land and implements of labor, and are compelled to work with the tools of others; but by no means is it established that this casual violation of the law of production is that very law itself.

In saying that this isolation of the agents of produce is the fundamental law of production, the economist is doing the very thing a zoölogist would do, who, upon seeing a great many siskins, with their wings cut, and kept in little cages, drawing water-barrels out of an imaginary well, should assert this was the most essential condition for the life of birds, and that their life is composed of these conditions.

However many siskins there may be kept in pasteboard houses with their wings cut, a zoölogist cannot acknowledge these houses to be the natural home of the birds. However great the number of working-people there may be driven from place to place, and deprived of their productions as well as the tools for their labor, the natural right of man to live upon the land, and to work with his own tools, is that which he needs, and it will remain so forever.

We have some who lay claim to the land and to the tools of working-men, just as there existed in former ages the claim of some men over the persons of others; but there may be no real division of men into lords and slaves as was anciently established, nor can there exist any division in the agents of production, in land and capital, as economists want to establish at present.

These very unlawful claims of some men over the liberty of others, science calls the natural condition of production. Instead of taking its fundamental principles from the natural properties of human societies, science took them from a particular case; and, desiring to justify this case, it recognized the right of some men to the land by which other men earned their living, and to the tools with which other men worked; in other words, it recognized as a right that which had never existed, and cannot exist, and which is in itself a contradiction, because the claim of the landowner to the land on which he does not labor is in essence nothing more than the right to use the land which he does not use; the claim on the tools of others is nothing more than a man assuming a right to work with implements with which he does not work.

Science, by isolating the agents of production, declares that the natural condition of a working-man — that is, of a man in the true sense of the word — is that unnatural condition in which he exists at present, as in ancient times, by the division of men into citizens and slaves, when it was asserted that the unnatural condition of slavery was the natural condition of life.

This very division, accepted by science only in order to justify the existing injustice, and the adjudging this division to be the foundation of all its inquiries, has for its result that science vainly tries to give some explanation of existing phenomena; and, denying the clearest and plainest answers to the questions that arise, gives answers which have no meaning in them at all.

The question of economical science is this: What is the reason of the fact that some men by means of money acquire an imaginary right to the land and capital, and may make slaves of those men who have no money? The answer which presents itself to common sense would be, that it is the result of money, the nature of which is to enslave men.

But science denies this, and says: This arises, not from the nature of money, but from the fact that some men have land and capital, and others have neither. We ask why persons who possess land and capital oppress such as possess neither? and we are answered, Because they do possess land and capital.

But this is just what we are inquiring about. Is not deprivation of land and tools enforced slavery? Life ceases not to put this essential question: and even science herself notices it, and tries to answer it, but does not succeed in doing so; proceeding from her own fundamental principles, she only turns herself round, as in a magic circle.

In order to give itself a satisfactory answer to the above question, science has first of all to deny that wrong division of the agents of production, to cease to acknowledge the result of the phenomena as being the cause of them; and she has to seek, first the more obvious, and then the remoter, causes of those phenomena which make up the whole.

Science must answer the question: What is the reason that some men are deprived of land and tools while others possess both? or, Why is it that land and tools are taken away from persons who labor upon the land and work with the tools?

As soon as science puts this question to herself, she will at once get new ideas which will transform all the previous ideas of that sham science, which has been moving in an unalterable circle of propositions, as, for instance, the miserable condition of working-people proceeding from the fact that it is miserable. For simple-minded persons, it must seem unquestionable that the obvious reason of the oppression of some men by others is this money. But science, denying this, says that money is only a medium of exchange, which has nothing in common with oppression or slavery.

Let us see whether it is so or not.

CHAPTER XVIII

WHENCE comes money? How is it that a nation always has money, and under what circumstances is it that a nation need not use money? There is a small tribe in Africa, and one in Australia, who live as lived the Sknepies and the Drevlyans in olden times.

These tribes lived and plowed, bred cattle, and cultivated gardens. We became acquainted with them only at the dawn of history. And history begins with recording the fact that some invaders appear on the stage. And invaders always do the same thing: they take away from the aborigines everything they can take,—cattle, corn, and stuffs; even make prisoners, male and female, and carry them away.

After some years the invaders appear again; but the people have not got over the consequences of their misfortune, and there is scarcely anything to take from them, so the invaders invent another and better means of making use of their victims.

These means are very simple, and naturally present themselves to the mind of every man. The *first* is personal slavery. There is a drawback to this, seeing the enforcers of it have to put everything into working order, and feed all the slaves; hence, naturally, there appears the *second.* The people are left on their own land, which becomes the recognized property of the invaders, who portion it out among the leading military men, in order that by means of these men they may utilize the labor of the people.

But this, too, has its drawback. It is not convenient to these officers to have an oversight over all the productions of the conquered people, and thus the *third* means is introduced, which is as primitive as the two former ones; and this is the levying of a certain obligatory tax which the conquered have to pay at stated periods.

The object of a conquest is to take from the conquered as much as possible of the products of their labor. It is evident that, in order to do this, the conquerors must take such articles as are the most valuable to the conquered, and which at the same time are not cumbersome, and are convenient for keeping—skins of animals and gold.

And the conqueror lays upon the family or the tribe

a tax in these skins or gold, which is to be paid at fixed times; and by means of this tribute, he utilizes the labor of the conquered people in the most convenient way.

Almost all the skins and all the gold are taken away from their original possessors, and therefore these are compelled to sell all they have amongst themselves to obtain gold and skins for their masters; that is, they have to sell their property and their labor.

This very thing happened in ancient times, in the Middle Ages, and occurs now too. In the ancient world, when the subjugation of one people by another was frequent, and owing to the equality of men not being acknowledged, personal slavery was the most widely spread means for compelling the service of others, and was the center of gravity in this compulsion. In the Middle Ages, feudalism — landownership and the servitude connected with it — partly takes the place of personal slavery, and the center of compulsion is transferred from persons to land; in modern times, since the discovery of America, the development of commerce, and the influx of gold, which is accepted as a universal medium of exchange, the tribute in money with the increase of the state power becomes the chief instrument for enslaving men, and upon it are now built all economical relationships.

In "The Literary Miscellany" is printed an article by Professor Yanjoul, in which he describes the recent history of the Fiji Islands. If I were trying to find the most pointed illustration of how in our time the forcible requirement of money became the chief instrument of the enslaving of some men by others, I could not imagine anything more striking and convincing than this trustworthy history, — history, based upon documents, of facts which are of recent occurrence.

In the South Sea Islands in Polynesia lives a race called Fiji. The group on which they live, says Professor Yanjoul, is composed of small isles, which all together occupy a space of about forty thousand square miles. Only half of these islands are inhabited, by one hundred and fifty thousand natives and fifteen hundred white men. The natives had been reclaimed from a savage state a long time ago, and are distinguished among other natives of Polynesia by their intellectual capacities; and they appear to be a nation capable of labor and development, which they have also proved by the fact that in a short period of time they became good workmen and breeders of cattle.

The inhabitants were well-to-do, but in the year 1859 the condition of this new state became desperate; the natives of Fiji, and their representative, Kokab, were in need of money. The money, forty-five thousand dollars, was wanted by the government of Fiji for the payment of a contribution or indemnification, which was demanded of them by the United States of America for violence done by Fijis to some citizens of the American Republic.

For this purpose the Americans sent a squadron, which unexpectedly took possession of some of the best islands, under the pretext that they would hold them as a guarantee, and threatened to bombard and ruin the towns if the indemnification were not paid over, upon a certain date, to the representatives of America.

The Americans were among the first colonists who, together with missionaries, came to the Fiji Islands. They chose and (under one pretext or another) took possession of the best pieces of land on the islands, and established there cotton and coffee plantations. They hired whole crowds of natives, binding them by contracts unknown to this half-civilized race; or acted through special contractors or purveyors of human merchandise.

Misunderstandings between such master planters and the natives, whom they considered almost as slaves, were unavoidable; it was some of these quarrels which served as a pretext for the American indemnification.

Notwithstanding their prosperity, the Fijis had preserved almost up to the present time the forms of so-called natural economy which existed in Europe during the Middle Ages: money was scarcely in circulation among the natives, and their trade had almost exclusively the character of barter, — one merchandise was exchanged for another, and a few social taxes and those of the state were taken out in productions. What were the Fiji Islanders with their King Kokab to do when the Americans required from them forty-five thousand dollars under the most terrible threat in the event of non-payment? To the Fijis the very figures appeared to be something inconceivable, to say nothing of the money itself, which they had never seen in such large quantities. After deliberating with other chiefs, Kokab made up his mind to apply to the queen of England, at first asking her to take the islands under her protection, and then plainly under her rule.

But the English regarded this request circumspectly, and were in no hurry to assist the half-savage monarch out of his difficulty. Instead of giving a direct answer, they sent, in 1860, special commissioners to make inquiries about the Fiji Islanders, in order to be able to decide whether it was worth while to annex them to the British possessions, and to lay out money to satisfy the American claims.

Meanwhile the American government continued to insist upon payment, and held as a pledge in their *de facto* dominion some of the best parts, and, having looked closely into the national wealth, raised their former claim to ninety thousand dollars, and threatened to increase it still if Kokab did not pay at once.

Being thus pushed on every side, the poor king, unacquainted with European means of credit accommodation, in accordance with the advice of European colonists, began to try to raise money in Melbourne, among the merchants, cost what it might, if even he should be obliged to yield up all his kingdom into private hands.

And so in Melbourne, in consequence of his application, a commercial society was formed. This joint-stock company, which took the name of the Polynesian Company, formed with the chiefs of the Fiji-Islanders a treaty upon terms the most advantageous to itself. It took upon itself the debt to the American government, and pledged itself to pay it by several instalments; for this the company received, according to the first treaty, one and then two hundred thousand acres of the best land, selected by themselves; the perpetual immunity from all taxes and dues for all its factories, operations, and colonies, and the exclusive right for a long period to establish in the Fiji Islands issuing-banks, with the privilege of printing unlimited numbers of notes.

Since this treaty, definitively concluded in the year 1868, there appeared in the Fiji Islands, along with their local government with Kokab at the head, another powerful authority, — a commercial factory, with large estates over all the islands, exercising a decided influence upon the government.

Up to this time the wants of the government of Kokab had been satisfied with the payment in natural productions, which consisted of various duties and a small customs-tax on goods imported. With the conclusion of the treaty, and the forming of the influential Polynesian Company, the king's financial circumstances had changed.

A considerable part of the best land in his dominion had passed into the hands of the company, his income from the land therefore diminished; on the other hand, the income from the customs-taxes also diminished, because the company obtained for itself an import and export of all kinds of goods free of customs-duties.

The natives — ninety-nine per cent of all the population — had always been bad payers of customs-duties, because they scarcely bought any of the European productions, except some stuffs and hardware; and now, from the freeing from customs-duties, along with the Polynesian Company, of many well-to-do Europeans, the income of King Kokab was reduced to *nil*, and he was obliged to take steps to resuscitate it if possible.

He began to consult his white friends as to how he was to avert the calamity, and they advised him to create the first direct tax in the country; and, in order, I suppose, to have less trouble about it, in money. The tax was established in the form of a general poll-tax, amounting to one pound for every man, and to four shillings for every woman, throughout the islands.

As we have already said, on the Fiji Islands there still exist a natural economy and a trade by barter. Very few natives possess money. Their wealth consists chiefly of various raw productions and cattle; whilst the new tax required the possession in a family of considerable sums of money at fixed times.

Up to that date a native had not been accustomed to any individual burden in the interests of his government, except personal obligations; all the taxes which had to be paid were paid by the community or village to which he belonged, and from the common fields from which he received his principal income.

One alternative was left to him, — to try to raise money from the European colonists; that is, to address himself either to the merchant or to the planter.

To the first he was obliged to sell his productions on the merchant's own terms, because the tax-collector required money at a certain fixed date, or he had even to raise money by selling his expected production, which enabled the merchant to take iniquitous interest. Or he had to address himself to the planter, and sell him his labor; that is, to become his workman; but the wages on the Fiji Islands were very low, owing, I suppose, to the exceptionally great offer of services.

They did not exceed one shilling per week for a grown-up man, or two pounds twelve shillings a year; and therefore, in order merely to get the money necessary for the payment for himself, not to speak of his family, a Fiji had to leave his house, his family, and his own land, and often go far away to another island, and there enslave himself to the planter for at least half a year in order to get the one pound necessary for the payment of the new tax; and as for the payment of taxes for his whole family, he had to look for it to some other means.

We can understand what was the result of such a state. From a hundred and fifty thousand of his subjects, Kokab collected in all six thousand pounds; and now there began a forcible extortion of taxes unknown till then, and a series of violent measures.

The local administration, which had been formerly incorruptible, soon made common cause with the European planters, who began to have their own way with the country. For non-payment, the Fijis were summoned to the court and were sentenced, not only to pay the expenses, but also to be sent to prison for not less than half a year. This prison was really the plantation of the first white man who chose to pay the tax-money and the legal expenses of the condemned.

Thus the white settlers received cheap labor to any amount. First this compulsory labor was fixed at not longer than half a year; but afterward the bribed judges found it possible to pass sentence for eighteen months, and then to renew the sentence.

Very quickly, in the course of a few years, the picture of the social condition of the inhabitants of Fiji was quite changed.

Whole districts, formerly flourishing, lost half of their population, and were greatly impoverished. All the male population, except the old and infirm, were working away from their homes for European planters, in order to get money necessary for the payment of taxes, or in consequence of the law court. The women on the Fiji Islands had scarcely ever worked in the fields; therefore, in the absence of the men, all farming was neglected, and went to ruin. In the course of a few years, half of the population of Fiji was transformed into slaves of the colonists.

In order to ease their situation, the Fiji Islanders again appealed to England. A new petition was got up, subscribed by a great many eminent persons and chiefs, praying to be annexed to England; and this was handed to the British consul. Meanwhile, England, thanks to her learned expedition, had time not only to investigate the affairs of the islands, but even to survey them, and duly to appreciate the natural riches of this fine corner of the globe.

Owing to all these circumstances, the negotiations

this time were crowned with full success; and in 1874, to the great dissatisfaction of the American planters, England officially took possession of the Fiji Islands, and added them to its colonies. Kokab died, and his heirs had a small pension assigned to them.

The administration of the islands was intrusted to Sir Hercules Robinson, the governor of New South Wales. In the first year of its annexation to England, the Fiji Islanders had not any self-government, but were under the direction of Sir Hercules Robinson, who had appointed an administrator for them. Taking the islands into their hands, the English government had to undertake the difficult task of gratifying various expectations raised by them.

The natives, of course, first of all expected the abolition of the hated poll-tax; one part of the white colonists (the Americans) looked with suspicion upon the British rule; and another part (those of English origin) expected all kinds of confirmations of their power over the natives, — permission to inclose the land, and so on. The English government, however, proved itself equal to the task; and its first act was to abolish forever the poll-tax, which had created the slavery of the natives in the interest of a few colonists. But here Sir Hercules Robinson had at once to face a difficult dilemma.

It was necessary to abolish the poll-tax, which had made the Fijis seek help of the English government; but, at the same time, according to English colonial policy, the colonies had to support themselves; they had to find their own means for covering the expenses of the government. With the abolition of the poll-tax, all the incomes of the Fijis (from customs-duties) did not amount to more than six thousand pounds, while the government expenses required at least seventy thousand a year.

And now Sir Hercules Robinson, having abolished the money tax, thought of a labor tax; but it did not yield the sum necessary for feeding him and his assistants. Matters did not mend until a new governor had been appointed, — Gordon, — who, in order to get out of the inhabitants the money necessary for keeping him and his functionaries, resolved not to demand money until it had come sufficiently into general circulation on the islands, but to take from the natives their productions, and to sell them himself.

This tragical episode in the lives of the Fijis is the clearest and best proof of what is the true meaning of money in our time.

In this case everything is illustrated, the first fundamental condition of slavery, — the guns, threats, murders, and plunder, and lastly, money, the means of subjugation which has taken the place of all other. That which in an historical sketch of economical development has to be investigated during centuries, here when all the forms of monetary violence have fully developed themselves, had been concentrated into a space of ten years. The drama begins thus: the American government sends ships with loaded guns to the shores of the islands whose inhabitants they want to enslave. The pretext of this threat is monetary; but the beginning of the tragedy is the leveling of guns against all the inhabitants, — wives, children, old people, and men, — though they have not committed any crime. "Your money or your life," — forty-five thousand dollars, then ninety thousand, or slaughter. But ninety thousand are not to be had. And now begins the second act: it is necessary to forego a slaughter, which would be bloody, terrible, and concentrated, in a short period; it is necessary to substitute a suffering less perceptible which can be laid upon all, and will last longer; and the natives with their representative seek to substitute for slaughter a slavery of money. They borrow money, and the planned means of enslaving men by money at once begins to operate like a disciplined army. In five years the thing is done, — men have not only lost their right to utilize their own land and their property, but also their liberty, — they have become slaves. Here begins act three. The situation is too painful; and the unfortunate ones are told they may change their master, and become slaves of another: there is not a thought about freedom from the slavery brought about by the means of money. And the people call for another master, to whom they give themselves up, asking him to improve their condition. The English come and see that dominion over these islands gives them the possibility of feeding their already too greatly multiplied parasites, and the English government takes possession of these islands and their inhabitants; but it does not take them in the form of personal slaves, it does not take even the land, nor distribute it among its assistants.

These old ways are not necessary now: only one thing is necessary, — taxes, which must be large enough on the one hand to prevent the working-men from freeing themselves from virtual slavery, and on the other hand to feed luxuriously a great number of parasites. The inhabitants must pay seventy thousand pounds sterling, — that is the fundamental condition upon which England consents to free the Fijis from the American despotism, and this is just what was wanting for the final enslaving of the inhabitants. But it turned out that the Fiji Islanders cannot under any circumstances pay these seventy thousand pounds in their present state. The claim is too great.

The English temporarily modify it, and take a part of it out in natural productions in order that in time, when money has come into circulation, they may receive the full sum. They do not behave like the former company, whose conduct we may liken to the first coming of savage invaders into an uncivilized land, when they want only to take as much as possible and then decamp: but England behaves like a more clear-sighted enslaver; she does not kill at one blow the goose with the golden eggs, but feeds her in order that she may continue to lay them. England at first relaxes the reins for her own interest that she may hold them forever afterward, and so has brought the Fiji Islanders into that state of permanent monetary thraldom in which all civilized European people now are, and from which their chance of escape is not apparent.

This phenomenon repeats itself in America, in China, in Central Asia; and it is the same in the history of the conquest of all nations.

Money is an inoffensive means of exchange when it is not collected with violence, or when loaded guns are not directed from the sea-shore against the defenseless inhabitants. As soon as it is taken by force of arms, the same thing must unavoidably take place which occurred on the Fiji Islands, and has always and everywhere repeated itself.

Such men as consider it their lawful right to utilize the labor of others, and who have the means of doing so, will achieve this by means of forcibly demanding such sums of money as will compel the oppressed to become the slaves of the oppressors.

And, moreover, that will happen which occurred between the English and the Fijis, — the extortioners will always, in their demand for money, rather exceed the limit to which the amount of the sum required must rise in order that the enslaving may take place more effectually. They will respect this limit only while they have moral sense and sufficient money for themselves; they will overstep it when they lose moral sense or require funds.

As for governments, they will always exceed this limit, — first, because for a government there exists no moral sense of justice; and secondly, because, as we all know, every government is in the greatest want of money, caused by wars and the necessity of giving gratuities to their allies. All governments are insolvent, and cannot help following a maxim expressed by a Russian statesman of the eighteenth century, — that the peasant must be sheared of his wool lest it should grow too long. All governments are hopelessly in debt, and this debt on an average (not taking in consideration its occasional diminution in England and America) is growing at a terrible rate. So also grow the budgets; that is, the necessity of struggling with other extortioners, and of giving presents to those who assist in extortion.

Wages do not increase, not because of the law of rent,

but because taxes collected with violence exist, in order to take away from men their superfluities, so that they may be compelled to sell their labor to satisfy them, the utilizing of their labor being the aim of raising them.

And their labor can only be utilized when on a general average the taxes required are more than the working-people are able to give without depriving themselves of all means of subsistence. The rising of wages would put an end to the possibility of enslaving; and therefore, as long as violence exists, wages can never rise. This simple and plain mode of action by some men toward others, political economists term *the iron law;* the instrument by which such action is performed, they call a medium of exchange; and money is this inoffensive medium of exchange necessary for men in their transactions with each other.

Why is it, then, that, whenever there is no violent demand for money taxes, there has never been, and can never be, money in its true signification; but, as among the Fiji Islanders, the Phœnicians, the Kirghis, and generally among men who do not pay taxes, as among the Africans, there is either a direct exchange of produce, or arbitrary standards of value, as sheep, hides, skins, and shells?

A definite kind of money, whatever it may be, will always become, not a means of exchange, but a means of ransoming from violence; and it begins to circulate among men only when a definite standard is compulsorily required from all.

It is only then that everybody equally wants it, and only then it receives any value.

Further, it is not the thing that is most convenient for exchange that receives any value, but that which is required by the government. If gold is demanded, gold becomes valuable; if knuckle-bones were demanded, they, too, would become valuable. If it were not so, why, then, has the issue of this means of exchange always been the prerogative of the government? The Fiji Islanders, for instance, have arranged among themselves their own means of exchange; well, then, let them be free to exchange what and how they like, and you, men possessing power, or the means of violence, do not interfere with this exchange. But instead you coin money, not allowing any one else to do so; or, as is the case with us, you merely print some notes, engraving upon them the heads of the tsars, sign them with a particular signature, and threaten to punish every falsification of them, distribute this money to your assistants, and require everybody to give you such money or such notes with such signatures, and so many of them that a working-man must give away all his labor in order to get these very notes or coins; and then you want to convince us that this money is necessary for us as a means of exchange.

All men are free, and none of them oppresses the others by keeping them in slavery; but there exist only money in society and an iron law, in consequence of which rent increases, and wages diminish down to a minimum. That half (nay, more than half) of the Russian peasants, in order to pay direct and indirect taxes and land taxes, enslave themselves to labor for the landowners or for manufacturers, does not at all signify (which is obvious); for the violent collection of poll-taxes and indirect and land taxes which are paid in money to the government and to its assistants, — the landowners, — compels the working-man to be in slavery to those who collect money; but it means that this money, as a means of exchange, and an iron law, exist.

Before the serfs were free, I could compel Ivan to do any work; and if he refused to do it, I could send him to the police-sergeant, and the latter would give him the rod till he submitted. And if I compelled Ivan to overwork himself, and did not give him either land or food, the matter would go up to the authorities, and I should have to answer for it.

But now that men are free, I can compel Ivan and Peter and Sidor to do every kind of work; and if they refuse to do it, I give them no money to pay taxes, and they will be flogged till they submit; besides this, I may also make a German, a Frenchman, a Chinaman, and an

Indian work for me by that means, so that, if they do not submit, I shall not give them money to hire land, or to buy bread, because they have neither land nor bread. And if I make them overwork themselves, or kill them with excess of labor, nobody will say a word to me about it; and, moreover, if I have read books on political economy, I shall be strongly persuaded that all men are free, and that money does not create slavery! Our peasants have long known that with a ruble one can hurt more than with a stick. But it is only political economists who do not want to see it.

To say that money does not create bondage is to say that half a century ago servitude did not create slavery. Political economists say that money is an inoffensive medium of exchange, notwithstanding the fact that, in consequence of possessing it, one man may enslave the other. Why, then, was it not said half a century ago that servitude was, in itself, an inoffensive medium of reciprocal services, notwithstanding the fact that by no lawful means could one man enslave another?

Some men give their manual labor; and the work of others consists in taking care of the physical and intellectual welfare of the slaves, and in superintending their efforts.

And, I fancy, some have really said this.

CHAPTER XIX

If the object of this sham, so-called science of Political Economy had not been the same as that of all other sciences of law, — the justification of violence, — it could not have avoided noticing the strange phenomenon that the distribution of wealth, and the depriving of some men of land and capital, and the enslaving of some men by others, depend upon money, and that it is only by means of money that some men utilize the labor of others, — in other words, enslave them.

I repeat it, a man who has money, may buy up and monopolize all the corn, and kill others with starvation, completely oppressing them, as it has frequently happened before our own eyes on a very large scale.

It would seem that we ought to look out for the connection of these occurrences with money; but science, with full assurance, asserts that money has no connection whatever with the matter in question.

Science says, money is as much an article of merchandise as anything else which has the value of its production, only with this difference, — that this article of merchandise is chosen as the more convenient medium of exchange for establishing values, for saving, and for making payments. One man has made boots, another has grown wheat, the third has bred sheep; and now, in order to exchange more conveniently, they put into circulation money, which represents the equivalent of labor; and by this medium they exchange the soles of boots for a loin of mutton, or ten pounds of flour.

Students of this sham science are very fond of picturing to themselves such a state of affairs; but there has never been such a condition in the world. Such an idea about society is like the idea about the primitive, prehistorical, perfect human state, which the philosophers cherished; but there has never existed such a state.

In all human societies where there has been money, there has been also the violence of the strong and the armed over the weak and the defenseless; and wherever there has been violence, there the standard of value, — money, — be it what it may, — either cattle or hides, or skins or metals, — must have lost unavoidably its significance as a medium of exchange, and received the meaning of a ransom from violence.

Without doubt, money possesses the inoffensive properties which science enumerates; but these properties it would have only in a society in which there was no violence, in an ideal state; but in such a society, money would not be found as a general measure of value; it has never existed, and could never exist, in a society which had not come under the general violence of the state.

In all societies known to us where there is money, it

receives the signification of the medium of exchange only because it serves as a means of violence. And its chief object is to act thus, and not as a mere medium. Where there is violence, money cannot be a regular medium of exchange, because it cannot be a measure of value. And it cannot be a measure of value, because, as soon as in a society one man can take away from another the productions of his labor, this measure is directly violated. If horses and cows, bred by one man, and violently taken away by others, were brought to a market, it is plain that the value of horses and cows there would no longer correspond with the labor of breeding them; and the value of all other things would also change in accordance with this change, and money would not determine their value.

Besides, if one man may acquire by force a cow or a horse or a house, he may by the same force acquire money itself, and with this money acquire all kinds of produce. If, then, money itself is acquired by violence, and spent to purchase things, money entirely loses its quality as a medium of exchange.

The oppressor who takes away money, and gives it for the production of labor, does not exchange anything, but by the means of labor takes away all that he wants.

But let us suppose that such an imaginary and impossible state of society really existed, in which, without a general violence of the state exercised over men, money is in circulation, — silver or gold serving as a measure of value and as a medium of exchange. All the savings in such a society are expressed by money. There appears in this society an oppressor in the shape of a conqueror. Let us suppose that this oppressor takes away the cows, horses, clothes, and the houses of the inhabitants, but, as it is not convenient for him to be in possession of all this, he will therefore naturally think of taking from these men that which represents among them all kinds of value, and is exchanged for all kinds of things, — money. And at once in this community, money will receive for the oppressor and his assistants another signification; its character as a medium of exchange will therefore cease in such a society.

The measure of the value of all things will always depend upon the pleasure of the oppressor.

The articles most necessary for him, and for which he gives more money, will receive a greater value, and *vice versa ;* so that, in a community exposed to violence, money receives at once its chief meaning, — it becomes a means of violence and a ransom from violence, and it will retain among the oppressed people its signification as a medium of exchange only so far as it is convenient for the oppressor. Let us picture the whole affair in a circle, thus: —

The serfs supply their landlord with linen, poultry, sheep, and daily labor.

The landlord substitutes money for these goods, and fixes the value of various articles sent in. Those who have no linen, corn, cattle, or manual labor to offer, may bring a definite sum of money.

It is obvious that, in the society of the peasants of this landlord, the price of various articles will always depend upon the landlord's pleasure. The landlord uses the articles collected among his peasants, and some of these articles are more necessary for him than others; accordingly, he fixes the prices for them, more or less. It is clear that the mere will and requirements of the landlord must regulate the prices of these articles among the payers. If he is in want of corn, he will set a high price for a fixed quantity of it, and a low price for linen, cattle, or work; and therefore those who have no corn will sell their labor, linen, and cattle to others, in order to buy corn to give to the landlord.

If the landlord chooses to substitute money for all kinds of claim, then the value of things will again depend, not upon the value of labor, but first upon the sum of money which the landlord will require,. and secondly upon the articles produced by the peasants which are more necessary to the landlord, and for which he will allow a higher price.

The money claim made by the landlord upon the

peasants would cease only to have any influence upon the prices of the articles when the peasants of this landlord should live separate from other people and have no connection with any one besides themselves and the landlord; and secondly, when the landlord employs money, not in purchasing things in his own village, but elsewhere. It is only under these two conditions that the prices of things, though changed nominally, would remain relatively the same, and money would have the signification of a measure of value and of a medium of exchange.

But if the peasants have any business connections with the inhabitants surrounding them, the prices of the articles of their produce, as sold to their neighbors, would depend upon the sum of money required from them by their landlord.

(If from their neighbors less money is required than from them, then their productions would be sold cheaper than the productions of their neighbors, and *vice versa.*) And again, the money demand made by the landlord upon his peasants would cease to have any influence upon the prices of the articles, only when the sums collected by the landlord were not spent in buying the productions of his own peasants. But if he spends money in purchasing from them, it is plain that the prices of various articles will constantly vary among them according as the landlord buys more of one thing than another.

Suppose one landlord has fixed a very high poll-tax, and his neighbor a very low one; it is clear that on the estate of the first landlord everything will be cheaper than on the estate of the second, and that the prices on either estate will depend only upon the augmentation and diminution of the poll-taxes. This is one influence of violence upon value.

Another, arising out of the first, consists in the relative value of all things. Suppose one landlord is fond of horses, and pays a high price for them; another is fond of towels, and offers a high figure for them. It is obvious that on the estate of either of these two landlords, the horses and the towels will be dear, and the prices for these articles will not be in proportion to those of cows or of corn. If to-morrow the collector of towels dies, and his heirs are fond of poultry, then it is obvious that the price of towels will fall, and that of poultry will rise.

Wherever there is in society the mastery of one man over another, there the meaning of money as the measure of value at once yields to the will of the oppressor, and its meaning as a medium of exchange of the productions of labor is replaced by another, that of the most convenient means of utilizing the labor of others.

The oppressor wants money neither as a medium of exchange, — for he will take whatever he wants without exchange, — nor as a measure of value, — for he will himself determine the value of everything, — but only for the convenience it affords of exercising violence; and this convenience consists in the fact that money may be saved up, and is the most convenient means of holding in slavery the majority of mankind.

It is not convenient to carry away all the cattle in order always to have horses, cows, and sheep whenever wanted, because they must be fed; the same holds good with corn, for it may be spoiled; the same with slaves, — sometimes a man may require thousands of workmen, and sometimes none. Money demanded from those who have not got it makes it possible to get rid of all these inconveniences, and to have everything that is required; this is why the oppressor wants money. Besides this, he wants money in order that his right to utilize another's labor may not be confined to certain men, but may be extended to all men who likewise require it.

When there was no money in circulation, each landlord could utilize the labor only of his own serfs; but when they agreed to demand from their peasants money which they had not, they were all enabled to appropriate without distinction the labor of the men on every estate.

Thus the oppressor finds it more convenient to press all his claims upon another's labor in the shape of money, and for this sole object is it desired. To the victim from whom it is taken away, money cannot be of use, either for the purpose of exchange, seeing he exchanges without money, as all nations have exchanged who had no government; nor for a measure of value, because this is fixed without him; nor for the purpose of saving, because the man whose productions are taken away cannot save; neither for payments, because an oppressed man will always have more to pay than to receive; and if he does receive anything, the payment will be made, not in money, but in articles of merchandise in either case; whether the workman takes goods out of his master's shop as remuneration for his labor, or whether he buys the necessaries of life with all his earnings in other shops, the money is required from him, and he is told by his oppressors that if he does not pay it, they will refuse to give him land or bread, or will take away his cow or his horse, or condemn him to work, or put him in prison. He can only free himself from all this by selling the productions of his toil, his own labor, or that of his children.

And this he will have to sell according to those prices which will be established, not by a regular exchange, but by the authority which demands money of him.

Under the conditions of the influence of tribute and taxes upon the prices which everywhere and always repeat themselves, as with the landowners in a narrow circle, so also with the state on a larger scale (in which the causes of the modification of prices are as obvious to us as it is obvious how the hands and feet of puppets are set in motion, to those who look behind the curtain and see who are the wire-pullers), — under these circumstances, to say that money is a medium of exchange and a measure of value is at least astonishing.

CHAPTER XX

ALL slavery is based solely on the fact that one man can deprive another of his life, and by threatening to do so compel him to do his will. We may see for certain that whenever one man is enslaved by another, when against his own will, and according to the will of another, he does certain actions, which are contrary to his inclination, the cause, if traced to its source, is nothing more nor less than a result of this threat. If a man gives to others all his labor, has not enough to eat, has to send his little children from home to work hard, leaves his family and devotes all his life to a hated and unnecessary task, as happens before our own eyes in the world (which we term civilized because we ourselves live in it), then we may certainly say that he does so only because not to do so would be equivalent to loss of life.

And therefore in our civilized world, where the majority of people, amidst terrible privations, perform hated labors unnecessary to themselves, the greater number of men are in slavery based upon the threat of being deprived of their existence. Of what, then, does this slavery consist? And wherein lies this power of threat?

In olden times the means of subjugation and the threat to kill were plain and obvious to all; the primitive means of enslaving men consisted then in a direct threat to kill with the sword.

An armed man said to an unarmed, "I can kill thee, as thou hast seen I have done to thy brother, but I do not want to do it: I will spare thee, — first, because it is not agreeable for me to kill thee; secondly, because, as well for me as for thee, it will be more convenient that thou shouldst labor for me than that I should kill thee. Therefore do all I order thee to do, but know that, if thou refusest, I will take thy life."

So the unarmed man submitted to the armed one, and did everything which he was ordered to do. The unarmed man labored, the armed threatened. This was that personal slavery which appeared first among all nations, and which still exists among primitive races.

This means of enslaving always begins the work; but when life becomes more complicated, it undergoes a change. With the complication of life, such a means presents great inconveniences to the oppressor. He, in order to appropriate the labor of the weak, has to feed and clothe them, and keep them able to work, and so the number of slaves is diminished; besides, this compels the enslaver to remain continually with the enslaved, driving him to work by the threat of murdering him. And thus is developed another means of subjugation.

Five thousand years ago (as we find in the Bible) this novel, convenient, and clever means of oppression was discovered by Joseph the Beautiful.

It is similar to that employed now in the menageries for taming restive horses and wild beasts.

It is hunger!

This contrivance is thus described in the Bible:—

Genesis xli. 48: And he gathered up all the food of the seven years, which were in the land of Egypt, and laid up the food in the cities; the food of the field, which was round about every city, laid he up in the same.

49. And Joseph gathered corn as the sand of the sea, very much, until he left numbering; for it was without number.

53. And the seven years of plenteousness, that was in the land of Egypt, were ended.

54. And the seven years of dearth began to come, according as Joseph had said: and the dearth was in all lands; but in all the land of Egypt, there was bread.

55. And when all the land of Egypt was famished, the people cried to Pharaoh for bread: and Pharaoh said unto all the Egyptians, Go unto Joseph; what he saith to you, do.

56. And the famine was over all the face of the

earth: and Joseph opened all the storehouses, and sold unto the Egyptians; and the famine waxed sore in the land of Egypt.

57. And all countries came into Egypt to Joseph for to buy corn; because that the famine was so sore in all lands.

Joseph, making use of the primitive means of enslaving men by the threat of the sword, gathered corn during the seven years of plenty in expectation of seven years of famine, which generally follow years of plenty, — men know all this without the dreams of Pharaoh, — and then by the pangs of hunger he more securely and conveniently made all the Egyptians and the inhabitants of the surrounding countries slaves to Pharaoh. And when the people began to be famished, he arranged matters so as to keep them in his power forever.

Genesis xlvii. 13: And there was no bread in all the land; for the famine was very sore, so that the land of Egypt and all the land of Canaan fainted by reason of the famine.

14. And Joseph gathered up all the money that was found in the land of Egypt, and in the land of Canaan, for the corn which they bought; and Joseph brought the money into Pharaoh's house.

15. And when money failed in the land of Egypt, and in the land of Canaan, all the Egyptians came unto Joseph, and said, Give us bread: for why should we die in thy presence? for the money faileth.

16. And Joseph said, Give your cattle; and I will give you for your cattle, if money fail.

17. And they brought their cattle unto Joseph: and Joseph gave them bread in exchange for horses, and for the flocks, and for the cattle of the herds, and for the asses: and he fed them with bread for all their cattle for that year.

18. When that year was ended, they came unto him the second year, and said unto him, We will not hide it from my lord, how that our money is spent; my lord

also hath our herds of cattle; there is not aught left in the sight of my lord, but our bodies, and our lands:

19. Wherefore shall we die before thine eyes, both we and our land? buy us and our land for bread, and we and our land will be servants unto Pharaoh: and give us seed, that we may live, and not die, that the land be not desolate.

20. And Joseph bought all the land of Egypt for Pharaoh; for the Egyptians sold every man his field, because the famine prevailed over them; so the land became Pharaoh's.

21. And as for the people, he removed them to cities from one end of the borders of Egypt even to the other end thereof.

22. Only the land of the priests bought he not; for the priests had a portion assigned them of Pharaoh, and did eat their portion which Pharaoh gave them: wherefore they sold not their lands.

23. Then Joseph said unto the people, Behold, I have bought you this day and your land for Pharaoh: lo, here is seed for you, and ye shall sow the land.

24. And it shall come to pass in the increase, that ye shall give the fifth part unto Pharaoh, and four parts shall be your own, for seed of the field, and for your food, and for them of your households, and for food for your little ones.

25. And they said, Thou hast saved our lives; let us find grace in the sight of my lord, and we will be Pharaoh's servants.

26. And Joseph made it a law over the land of Egypt unto this day, that Pharaoh should have the fifth part; except the land of the priests only, which became not Pharaoh's.

Formerly, in order to appropriate labor, Pharaoh had to use violence toward them; but now, when the stores and the land belonged to Pharaoh, he had only to keep these stores by force, and by means of hunger compel men to labor for him.

All the land now belonged to Pharaoh, and he had

all the stores (which were taken away from the people); and therefore, instead of driving them to work individually by the sword, he had only to keep food from them, and they were enslaved, not by the sword, but by hunger.

In a year of scarcity, all men may be starved to death at Pharaoh's will; and in a year of plenty, all may be killed who, from casual misfortunes, have no stores of corn.

And thence comes into operation the second means of enslaving, not directly with the sword, — that is, by the strong man driving the weak one to labor under threat of killing him, — but by the strong one having taken away from the weak the stores of corn which, keeping by the sword, he compels the weak to work for.

Joseph said to the hungry men, "I could starve you to death, because I have the corn; but I will spare your life, but only under the condition that you do all I order you for the food which I will give you." For the first means of enslaving, the oppressor needs only soldiers to ride to and fro among the inhabitants, and under threat of death make them fulfil the requirements of their master. And thus the oppressor has only to pay his soldiers; but with the second means, besides these the oppressor must have different assistants for keeping and protecting the land and stores from the starving people.

These are the Josephs and his stewards and distributers. And the oppressor has to reward them, and to give Joseph a dress of fine linen, a gold ring, and servants, and corn and silver to his brothers and relatives. Besides this, from the very nature of this second means, not only the stewards and their relations, but all those who have stores of corn, become participators in this violence, just as by the first means, based upon crude force, every one who has arms becomes a partner in tyranny; so by this means, based upon hunger, every one who has stores of provision shares in it, and has power over those who have no stores.

The advantage of this means over the former for the oppressor consists, first and chiefly, in the fact that he need no longer compel the working-men by force to do his will, for they themselves come to him, and sell themselves to him; secondly, in the circumstance that fewer men escape from his violence: the drawback is that he has to employ a greater number of men. For the oppressed the advantage of it consists in the fact that they are no longer exposed to rough violence, but are left to themselves, and can always hope to pass from being the oppressed to become oppressors in their turn, which they sometimes really do by fortunate circumstances. The drawback for them is that they can never escape from participating in the oppression of others.

This new means of enslaving generally comes into operation together with the old one; and the oppressor lessens the one and increases the other according to his desires.

But this does not fully satisfy the man who wishes to have as little trouble and care as possible, and to take away as much as possible of the productions of labor of as many working-people as he can find, and to enslave as many men as possible; and therefore a third means of oppression is evolved.

This is the slavery of taxation, and, like the second, it is based upon hunger; but to the means of subduing men by depriving them of bread, is added the privation of other necessaries of life.

The oppressor requires from the slaves such a quantity of money which he himself has coined, that, in order to obtain it, the slaves are compelled to sell not only stores of corn in greater quantity than the fifth part which was fixed by Joseph, but the first necessaries of life as well, — meat, skins, wool, clothes, firewood, even their dwellings; and therefore the oppressor always keeps his slaves in his power, not only by hunger, but by hunger, thirst, cold, and other privations.

And then the third means of slavery comes into operation, a monetary, a tributary one, consisting in the oppressor saying to the oppressed, "I can do with each of you just what I like, I can kill and destroy you by taking away the land by which you earn your living; I can, with this money which you must give me, buy all the corn upon which you feed, and sell it to strangers, and at any time annihilate you by starvation; I can take from you all that you have, — your cattle, your houses, your clothes; but it is neither convenient nor agreeable for me to do so, and therefore I let you alone, to work as you please; only give me so much of the money which I demand of you, either as a poll-tax, or according to the quantity of your food and drink, or your clothes or your houses. Give me this money, and do what you like among yourselves, but know that I shall neither protect nor maintain widows nor orphans nor invalids nor old people, nor such as have been burned out; I shall only protect the regular circulation of this money. This right will always be mine, to protect only those who regularly give me the fixed number of these pieces of money; as to how or where you get it, I will not in the least trouble myself." And so the oppressor distributes these pieces of money as an acknowledgment that his demand has been complied with.

The second means of enslaving consists in that, having taken away the fifth part of the harvest, and collected stores of corn, the Pharaoh, besides the personal slavery by the sword, receives, by his assistants, the possibility of dominion over the working-people during the time of famine, and over some of them forever from misfortunes which happen to them.

The third means consists in this: Pharaoh requires from the working-people more money than the value of the fifth part of corn which he took from them; he, together with his assistants, gets a new means of dominion over the working-class, not merely during the famine and their casual misfortunes, but permanently. By the second means, men retain stores of corn which help them to bear indifferent harvests and casual misfortunes without going into slavery; by the third, when there are more demands, the stores, not of corn only, but of all other necessaries of life, are taken away from them, and at the first misfortune a working-man, having neither stores of corn, nor any other stores which he might have exchanged for corn, falls into slavery to those who have money.

For the first, an oppressor need have only soldiers, and share the booty with them; for the second, he must have, besides the protectors of the land and the stores of corn, collectors and clerks for the distribution of this corn; for the third, he must have, besides the soldiers for keeping the land and his property, collectors of taxes, assessors of direct and indirect taxation, supervisors, custom-house clerks, managers of money, and coiners of it.

The organization of the third means is much more complicated than that of the second. By the second, the getting in of corn may be leased out, as was the case in olden times and is still in Turkey; but by putting taxes on men, there is need of a complicated administration, which has to insure that the taxes are rightly levied. And therefore, by the third means, the oppressor has to share the plunder with a still greater number of men than by the second; besides, according to the very nature of the thing, all those men of the same or of the foreign country who possess money become sharers with the oppressed.

The advantage of this means over the first and second consists in the following fact: chiefly that by it there is no need of waiting for a year of scarcity, as in the time of Joseph, but years of famine are established forever, and (whilst by the second method the part of the labor which is taken away depends upon the harvest, and cannot be augmented *ad libitum*, because if there is no corn, there can be nothing to take) by the new monetary method the requirement can be brought to any desired limit, for the demand for money can always be satisfied, because the debtor, in order to satisfy it, will sell his cattle, clothes, or houses. The chief advantage of this means to the oppressor consists in the fact that by it he can take away the greatest quantity of labor and in the most convenient way; for a money-tax, like a screw, may easily and conveniently be screwed up to the utmost limit, and golden eggs be obtained though the bird that lays them is all but dead.

Another of its advantages for the oppressor is that its violence reaches all those also who, by possessing no land, escaped from it formerly by giving only a part of their labor for corn; and now, besides that part which they give for corn, they must give another part for taxes. A drawback for the oppressor is that he has to share the plunder with a still greater number of men, not only with his direct assistants, but also with all those men of his own country, and even foreign countries, who may have the money which is demanded from the slaves.

Its advantage for the oppressed is only that he is allowed greater independence: he may live wherever he chooses, do whatever he likes; he may sow or not sow; he has not to give any account of his labor; and if he has money, he may consider himself entirely free, and constantly hope, though only for a time, when he has money to spare, to obtain not only an independent position, but even to become an oppressor himself.

The drawback is that, on a general average, the situation of the oppressed becomes much worse, and they are deprived of the greater part of the productions of their labor, because by it the number of those who utilize the labor of others increases, and therefore the burden of keeping them falls upon a smaller number of men. This third means of enslaving men is also a very old one, and comes into operation with the former two without entirely excluding them.

All three have always been in operation. All may be likened to screws, which secure the board which is laid upon the working-people, and which presses them down. The fundamental or middle screw, without which the other screws could not hold, which is first screwed up, and which is never slackened, is the screw of personal slavery, the enslaving of some men by others under threat of slaughter; the second, which is screwed up after the first, is that of enslaving men by taking away the land and stores of provisions from them, such abduction being maintained under threat to murder; and the third screw is slavery enforced by the requirement of certain coins; and this demand is also maintained under threat of murder.

These three screws are made fast, and it is only when one of them is tightened that the two others are slackened. For the complete enslaving of the working-man, all three are necessary; and in our society, all three are in operation together. The first means by personal slavery under the threat of murder by the sword has never been abolished, and never will be so long as there is oppression, because all kinds of oppression are based upon this alone. We are all very sure that personal slavery is abolished in our civilized world; that the last remnant of it has been annihilated in America and in Russia, and that it is only among barbarians that real slavery exists, and that with us it is no longer in being.

We forget only one small circumstance,—those hundreds of millions of standing troops, without which no state exists, and with the abolition of which all the economical organization of each state would inevitably fall to pieces. Yet what are these millions of soldiers but the personal slaves of those who rule over them? Are not these men compelled to do the will of their commanders, under the threat of torture and death,—a threat often carried out? the difference consisting only in the fact that the submission of these slaves is not called slavery, but discipline; the only difference being that slaves are so from their birth, and soldiers only during a more or less short period of their so-called service.

Personal slavery, therefore, is not only not abolished in our civilized world, but, under the general system of recruiting, it has become confirmed of late years; and as it has always existed, so it has remained, having only somewhat changed from its original form. And it cannot but exist, because, so long as there is the enslaving of one man by another, there will be this personal slavery too, that which under threat of the sword maintains the serfdom of landownership and taxes.

It may be that this slavery, that is, of troops, is necessary, as it is said, for the defense and the glory of the country; but this kind of utility is more than doubtful, because we see how often in the case of unsuccessful wars it serves only for the subjugation and shame of the country; but the expediency of this slavery for maintaining that of the land and taxes is unquestionable.

If Irish or Russian peasants were to take possession of the land of the landowners, troops would be sent to dispossess them.

If you build a distillery or a brewery, and do not pay excise, then soldiers will be sent to shut it up. Refuse to pay taxes, the same thing will happen to you.

The second screw is the means of enslaving men by taking away from them the land and their stores of provisions. This means has also been always in existence wherever men are oppressed; and, whatever changes it may undergo, it is everywhere in operation.

Sometimes all the land belongs to the sovereign, as is the case in Turkey, and there one-tenth is given to the state treasury. Sometimes a part of the land belongs to the sovereign, and taxes are raised upon it. Sometimes all the land belongs to a few people, and is let out for labor, as is the case in England. Sometimes more or less large portions of the land belong to the landowners, as is the case in Russia, Germany, and France. But wherever there is enslaving, there exists also the appropriation of the land by the oppressor. This screw is slackened or tightened according to the condition of the other screws.

Thus, in Russia, when personal slavery was extended to the majority of working-people, there was no need of land slavery; but the screw of personal slavery was slackened in Russia only when the screws of land and tax slavery were tightened.

In England, for instance, the land slavery is preëminently in operation, and the question about the nation alizing of the lands consists only in the screw of taxation being tightened in order that the screw of land appropriation may be slackened.

The third means of enslaving men, by taxes, has also been in operation for ages; and in our days, with the extension of uniform standards of money and the strengthening of the state power, it has received only a particular influence.

This means is so worked out in our days, that it tends to substitute the second means of enslaving, — the land monopoly.

This is the screw by the tightening of which the screw of land slavery is slackened, as is obvious from the politico-economical state of all Europe.

We have, in our lifetime, witnessed in Russia two transformations of slavery: when the serfs were liberated, and their landlords retained the right to the greater part of the land, the landlords were afraid that they were going to lose their power over their slaves; but experience has shown that, having let go the old chain of personal slavery, they had only to seize another, — that of the land. A peasant was short of corn, he had not enough to live on; and the landlord had land and stores of corn, and therefore the peasant still remained the same slave.

Another transformation was caused by the government screw of taxation being pressed home, when the majority of working-people, having no stores, were obliged to sell themselves to their landlords and to the factories. The new form of oppression held the people still tighter, so that nine-tenths of the Russian working-people are working for their landlords and in the factories to pay these taxes. This is so obvious that, if the government were not to raise taxes for one year only, all labor would be stopped in the fields of the landlords and in the factories. Nine-tenths of the Russian people hire themselves out during and before the collection of taxes. All these three means have never ceased to operate, and are still in operation; but men are inclined to ignore them, and new excuses are invented fcr them.

And what is most remarkable of all is this, that the very means on which, at the moment in question, everything is based, that screw which is screwed up tighter than all others, which holds everything, is not noticed so long as it holds. When in the ancient world all the economical administration was upheld by personal slavery, the greatest intellects did not notice it. To Plato, as well as to Xenophon and Aristotle and to the Romans, it seemed that it could not be otherwise, and that slavery was an unavoidable and natural result of wars, without which the existence of mankind could not be thought of. So also in the Middle Ages and up to the present time, men have not apprehended the meaning of landownership, upon which depended all the economical administration of their time.

So also, at present, no one sees, or wants to see, that in our time the enslaving of the majority of the people depends upon taxes collected by the government from its own land slaves, taxes collected *by the troops*, by the very same troops, which are maintained by means of these taxes.

CHAPTER XXI

No wonder that the slaves themselves, who have always been enslaved, do not understand their own position, and that this condition in which they have always been living is considered by them to be that natural to human life, and that they hail as a relief any change in their form of slavery; no wonder that their owners sometimes quite sincerely think they are, in a measure, freeing the slaves by slackening one screw, though they are compelled to do so by the over-tension of another.

Both become accustomed to their state; and one part, — the slaves, — never having known what freedom is, merely seek an alleviation, or only the change of their condition; the other, — the owners, — wishing to mask their injustice, try to assign a particular meaning to those new forms of slavery which they enforce in place of older ones: but it is wonderful how the majority of the investigators of the economical conditions of the life of the people fail to see that which forms the basis of all the economical conditions of a people.

It would seem that the duty of a true science was to try to ascertain the connection of the phenomena and general cause of a series of occurrences. But the majority of the representatives of modern Political Economy are doing just the reverse of this: they carefully hide the connection and meaning of the phenomena, and avoid answering the most simple and essential questions.

Modern Political Economy, like an idle, lazy carthorse, goes well only downhill, when it has no collar-work; but as soon as it has anything to draw, it at once refuses, pretending it has to go somewhere aside after its own business. When any grave, essential question is put to Political Economy, scientific discussions are started about some matter or other, which does not in the least concern the question.

You ask, How are we to account for a fact so unnatural, monstrous, unreasonable, and not useless only, but harmful, that some men can eat or work only in accordance with the will of other men?

And you are gravely answered, Because some men must arrange the labor and the feeding of others, — such is the law of production.

You ask, What is this right of property, according to which some men appropriate to themselves the land, food, and instruments of labor belonging to others? You are again gravely answered, This right is based upon the protection of labor, — that is, the protection of some men's labor is effected by taking possession of the labor of other men.

You ask, What is that money which is everywhere coined and stamped by the governments, by the authorities, and which is so exorbitantly demanded from the working-people, and which in the shape of national debts is levied upon the future generations of workingmen? And further, has not this money, demanded from the people in the shape of taxes, raised to the utmost pitch, has not this money any influence upon the economical relationships of men, — between the payers and the receivers? And you are answered in all seriousness, Money is an article of merchandise like sugar, or chintz; and it differs from other articles only in the fact that it is more convenient for exchange.

As for the influence of taxes upon the economical conditions of a people, it is a different question altogether: the laws of production, exchange, and distribution of wealth are one thing, but taxation is quite another. You ask whether it has any influence upon the economical conditions of a people that the government can arbitrarily raise or lower prices, and, having augmented the taxes, can enslave all those who have no land? The pompous answer is, The laws of production, exchange, and distribution of wealth are one science, — Political Economy; and taxes, and, generally speaking, State Economy, come under another head, — the Law of Finance.

You ask finally, Is there no influence exercised upon economical conditions by the circumstance that all the people are in bondage to the government, and that this government can arbitrarily ruin all men, take away all the productions of men's labor, and even carry the men themselves away from their labor into military slavery? You are answered, That this is altogether a different question, belonging to the State Law.

The majority of the representatives of science discuss quite seriously the laws of the economical life of a people, while all the functions and activities of this life are dependent upon the will of the oppressor; while at the same time, recognizing the influence of the oppressor as a natural condition of the life of a people, they do the same thing that an investigator of the economical conditions of the life of the personal slaves of different masters would do, were he not to consider the influence exercised upon the life of these slaves by the will of that master who compels them to labor upon this or that thing, and who drives them from one place to another, according to his pleasure, who feeds them or neglects to do so, who kills them or leaves them alive.

A dreadful superstition has been long, and is still, in existence, — a superstition which has done more harm to men than all the most terrible religious superstitions.

And so-called science supports this superstition with all its power, and with the utmost zeal. This superstition resembles exactly the religious one, and consists in affirming that, besides the duties of man to man, there are still more important duties toward an imaginary being, which theologians call God, and political science the State.

The religious superstition consists in this: That the sacrifices, sometimes of human lives, offered to this imaginary being, are necessary, and that they can and ought to be enforced by every means, even by violence. The political superstition consists in this: That, besides the duties of man to man, there exist still more important duties to an imaginary being; and the offerings, very often of human lives, brought to this imaginary being, — the State, — are also necessary, and can and ought to be enforced by every means, even by violence.

This very superstition, which was formerly encouraged by the priests of different religions, is now sustained by so-called science.

Men are thrown into slavery, into the most terrible slavery, worse than has ever before existed; but so-called science tries to persuade men that such is necessary, and cannot be avoided.

The state must exist for the welfare and business of the people, to rule and protect them from their enemies.

For this purpose the state wants money and troops. Money must be subscribed by all the citizens of the state. And hence all the relationships of men must be considered under the conditions of the existence of the state.

"I want to help my father by my labor," says a common, unlearned man. "I want also to marry; but, instead, I am taken and sent to Kazan, to be a soldier for six years. I leave the military service. I want to plow the ground, and earn food for my family; but I am not allowed to plow for one hundred versts around me, unless I pay money, which I have not got, and pay it to those men who do not understand how to plow, and who require for the land so much money, that I must give them all my labor to procure it: however, I still manage to save something and I want to give my savings to my children; but a police sergeant comes to me, and takes from me all I had saved for taxes; I earn a little more, and am again deprived of it. All my economical activity is under the influence of state demands; and it appears to me that the amelioration of my position, and that of my brethren, will follow our liberation from the demands of the state."

But he is told such reasoning is the result of his ignorance.

Study the laws of production, exchange, and distribution of wealth, and do not mix up economical questions with those of the state.

The phenomena which you point to are not at all a constraint put upon your freedom; but they are those necessary sacrifices which you, along with others, must make for your own freedom and welfare.

"But my son has been taken away from me," says again a common man, "and they threaten to take away all my sons as soon as they are grown up; they took him away by force, and drove him to face the enemy's guns into some country which we have never heard of, and for an object which we cannot understand.

"And as for the land which they do not allow us to plow, and for want of which we are starving, it belongs to a man who got possession of it by force and whom we have never seen, and whose affairs we cannot even understand. And the taxes, to collect which the police sergeant has by force taken away my cow from my children, so far as I know, will go over to this same man who took my cow away, and to various members of committees, and of departments which I do not know of and in the utility of which I do not believe. How is it, then, that all these acts of violence secure my liberty, and all this evil is to procure good?"

You may compel a man to be a slave, and to do that which he considers to be evil for himself, but you cannot compel him to think that in suffering violence he is free, and that the obvious evil which he endures constitutes his good.

Yet this seemingly impossible thing has been done in our days.

The government, that is, the armed oppressors, decide what they want from those whom they oppress (as in the case of England and the Fiji Islanders): they decide how much labor they want from their slaves, — they decide how many assistants they will need in collecting the fruits of this labor; they organize their assistants in the shape of soldiers, landowners, and collectors of taxes.

And the slaves give their labor, and, at the same time, believe that they give it, not because their masters demand it, but for the sake of their own freedom and welfare; and that this service and these bloody sacrifices to the divinity called State are necessary, and that, barring this service to their Deity, they are free. They believe it because the same had been formerly said in the name of religion by the priests, and is now said in the name of so-called science — by learned men.

But one need only cease to believe what is said by other men, who call themselves priests or learned men, in order that the absurdity of such an assertion may become obvious.

The men who oppress others assure them that this oppression is necessary for the state, — and the state is necessary for the freedom and welfare of men; so that it appears that the oppressors oppress men for the sake of their freedom, and do them evil for the sake of good. But men are furnished with reason in order to understand wherein consists their own good, and to do it willingly.

As for the acts, the goodness of which is not intelligible to men, and to which they are compelled by force, such cannot serve for their good, because a reasoning being may consider as good only the thing which appears so to his reason. If men from passion or folly are driven to evil, all that those who are not so driven can do is to persuade men as to what constitutes their real good. You may try to persuade men that their welfare will be greater when they are all become soldiers, are deprived of land, and have given their whole labor away for taxes; but until all men consider this condition to be their welfare, and undertake it willingly, one cannot call such a state of things the common welfare of men.

The willing acceptance of a condition by men is the sole criterion of its good. And the lives of men abound with such acts. Ten workmen buy tools in common, in order to work together with them, and in so doing they are undoubtedly benefiting themselves; but we cannot suppose that if these ten workmen were to compel an eleventh, by force, to join in their association, they would insist that their common welfare will be the same for him.

And so with gentlemen who agree to give a subscription dinner at a pound a head to a mutual friend, — no one can assert that such a dinner will benefit a man who, against his will, has been obliged to pay a sovereign for it; and so with peasants who decide, for their common convenience, to dig a pond.

For those who consider the existence of such more valuable than the labor spent upon it, the digging of it will be a common good. But to the one who considers the existence of the pond of less value than a day's harvesting, in which he is behindhand, the digging of it will appear evil. The same holds good with roads, churches, and museums, and with all various social and state affairs.

All such work may be good for those who consider it good, and who therefore freely and willingly perform it, — the dinner which the gentlemen give, the pond which the peasants dig. But the work to which men must be driven by force ceases to be a common good precisely by the fact of such violence. All this is so plain and simple, that if men had not been so long deceived, there would be no need to explain it

Suppose we live in a village where all the inhabitants have agreed to build a viaduct over the morass which is a danger to them. We agree together, and promise to give from each house so much in money or wood or days of labor. We agree to do this because the making of this road is more advantageous to us than what we exchange for it; but among us there are some for whom it is more advantageous to do without a road than to spend money on it, or who, at all events, think it is so. Can the compelling of these men to make the way make it of advantage to them? Obviously not; because those who considered that their joining by choice in making the way would have been to their disadvantage, will consider it, *a fortiori*, still more disadvantageous when they are compelled to do so. Suppose, even, that we all without exception were agreed, and promised so much money or labor from each house, but that it happened that some of those who had promised did not give what they agreed on, their circumstances having meanwhile changed, so that it is more advantageous for such now to be without the road than to spend money on it; or that they have simply changed their mind about it, or even calculate that others will make the road without them, and that they will pass over it. Can the compelling of these men to join in the labor make them consider the sacrifices enforced upon them their own good?

Obviously not; because if such have not fulfilled what they have promised, owing to a change in their circumstances, so that now the sacrifices for the sake of the road outbalance their gain by it, the compulsory sacrifices of such would be only a worse evil. But if those who refuse to join in building the bridge have in view the utilizing of the labor of others, then in this case also the compelling them to make a sacrifice would be only a punishment on a supposition, and their object, which nobody can prove, will be punished before it is made apparent; but in neither case can the compelling them to join in a work undesired by them be good for them.

And if it be so with sacrifices for a work comprehensible by all, obvious and undoubtedly useful to all, as a road over a morass, how still more unjust and unreasonable is the compelling of millions of men to make sacrifices, the object of which is incomprehensible, imperceptible, and often undoubtedly harmful, as is the case with military service and with taxes.

But it is believed that what appears to every one to be an evil is a common good: it appears that there are men, a small minority, who alone know what the common good consists in, and, notwithstanding the fact that all other men consider this common good to be an evil, this minority can compel other men to do whatever they may consider to be for the common good. This constitutes the chief superstition and the chief deceit, which hinders the progress of mankind toward the True and the Good.

The nursing of this superstitious deceit has been the object of political sciences in general, and of so-called Political Economy in particular.

Many are making use of it in order to hide from men the state of oppression and slavery in which they now are.

The way they set about doing so is by starting the theory that violence, connected with the economy of social slavery, is a natural and unavoidable evil, and men thereby are deceived, and turn their eyes from the real causes of their misfortunes.

Slavery has long been abolished. It has been abolished as well in Rome as in America, and among ourselves; but the word only has been abolished, and not the evil.

Slavery is the violent freeing of some men from the labor necessary for satisfying their wants, which transfers this labor to others; and wherever there is a man who does not work, not because others willingly and lovingly work for him, but because he has the possibility, while not working himself, to make others work for him, there is slavery.

And wherever there are, as is the case with all European societies, men who by means of violence utilize the labor of thousands of others, and consider such to be their right, and others who submit to this violence considering it to be their duty, — there is slavery in its most dreadful proportions.

Slavery does exist. In what, then, does it consist? In that by which it has always consisted, and without which it cannot exist at all, — in the violence of a strong and armed man over a weak and unarmed one.

Slavery with its three fundamental modes of operation, — personal violence, soldiery, land-taxes, — maintained by soldiery, and direct and indirect taxes put upon all the inhabitants, and so maintained, is still in operation now as it has been before.

We do not see it, because each of these three forms of slavery has received a new justification, which hides its meaning from us.

The personal violence of armed over unarmed men received its justification in the defense of the country from its imaginary enemies, while in its essence it has the one old meaning, — the submission of the conquered to the oppressors.

The taking away by violence from the laborers of their land was justified as a recompense for services rendered to an imaginary common welfare, and is confirmed by the right of heritage; but in reality it is the same depriving men of land and enslaving them, which has been performed by the troops.

And the last, the monetary violence by means of taxes, the strongest and most effective in our days, had received a most wonderful justification.

The depriving men of the possession of their liberty and of all their goods is said to be done for the sake of the common liberty and of the common welfare. But in fact it is the same slavery, only an impersonal one.

Wherever violence is turned into law, there is slavery.

Whether violence finds its expression in the circumstance that princes with their courtiers come, kill, and burn down villages, or in the fact that the slaveowners take labor or money for the land from their slaves, and enforce payment by means of armed men, or by putting taxes on others, and riding armed to and fro in the villages, or in the circumstance of a home department collecting money through governors and police sergeants, — in one word, as long as violence is maintained by the bayonet, there will be no distribution of wealth, but it will all be accumulated among the oppressors. As a striking illustration of the truth of this assertion, the project of Mr. George as to the nationalization of the land may serve us.

Mr. George proposes to recognize all the land as the property of the state, and therefore to substitute the land-rent for all the taxes, direct and indirect. That is, that every one who utilizes the land would have to pay to the state the value of its rent.

What would be the result? The land slavery would be quite abolished within the limits of the state, and the land would belong to the state, — English land to England, American to America, and so on; so that there would be a slavery which would be determined by the quantity of utilized land. It might be that the condition of some laborers would improve, but while a forcible demand for rent remained, the slavery would remain too.

The laborer, after a bad harvest, being unable to pay the rent required from him, in order not to lose everything and to retain the land, would be obliged to enslave himself to any one who happened to have the money. If a pail leaks, there must be a hole. On looking to the bottom of the pail, we may imagine that water runs from different holes; but however many imaginary holes we tried to stop from without, the water would not cease running.

In order to put a stop to this leakage, we must find the place out of which water runs, and stop it from the inside. The same holds good with the proposed means of stopping the irregular distribution of wealth, — the holes through which the wealth runs away from the people.

It is said, Organize working-men's corporations, make capital social property, make land social property. All this is only the mere stopping from the outside of those holes from which we fancy water runs away. In order to stop wealth going from the hands of working-men to those of non-working-men, it is necessary to try to find out from inside the hole through which this leakage takes place. This hole is the violence of armed over unarmed men, the violence of troops, by means of which men are carried away from their labor, and the land, and the productions of labor, taken away from men.

As long as there is an armed man with the acknowledgment of his right to kill another man, whoever he may be, so long will there also exist an unjust distribution of wealth, — in other words, slavery.

CHAPTER XXII

I ALWAYS wonder at the often repeated words, "Yes, it is all true in theory, but how is it in practice?" As though this theory was a mere collection of good words, needful for conversation, and not as though all practice — that is, all activity of life — was inevitably based upon it.

There must have been in the world an immense number of foolish theories, if men employed such wonderful reasoning.

You know that theory is what a man thinks about a thing, and practice is what he does. How can it be that a man should think that he ought to act in one way, and then do quite the reverse? If the theory of baking bread consists in this, that first of all one must knead the dough, then put it by to rise, then any one knowing this would be a fool to do the reverse. But with us it has come into fashion to say, "All this is very well in theory, but how would it be in practice?"

In all that has occupied me, practice has unavoidably followed theory, not mainly in order to justify it, but because it cannot help doing so; if I have understood the affair upon which I have meditated, I cannot help doing it in the way in which I have understood it.

I wished to help the needy, only because I had money

to spare; and I shared the general superstition that money is the representative of labor, and, generally speaking, something lawful and good in itself. But, having begun to give this money away, I saw that I was only drawing bills of exchange collected by me from poor people; that I was doing the very thing the old landlords used to do in compelling some of their serfs to work for other serfs.

I saw that every use of money, whether buying anything with it, or giving it away gratis, is a drawing of bills of exchange on poor people, or passing them to others to be drawn by them. And therefore I clearly understood the foolishness of what I was doing, in helping the poor by exacting money from them.

I saw that money in itself was not only not a good thing, but obviously an evil one, depriving men of their chief good, labor, and the utilizing of their labor, and that this very good I cannot give to any one, because I am myself deprived of it: I have neither labor, nor the happiness of utilizing my labor.

It might be asked by some, "What is there so peculiarly important in abstractly discussing the meaning of money?" But this argument which I have opened, is not merely for the sake of discussion, but in order to find an answer to the vital question, which had caused me so much suffering, and on which my life depended, in order to discover what I was to do.

As soon as I understood what riches are, what money is, at once it became plain and unquestionable to me what all men must do. In reality I merely came to realize what I have long known, — that truth which has been transmitted to men from the oldest times, by Buddha, by Isaiah, by Laotse, and by Socrates, and particularly clearly and definitely by Jesus Christ, and His predecessor John the Baptist.

John the Baptist, in answer to men's question, "What shall we do, then?" answered plainly and briefly, "He that hath two coats, let him impart to him that hath none; and he that hath meat, let him do likewise." (Luke iii. 10, 11.)

The same thing, and with still greater clearness, said Christ, — blessing the poor, and uttering woes on the rich. He said that no man can serve God and mammon.

He forbade His disciples not only to take money, but also to have two coats. He said to the rich young man that he could not enter into the kingdom of God, because he was rich, and that it is easier for a camel to go through the needle's eye, than for a rich man to enter the kingdom of God.

He said that he who would not leave everything — his houses and children and his fields — in order to follow Him, was not His disciple. He spoke a parable about a rich man who had done nothing wrong (like our own rich people), but merely dressed well, ate and drank well, yet by this lost his own soul; and about a beggar named Lazarus, who had done nothing good, and who had saved his soul by his beggar's life.

This truth had long been known to me; but the false teaching of the world had so cunningly hidden it, that it became a theory in the sense which men like to attach to this word, — that is, a pure abstraction. But as soon as I succeeded in pulling down in my consciousness the sophistry of the world's teaching, then theory became one with practice, and the reality of my life became its unavoidable result.

I understood that man, besides living for his own good, must work for the good of others; that if we were to draw our comparison from the world of animals, as some men are so fond of doing in justifying violence and contest by the law of the struggle for existence, we must take this comparison also from the lives of social animals like bees; and therefore man, saying nothing of his love to his neighbors incumbent upon him, as well by reason as by his very nature, is called upon to serve his fellows and their common object.

I understood that this is the natural law of man, by fulfilling which he can alone fulfil his calling, and therefore be happy. I understood that this law has been and is being violated by the fact that men by violence (as robber-bees) free themselves from labor, and utilize the labor of others, using this labor not for the common purpose, but for the personal satisfaction of their constantly increasing lusts, and also, like robber-bees, they perish thereby. I understood that the misfortune of men comes from the slavery in which some men are kept by others. I understood that this slavery is brought about in our days by the violence of military force, by the appropriation of land, and by the exaction of money.

And, having understood the meaning of all these three instruments of modern slavery, I could not help desiring to free myself from any share in it.

When I was a landlord, possessing serfs, and came to understand the immorality of such a position, I, along with other men who had understood the same thing, tried to free myself from it. Failing to do so, I endeavored to assert my claims as a slaveowner as little as possible, and to live, and to let other people live, as if such claims did not exist, and at the same time, by trying every means, to suggest to other slaveowners the unlawfulness and inhumanity of their imaginary rights.

I cannot help doing the same now with reference to existent slavery; that is, I try as little as possible to assert my claims while I am unable to free myself from such power of claim which gives me landownership and money, raised by the violence of military force, and at the same time by all means in my power to try to suggest to other men the unlawfulness and inhumanity of these imaginary rights.

The share in enslaving men, from the standpoint of a slaveowner, consists in utilizing the labor of others; it is quite the same, whether the enslaving is based upon a claim to the person of the slave, or upon the possession of land or money. And therefore, if a man really does not like slavery, and does not desire to be a partaker in it, the first thing which he must do is this: neither utilize men's labor by serving the government, nor possess land or money.

The refusal of all the means in use for utilizing another's labor will unavoidably bring such a man to the necessity, on the one hand, of lessening his wants, and, on the other, of doing himself what formerly was done for him by others. And this so simple inference at once puts an end to all three causes which prevent our helping the poor, which I discovered in seeking the cause of my non-success.

The first cause was the accumulation of people in towns, and the absorption there of the productions of the country.

All that a man needs is not to desire to utilize another's labor by serving the government, possessing land and money, and then, according to his strength and ability, to satisfy unaided his own wants, and the idea of leaving his village would never enter his mind, because in the country it is easier for him personally to satisfy his wants, while in a town everything is the production of the labor of others; in the country a man will always be able to help the needy, and will not experience that feeling of being useless which I felt in the town when I wanted to help men, not with my own, but with other men's labors.

The second cause was the estrangement between the poor and the rich. A man need only not desire to utilize other men's labor by serving the government, possessing land and money, and he would be compelled himself to satisfy his wants, and at once involuntarily that barrier would be pushed down which separates him from the working-people, and he would be one with the people, standing shoulder to shoulder with them, and seeing the possibility of helping them.

The third cause was shame, based upon the consciousness of the immorality of possessing money with which I wanted to help others. A man needs only not to desire to utilize another man's labor by serving the government, possessing land and money, and he will never have that superfluous "fool's money," the fact of possessing which made those who wanted money ask me for pecuniary assistance, which I was not able to satisfy, and called forth in me the consciousness of my unrighteousness.

CHAPTER XXIII

I SAW that the cause of the sufferings and depravity of men lies in the fact that some men are in bondage to others; and therefore I came to the obvious conclusion that if I want to help men, I have first of all to leave off causing those very misfortunes which I want to remedy, — in other words, I must not share in the enslaving of men.

I was led to the enslaving of men by the circumstance that from my infancy I had been accustomed not to work, but to utilize the labor of others, and I have been living in a society which is not only accustomed to this slavery, but justifies it by all kinds of sophistry, clever and foolish.

I came to the following simple conclusion, that, in order to avoid causing the sufferings and depravity of men, I ought to make other men work for me as little as possible, and to work myself as much as possible.

It was by this roundabout way that I arrived at the inevitable conclusion at which the Chinese arrived some thousand years ago, and which they express thus: "If there is one idle man, there must be another who is starving."

I came to that simple and natural conclusion, that if I pity the exhausted horse on whose back I ride, the first thing for me to do, if I really pity him, is to get off him and walk. This answer which gives such complete satisfaction to the moral sense, has been always before my eyes, as it is before the eyes of every one, but we do not all see it.

In seeking to heal our social diseases we look everywhere, — in the governmental, anti-governmental, scientific, and philanthropic superstitions, — and yet we do not see that which meets the eyes of every one. We fill our drains with filth, and require other men to clean them, and pretend to be very sorry for them, and we want to ease their work, and are inventing all sorts of devices except one, the simplest; namely, that we should ourselves remove our slops so long as we find it necessary to produce them in our rooms.

For one who really suffers from the sufferings of other men surrounding him, there exists a most clear, simple, and easy means, the only one sufficient to heal this evil, and to confer a sense of the lawfulness of one's life. This means is that which John the Baptist recommended when he answered the question, "What shall we do, then?" and which was confirmed by Christ, not to have more than one coat, and not to possess money, — that is, not to profit by another man's labor; and in order not to utilize another's labor, we must do with our own hands all that we can do. This is so plain and simple! But this is plain and simple and clear, only when our wants are also plain, and when we ourselves are still sound, and not corrupted to the backbone by idleness and laziness.

I live in a village, lie by the stove, and tell my neighbor, who is my debtor, to light it. It is obvious that I am lazy, take my neighbor away from his own work, and I at last feel ashamed of it; and besides, it grows dull for me to be always lying down when my muscles are strong and accustomed to work, and I go to fetch the wood myself.

But slavery of all kinds has been going on so long, so many artificial wants have grown about it, so many people with different degrees of familiarity with these wants are interwoven one with another, through so many generations men have been spoiled and made effeminate, such complicated temptations and justifications of luxury and idleness have been invented by men, that for one who stands on the top of the pyramid of idle men, it is not at all so easy to understand his sin as it is for the peasant who compels his neighbor to light his stove.

Men who stand at the top find it most difficult to understand what is required of them. They become giddy from the height of the structure of lies on which they stand when they look at that spot on the earth to which they must descend, in order to begin to live, not righteously, but only not quite inhumanly; and that is why this plain and clear truth appears to these men so strange.

A man who employs ten servants in livery, coachmen and cooks, who has pictures and pianos, must certainly regard as strange and even ridiculous the simple preliminary duty of, I do not say a good man, but of every man who is not a beast, to hew that wood with which his food is cooked and by which he is warmed; to clean those boots in which he carelessly stepped into the mud; to bring that water with which he keeps himself clean, and to carry away those slops in which he has washed himself.

But besides the estrangement of men from the truth, there is another cause which hinders men from seeing the duty of doing the most simple and natural physical work; that is, the complicity and interweaving of the conditions in which a rich man lives.

This morning I entered the corridor in which the stoves are heated. A peasant was heating the stove which warmed my son's room. I entered his bedroom: he was asleep, and it was eleven o'clock in the morning. The excuse was, "To-day is a holiday; no lessons." A stout lad of eighteen years of age, having overeaten himself the previous night, is sleeping until eleven o'clock; and a peasant of his age, who had already that morning done a quantity of work, was now lighting the tenth stove. "It would be better, perhaps, if the peasant did not light the stove to warm this stout, lazy fellow!" thought I; but I remembered at once that this stove also warmed the room of our housekeeper, a woman of forty years of age, who had been working the night before till three o'clock in the morning, to prepare everything for the supper which my son ate; and then she put away the dishes, and, notwithstanding this, got up at seven.

She cannot heat the stove herself: she has no time for that. The peasant is heating the stove for her too. And under her name my lazy fellow is being warmed.

True, the advantages of all are interwoven; but without much consideration the conscience of each will say,

On whose side is the labor, and on whose the idleness! But not only does conscience tell this, the account-book also tells it: the more money one spends, the more people work. The less one spends, the more one works one's self. My luxurious life gives means of living to others. Where should my old footman go, if I were to discharge him? What! every one must do everything for himself? Make his coat as well as hew his wood? And how about a division of labor? And industry and social undertakings? And, last of all, come the most horrible of words, — civilization, science, art!

CHAPTER XXIV

LAST March I was returning home late in the evening. On turning into a by-lane, I perceived on the snow, in a distant field, some black shadows. I should not have noticed this but for the policeman, who stood at the end of the lane, and cried in the direction of the shadows, "Vasili, why don't you come along?"

"She won't move," answered a voice; and thereupon the shadows came toward the policeman. I stopped and asked him: —

"What is the matter?"

He said, "We have got some girls from Rzhanoff's house, and are taking them to the police station; and one of them lags behind, and won't come along."

A night-watchman in sheepskin coat appeared now, leading a girl who slouched along, while he prodded her from behind. I, the watchman, and the policeman were wearing winter coats; she alone had none, having only her gown on. In the dark, I could distinguish only a brown dress, and a kerchief round her head and neck. She was short, like most starvelings, and had a broad, clumsy figure.

"We are n't going to stay here all night for you, you hag! Get on, or I 'll give it you!" shouted the policeman. He was evidently fatigued, and tired of her. She walked some paces, and stopped again.

The old watchman, a good-natured man (I knew him) pulled her by the hand. "I 'll wake you up! come along!" said he, pretending to be angry. She staggered, and began to speak, with a creaking, hoarse voice: "Let me be; don't you push. I 'll get on myself."

"You 'll be frozen to death," he returned.

"A girl like me won't be frozen; I 've lots of hot blood."

She meant it as a joke, but her words sounded like a curse. By a lamp which stood not far from the gate of my house, she stopped again, leaned back against the paling, and began to seek for something among her petticoats with awkward, frozen hands. They again shouted to her; but she only muttered, and continued searching. She held in one hand a crumpled cigarette, and matches in the other. I remained behind her; I was ashamed to pass by, or to stay and look at her. But I made up my mind, and came up to her. She leaned with her shoulder against the paling, and vainly tried to light a match on it.

I looked narrowly at her face. She was indeed a starveling, and appeared to me to be a woman of about thirty. Her complexion was dirty; her eyes small, dim, and bleared with drinking; she had a squat nose; her lips were wry and slavering, with downcast angles; from under her kerchief fell a tuft of dry hair. Her figure was long and flat; her arms and legs short.

I stopped in front of her. She looked at me and smiled, as if she knew all that I was thinking about. I felt that I ought to say something to her. I wanted to show her that I pitied her.

"Have you parents?" I asked. She laughed hoarsely, then suddenly stopped, and, lifting her brows, began to look at me steadfastly.

"Have you parents?" I repeated.

She smiled with a grimace which seemed to say, "What a question for him to put!"

"I have a mother," she said at last; "but what 's that to you?"

"And how old are you?"

"I am over fifteen," said she, at once answering a question she was accustomed to hear.

"Come, come! go on; we shall all be frozen for you; the deuce take you!" shouted the policeman; and she edged off from the paling, and staggered on along the lane to the police station; and I turned to the gate, and entered my house, and asked whether my daughters were at home. I was told that they had been to an evening party, had enjoyed themselves much, and now were asleep.

The next morning I was about to go to the police station to inquire what had become of this unhappy girl; and I was ready to start early enough, when one of those unfortunate men called, who from weakness have dropped out of the gentlemanly line of life to which they have been accustomed, and who rise and fall by turns. I had been acquainted with him three years. During this time he had several times sold everything he had,—even his clothes; and, having just done so again, he passed his nights temporarily in Rzhanoff's house, and his days at my lodgings. He met me as I was going out, and without listening to me, began at once to tell me what had happened at Rzhanoff's house the night before.

He began to relate it, yet had not got through one-half, when, all of a sudden, he, an old man who had gone through much in his life, began to sob, and ceasing to speak turned his face away from me. This was what he related. I ascertained the truth of his story on the spot, where I learned some new particulars, which I shall relate too.

A washerwoman thirty years of age, fair, quiet, good-looking, but delicate, passed her nights in that night-lodging on the ground floor in No. 32, where my friend slept among various shifting night-lodgers, men and women, who for five kopeks slept with each other.

The landlady at this lodging was the mistress of a boatman. In summer her lover kept a boat, and in winter they earned their living by letting lodgings to night-lodgers, at three kopeks without a pillow, and at five kopeks with one.

The washerwoman had been living here some months, and was a quiet woman; but lately they began to object to her because she coughed and prevented the other lodgers from sleeping. An old woman in particular, eighty years old, half silly, and also a permanent inmate of this lodging, began to dislike the washerwoman, and kept annoying her, because she disturbed her sleep; for all night she coughed like a sheep.

The washerwoman said nothing. She owed for rent, and felt herself guilty, and was therefore compelled to endure. She began to work less and less, for her strength failed her; and that was why she was unable to pay her rent. She had not been to work at all the whole of the last week; and she had been making the lives of all, and particularly of the old woman, miserable by her cough.

Four days ago the landlady gave her notice to leave. She already owed sixty kopeks, and could not pay them, and there was no hope of doing so; and other lodgers complained of her cough.

When the landlady gave the washerwoman notice, and told her she must go away if she did not pay the rent, the old woman was glad, and pushed her out into the yard. The washerwoman went away, but came back again in an hour, and the landlady had not the heart to send her away again. . . . During the second and the third day the landlady left her there. "Where shall I go?" she kept saying. On the third day, the landlady's lover, a Moscow man, who knew all the rules and regulations, went for a policeman. The policeman, with a sword and a pistol slung on a red cord, came into the lodging, and quietly and politely turned the washerwoman out into the street.

It was a bright, sunny, but frosty day in March. The melting snow ran down in streams, the house-porters were breaking the ice. The hackney sledges bumped on the ice-glazed snow, and creaked over the stones. The washerwoman went up the hill on the sunny side, got to the church, and sat down in the sun at the church porch. But when the sun began to go down behind the houses, and the pools of water began to be covered over with a thin sheet of ice, the washerwoman felt chilly and terrified. She got up and slowly walked on. . . . Where? Home, — to the only house in which she had been living lately.

While she was walking there, several times resting herself, it began to get dark. She approached the gate, turned into it, her foot slipped, she gave a shriek, and fell down.

One man passed by, then another. "She must be drunk," they thought. Another man passed, and stumbled up against her, and said to the house-porter, "Some tipsy woman is lying at the gate. I very nearly broke my neck over her. Won't you take her away?"

The house-porter came. The washerwoman was dead. Such was what my friend related to me.

The reader will perhaps fancy I have picked out particular cases in the prostitute of fifteen years of age and the story of this washerwoman; but let him not think so: this really happened in one and the same night. I do not exactly remember the date, only it was in March, 1884.

Having heard my friend's story, I went to the police station, intending from there to go to Rzhanoff's house to learn all the particulars of the washerwoman's story. The weather was fine and sunny; and again under the ice of the previous night, in the shade, you could see the water running; and in the sun, in the square, everything was melting fast. The trees of the garden appeared blue from over the river; the sparrows that were reddish in winter, and unnoticed then, now attracted people's attention by their merriness; men also tried to be merry, but they all had too many cares. The bells of the churches sounded; and blending with them from the barracks were heard sounds of shooting, — the hiss of the rifle-balls, and the crack when they struck the target.

I entered the police station. There some armed

men — policemen — led me to their chief. He, also armed with a sword, saber, and pistol, was busy giving some orders about a ragged, trembling old man who was standing before him and from weakness could not clearly answer what was asked of him. Having done with the old man, he turned to me. I inquired about the girl of last night. He first listened to me attentively, then he smiled, not only because I did not know why they were taken to the police station, but more particularly at my astonishment at her youth. "Goodness! there are some of twelve, thirteen, and fourteen years of age often," said he, in a lively tone.

To my question about my friend of yesterday, he told me that she had probably been already sent to the committee (if I understood him right). To my question where such passed the night, he gave a vague answer. The one about whom I spoke he did not remember. There were so many of them every day.

At Rzhanoff's house, in No. 32, I already found the clerk reading prayers over the dead laundrywoman. She had been brought in and laid on her former pallet; and the lodgers, all starvelings themselves, contributed money for the prayers, the coffin, and the shroud; the old woman had dressed her, and laid her out. The clerk was reading something in the dark; a woman in a cloak stood holding a wax taper; and with a similar wax taper stood a man (a gentleman, it is fair to state), in a nice greatcoat, trimmed with an Astrachan collar, in bright goloshes, and he had on a starched shirt. That was her brother. He had been hunted up.

I passed by the dead to the landlady's room, in order to ask her all the particulars. She was afraid of my questions, — afraid probably of being charged with something; but by and by she grew talkative, and told me all. On passing by again, I looked at the dead body. All the dead are beautiful; but this one was particularly so, and touching in her coffin, with her clear, pale face, with closed, swollen eyes, sunken cheeks, and fair, soft hair over her high forehead; her face looked weary, but kind, and not sad at all, but rather astonished. And indeed, if the living do not see, the dead may well be astonished.

On the day I wrote this, there was a great ball in Moscow. On the same night I left home after eight o'clock. I live in a locality surrounded by factories; and I left home after the factory whistle had sounded, and when, after a week of incessant work, people were freed for their holiday. Factory men passed by me, and I by them, all turning their steps to the public houses and inns. Many were already tipsy; many more were with women.

Every morning at five I hear each of the whistles, which means that the labor of women, children, and old people has begun. At eight o'clock another whistle, — this means half an hour's rest; at twelve the third whistle, — this means an hour for dinner. At eight o'clock the fourth whistle, indicating cessation from work. By a strange coincidence, all the three factories in my neighborhood produce only the articles necessary for balls.

In one factory — the one nearest to me — they make nothing but stockings; in the other opposite, silk stuffs; in the third, perfumes and pomades.

One may, on hearing these whistles, attach to them no other meaning than that of the indication of time. "There, the whistle has sounded: it is time to go out for a walk."

But one may associate with them also the meaning they in reality have,— that at the first whistle at five o'clock in the morning, men and women, who have slept side by side in a damp cellar, get up in the dark, and hurry away into the noisy building, and take their part in a work of which they see neither cessation nor utility for themselves, and work often so in the heat, in suffocating exhalations, with very rare intervals of rest, for one, two, or three, or even twelve and more hours. They fall asleep, and get up again, and again do this work, meaningless for themselves, to which they are compelled exclusively by want. And so it goes on from one week to another, interrupted only by holidays.

And now I saw these working-people freed for one of these holidays. They go out into the street; everywhere there are inns, public houses, and gay women. And they, in a drunken state, pull each other by the arms, and carry along with them girls like the one whom I saw conducted to the police station; they hire hackney-coaches, and ride and walk from one inn to another, and abuse each other, and totter about, and say they know not what.

Formerly, when I saw the factory people knocking about in this way, I used to turn aside with disgust, and almost reproached them; but since I hear these daily whistles, and know what they mean, I am only astonished that all these men do not come into the condition of utter beggars, with whom Moscow is filled; and the women into the position of the girl whom I had met near my house.

Thus I walked on, looking at these men, observing how they went about the streets till eleven o'clock. Then their movements became quieter; there remained here and there a few tipsy people, and I met some men and women who were being conducted to the police station. And now, from every side, carriages appeared, all going in one direction. On the coach-box sat a coachman, sometimes in a sheepskin coat; and a footman — a dandy with a cockade. Well-fed trotters, covered with cloth, ran at the rate of fifteen miles an hour; in the carriages sat ladies wrapped in shawls, and taking great care not to spoil their flowers and their toilets. All, beginning with the harness on the horses, carriages, gutta-percha wheels, the cloth of the coachman's coat, down to the stockings, shoes, flowers, velvet, gloves, scents,— all these articles have been made by those men, some of whom fell asleep on their own pallets in their mean rooms, some in night-houses with prostitutes, and others in the police station.

The ball-goers drive past these men, in and with things made by them; and it does not even enter into their minds that there could possibly be any connection between the ball they are going to and these tipsy people, to whom their coachmen shout out so angrily. With quite easy minds, and assurance that they are doing nothing wrong, they enjoy themselves at the ball.

Enjoy themselves!

From eleven o'clock in the evening till six in the morning, in the very depth of the night, while with empty stomachs men are lying in night-lodgings, or dying as the washerwoman had done!

The enjoyment of the ball consists in women and girls uncovering their bosoms, putting on artificial protuberances, and altogether getting themselves up in a way that no girl and no woman who is not yet depraved would, on any account, appear before men; and in this half-naked condition, with uncovered bosoms, and arms bare up to the shoulders, with dresses puffed behind and tight round the hips, in the brightest light, women and girls, whose first virtue has always been modesty, appear among strange men, who are also dressed in indecently tight-fitting clothes, and with them, to the sound of exciting music, embrace each other, and pivot round and round. Old women, often also half-naked like the younger ones, are sitting looking on, and eating and drinking; the old men do the same. No wonder it is done at night, when every one else is sleeping, so that no one may see it!

But this is not done in order to hide it; there is nothing indeed to hide; all is very nice and good; and by this enjoyment, in which is swallowed up the painful labor of thousands, not only is nobody harmed, but by this very thing poor people are fed! The ball goes on very merrily, maybe, but how did it come to do so? When we see in society or among ourselves one who has not eaten, or is cold, we are ashamed to enjoy ourselves, and cannot begin to be merry until he is fed, saying nothing of the fact that we cannot imagine that there are such people who can enjoy themselves by means of anything which produces the sufferings of others.

We are disgusted, and we do not understand the enjoyment of naughty boys who have squeezed a dog's tail into a piece of split wood. How is it, then, that in our enjoyments we become blind, and do not see that cleft in which we have pinched those men who suffer for our enjoyment?

We know that each woman at this ball whose dress costs a hundred and fifty rubles was not born at the ball, but she has lived also in the country, has seen peasants, knows her own nurse and maid, whose fathers and brothers are poor, for whom earning one hundred and fifty rubles to build a cottage with is the end and aim of a long, laborious life; she knows this; how can she, then, enjoy herself, knowing that on her half-naked body she is wearing the cottage which is the dream of her housemaid's brother?

But let us suppose she has not thought about this: she cannot help knowing that velvet and silk, sweetmeats and flowers, and laces and dresses, do not grow of themselves, but are made by men.

It would seem she could not help knowing that men make all this, and under what circumstances, and why. She cannot help knowing that her dressmaker, whom she has been scolding to-day, has made this dress not at all out of love to her, therefore she cannot help knowing that all those things were made — her laces, flowers, and velvet — from sheer want.

But perhaps she is so blinded that she does not think of all this. Well, but, at all events, she could not help knowing that five people, old, respectable, often delicate men and women, have not slept all night, and have been busy on her account. This, also, she could not help knowing, — that on this night there were twenty-eight degrees of frost, and that her coachman — an old man — was sitting in this frost all night, upon his coach-box.

If these young women and girls, from the hypnotic influence of the ball, fail to see all this, we cannot judge them. Poor things! they consider all to be good which is pronounced so by their elders. How do these elders explain their cruelty? They, indeed, always answer in the same way: "I compel no one; what I have,

I have bought; footmen, chambermaids, coachman, I hire. There is no harm in engaging and in buying. I compel none; I hire; what wrong is there in that?"

Some days ago I called on a friend. Passing through the first room, I wondered at seeing at a table two females, for I knew my acquaintance was a bachelor. A skinny, yellow, elderly-looking woman, about thirty, with a kerchief thrown over her shoulder, was briskly doing something over the table with her hands, jerking nervously, as if in a fit. Opposite to her sat a little girl, who was also doing something, jerking in the same way. They both seemed to be suffering from St. Vitus's dance. I came nearer and looked closer to see what they were about.

They glanced up at me, and then continued their work as attentively as before.

Before them were spread tobacco and cigarettes. They were making cigarettes. The woman rubbed the tobacco fine between the palms of her hands, caught it up by a machine, put on the tubes, and threw them to the girl. The girl folded the papers, put them over the cigarette, threw it aside, and took up another.

All this was performed with such speed, with such dexterity, that it was impossible to describe it. I expressed my wonder at their quickness. "I have been at this business fourteen years," said the woman.

"Is it hard work?"

"Yes; my chest aches, and the air is choky with tobacco."

But it was not necessary for her to have said so: you need only have looked at her or at the girl. The latter had been at this business three years; but any one not seeing her at this work would have said that she had a strong constitution, which was already beginning to be broken.

My acquaintance, a kind-hearted man of liberal views, hired these women to make him cigarettes at two rubles and a half a thousand. He has money, and he pays it away for this work: what harm is there in it?

My acquaintance gets up at twelve. His evenings,

from six to two, he spends at cards or at the piano; he eats and drinks; other people do all the work for him. He has devised for himself a new pleasure, — smoking. I can remember when he began to smoke. Here are a woman and a girl, who scarcely earn their living by transforming themselves into machines, and pass all their lives in breathing tobacco, thus ruining their lives. He has money which he has not earned, and he prefers playing at cards to making cigarettes for himself. He gives these women money, only under the condition that they continue to live as miserably as they have been living, in making cigarettes for him.

I am fond of cleanliness; and I give money, only under the condition that the washerwoman washes my shirts, which I change twice a day; and the washing of these shirts having taxed the utmost strength of the washerwoman, she has died.

What is wrong in this?

Men who buy and hire will continue doing so whether I do or not; they will force other people to make velvets and dainties, and will buy them whether I do or not; so also they will hire people to make cigarettes and to wash shirts. Why should I, then, deprive myself of velvets, sweetmeats, cigarettes, and clean shirts, when their production is already set in going.

A crowd, maddened with the passion of destruction, will employ this very reasoning. It leads a pack of dogs, when one of their number runs against another and knocks it down, to attack it and tear it to pieces. Others have already begun, have done a little mischief; why should n't I, too, do the same? What can it possibly signify if I wear a dirty shirt, and make my cigarettes myself? Could that help any one? Ask men who desire to justify themselves.

Had we not wandered so far from truth, it would be needless to answer this question; but we are so entangled that such a question seems natural to us, and, therefore, though I feel ashamed, I must answer it.

What difference would it be if I should wear my shirt

a week instead of one day, and make my cigarettes myself, or leave off smoking altogether?

The difference would be this, — that a certain washer-woman, and a certain cigarette-maker, would exert themselves less, and what I gave formerly for the washing of my shirt, and for the making of my cigarettes, I may give now to that or to another woman; and working-people who are tired by their work, instead of overworking themselves, will be able to rest and to have tea. But I have heard objections to this, so averse are the rich and the luxurious to understand their position.

They reply, "If I should wear dirty linen, leave off smoking, and give this money away to the poor, then this money would be all the same taken away from them, and my drop will not help to swell the sea."

I am still more ashamed to answer such a reply, but at the same time I must do so. If I came among savages who gave me chops which I thought delicious, but the next day I learned (perhaps saw, myself) that these delicious chops were made of a human prisoner who had been slain in order to make them; and if I think it bad to eat men, however delicious the cutlets may be, and however general the custom to eat men among the persons with whom I live, and however small the utility to the prisoners who have been prepared for food my refusal to eat them may be, I shall not and will not eat them.

Maybe I shall eat human flesh when urged by hunger; but I shall not make a feast of it, and shall not take part in feasts with human flesh, and shall not seek such feasts, and be proud of my partaking of them.

CHAPTER XXV

But what is to be done, then? Is it we who are to blame? And if not, who is?

We say, It is not we who have done all this; it has been done of itself; as children say when they break anything, that it broke itself. We say that as towns are already in existence, we, who are living there, must feed men by buying their labor. But that is not true. It need only be observed how we live in the country, and how we feed people there.

Winter is over; Easter is past. In town the same orgies of the rich go on, — on the boulevards, in gardens, in the parks, on the river, music, theaters, riding, illuminations, fireworks; but in the country it is still better, — the air is purer; the trees, the meadows, the flowers, are fresher. We must go where all is budding and blooming. And now the majority of rich people, who utilize other men's labor, go into the country to breathe the purer air, to look at the meadows and woods. And here in the country among humble villagers, who feed upon bread and onions, work eighteen hours every day, and have neither sufficient sleep nor clothes, rich people take up their abode. No one tempts these people: here are no factories, and no idle hands, of which there are so many in town, and which we imagine we feed by giving them work to do. Here people never can do their own work in time during the summer; and not only are there no idle hands, but much property is lost for want of hands; and an immense number of men, children, old people, and women with child overwork themselves.

How, then, do rich people order their lives here? Thus: If there happens to be an old mansion, built in the time of the serfs, then this house is renewed and embellished, if there is not, one is built of two or three stories. The rooms, which are from twelve to twenty and more in number, are all about sixteen feet high. The floors are inlaid; in the windows are put single panes of glass, expensive carpets on the floors; expensive furniture is procured, — a sideboard, for instance, costing from twenty to sixty pounds. Near the mansion, roads are made; flower-beds are laid out; there are croquet-grounds, giant-strides, reflecting-globes, conservatories, and hothouses, and always luxurious stables. All is painted in colors, prepared with the very oil which old people and children lack for their porridge. If a rich man can afford it he buys such a house for himself; if he cannot, he hires one; but however poor and however liberal a man of our circle may be, he always takes up his abode in the country in such a house, for building and keeping which it is necessary to take away dozens of working-people who have not enough time to do their own business in the field in order to earn their living.

Here we cannot say that factories are already in existence and will continue so, whether we made use of their work or no; we cannot say that we are feeding idle hands; here we plainly establish the factories for making things necessary for us, and simply make use of the surrounding people; we divert the people from work necessary for them, as for us and for all, and by such system deprave some and ruin the lives and health of others.

There lives, let us say, in a village, an educated and respectable family of the upper class, or that of a government officer. All the members of it and the visitors assemble toward the middle of June, because up to June they had been studying and passing their examinations: they assemble when mowing begins, and they stay until September, until the harvest and sowing time. The members of the family (as almost all men of this class) remain in the country from the beginning of the urgent work, — harvest-time, — not to the end of it, indeed, because in September the sowing goes on, and the digging up of potatoes, but till labor begins to slacken. During all the time of their stay, around them and close by, the peasants' summer work has been proceeding, the strain of which, however much we may have heard or read of it, however much we may have looked at it, we can form no adequate idea of without having experienced it ourselves.

And the members of the family, about ten persons, have been living as they did in town, if possible still worse than in town, because here in the village they are supposed to be resting (after doing nothing), and offer no pretense in the way of work, and no excuse for their idleness.

In the middle of the summer, when people are forced from want to feed on kvas, and bread and onions, begins the mowing-time. Gentlefolks, who live in the country, see this labor, partly order it, partly admire it; enjoy the smell of the drying hay, the sound of the women's songs, the noise of the scythes, and the sight of the rows of mowers and of the women raking. They see this as well near their house as when they, with young people and children, who do nothing all the day long, drive well-fed horses a distance of a few hundred yards to the bathing-place.

The work of mowing is one of the most important in the world. Nearly every year, from want of hands and of time, the meadows remain half cut, and may remain so till the rains begin; so that the degree of intensity of the labor decides the question whether twenty or more per cent will be added to the stores of men, or whether this hay will be left to rot and spoil while yet uncut.

And if there is more hay, there will be also more meat for old people, and milk for children; thus matters stand in general; but in particular for each mower here is decided the question of bread and milk for himself and for his children during the winter.

Each of the working-people, male and female, knows it; even the children know that this is an important business, and that one ought to work with all one's strength, carry a jug with kvas for the father to the mowing-place, and, shifting it from one hand to another, run barefoot as quickly as possible, a distance of perhaps a mile and a half from the village, in order to be in time for dinner, that father may not grumble. Every one knows that, from the mowing to the harvest, there will be no interruption of labor, and no time for rest. And besides mowing, each has some other business to do, — to plow up new land, and to harrow it; the women have cloth to make, bread to bake, and the washing to do; and the peasants must drive to the mill and to market; they have the official affairs of their community to attend to; they have also to provide the local government officials with means of locomotion, and to pass the night in the fields with the pastured horses.

All, old and young and sick, work with all their strength.

The peasants work in such a way that, when cutting the last rows, the mowers — weak people, growing youths, old men — are so tired that, having rested a little, it is with great pain they begin anew; the women, often with child, work hard too.

It is a strained, incessant labor. All work to the utmost of their strength, and use not only all their provisions, but what they have in store: during harvest-time all the peasants grow thinner, although they never were very stout.

There is a small company laboring in the hayfield, three peasants, — one of them an old man; another his nephew, who is married; and the third the village bootmaker, a thin, wiry man. Their mowing this morning decides their fate for the coming winter, whether they will be able to keep a cow and pay taxes. This is their second week's work. The rain hindered them for a while. After the rain had left off, and the water had dried up, they decided on making hayricks; and in order to do it quicker, they decided that two women must rake to each scythe. With the old man came out his wife, fifty years of age, worn out with labor and the bearing of eleven children, deaf, but still strong enough for work; and his daughter, thirteen years of age, a short but brisk and strong little girl.

With the nephew came his wife, — a tall woman, as strong as a peasant; and his sister-in-law, — a soldier's wife, who was with child. With the bootmaker came his wife, — a strong working-woman; and her mother, — an old woman about eighty, who for the rest of the year used to beg.

They all draw up in a line, and work from morning to evening in the burning sun of June. It is steaming hot, and a thunder-shower is threatening. Every moment of work is precious. They have not wished to leave off working, even in order to fetch water or kvas

A small boy, the grandson of the old woman, brings them water. The old woman is evidently anxious only on one point, — not to be obliged to cease working. She does not let the rake out of her hands, and moves about with great difficulty. The little boy, quite bent under the jug with water, heavier than he himself, walks with short steps on his bare feet, and carries the jug, with many shifts. The little girl takes on her shoulders a load of hay, which is also heavier than herself; walks a few paces, and stops, then throws it down, having no strength to carry it farther. The old man's wife rakes together unceasingly, her kerchief loosened from her disordered hair: she carries the hay, breathing heavily, and staggering under the burden; the cobbler's mother is only raking, but this also is beyond her strength; she slowly drags her ill-shod feet, and looks gloomily before her, like one at the point of death. The old man purposely sends her far away from the others, to rake about the ricks, in order that she may not attempt to compete with them; but she does not leave off working, but continues with the same dead, gloomy face as long as the others.

The sun is already setting behind the wood, and the ricks are not yet in order; there is much still to be done.

All feel that it is time to leave off working, but no one says so, each waiting for the other to suggest it. At last, the bootmaker, realizing that he has no more strength left, proposes to the old man to leave the ricks till to-morrow, and the old man agrees to it; and at once the women go to fetch their clothes, their jugs, their pitch-forks; and the old woman sits down where she was standing, and then lays herself down with the same fixed stare on her face. But as the women go away, she gets up groaning, and, crawling along, follows them.

Let us turn to the country-house. The same evening, when from the side of the village were heard the rattle of the scythes of the toil-worn mowers who were returning from work, the sounds of the hammer against the anvil, the cries of women and girls who had just had time to put away their rakes, and were already running to drive the cattle in, — with these blend other sounds from the country-house. Drin, drin, drin! goes the piano; a Hungarian song is heard through the noise of the croquet-balls; before the stable an open carriage is standing, harnessed with four fat horses, which has been hired for twenty shillings to bring some guests a distance of ten miles.

Horses standing by the carriage rattle their little bells. Before them hay has been thrown, which they are scattering with their hoofs, the same hay which the peasants have been gathering with such hard labor. In the yard of this mansion there is movement; a healthy, well-fed fellow in a pink shirt, presented to him for his service as a house-porter, is calling the coachmen, and telling them to harness and saddle some horses. Two peasants, who live here as coachmen, come out of their room, and go in an easy manner, swinging their arms, to saddle horses for the ladies and gentlemen. Still nearer to the house the sounds of another piano are heard. It is the music-mistress, who lives in the family to teach the children, practising her Schumann. The sounds of one piano jangle with those of another. Quite near the house walk two nurses; one is young, another old; they lead and carry children to bed; these children are of the same age as those who ran from the village with jugs. One nurse is English: she cannot speak Russian. She was engaged to come from England, not from being distinguished by some peculiar qualities, but simply because she does not speak Russian. Farther on is another person, a Frenchwoman, who is also engaged because she does not know Russian. Farther on a peasant, with two women, is watering flowers near the house; another is cleaning a gun for one of the young gentlemen. Here two women are carrying a basket with clean linen, — they have been washing for all these gentlefolks. In the house two women have scarcely time to wash the plates and dishes after the company, who have just done eating; and two peasants in evening clothes are running up and down the stairs, serving coffee, tea, wine, seltzer-water, etc. Up-stairs a table is spread. A meal has just ended; and another will soon begin, to continue till cock-crow, and often till morning dawns. Some are sitting smoking, playing cards; others are sitting and smoking, engaged in discoursing liberal ideas of reform; and others, again, walk to and fro, eat, smoke, and not knowing what to do, have made up their mind to take a drive.

The household consists of fifteen persons, healthy men and women; and thirty persons, healthy working-people, male and female, labor for them. And this takes place there, where every hour, and each little boy, are precious.

This will be so, also, in July, when the peasants, not having had their sleep out, will mow the oats at night, in order that it may not be lost, and the women will get up before dawn in order to finish their threshing in time; when this old woman, who had been exhausted during the harvest, and the woman with child, and the little children, all will again overwork themselves, and when there is a great want of hands, horses, carts, in order to house this corn upon which all men feed, of which millions of poods are necessary in Russia in order that men should not die: during even such a time, the idle lives of ladies and gentlemen will go on. There will be private theatricals, picnics, hunting, drinking, eating, piano-playing, singing, dancing, — in fact, incessant orgies.

Here, at least, it is impossible to find any excuse from the fact that all this had been going on before: nothing of the kind had been in existence. We ourselves carefully create such a life, taking bread and labor away from the work-worn people. We live sumptuously, as if there were no connection whatever between the dying washerwoman, child-prostitute, women worn out by making cigarettes, and by all the intense labor around us which is inadequate to their unnourished strength. We do not want to see the fact that if there were not our idle, luxurious, depraved lives, there would not be this labor disproportioned to the strength of people, and that if there were not this labor we could not go on living in the same way.

It appears to us that their sufferings are one thing, and our lives another, and that we, living as we do, are innocent and pure as doves. We read the description of the lives of the Romans, and wonder at the inhumanity of a heartless Lucullus, who gorged himself with fine dishes and delicious wines while people were starving; we shake our heads, and wonder at the barbarism of our grandfathers, — the serf-owners, — who provided themselves with orchestras and theaters, and employed whole villages to keep up their gardens. From the height of our greatness we wonder at their inhumanity. We read the words of Isaiah v. 8, Woe unto them that join house to house, that lay field to field, till there be no room, and ye be made to dwell alone in the midst of the land.

11. Woe unto them that rise up early in the morning, that they may follow strong drink; that tarry late into the night, till wine inflame them!

12. And the harp, and the lute, the tabret, the pipe, and wine, are in their feasts: but they regard not the work of the Lord, neither have they considered the operation of his hands.

18. Woe unto them that draw iniquity with cords of vanity, and sin as it were with a cart rope.

20. Woe unto them that call evil good, and good evil; that put darkness for light, and light for darkness; that put bitter for sweet, and sweet for bitter!

21. Woe unto them that are wise in their own eyes, and prudent in their own sight!

22. Woe unto them that are mighty to drink wine, and men of strength to mingle strong drink:

23. Which justify the wicked for reward, and take away the righteousness of the righteous from him!

We read these words, and it seems to us that they have nothing to do with us. We read in the Gospel, Matthew iii. 10: And even now is the ax laid unto the root of the tree: every tree therefore that bringeth not forth good fruit is hewn down, and cast into the fire.

And we are quite sure that the good tree bearing good fruit is we ourselves, and that those words are said, not to us, but to some other bad men.

We read the words of Isaiah vi. 10: Make the heart of this people fat, and make their ears heavy, and shut their eyes; lest they see with their eyes, and hear with their ears, and understand with their heart, and turn again, and be healed.

11. Then said I, Lord, how long? And he answered, Until cities be waste without inhabitant, and houses without man, and the land become utterly waste.

We read and are quite assured that this wonderful thing has not happened to us, but to some other people. But it is for this very reason we do not see that this has happened to and is taking place with us. We do not hear, we do not see, and do not understand with our heart. But why has it so happened?

CHAPTER XXVI

How can a man who considers himself to be, we will not say a Christian, or an educated and humane man, but simply a man not entirely devoid of reason and of conscience, — how can he, I say, live in such a way that, not taking part in the struggle of all mankind for life, he only swallows up the labor of others, struggling for existence, and by his own claims increases the labor of those who struggle, and the number of those who perish in struggle?

And such men abound in our so-called Christian and cultured world; and not only do they abound in our world, but the very ideal of the men of our Christian, cultured world is to get the largest amount of property, — that is, wealth, — which secures all comforts and idleness of life by freeing its possessors from the struggle for existence, and enabling them, as much as possible, to profit by the labor of those brothers of theirs who perish in that struggle.

How could men have fallen into such astounding error?

How could they have come to such a state that they can neither see nor hear nor understand with their heart that which is so clear, obvious, and certain?

One need only think for a moment in order to be terrified at the contradiction of our lives to what we profess to believe, we, whether we be Christian or only humane, educated people. Be it God or a law of nature that governs the world and men, good or bad, the position of men in this world, so long as we know it, has always been such that naked men, without wool on their bodies, without holes in which to take refuge, without food which they might find in the field like Robinson Crusoe on his island, are put into a position of a continual and incessant struggle with nature in order to cover their bodies by making clothes for themselves, to protect themselves by a roof over their heads, and to earn food in order twice or thrice a day to satisfy their hunger and that of their children and their parents.

Wherever and whenever and to whatever extent we observe the lives of men, whether in Europe, America, China, or Russia; whether we take into consideration all mankind, or a small portion, whether in olden times in a nomad state, or in modern times with steam-engines, steam-plows, sewing-machines, and electric light, — we shall see one and the same thing going on, — that men, working constantly and incessantly, are not able to get clothes, shelter, and food for themselves, their little ones, and the old, and that the greatest number of men as well in olden times as now perish from want of the necessaries of life and from overwork.

Wherever we may live, if we draw a circle around us, of a hundred thousand, or a thousand, or ten, or even one mile's circumference, and look at the lives of those men who are inside our circle, we shall find half-starved children, old people male and female, pregnant women, sick and weak persons, working beyond their strength, and who have neither food nor rest enough to support them, and who, for this reason, die before their time: we shall see others full-grown, who are even killed by dangerous and hurtful tasks.

Since the world has existed, we find that men with great efforts, sufferings, and privations have been struggling for their common wants, and have not been able to overcome the difficulty.

Besides, we also know that every one of us, wherever and however he may live, *nolens volens*, is every day, and every hour of the day, absorbing for himself a part of the labor done by mankind.

Wherever and however he lives, his house, the roof over him, do not grow of themselves; the firewood in his stove does not get there of itself; the water did not come of itself either; and the baked bread does not fall down from the sky; his dinner, his clothes, and the covering for his feet, all this has been made for him, not only by men of past generations, long dead, but it is being done for him now by those men of whom hundreds and thousands are fainting away and dying, in vain efforts to get for themselves and for their children sufficient shelter, food, and clothes, — means to save themselves and their children from suffering and a premature death.

All men are struggling with want. They are struggling so intensely that always around them their brethren, fathers, mothers, children, are perishing. Men in this world are like those on a dismantled or water-logged ship, with a short allowance of food; all are put by God, or by nature, in such a position that they must husband their food, and unceasingly war with want.

Each interruption in this work of every one of us, each absorption of the labor of others useless for the common welfare, is ruinous, alike for us and them.

How is it that the majority of educated people, without laboring, are quietly absorbing the labors of others, necessary for their own lives, and are considering such an existence quite natural and reasonable?

If we are to free ourselves from the labor proper and

natural to all, and lay it on others, at the same time not considering ourselves to be traitors and thieves, we can do so only by two suppositions,— first, that we (the men who take no part in common labor) are different beings from working men, and have a peculiar destiny to fulfil in society (like drone bees, which have a different function from the working bees); or secondly, that the business which we (men freed from the struggle for existence) are doing for other men is so useful for all that it undoubtedly compensates for that harm which we do to others in overburdening them.

In olden times, men who utilized the labor of others asserted, first, that they belonged to a different race; and secondly, that they had from God a peculiar mission,—caring for the welfare of others; in other words, to govern and teach them: and therefore they assured others, and partly believed themselves, that the business they did was more useful and more important for the people than those labors by which they profit. This justification was sufficient so long as the direct interference of God in human affairs, and the inequality of human races, was undoubted.

But with Christianity, and the consciousness of the equality and unity of all men proceeding from it, this justification could no longer be expressed in its previous form.

It was no longer possible to assert that men are born of different kind and quality, and having a different destiny; and the old justification, though still held by some, has been little by little destroyed, and has now almost entirely disappeared.

But though the justification disappeared, the fact itself, of the freeing of some men from labor, and the appropriation by them of other men's labor, remained the same for those who had the power of enforcing it. For this existing fact, new excuses have constantly been invented, in order that, without asserting the difference of human beings, men might be able to free themselves from personal labor with apparent justice. A great many such justifications have been invented.

However strange it may seem, the main object of all that has been called science, and the ruling tendency of science, has been the seeking out of such excuse.

This has been the object of the theological sciences and of the science of law; this was the object of so-called philosophy, and this became lately the object of modern rationalistic science. All the theological subtleties which aimed at proving that a certain church is the only true successor of Christ, and that, therefore, she alone has full and uncontrolled power over the souls and bodies of men, had in view this very object.

All the legal sciences — those of state law, penal law, civil law, and international law — have this sole aim; the majority of philosophical theories, especially that of Hegel, which reigned over the minds of men for such a long time, and maintained the assertion that everything which exists is reasonable, and that the state is a necessary form of the development of human personality, had only this one object in view.

Comte's positive philosophy and its outcome, the doctrine that mankind is an organism; Darwin's doctrine of the struggle for existence, directing life and its conclusion, the teaching of diversity of human races, the now so popular anthropology, biology, and sociology, — all have the same aim. These sciences have become favorites, because they all serve for the justification of the existing fact of some men being able to free themselves from the human duty of labor, and to consume other men's labor.

All these theories, as is always the case, are worked out in the mysterious sanctums of augurs, and in vague, unintelligible expressions are spread abroad among the masses, and adopted by them.

As in olden times, the subtleties of theology, which justified violence in church and state, were the special property of priests; and in the masses of the people, the conclusions, taken by faith, and ready made for them, were circulated, that the power of kings, clergy, and nobility was sacred; so afterward, the philosophical and legal subtleties of so-called science became the property of the priests of science; and through the masses only the ready-made conclusions, accepted by faith, that social order (the organization of society) must be such as it is, and cannot be otherwise, was diffused.

So it is also now: it is only in the sanctuaries of the modern sages that the laws of life and development of organisms are analyzed. Whereas in the crowd, the ready-made conclusion accepted on trust, that division of labor is a law, confirmed by science, is circulated, and that thus it must be that some are starving and toiling, and others eternally feasting, and that this very ruin of some and feasting of others is the undoubted law of man's life, to which we must submit.

The current justification of their idleness of all so-called educated people, with their various activities, from the railway proprietor down to the author and artist, is this: We men who have freed ourselves from the common human duty of taking part in the struggle for existence, are furthering progress, and so we are of great use to all human society, of such use that it counterbalances all the harm we do the people by consuming their labor.

This reasoning seems to the men of our day to be not at all like the reasoning by which the former non-workers justified themselves; just as the reasoning of the Roman emperors and citizens, that but for them the civilized world would go to ruin, seemed to them to be of quite another order to that of the Egyptians and Persians, and so also an exactly similar kind of reasoning seemed in turn to the knights and clergy of the Middle Ages totally different from that of the Romans.

But it only seems to be so. One need but reflect upon the justification of our time in order to ascertain that in it there is nothing new. It is only a little differently dressed up, but it is the same because it is based upon the same principle. Every justification of one man's consumption of the labor of others, while producing none himself, as with Pharaoh and his soothsayers, the emperors of Rome and those of the Middle Ages and their citizens, knights, priests, and clergy, always consists in these two assertions: First, we take the labor of the masses, because we are a peculiar people, called by God to govern them, and to teach them divine truths; secondly, those who compose the masses cannot be judges of the measure of labor which we take from them for the good we do them, because, as it has been said by the Pharisees, "This multitude which knoweth not the law are accursed." (John vii. 49.)

The people do not understand wherein lies their good, and therefore they cannot be judges of the benefits done to them. The justification of our time, notwithstanding all apparent originality, in fact consists of the same fundamental assertions: First, we are a peculiar people, — we are an educated people, — we further progress and civilization, and by this fact, we procure for the masses a great advantage. Secondly, the uneducated crowd does not understand that advantage which we procure for them, and therefore cannot be judges of it.

The fundamental assertions are the same. We free ourselves from labor, appropriate the labor of others, and by this increase the burden of our fellows, and assert that in compensation for this we bring them a greater advantage, of which they, owing to their ignorance, cannot be judges.

Is it not, then, the same thing? The only difference lies in this, that formerly the citizens, the Roman priests, the knights, and the nobility had claims on other men's labor, and now these claims are put forward by a caste who term themselves educated.

The lie is the same, because the men who justify themselves are in the same false position. The lie consists in the fact that, before beginning to reason about the advantages conferred on the people by men who have freed themselves from labor, certain men, Pharaohs, priests, or we ourselves, — educated people, — assume this position, and only afterward excogitate a justification for it.

This very position of some men who oppressed others, in former times as now, serves as a universal basis. The difference of our justification from the ancient ones consists only in the fact that it is more false, and less well grounded. The old emperors and popes, if they themselves and the people believed in their divine calling, could plainly explain why they were the men to control the labor of others: they said that they were appointed by God Himself for this very thing, and from God they had a commandment to teach the people divine truths revealed to them, and to govern them.

But modern, educated men, who do not labor with their hands, acknowledging the equality of all men, cannot explain why they in particular and their children (for education is only by money; that is, by power) are those lucky persons who are called to an immaterial, easy utility, out of those millions who by hundreds and thousands are perishing in making it possible for them to be educated. Their only justification consists in this, that they, such as they now are, instead of doing harm to the people by freeing themselves from labor, and by swallowing up labor, bring to the people an advantage unintelligible to them, which compensates for all the evil perpetrated upon them.

CHAPTER XXVII

The theory by which men who have freed themselves from personal labor justify themselves, in its simplest and most exact form, is this: We men, having freed ourselves from work, and having by violence appropriated the labor of others, find ourselves better able to benefit them; in other words, certain men, for doing the people a palpable and comprehensible harm, — utilizing by violence their labor, and thereby increasing the difficulty of their struggles with nature, — do to them an impalpable and incomprehensible good.

This proposition is a very strange one; but men, as well of former as also of modern times, who have lived on the labors of working-men, believe it, and calm their conscience by it. Let us see in what way it is justified in different classes of men, who have freed themselves from labor in our own days.

I serve men by my activity in state or church, — as king, minister, archbishop; I serve men by my trading or by industry; I serve men by my activity in the departments of science or art.

By our activities we are all as necessary to the people as they are to us.

So say various men of to-day, who have freed themselves from laboring.

Let us consider *seriatim* those principles upon which they base the usefulness of their activity.

There are only two indications of the usefulness of any activity of one man for another: an exterior indication, — the acknowledgment of the utility of activity by those to whom it is produced; and an interior indication, — the desire to be of use to others lying at the root of the activity of the one who is trying to be of use.

Statesmen (I include the Church dignitaries appointed by the government in the category of statesmen) are of use to those whom they govern. The emperor, the king, the president of a republic, the prime minister, the minister of justice, the minister of war, the minister of public instruction, the bishop, and all under them, who serve the state, all live, having freed themselves from the struggle of mankind for existence, and having laid all the burden of this struggle upon other men, upon the ground that their non-activity compensates for this.

Let us apply the first indication to those for whose welfare the activity of statesmen is bestowed. Do they, I ask, recognize the usefulness of this activity?

Yes, it is recognized: most men consider statesmanship necessary to them; the majority recognize the usefulness of this activity in principle; but in all its manifestations as known to us, in all particular cases as known to us, the usefulness of each of the institutions and of each of the manifestations of this activity is not only denied by those for whose advantage it is performed, but they assert that this activity is even pernicious and hurtful. There is no state function or social activity which is not considered by many men to be hurtful; there is no institution which is not considered pernicious, — courts of justice, banks, local self-government, police, clergy. Every state activity, from the minister down to the policeman, from the bishop to the sexton, is considered by some men to be useful, and by others to be pernicious. And this is the case, not only in Russia, but throughout the world, in France as well as in America.

All the activity of the republican party is considered pernicious by the radical party, and *vice versa:* all the activity of the radical party, if the power is in their hands, is considered bad by the republican and other parties. But not only is it a fact that the activity of statesmen is never considered by all men to be useful: their activity has, besides, this peculiarity, that it must always be carried on by violence, and that, in order to attain this end, there are necessary, murders, executions, prisons, taxes raised by force, and so on.

It therefore appears that, besides the fact that the usefulness of state activity is not recognized by all men, and is always denied by one portion of men, this usefulness has the peculiarity of vindicating itself always by violence.

And therefore the usefulness of state activity cannot be confirmed by the fact that it is recognized by those men for whom it is performed.

Let us apply the second test: let us ask statesmen themselves, from the tsar down to the policeman, from the president to the secretary, from the patriarch to the sexton, begging for a sincere answer, whether in occupying their respective positions, they have in view the good which they wish to do for men, or something else. In their desire to fill the situation of a tsar, a president, a minister, a police-sergeant, a sexton, a teacher, are they moved by the desire of being useful to men, or for their own personal advantage? And the answer of sincere men would be that the chief motive is their own personal advantage.

And so it appears that one class of men, who utilize the labor of others who perish by their labors, compensate for such an undoubted evil by an activity which is always considered by a great many men to be not only useless, but pernicious; which cannot be voluntarily accepted by men, but to which they must always be compelled, and the aim of which is not the benefit of others, but the personal advantage of those men who perform it.

What is it, then, that confirms the theory that state activity is useful for men? Only the fact that those men who perform it, firmly believe it to be useful, and that it has been always in existence; but so have always been not only useless institutions, but very pernicious ones, like slavery, prostitution, and wars.

Business people (merchants, manufacturers, railway proprietors, bankers, landowners) believe in the fact that they do a good which undoubtedly compensates for the harm done by them. Upon what grounds do they believe it? To the question by whom the usefulness of their activity is recognized, men in church and in state are able to point to the thousands and millions of working-people who in principle recognize the usefulness of state and church activity; but to whom will bankers, distillers, manufacturers of velvet, of bronzes, of looking-glasses, to say nothing of guns, — to whom will they point when we ask them is their usefulness recognized by the majority?

If there can be found men who recognize the usefulness of manufacturing chintzes, rails, beer, and such like things, there will be found also a still greater number of men who consider the manufacture of these articles pernicious.

And as for the activity of merchants who raise the prices of all articles, and that of landowners, nobody would even attempt to justify it.

Besides, this activity is always associated with the harm done to working-people and with violence, if less direct than that of the state, yet just as cruel in its consequences; for the activities displayed in industry and in trade are entirely based upon taking advantage of the wants of working-people in every form, in order to compel working-men to hard and hated labor; to buy all goods cheap, and to sell to the people the articles necessary for them at the highest possible price, and to raise the interest on money. From whatever point we consider their activity, we see that the usefulness of business-men is not recognized by those for whom it is expended, neither in principle nor in particular cases; and by the majority their activity is considered to be directly pernicious. If we were to apply the second test, and to ask, What is the chief motive of the activity of business-men? we should receive a still more determinate answer than that on the activity of statesmen.

If a statesman says that besides a personal advantage he has in view the common benefit, we cannot help believing him, and each of us knows such men; but a business-man, from the very nature of his occupations, cannot have in view a common advantage, and would be ridiculous in the sight of his fellows if he were in his business aiming at something besides the increasing of his own wealth and the keeping of it. And, therefore, working-people do not consider the activity of business-men of any help to them. Their activity is associated with violence toward such people; and its object is not their good, but always and only personal advantage; and lo! strange to say, these business-men are so assured of their own usefulness that they boldly, for the sake of this imaginary good, do an undoubted obvious harm to working-men by extricating themselves from laboring, and consuming the labor of the working-classes. Men of science and of art have freed themselves from laboring by putting this labor on others, and live with a quiet conscience, thinking they bring a sufficient advantage to other men to compensate for it.

On what is their assurance based? Let us ask them as we have done statesmen and business-men.

Is the utility of the arts and sciences recognized by all, or even by the majority of working-people?

We shall receive a very deplorable answer. The activity of men in church and state is recognized to be useful in theory by almost all, and in application by the majority of those for whom it is performed; the activity of business-men is recognized as useful by a small number of working-people; but the activity of men of science and of art is not recognized to be useful by any of the working-class. The usefulness of their activity is recognized only by those who are engaged in it, or who desire to practise it. Those who bear upon their shoulders all the labor of life, and who feed and clothe the men of science and art, cannot recognize the usefulness of the activity of these men, because they cannot even form any idea about an activity which always appears to working-men useless and even depraving.

Thus, without any exception, working-people think the same of universities, libraries, conservatories, picture and statue galleries, and theaters, which are built at their expense.

A working-man considers this activity to be so decidedly pernicious that he does not send his children to be taught; and in order to compel people to accept this activity, it has been everywhere found necessary to introduce a law compelling parents to send the children to school.

A working-man always looks at this activity with ill-will, and only ceases to look at it so when he ceases to be a working-man, and having saved money, and been educated, he passes out of the class of working-people into the class of men who live upon the necks of others.

And notwithstanding the fact that the usefulness of the activity of men of science and art is not recognized, and even cannot be recognized, by any workman, these men are all the same compelled to make a sacrifice for such an activity.

A statesman simply sends another to the guillotine or to prison; a business-man, utilizing the labor of another, takes away from him his last resource, leaving him the alternative of starvation, or labor destructive of his health and life; but a man of science or of art seemingly compels nobody to do anything: he merely offers the good he has done to those who are willing to take it; but, in order to be able to make his productions undesirable to the working-people, he takes away from the people, by violence, through the statesmen, the greatest part of their labor for the building and keeping open of academies, universities, colleges, schools, museums, libraries, conservatories, and for the wages for himself and his fellows.

But if we were to ask men of science and art about the object which they are pursuing in their activity, we should receive the most astonishing replies.

A statesman would answer that his aim was the common welfare; and in his answer, there would be an admixture of truth confirmed by public opinion.

In the answer of the business-man, that his aim was social welfare, there would be less probability; but we could admit even this also.

But the answer of men of science and art strikes one at once by its want of proof and by its effrontery. Such men say, without bringing any proofs, just as priests used to do in olden times, that their activity is the most important of all, and the most necessary for all men, and that without it all mankind would go to ruin. They assert that it is so, notwithstanding the fact that nobody except they themselves either understands or acknowledges their activity, and notwithstanding the fact that, according to their own definition, true science and true art should not have a utilitarian aim.

These men are occupied with the matter they like, without troubling themselves what advantage will come out of it to men; and they are always assured that they are doing the most important thing, and the most necessary for all mankind.

So that while a sincere statesman, acknowledging that the chief motive of his activity is a personal one, tries to be as useful as possible to the working-people; while a business-man, acknowledging the egotism of his activity, tries to give it an appearance of being one of universal utility, — men of science and art do not consider it necessary to seem to shelter themselves under a pretense of usefulness: they deny even the object of usefulness, so sure are they, not only of the usefulness, but even of the sacredness, of their own business.

And now it turns out that the third class of men, who have freed themselves from labor, and have laid it on other men, are occupied with things which are totally incomprehensible to working-people, and which these people consider to be trifles, and often very pernicious trifles; and are occupied with these things without any consideration of their usefulness, but merely for the gratification of their own pleasure: it turns out that these men are, from some reason or other, quite assured that their activity will always produce that without which working-people would never be able to exist.

Men have freed themselves from laboring for their living, and have thrown the work upon others, who perish under it; they utilize this labor, and assert that their occupations, which are incomprehensible to all other men, and which are not directed to useful aims, compensate for all the evil they are doing to men by freeing themselves from the labor of earning their livelihood, and swallowing up the labor of others.

The statesman, in order to compensate for that undoubted and obvious evil which he does to man by freeing himself from the struggle with nature, and by appropriating the labor of others, does men another obvious and undoubted harm by countenancing all sorts of violence.

The business-man, in order to compensate for that undoubted and obvious harm which he does to men by using up their labor, tries to earn for himself as much wealth as possible; that is, as much of other men's labor as possible.

The man of science and art, in compensating for the same undoubted and obvious harm which he does to working-people, is occupied with matters to which he feels attracted, and which is quite incomprehensible to working-people, and which, according to his own assertion, in order to be a true one, ought not to aim at usefulness.

And therefore, all these men are quite sure that their right of utilizing other men's labor is secure. Yet it seems obvious that all those men who have freed themselves from the labor of earning their livelihood have no ground for doing this.

But, strange to say, these men firmly believe in their own righteousness, and live as they do with an easy conscience. There must be some plausible ground, some false belief, at the bottom of such a profound error.

CHAPTER XXVIII

And in reality the position in which men, living by other men's labor, are placed, is based, not only upon a certain belief, but upon an entire doctrine; and not only on one doctrine, but on three, which have grown one upon another during centuries, and are now fused together into an awful deceit, or humbug as the English call it, which hides from men their unrighteousness.

The oldest of these in our world, which justifies the treason of men against the fundamental duty of labor to earn their livelihood, was the Church-Christian doctrine, according to which men, by the will of God, differ one from another, as the sun differs from the moon and the stars, and as one star differs from another. Some men God ordains to have dominion over all; others to have power over many; others, still, over a few; and the remainder are ordained by God to obey.

This doctrine, though already shaken to its foundations, still continues to influence some men, so that many who do not accept it, who often even ignore the existence of it, are, nevertheless, guided by it.

The second is what I cannot help terming the State-philosophical doctrine. According to it, as fully developed by Hegel, all that exists is reasonable, and the established order of life is constant and sustained, not merely by men, but as the only possible form of the manifestation of the spirit, or generally, of the life of mankind.

This doctrine, too, is no longer accepted by men who direct social opinion, and it holds its position only by the property of inertia.

The last doctrine, which is now ruling the minds of men, and on which is based the justification as well of leading statesmen as also of leading men of business and of science and art, is a scientific one, not in the evident sense of the word, meaning knowledge generally, but in the sense of a knowledge peculiar in form as well as in matter, termed science in particular. On this new doctrine particularly is based in our days the justification of man's idleness, hiding from him his treason against his calling.

This new doctrine appeared in Europe contemporaneously with a large class of rich and idle people, who served neither the church nor the state, and who were in want of a justification of their position.

Not very long ago in France, before the revolution in Europe, it was always the case that all non-working-people, in order to have a right to utilize other men's labor, were obliged to have some definite occupation,— to serve in the church, the state, or the army.

Men who served the government, governed the people; those who served the church, taught the people divine truths; and those who served the army, protected the people.

Only these three classes of men — the clergy, the statesmen, and the military men — claimed for themselves the right of utilizing working-men's labor, and they could always point out their services to the people: the remaining rich men, who had not this justification, were despised, and, feeling their own want of right, were ashamed of their wealth and of their idleness. But as time went on, this class of rich people who did not belong either to the clergy, to the government, or to the army, owing to the vices of these three classes, increased in number, and became a powerful party. They were in want of a justification of their position. And one was invented for them. A century had not elapsed when the men who did not serve either the state or the church, and who took no part whatever in their affairs, received the same right to live by other men's labor as the former classes; and they not only left off being ashamed of their wealth and idleness, but began to consider their position quite justified. And the number of such men has increased and is still increasing in our days.

And the most wonderful of all is this, that these men, the same whose claims to be freed from laboring were unrecognized not long ago, now consider themselves alone to be fully right, and are attacking the former three classes, — the servants of the church, state, and army, — alleging their exemption from labor to be unjust, and often even considering their activity to be directly pernicious. And what is still more wonderful is this, that the former servants of church, state, and army do not now lean upon the divineness of their calling, nor even upon the philosophy which considers the state necessary for individual development, but they set aside these supports which have so long maintained them, and are now seeking the same supports on which the new reigning class of men, who have found a novel justification, stands, and at the head of which are the men of science and art.

If a statesman now sometimes, appealing to old memories, justifies his position by the fact that he was set in it by God, or by the fact that the state is a form of the development of personality, he does it because he is behind the age, and he feels that nobody believes him.

In order to justify himself effectually, he ought to find now neither theological nor philosophical, but other new, scientific supports.

It is necessary to point to the principle of nationalities, or to that of the development of an organism; and to gain over the ruling class, as in the Middle Ages it was necessary to gain over the clergy, and as at the end of the last century it was necessary to obtain the sanction of philosophers, as seen in the case of Frederick the Great and Catherine of Russia. If now a rich man, after the old fashion, says sometimes that it is God's providence which makes him rich, or if he points to the importance of a nobility for the welfare of a state, he does it because he is behind the times.

In order to justify himself completely, he must point to his furthering progress and civilization by improving the modes of production, by lowering the prices of consumption, by establishing an intercourse between nations. A rich man ought to think and to speak in scientific language, and, as the clergy formerly, he has to offer sacrifices to the ruling class: he must publish magazines and books, provide himself with a picture gallery, a musical society, a kindergarten, or a technical school. The ruling class is the class of learned men and artists of a definite character. They possess complete justification for having freed themselves from laboring; and upon this justification (as in former times upon the theological justification and afterward upon the philosophical one) all is based; and it is these men who now give the diploma of exemption to other classes.

The class of men who now feel completely justified in freeing themselves from labor, is that of men of science and particularly of experimental, positive, critical, evolutional science, and of artists who develop their ideas according to this tendency.

If a learned man or an artist, after the old fashion, speaks nowadays about prophecy, revelation, or the manifestation of the spirit, he does so because he is behind the age, but he will not succeed in justifying himself: in order to stand firm he must try to associate his activity with experimental, positive, critical science, and he must make this science the fundamental principle of his activity. Then only would the science or the art with which he is occupied appear to be a true one, and he would then stand in our days on firm ground, and then will there be no doubt as to the usefulness he is bringing to mankind. The justification of all those who have freed themselves from laboring is based upon experimental, critical, positive science.

The theological and philosophical explanations have already had their day: they timidly and bashfully now introduce themselves to notice, and try to humor their scientific usurper, which, however, boldly knocks down and destroys the remnants of the past, everywhere taking its place, and with assurance in its own firmness lifts aloft its head.

The theological justification maintained that men by their destination are called, — some to govern, others to obey; some to live sumptuously, others to labor; and therefore those who believed in the revelation of God could not doubt the lawfulness of the position of those men who, according to the will of God, are called to govern and to be rich.

The state-philosophical justification used to say, The state with all its institutions and differences of classes, according to rights and possessions, is that historical form which is necessary for the right manifestation of the spirit in mankind; and therefore the situation which every one occupies in state and in society according to his rights and to his possessions must be such as to insure the sound life of mankind.

The scientific theory says, All this is nonsense and superstition: the one is the fruit of the theological period of thought, and the other of the metaphysical period.

For the study of the laws of the life of human societies, there is only one sure method, — that of a positive, experimental, critical science. It is only sociology based upon biology, based again upon all other positive sciences, which is able to give us new laws of the life of mankind. Mankind, or human societies, are organisms either already perfect, or in a state of development subject to all the laws of the evolution of organisms. One of the first of these laws is the division of labor among the portions of the organs. If some men govern, and others obey, some live in opulence, and others in want, then this takes place, neither according to the will of God, nor because the state is the form of the manifestation of personality, but because in societies as in organisms a division of labor takes place which is necessary for the life of the whole. Some men perform in societies the muscular part of labor, and others the mental.

Upon this doctrine is built the ruling excuse of the age.

CHAPTER XXIX

CHRIST teaches men in a new way, and this teaching is written down in the Gospels.

It is first persecuted, and then accepted; and upon it at once a complete system of theological dogma is invented, which is thereafter accepted for the teaching of Christ. The system is absurd, it has no foundation; but by virtue of it, men are led to believe that they may continue to live in an evil way, and none the less be Christians. And this conclusion is so agreeable to the mass of weak men, who have no affection for moral effort, that the system is eagerly accepted, not only as true, but even as the Divine truth as revealed by God Himself. And the invention becomes the groundwork on which for centuries theologians build their theories.

Then by degrees these learned men diverge by various channels into special systems of their own, and finally endeavor to overthrow each others' theories. They begin to feel there is something amiss, and cease to understand what they themselves are talking about. But the crowd still requires them to expound its favorite instruction; and thus the theologians, pretending both to understand and believe what they are saying, continue to dispense it.

In process of time, however, the conclusions drawn from theological conceptions cease to be necessary to the masses, who, then, peeping into the very sanctuaries of their augurs, discover them to be utterly void of those glorious and indubitable truths which the mysteries of theology had seemed to suggest.

The same happened to philosophy, not in the sense of the wisdom of men like Confucius or Epictetus, but with professional philosophy, when it humored the instincts of the crowd of rich and idle people. Not long ago, in the learned world, a moral philosophy was in fashion, according to which it appeared that everything that is, is reasonable; that there is neither good nor evil; that man has not to struggle with evil, but has merely to manifest the spirit, some in military service, some in courts of justice, and some on the violin.

Many and various were the expressions of human wisdom, and as such were known to the men of the nineteenth century,—Rousseau, Pascal, Lessing, and Spinoza; and all the wisdom of antiquity was expounded, but none of its systems laid hold of the crowd. We cannot say that Hegel's success was due to the harmony of his theory. We had no less harmonious theories from Descartes, Leibnitz, Fichte, and Schopenhauer.

There was only one reason for the fact that this doctrine became for a short time the belief of the civilized world, the same which had caused the success of theology; to wit, that the deductions of this philosophical theory humored the weak side of men's nature. It said, All is reasonable, all is good; nobody is to blame for anything.

And as at first with the church upon theological foundations, so also, with the philosophy of Hegel for a base, a Babel's tower was built (some who are behind the age are still sitting upon it); and here again was a confusion of tongues, men feeling that they themselves did not know of what they were talking, but trying to conceal their ignorance, and to keep their prestige before the crowd.

When I began life, Hegelianism was the order of the day; it was in the very air you breathed; it found its expression in newspapers and magazines, in lectures upon history and upon law, in novels, in tracts, in art, in sermons, in conversation. A man who did not know Hegel, had no right to open his mouth; those who desired to learn the truth, were studying Hegel,—everything pointed to him; and lo! forty years have elapsed, and nothing is left of him; there is no remembrance of him; all is as though he had never existed. And the most remarkable of all is that, as false Christianity, so also Hegelianism has fallen, not because some one had refuted or overthrown it,—no, it is now as it was before,

– but both have only become no longer necessary for the learned, educated world.

If, at the present time, any man of culture is questioned about the system of theological dogma, he will neither contradict nor argue, but will simply ask, "Why should I believe these dogmas?" — "What good are they to me?"

So also with Hegelianism. No one of our day will argue its theses. He will only inquire, "What Spirit?" "Where did it come from?" "With what purpose?" "What good will it do me?" Not very long ago the sages of Hegelianism were solemnly teaching the crowd; and the crowd, understanding nothing, blindly believed all, finding the confirmation of what suited them, and thinking that what seemed to them to be not quite clear, or even contradictory, on the heights of philosophy was clearer than day; but time went on, the theory was worn out, a new one appeared in its place, the former one was no longer demanded, and again the crowd looked into the mysterious temples of the augurs, and saw there was nothing there, and that nothing had ever been there but words, very dark and meaningless.

(This happened within my memory.) These things happened, we are told, because they were ravings of the theological and metaphysical period; but now we have a critical, positive science, which will not deceive us, because it is based upon induction and experience. Now our knowledge is no longer uncertain as it formerly was, and it is only by following it that one can find the answer to all the questions of life.

But this is exactly the same that was said by the old teachers, and they certainly were no fools, and we know that among them were men of immense intellect; and within my memory the disciples of Hegel said exactly the same thing, with no less assurance and no less acknowledgment on the side of the crowd of so-called educated people. And such men as our Herzen, Stankievich, Byelinsky, were no fools either. But why, then, has this wonderful thing happened, that clever men preached with the greatest assurance, and the crowd accepted with veneration such groundless and meaningless doctrines? The reason of it is only that these doctrines justified men in their bad mode of living.

A very commonplace English writer, whose books are now almost forgotten and recognized as the emptiest of all empty ones, wrote a tract upon population, in which he invented an imaginary law that the means of living does not increase with increase of population. This sham law the author dressed out with formulæ of mathematics, which have no foundation whatever, and published it. Judged by the lightness of mind and the want of talent displayed in this treatise, we might suppose that it would have passed unnoticed, and been forgotten as all other writings of the same author have been; but it turned out quite differently. The author who wrote it became at once a scientific authority, and has maintained this high position for nearly half a century. Malthus! The Malthusian theory,—the law of the increase of population in geometrical progression and the increase of means of living in arithmetical progression, and the natural and prudent means of restraining the increase of population,—all these became scientific, undoubted truths which have never been verified, but being accepted as axioms, have served for further deductions.

Thus learned, educated men were deceived; whereas in the crowd of idle men, there was a devout trust in the great laws discovered by Malthus. How, then, did this happen? These seem to be scientific deductions, which had nothing in common with the instincts of the crowd.

But this is so only to those who believe science to be something self-existent, like the Church, not liable to errors, and not merely the thoughts of weak men liable to mistakes, who only for importance' sake call by a pompous word, *science*, their own thoughts and words. It was only necessary to draw practical conclusions from the Malthusian theory in order to see that it was quite a human one with very determinate aims.

The deductions which followed directly from this

theory were the following: The miserable condition of working-people does not come from the cruelty, egotism, and unreasonableness of rich and strong men, but it exists according to an unchangeable law which does not depend upon man, and, if anybody is to blame, it is the starving working-people themselves: why do these fools come into the world when they know that they will not have enough to eat? and therefore the wealthy and powerful classes are not at all to blame for anything, and they may quietly continue to live as they have done.

This conclusion, precious to the crowd of idle men, induced all learned men to overlook the incorrectness and total arbitrariness of the deductions; and the crowd of educated idle people, instinctively guessing to what these deductions led, greeted the theory with delight, set upon it the seal of truth, and cherished it during half a century. The reason for all this was that these doctrines justified men in their bad mode of life.

Is not the same cause at the bottom of the self-assurance of men of positive, critical, experimental science, and of the reverent regard of the crowd to what they preach? At first it appears strange that the theory of evolution justifies men in their unrighteousness, and that the scientific theory has only to do with facts, and does nothing else than observe facts. But it only seems so.

So it had been with theological teaching: theology seemed to be occupied only with doctrines, and to have nothing to do with the lives of men; so it had been with philosophy, which also seemed to be occupied only with facts.

So it had been with the teaching of Hegel on a large scale, and with the theory of Malthus on a small one. Hegelianism seemed to be occupied merely with its logical constructions, and to have nothing to do with the lives of men; so with the theory of Malthus, which seemed to be occupied exclusively with statistics.

But it only seemed so.

Modern science is also occupied exclusively with facts: it studies facts.

But what facts? Why such facts, and not others?

The men of modern science are very fond of speaking with a solemn assurance, "We study facts alone," imagining that these words have some meaning.

To study facts alone is quite impossible, because the number of facts which may be objects of our study is countless, in the strict sense of the word.

Before beginning to study facts, one must have some theory, according to which facts are studied; that is, these or those being selected from the countless number of facts. And this theory indeed exists, and is even very definitely expressed, though many of the agents of modern science ignore it; that is, do not want to know it, or really do not know it, and sometimes pretend not to know it.

Thus matters stood before with all most important beliefs.

The foundations of each are always given in theory; and so-called learned men seek only for further deductions from various foundations given to them, though sometimes ignoring even these.

But a fundamental theory must always be present. So is it also now: modern science selects its facts upon the ground of a determinate theory, which sometimes it knows, sometimes does not wish to know, sometimes really does not know; but it exists. And the theory is this: All mankind is an undying organism; men are particles of the organs of this organism, having each his special calling for the service of the whole. As the cells, growing into an organism, divide among themselves the labor of the struggle for existence of the whole organism, increase one capacity, and diminish another, and all together form an organ in order better to satisfy the wants of the whole organism; and as among social animals,— ants and bees,— the individuals divide the labor among themselves (queen bees lay eggs, drone bees fecundate, working-bees labor for the life of the whole), — so also in mankind and in human societies there takes place the same differentiation and integration of the parts. And, therefore, in order to find the law of man's life, we must study the laws of the lives and development of organisms. And in these we find the following laws: That each phenomenon is followed by more than one consequence; the failure of uniformity; the law of uniformity and diversity; and so on. All this seems to be very innocent, but we need only draw deductions from these observations of facts in order to see at once to what they are tending.

These facts lead to one thing, — the acknowledgment that the existence in human societies of division of activities is organic; that is, necessary. And they therefore induce us to consider the unjust position in which we are, who have freed ourselves from laboring, not from the point of reasonableness and justice, but merely as an indubitable fact which confirms a general law. Moral philosophy used also to justify every cruelty and wickedness; but there it turned out to be philosophical, and therefore incorrect: but according to science, the same thing turns out to be scientific, and therefore unquestionable.

How, then, can we help accepting such a fine theory! We need only look at human society merely as at an object of observation, and we may quietly devour the labor of perishing men, calming ourselves with the idea that our activity as a dancing-master, a lawyer, a doctor, a philosopher, an actor, an investigator of the theory of mediumism and of forms of atoms, and so on, is a functional activity of the organism of mankind, and therefore there cannot be a question whether it is just that I should live doing only what is pleasant, as there can be no question whether the division of labor between a mental and a muscular cell is just or not. How, then, can we help accepting such a nice theory which enables us afterward forever to put our conscience into our pockets, and live a completely unbridled, animal life, feeling under our feet a firm, scientific support? And it is upon this new belief that the justification of idleness and the cruelty of men is built.

CHAPTER XXX

This doctrine had its commencement about half a century ago. Its chief founder was the French philosopher Comte. Comte, being a lover of systematic theory, and at the same time a man of religious tendency, was impressed by the then new physiological researches of Bichat; and he conceived the old idea, expressed in bygone days by Menenius Agrippa, that human societies, indeed all human-kind, may be regarded as one whole, an organism; and men, — as live particles of separate organs, each having his definite destination to fulfil in the service of the whole organism.

Comte was so fascinated by this idea, that he founded upon it his philosophical theory; and this theory so captivated him, that he quite forgot that the point of departure he had started from was no more than a pretty comparison, suitable enough in a fable, but in no way justifiable as the foundation of a science. As often happens, he took his pet hypothesis for an axiom, and so imagined that his whole theory was based upon the most firm and positive foundations.

According to his theory, it appeared that, as mankind is an organism, therefore the knowledge of what man is and what ought to be his relation to the world is only possible through a knowledge of the properties of this organism. In order to learn these properties, man is fitted to make observations upon the lower organisms, and draw deductions from their lives.

Therefore, first, the true and exclusive method of science, according to Comte, is the inductive one, and science is only science when it has experiment for its basis; secondly, the final aim and the summit of science becomes the new science concerning the imaginary organism of mankind, or the organic being, — mankind; this new hypothetic science is sociology; from this view of science, it generally turns out that all former knowledge was false, and that the whole history of mankind, in the sense of its self-consciousness, divides itself into three, or rather into two, periods: first, the theological and metaphysical period, from the beginning of the world to Comte; and secondly, the modern period of true science, positive science, beginning with Comte.

All this was very well, but there was a single mistake in it; it was this: that all this edifice was built upon the sand, upon an arbitrary and incorrect assertion that mankind, collectively considered, was an organism. This assertion was arbitrary, because there is no more reason why, if we acknowledge the existence of mankind to be an organism, we should refuse to allow the correctness of all the various theological propositions.

It was incorrect, because to the idea of mankind, that is, of men, the definition of an organism was incorrectly added, whereas mankind lacks the essential characteristic of an organism, — a center of sensation or consciousness. We call an elephant, as well as a bacterium, organisms, only because we suppose by analogy in these beings unification of sensations or consciousness. As for human societies and mankind, they lack this essential; and, therefore, however many other general character signs we may find out in mankind and in an organism, without this the acknowledgment of mankind to be an organism is incorrect.

But notwithstanding the arbitrariness and incorrectness of the fundamental proposition of positive philosophy, it was accepted by the so-called educated world with great sympathy, because of that great fact important for the crowd, that it afforded a justification of the existing order of things by recognizing the lawfulness of the existing division of labor; that is of violence in mankind. It is remarkable in this respect that from the writings of Comte, composed of two parts, — a positive philosophy and a positive politics, — by the learned world, only the first part was accepted, that which justified upon new experimental principles the existing evil in human society; the second part, treating of the moral altruistic duties following from this recognition of mankind to be an organism, was considered not only to be unimportant, but even unscientific.

Here the same thing was repeated which occurred with the two parts of Kant's writings: the "Critique of Pure Reason" was accepted by science; but the "Critique of Practical Reason," that part which contains the essence of moral doctrine, was rejected. In the teaching of Comte, that was recognized to be scientific which humored the reigning evil.

But the positive philosophy, accepted by the crowd, based upon an arbitrary and incorrect supposition, was by itself too ill-grounded, and therefore too unsteady, and could not be sustained by itself.

And now among all the idle play of ideas of so-called men of science, there also appeared a similarly arbitrary and incorrect assertion, not a new one at all, to the effect that all living beings, that is, organisms, proceed one from another; not only one organism from another, but one organism from many; that during a very long period, a million of years for instance, not only a fish and a duck may have proceeded from one and the same forefather, but also one organism might have proceeded from many separate organisms; so, for instance, out of a swarm of bees a single animal may proceed. And this arbitrary and incorrect assertion was accepted by the learned world with still greater sympathy.

This assertion was an arbitrary one, because nobody has ever seen how one kind of organism is made from others; and therefore the hypothesis about the origin of species will always remain a mere supposition, and never will become an experimental fact.

This hypothesis was incorrect because the solution of the problem of the origin of species by the theory that they had their origin in the law of inheritance and accommodation during an infinitely long time, was not at all a solution of the problem, but the mere iteration of the question in another form.

According to the solution of this problem by Moses (in opposition to which consists all the object of Comte's theory), it appeared that the variety of the species of living beings proceeded from the will of God and His infinite omnipotence: according to the theory of evolution, it appears that the variety of species of living beings proceeded by themselves in consequence of the infinite variety of conditions of inheritance and environment in an infinite period of time.

The theory of evolution, speaking plainly, asserts only that by chance in an infinite period of time anything you like may proceed from anything else you choose.

This is no answer to the question; it is simply the same question put differently: instead of will is put chance, and the coefficient of the infinite is transferred from omnipotence to time.

But this new assertion, enforced by Darwin's followers in an arbitrary and inaccurate spirit, maintained the former assertion of Comte, and therefore it became a revelation for our time, and the foundation of all sciences, even that of the history of philosophy and religion; and besides, according to the *naïve* confession of the very founder of Darwin's theory, this idea was awakened in him by the law of Malthus; and therefore he pointed to the struggle for existence of not only men, but of all living beings, as to a fundamental law of every living thing. And this was exactly what was wanted by the crowd of idle people for their own justification.

Two unstable theories which could not stand upon their own feet supported each other, and received a show of stability. Both the theories bore in them a sense, precious for the crowd, that for the existing evil in human societies men are not to be blamed, that the existing order is what ought to be, and thus the new theory was accepted by the crowd in the sense which was wanted by them, with full confidence and unprecedented enthusiasm.

And so the new scientific doctrine was founded upon two arbitrary and incorrect propositions, which were accepted in the same way as dogmas of faith are accepted. Both in matter and form, this new doctrine is remarkably similar to the Church-Christian one. In matter, the similarity lies in the fact that, in both doctrines alike, a fantastical meaning is attached to really existing things, and this artificial meaning is taken as the object of our research.

In the Church-Christian doctrine, the Christ which did really exist is screened away by a whole system of fantastical theological dogmas; in the positive doctrine, to the really existing fact of live men is attributed the fantastical attributes of an organism.

In form, the similarity of these two doctrines is remarkable, since, in both cases, a theory emanating from one class of men is accepted as the only and infallible truth. In the Church-Christian doctrine, the Church's way of understanding God's revelation to men is regarded as the sacred and only true one. In the doctrine of positivism, certain men's way of understanding science is regarded as absolutely correct and true.

As the Church-Christians regard the foundation of their church as the only origin of the true knowledge of God, and only out of a kind of courtesy admit that former believers may also be regarded as having formed a church; so in precisely the same manner does positive science, according to its own statement, place its origin in Comte: and its representatives, also only out of courtesy, admit the existence of previous science, and that only as regarding certain thinkers, as, for instance, Aristotle. Both the Church and positive science altogether exclude the ideas of all the rest of mankind, and regard all knowledge outside their own as erroneous.

In our time, the old dogma of evolution comes in with new importance to help the fundamental dogma of Comte concerning the organism of mankind; and from these two elements a new scientific doctrine has been formed. If it is not quite clear to a believer in the organism of mankind why a collection of individuals may be counted as an organism, the dogma of evolution is charged with the explanation. This dogma is needed to reconcile the contradictions and certainties of the first: mankind is an organism, and we see that it does not contain the chief characteristic of an organism; how must we account for it?

Here the dogma of evolution comes in, and explains, Mankind is an organism in a state of development. If you accept this, you may then consider mankind as such.

A man who is free from the positive superstition cannot even understand wherein lies the interest of the theory of the origin of species and of evolution; and this interest is explained, only when we learn the fundamental dogma, that mankind is an organism. And as all the subtleties of theology are intelligible only to those who believe in its fundamental dogmas, so also all the subtleties of sociology, which now occupy the minds of all men of this recent and profound science, are intelligible only to believers.

The similarity between these two doctrines holds good yet further. Being founded upon dogmas accepted by faith, these doctrines neither question nor analyze their own principles, which, on the other hand, are used as starting-points for the most extraordinary theories. The preachers of these call themselves, in theology, sanctified; in positive knowledge, scientific; in both cases, infallible. And at the same time, they attain the most peremptory, incredible, and unfounded assertions, which they give forth with the greatest pomp and seriousness, and which are with equal pomp and seriousness contradicted in all their details by others who do not agree, and yet who equally recognize the fundamental dogmas.

The Basil the Great of scientific doctrine, Spencer, in one of his first writings expresses these doctrines thus: Societies and organisms, says he, are alike in the following points: First, in that, being conceived as small aggregates, they imperceptibly grow up in mass, so that some of them become ten thousand times bigger than their originals.

Secondly, in that, while in the beginning they have such simple structure that they may almost be considered as structureless, in their growth they develop an ever increasing complexity of structure.

Thirdly, in that, though in their early undeveloped

period there does not exist among them any dependence of particles one upon another, these particles by and by acquire a mutual dependence, which at last becomes so strong that the activity and the life of each part is possible only with the activity and the lives of all others.

Fourthly, in this, that the life and the development of society is more independent and longer than the life and the development of every unit which goes to form it, and which are separately born and growing and acting and multiplying and dying while the political body formed of them continues to live one generation after another, developing in mass, in perfection of structure, and in functional activity.

Then follow the points of difference between organisms and societies, and it is demonstrated that these differences are only seeming ones, and that organisms and societies are quite similar. For an impartial man the question at once arises, What are you, then, speaking about? Why is mankind an organism, or something similar?

You say that societies are similar to organisms according to these four points; but even this comparison is incorrect. You take only a few characteristics of an organism, and you then apply them to human societies. You produce four points of similarity, then you take the points of difference which you say are only seemingly so, and you conclude that human societies may be considered as organisms.

But this is nothing else than an idle play of dialectics. Upon this ground we may consider as organism everything we choose. I take the first thing which comes to my mind, — a forest, — as it is planted in a field and grows up: first beginning as a small aggregate, it imperceptibly increases in mass. This is also the case with fields, when, after being planted, they are gradually covered with forest trees. Secondly, in the beginning the structure of an organism is simple, then the complexity increases, and so on.

The same is the case with the forest: at first there are only birch trees, then hazel, and so on; first all the trees grow straight, and afterward they interlace their branches. Thirdly, the dependence of the parts increases so that the life of each part depends upon the lives and activities of all the others: it is exactly the same with the forest; the nut tree warms the trunks (if you hew it down, the other trees will be frozen in winter), the underwood keeps off wind, the seed trees continue the species, the tall and leafy ones give shadow, and the life of each tree depends upon that of the rest. Fourthly, separate parts may die, but the whole organism continues to live. Separate trees perish, but the forest continues in life and growth. The same holds good with the example so often brought by the defenders of the scientific doctrine. Cut off an arm, — the arm will die: we may say remove a tree from the shadow and the ground of a forest, it will die.

Another remarkable similarity between this scientific doctrine and the Church-Christian one — as also in the case of any other theory founded upon propositions accepted through faith — lies in their capacity of being proof against logic.

After having demonstrated that by this theory a forest may be considered as an organism, you think you have proved to the followers of the theory of organisms the incorrectness of their definition? Not at all. Their definition of an organism is so inexact and dilatable, that they can apply it to everything they like.

Yes, they will say, you may consider the forest, too, as an organism. A forest is a mutual coöperationship of the individuals who do not destroy each other; an aggregate: its parts can also pass into a closer relationship, and by differentiation and integration it may become an organism.

Then you will say that, in that case, the birds too and the insects, and the herbs of this forest, which mutually coöperate and do not destroy each other, may be considered with the trees to be an organism. They would agree to this too. According to their theory, we may consider as an organism every collection of living beings which mutually coöperate, and do not destroy one another. You may establish a connection and coöperation between everything you like, and, according to evolution, you may assert that from anything may proceed anything else you like, if a long enough period is granted.

It is quite impossible to prove to a believer in a theological doctrine, that his doctrine is false. But one may tell him that if one man arbitrarily asserts one dogma, another has the same right arbitrarily to invent and assert another. One may say the same thing with yet better ground to the followers of positive and evolutional science. Upon the basis of this science one could undertake to prove anything one liked. And the strangest thing of all is that this same positive science regards the scientific method as a condition of true knowledge, and that it has itself defined the elements of the scientific method. It professes that common-sense is the scientific method. And yet common-sense itself discloses at every step the fallacies of this doctrine. The moment those who occupied the position of saints felt that there was no longer anything sacred left in them, like the Pope and our own Synod, they immediately called themselves not merely sacred, but "most sacred." The moment science felt that it had given up common-sense, it called itself the science of reason, the only really scientific science.

CHAPTER XXXI

The division of labor is the law pervading every existing thing, therefore it must exist in human societies too.

That may be so; but the question still remains, whether the now existing division of labor in human society is that division which ought to be. And when men consider a certain division of labor to be reasonable and just, no science whatever can prove to men that there ought to be that which they consider to be unreasonable and unjust.

The theological theory demonstrated that power is of

God, and it very well may be so. But the question still remains, To whom is the power given, — to Catherine the Empress, or to the rebel Pugatchof? And no theological subtleties whatever can solve this difficulty. Moral Philosophy demonstrated that a state is merely a form of the social development of the individual; but the question still remains, Can the state of a Nero or that of a Gengis Khan be considered a form of such development? And no transcendental words whatever can solve the difficulty.

It is the same with scientific science also. The division of labor is the condition of the life of organisms and of human societies; but what have we to consider in these human societies to be an organic division of labor? And however much science studies the division of labor in the molecules of a tapeworm, all these observations cannot compel men to acknowledge a division of labor to be correct which cannot be admitted by their reason and conscience. However convincing may be the proofs of the division of labor in the cells of investigated organisms, a man, if he has not yet lost his reason, will say it is wrong that some should only weave cloth all their life long, and that this is not a division of labor, but oppression of a human being.

Herbert Spencer and others say that, as there are a whole population of weavers, therefore the weaver's activity is the organic division of labor. Saying this, they use a similar line of reasoning as do theologians. There is a power, and therefore it is of God, whatever it may be: there are weavers, therefore they exist as a result of the law of division of labor. There might be some sense in this if the power and the position of weavers were created by themselves; but we know that they are not, but that it is we who create them. Well, then, we ought to ascertain whether we have established this before-mentioned power according to the will of God, or of ourselves, and whether we have called these weavers into being by virtue of some organic law, or from some other cause.

Here are men earning their living by agriculture, as

it is proper for all men to do: one man has arranged a smith's forge, and mended his plow; his neighbor comes to him, and asks him to mend his plow, too, and promises to give labor or money in return. A second comes with a similar request; others follow; and in the society of these men, a form of division of labor arises: thus, one man becomes a smith.

Another man has taught his children well; his neighbor brings him his children, and asks him to teach them, and thus a teacher is formed; but the smith as well as the teacher become, and continue to be, such, only because they were asked, and they remain such as long as people require their trades. If it happens that too many smiths and teachers appear, or if their labor is no longer wanted, they at once, according to common-sense, throw aside their trade, and become laborers again, as it everywhere always happens where there is no cause for the violation of a right division of labor.

Men who behave in such a way are directed both by their reason and their conscience; and therefore we who are endowed with reason and conscience, all agree that such a division of labor is a right one. But if it were to happen that smiths, having the possibility of compelling other men to labor for them, were to continue to make horseshoes when there was no longer a demand for them, and teachers were to wish to continue to teach when there was nobody to be taught, so to every impartial man endowed with reason and conscience it would become obvious that such is not real division of labor, but a usurpation of other men's labor; because such a division could no longer be tested satisfactorily by that sole standard by which we may know whether it is right or not, — the demand of such labor by other men, and a voluntary compensation offered for it by them. And exactly such an overplus, however, is that which scientific science terms a division of labor.

Men do that which others do not require, and they ask to be fed for this, and say it is just, because it is division of labor. That which forms the chief social evil of a people, not only with us alone, is the countless number of government functionaries: that which is the cause of the economical misery of our days is what is called in England over-production (that is, the production of an enormous quantity of articles, wanted by nobody, and which no one knows how to get rid of). All this comes simply from this strange idea about the division of labor.

It would be very strange to see a bootmaker who considered that men were bound to feed him because, forsooth, he continued to produce boots wanted by no one; but what shall we say about those men in government, church, science, and art, who not only do not produce anything tangibly useful for the people, and whose produce is wanted by nobody, and who as boldly require to be well fed and clothed on account of the division of labor?

There may be some sorcerers, for whose activity there is a demand, and to whom men give cakes and spirits; but we cannot even imagine the existence of such sorcerers who, while their sorcery is not wanted by anybody, require to be fed simply because they wish to practise their art. And this very thing is the case in our world with men in church and state, with men of science and art. And all this proceeds from that false conception of the division of labor which is defined, not by reason and conscience, but by deductions to which men of science so unanimously resort.

The division of labor, indeed, has always existed; but it is correct only when man decides wherein it ought to consist by his reason and conscience, and not by his making observation upon it. And the conscience and the reason of all men solve this question in the simplest and surest way. They always decide that question by recognizing the division of labor to be a right one only when the special activity of a man is so necessary to others, that they, asking him to serve them, freely offer to feed him in compensation for what he will do for them. But when a man from his infancy up to his thirtieth year lives upon the shoulders of other men, promising to do, when he finishes his studies, something very useful which nobody has ever asked him for, and then for the rest of his life lives in the same way, promising only to do presently something which nobody asks him to do, this would not be a true division of labor, but, as it really is, only a violation by a strong man of the labor of others, — the same appropriation of others' labor by a strong man which formerly theologians called divine destination; philosophers, inevitable conditions of life; and now scientific science, the organic division of labor.

All the importance of the ruling science consists in this alone. This science becomes now the dispenser of diplomas for idleness, because she alone in her temples analyzes and determines what activity is a parasitic and what an organic one in the social organism. As if men could not, each for himself, much better decide it, and more quickly, too, by consulting his reason and conscience.

And as formerly, both for the clergy and then for statesmen, there could not have been any doubt as to who were most necessary for other people, so now for the men of positive science it seems that there cannot be any doubt about this, that their own activity is undoubtedly an organic one: they, factors of science and art, are the cells of the brain, the most precious cells of all the human organism. Let us leave them to reign, eat and drink, and be feasted, as priests and sophists of old have done before them, as long as they do not deprave men!

Since men exist as reasonable creatures, they have discriminated good from evil, making use of what has been done in this direction before them by others, struggled with evil, seeking a true and better way, and slowly but unceasingly have been advancing in this way. And always across it various deceits stood before them, which had in view to show them that this struggle was not at all necessary for them, but that they should submit to the tide of life. There existed the awful old deceits of the Church; with dreadful struggle and effort men little by little got rid of them: but scarcely had they done so when in the place of the old deceit arose a new one, — a state and philosophical one. Men freed themselves out of these too.

And now a new deceit, a still worse one, springs up in their path, — the scientific one.

This new deceit is exactly such as the old ones were: its essence consists in the substitution for reason and conscience of something external; and this external thing is observation, as in theology it was revelation.

The snare of this science consists in this, that having shown to men the most barefaced perversions of the activity of reason and conscience, it destroys in them confidence in both reason and conscience. Things which are the property of conscience and reason are now to be discerned by observation alone: these men lose the conception of good and evil, and become unable to understand those expressions and definitions of good and evil which have been worked out by all the former existence of mankind.

All that reason and conscience say to themselves, all that they said to the highest representatives of men since the world has existed, all this in their slang is conditional and subjective. All this must be left behind.

It is said by reason, one cannot apprehend the truth, because reason is liable to error: there is another way, unmistakable and almost mechanical, — one ought to study facts upon the ground of science, that is, upon two groundless suppositions, positivism and evolution, which are given out to be most undoubted truths. And the ruling science, with mock solemnity, asserts that the solving of all the questions of life is only possible through studying the facts of nature, and especially those of organisms.

The credulous crowd of youth, overwhelmed by the novelty of this authority, not only not destroyed, but not yet even touched by critics, rush to the study of these facts of natural sciences to that only way which, according to the assertion of the ruling doctrine, alone can lead to the elucidation of all questions of life. But the farther the students proceed in this study, the farther do they remove, not only the possibility of solving the questions of life, but even the very thought of this solution; the more they grow accustomed, not so much to observe themselves, as to believe upon their word other men's observations (to believe in cells, in protoplasm, in the fourth dimension of matter, and so on); the more the form hides from them the contents; the more they lose the consciousness of good and evil, and the capacity of understanding those expressions and definitions of good and evil which have been worked out by all the former career of mankind; the more they appropriate to themselves that special scientific slang of conditional expressions which have no common human meaning in them; the farther and farther they get into the thick forest of observations which is not lighted up by anything; the more they lose the capacity, not only of an independent thinking, but even of understanding other men's fresh human ideas which are not included in their Talmud: but chiefly they pass their best years in losing the habit of life, that is, of laboring, and accustom themselves to consider their own position justified, and thus become physically good-for-nothing parasites, and mentally dislocate their brains, and lose all power of thought-productiveness.

And so by degrees, their capacities more and more blunted, they acquire self-assurance, which deprives them forever of the possibility of returning to a simple, laborious life, to any plain, clear, common, human manner of thinking.

CHAPTER XXXII

The division of labor in human society has always existed, and I dare say always will exist; but the question for us is, not whether or not it has been and will still continue, but what should guide us to arrange that this division may be a right one.

If we take the facts of observation for our standard, we must refuse to have any standard at all: every division of labor which we see among men, and which may seem to us to be a right one, we shall consider right; and this is what the ruling scientific science is leading us to.

Division of labor!

Some are occupied with mental and spiritual, others with muscular and physical, labor.

With what an assurance do men express this! They wish to think so, and that seems to them in reality a correct exchange of services which is only the very apparent ancient violence.

Thou, or rather you (because it is always many who have to feed one), — you feed me, dress me, do for me all this rough labor, which I require of you, to which you are accustomed from your infancy, and I do for you that mental work to which I have already become accustomed. Give me bodily food, and I will give you in return the spiritual.

The statement seems to be a correct one; and it would really be so if only such exchange of services were free, if those who supply the bodily food were not obliged to supply it before they get the spiritual. The producer of the spiritual food says, In order that I may be able to give you this food, you must feed me, clothe me, and remove all filth from my house.

But as for the producer of bodily food, he must do it without making any claims of his own, and he has to give bodily food whether he receive spiritual food or not. If the exchange were a free one, the conditions on both sides would be equal. We agree that spiritual food is as necessary to man as bodily. The learned man, the artist, says, Before we can begin to serve men by giving them spiritual food, we want men to provide us with bodily food.

But why should not the producers of this latter say, Before we begin to serve you with bodily food, we want spiritual food; and until we receive it, we cannot labor?

You say, I require the labor of a plowman, a smith, a bootmaker, a carpenter, masons, and others, in order that I may prepare the spiritual food I have to offer.

Every workman might say, too, Before I go to work, to prepare bodily food for you, I want the fruits of the spirit. In order to have strength for laboring, I require a religious teaching, the social order of common life, application of knowledge to labor, and the joys and comforts which art gives. I have no time to work out for myself a teaching concerning the meaning of life, — give it to me.

I have no time to think out statutes of common life which would prevent the violation of justice, — give me this too. I have no time to study mechanics, natural philosophy, chemistry, technology; give me books with information as to how I am to improve my tools, my ways of working, my dwelling, the heating and lighting of it. I have no time to occupy myself with poetry, with plastic art, or music; give me those excitements and comforts necessary for life; give me these productions of the arts.

You say it is impossible for you to do your important and necessary business if you were to be deprived of the labor working-people do for you; and I say, a workman may declare, It is impossible for me to do my important and necessary business, not less important than yours, — to plow, to cart away refuse, and clean *your* houses, — if I be deprived of a religious guidance corresponding to the wants of my intellect and my conscience, of a reasonable government which would secure my labor, of information for easing my labor, and the enjoyment of art to ennoble it. All you have offered me in the shape of spiritual food is not only of no use to me whatever, but I cannot even understand to whom it could be of any use. And until I receive this nourishment, proper for me as for every man, I cannot produce bodily food to feed you with.

What if the working-people should speak thus? And if they said so, it would be no jest, but the simplest justice. If a working-man said this, he would be far more in the right than a man of intellectual labor; because the labor produced by the working-man is more urgent and more necessary than that done by the producer of intellectual work, and because a man of intellect is hindered by nothing from giving that spiritual food which he promised to give, but the working-man is hindered in giving the bodily food by the fact that he himself is short of it.

What, then, should we, men of intellectual labor, answer, if such simple and lawful claims were made upon us? How should we satisfy these claims? Should we satisfy the religious wants of the people by the catechism of Philaret, by sacred histories of Sokolof, by the literature sent out by various monasteries and St. Isaak's cathedral? And should we satisfy their demand for order by the Code of Laws, and cassation verdicts of different departments, or by statutes of committees and commissions? And should we satisfy their want of knowledge by giving them spectrum analysis, a survey of the Milky Way, speculative geometry, microscopic investigations, controversies concerning spiritualism and mediumism, the activity of academies of science? How should we satisfy their artistic wants? By Pushkin, Dostoyevsky, Turgenief, L. Tolstoï, by pictures of French *salons*, and of those of our artists who represent naked women, satin, velvet, and landscapes, and pictures of domestic life, by the music of Wagner, and that of our own musicians?

All this is of no use, and cannot be of any use, because we, with our right to utilize the labor of the people, and absence of all duties in our preparation of their spiritual food, have quite lost from sight the single destination our activity should have.

We do not even know what is required by the working-man; we have even forgotten his mode of life, his views of things, his language; we have even lost sight of the very working-people themselves, and we study them like some ethnographical rarity or newly discovered continent. Now, we, demanding for ourselves bodily food, have taken upon ourselves to provide the spiritual; but in consequence of the imaginary division of labor, according to which we may not only first take our dinner, and afterward do our work, but may during many generations dine luxuriously, and do no work, — in the way of compensation for our food we have prepared something which is of use, as it seems to us, for ourselves and for science and art, but of no use whatever for those very people whose labor we consume under the pretext of providing them in return with intellectual food, and not only of no use, but quite unintelligible and distasteful to them.

In our blindness we have to such a degree left out of sight the duty which we took upon us, that we have even forgotten for what our labor is being done; and the very people whom we undertook to serve, we have made an object of our scientific and artistic activities. We study them and represent them for our own pleasure and amusement: we have quite forgotten that it is our duty, not to study and depict, but to serve them.

We have to such a degree left out of sight the duty which we assumed, that we have not even noticed that other people do what we undertook in the departments of science and art, and that our place turns out to be occupied.

It appears that, while we have been in controversy, now about the immaculate conception, and now about spontaneous generation of organisms; now about spiritualism, and now about the forms of atoms; now about pangenesis, now about protoplasms, and so on, — the rest of the world none the less required intellectual food, and the abortive outcasts of science and art began to provide for the people this spiritual food by order of various speculators who had in view exclusively their own profit and gain.

Now, for some forty years in Europe, and ten years in Russia, millions of books and pictures and songs have been circulating; shows have been opened; and the people look and sing, and receive intellectual food, though not from those who promised to provide it for them; and we, who justify our idleness by the need for that intellectual food which we pretend to provide for the people, are sitting still, and taking no notice.

But we cannot do so, because our final justification has vanished from under our feet. We have taken upon ourselves a peculiar department: we have a peculiar functional activity of our own. We are the brain of the people. They feed us, and we have undertaken to teach them. Only for the sake of this have we freed ourselves from labor. What, then, have we been teaching them? They have waited years, tens of years, hundreds of years. And we are still conversing among ourselves, and teaching each other, and amusing ourselves, and have quite forgotten them; we have so totally forgotten them, that others have taken upon themselves to teach and amuse them, and we have not even become aware of this in our flippant talk about division of labor: and it is very obvious that all our talk about the utility we offer to the people was only a shameful excuse.

CHAPTER XXXIII

THERE was a time when the Church guided the intellectual life of the men of our world. The Church promised men happiness, and, in compensation for this, she freed herself from taking part in mankind's common struggle for life.

And, as soon as she did so, she went astray from her calling, and men turned away from her. It was not the errors of the Church which caused her ruin, but the fact that her ministers had violated the law of labor with the help of the secular power in the time of Constantine, and their claim to idleness and luxury gave birth to her errors.

As soon as she obtained this right, she began to care for herself, and not for man, whom she had taken upon herself to serve. The ministers of the Church gave themselves up to idleness and depravity.

The state took upon itself to guide men's lives. The state promised men justice, peace, security, order, satisfaction for common intellectual and material wants, and in compensation men who served the state freed themselves from taking part in the struggle for life. And the state's servants, as soon as they were enabled to utilize other men's labor, have acted in the same way as the ministers of the Church.

They had not in view the people; but the state servants, from kings down to the lowest functionaries, in Rome, as well as in France, England, Russia, and America, gave themselves over to idleness and depravity.

And men lost their faith in the state, and now anarchy is seriously advocated as an ideal.

The state lost its prestige among men, only because its ministers claimed the right of utilizing for themselves the people's labor.

Science and art have done the same with the assistance of the state power which they took upon themselves to sustain. They have also claimed and obtained for themselves the right of idleness, and of utilizing other men's labor, and have also been false to their calling. And their errors also proceeded only from the fact that their ministers, pointing to a falsely conceived principle of the division of labor, claimed for themselves the right to utilize the work of the people, and so lost the meaning of their calling, making the aim of their activity, not the utility of the people, but a mysterious activity of science and art; and also, like their forerunners, they have given themselves over to idleness and depravity, though not so much to a fleshly, as to an intellectual, corruption.

It is said science and art have done much for mankind.

This is quite true.

Science and art also have done much for mankind, not because, but in spite of, the fact that men of science and art, under the pretext of division of labor, live upon the shoulders of the working-people.

The Roman Republic was powerful, not because its citizens were able to lead a life of depravity, but because it could number amongst them men who were virtuous.

The same is the case with science and art.

Science and art have effected much for mankind, not because their ministers had sometimes formerly, and have always at present, the possibility of freeing themselves from laboring, but because men of genius, not utilizing these rights, have forwarded the progress of mankind.

The class of learned men and artists who claim, on account of a false division of labor, the right of utilizing other men's labor, cannot contribute to the progress of true science and true art, because a lie can never produce a truth.

We are so accustomed to our pampered or debilitated representatives of intellectual labor, that it would seem very strange if a learned man or an artist were to plow or cart manure. We think that, were he to do so, all would go to ruin; that all his wisdom would be shaken out of him, and the great artistic images he carries in his breast would be soiled by the manure: but we are so accustomed to our present conditions that we do not wonder at our ministers of science, that is, ministers and teachers of truth, compelling other people to do for them that which they could very well do themselves, passing half their time eating, smoking, chattering in "liberal" gossip, reading newspapers, novels, visiting theaters; we are not surprised to see our philosopher in an inn, in a theater, at a ball; we do not wonder when we learn that those artists who delight and ennoble our souls, pass their lives in drunkenness, in playing cards, in company with loose women, or do things still worse.

Science and art are fine things: but, just because they are fine things, men ought not to spoil them by associating them with depravity; by freeing themselves from man's duty to serve by labor, his own life and the lives of other men.

Science and art have forwarded the progress of mankind. Yes; but this was not done by the fact that men of science and art, under the pretext of a division of labor, taught men by word, and chiefly by deed, to utilize by violence the misery and sufferings of the people, in order to free themselves from the very first and unquestionable human duty of laboring with their hands in the common struggle of mankind with nature.

CHAPTER XXXIV

"BUT it is," you say, "this very division of labor, the freeing men of science and of art from the necessity of earning their bread, that has rendered possible that extraordinary success in science which we see in our days.

"If everybody were to plow, these enormous results would not be attained; there would not be those astonishing successes which have so enlarged man's power over nature; there would not be those discoveries in astronomy which so strike the minds of men and promote navigation; there would be no steamers, railways, wonderful bridges, tunnels, steam-engines, and telegraphs, photographs, telephones, sewing-machines, phonographs, electricity, telescopes, spectroscopes, micronscopes, chloroform, Lister bandages, carbolic acid."

I will not attempt to enumerate all the things of which our century is so proud. This enumeration, and the ecstasy of contemplation of ourselves and of our great deeds, you may find in almost every newspaper and popular book.

These raptures of self-contemplation are so often repeated, and we are so seldom tired of praising ourselves, that we really come to believe, with Jules Verne, that science and art have never made such progress as in our time. And all this is rendered possible only by division of labor: how can we, then, avoid countenancing it?

Let us suppose that the progress of our century is indeed striking, astonishing, extraordinary; let us suppose that we, too, are particularly lucky in living at such an extraordinary time: but let us try to ascertain the value of these successes, not by our own self-contentment, but by the very principle of the division of labor; that is, by that intellectual labor of men of science for the advantage of the people which has to compensate for the freeing men of science and art from labor.

All this progress is very striking indeed; but owing to some unlucky chance, recognized, too, by men of science, this progress has not as yet ameliorated, but it has rather deteriorated, the condition of working-men.

Though a working-man, instead of walking, can use the railway, it is this very railway which has caused his forest to be burned, and has carried away his bread from under his very nose, and put him into a condition which is next door to slavery to the railway proprietor.

If, thanks to the engines and steam-machines, a working-man can buy cheap, and poor calico, it will be these very engines and machines which have deprived him of his wages, and brought him to a state of entire slavery to the manufacturer.

If there are telegraphs, which he is not forbidden to use, but which he does not use because he cannot afford it, then each of his productions, the value of which fluctuates, is bought up from under his very eyes by capitalists at low prices, thanks to the telegraph, before the working-man even becomes aware that the article is in demand.

Though there are telephones and telescopes, novels, operas, picture-galleries, and so on, the life of the working-man is not at all improved by any of them, because all, owing to the same unlucky chance, are beyond his reach. So that, after all, these wonderful discoveries and productions of art, if they have not made the life of working-people worse, have by no means improved it: on this the men of science are agreed.

So that, if to the question as to the reality of the successes attained by the sciences and arts, we apply, not our rapture of self-contemplation, but the very standard on which the ground of the division of labor is defended, — utility to the working world, — we shall see that we have not yet any sound reason for the self-contentment to which we consign ourselves so willingly.

A peasant uses the railway; a peasant's wife buys calico; in the cottage a lamp, and not a pine-knot, burns; and the peasant lights his pipe with a match, — this is comfortable; but what right have I from this to say that railways and factories have done good to the people?

If a peasant uses the railway, and buys a lamp, calico, and matches, he does it only because we cannot forbid his doing so: we all know very well that railways and factories have never been built for the use of the people; why, then, should the casual comfort a working-man obtains by chance be brought forward as a proof of the usefulness of these institutions to the people?

We all know very well that if those engineers and capitalists who build a railway or a factory have been thinking about working-people, they have been thinking only how to make the best possible use of them. And we see they have fully succeeded in doing so as well in Russia as in Europe and America.

In every hurtful thing there is something useful. After a house has been burned down, we may sit and warm ourselves, and light our pipes with one of the firebrands; but should we therefore say that a conflagration is beneficial?

Whatever we do, let us not deceive ourselves. We all know very well the motives for building railways, and for producing kerosene and matches. An engineer builds a railway for the government, to facilitate wars, or for the capitalists for financial purposes. He makes machines for manufacturers for his own advantage, and for the profit of capitalists. All that he makes or excogitates he does for the purpose of the government, the capitalists, and other rich people. His most skilful inventions are either directly harmful to the people, as guns, torpedoes, solitary prisons, and so on; or they are not only useless, but quite inaccessible to them, as electric light, telephones, and the innumerable improvements of comfort; or, lastly, they deprave the people, and rob them of their last kopek, that is, their last labor, for spirits, wine, beer, opium, tobacco, calicoes, and all sorts of trifles.

But if it happens sometimes that the inventions of men of science, and the works of engineers, are of any use to the people, as, for instance, railways, calicoes, steel, scythes, it only proves that, in this world of ours, all things are mutually connected together, and that, out of every hurtful activity, there may arise an accidental good for those to whom this activity was hurtful.

Men of science and of art can say that their activity is useful for the people, only if they have aimed in their activity at serving the people, as they do now to serve governments and capitalists.

We could have said that, only if men of science and art made the wants of the people their object; but such is not the case.

All learned men are occupied with their sacred business, which leads to the investigation of protoplasms, the spectrum analysis of stars, and so on: but concerning investigations as to how to set an ax, or with what kind it is more advantageous to hew; which saw is the most handy; with what flour bread shall be made, how it may best be kneaded, how to set it to rise; how to heat and to build stoves; what food, drink, crockery-ware, it is best to use; what mushrooms may be eaten, and how they may be prepared more conveniently,—science has never troubled itself.

And yet all this is the business of science.

I know that, according to its own definition, science must be useless; but this is only an excuse, and a very impudent one.

The business of science is to serve people. We have invented telegraphs, telephones, phonographs, but what improvements have we made in the life of the people? We have catalogued two millions of insects! but have we domesticated a single animal since biblical times, when all our animals had long been domesticated, and still the elk and the deer, and the partridge and the grouse and the wood-hen, are wild?

Botanists have discovered the cells, and in the cells protoplasms, and in protoplasms something else, and in this something else again.

These occupations will evidently never end, and therefore learned men have no time to do anything useful. And hence from the times of the ancient Egyptians and Hebrews, when wheat and lentils were already cultivated, down to the present time, not a single plant has been added for the nourishment of the people except potatoes, and these have not been discovered by science. We have invented torpedoes, house-drains; but the spinning-wheel, weaving-looms, plows and ax-handles, flails and rakes, buckets and well-sweeps, are still the same as in the time of Rurik.

And if some things have been improved, it is not the learned who have done it.

The same is the case with art. We have praised up many great writers, have carefully sifted these writers, and have written mountains of critiques and criticisms upon critics; we have collected pictures in galleries, and we have thoroughly studied all the schools of art; and we have such symphonies and operas that we ourselves are tired of listening to; but what have we added to the folk-lore, legends, tales, songs? what pictures, what music, have we created for the people?

Books and pictures are published, and harmoniums are made, for the people, but we do not care for either.

That which is most striking and obvious is the false tendency of our science and art, which manifests itself in those departments which, according to their own propositions, would seem to be useful to people, and which, owing to this tendency, appear rather pernicious than useful. An engineer, a surgeon, a teacher, an artist, an author, seem by their very professions to be obliged to serve the people, but what do we see?

With the present tendency, they can bring to the people nothing but harm. An engineer and a mechanic must work with capital: without capital they are good for nothing.

All their informations are such that, in order to make use of them, they need capital and the employment of working-people on a large scale, to say nothing of the fact that they themselves are accustomed to spend from fifteen hundred to two thousand rubles a year, and therefore they cannot go to a village, since no one there can give them any such remuneration: they, from their very occupations, are not fit for the service of the people.

They understand how to calculate by means of the highest mathematics the arch of a bridge, how to calculate power and the transfer of power in an engine, and so on: but they will be at a loss to meet the plain requirements of popular labor; they do not know how to improve the plow or the cart; how to make a brook passable, taking into consideration the conditions of a working-man's life.

They know and understand nothing of all this, less even than does the poorest peasant. Give them workshops, plenty of people, order engines from abroad, then they will arrange these matters. But to find out how to ease the labor of millions of people in their present condition, they do not know, and cannot do it; and accordingly, by their knowledge and habits and wants, they are not at all fit for this business. A surgeon is in a still worse condition. His imaginary science is such that he understands how to cure those only who have nothing to do, and who may utilize other men's labor. He requires a countless number of expensive accessories, instruments, medicines, sanitary dwellings, food, and drains, in order that he may act scientifically: besides his fee, he demands such expenses that, in order to cure one patient, he must kill with starvation hundreds of those who bear this expense.

He has studied under eminent persons in the capital cities, who attend only to such patients whom they may take into hospitals, or who can afford to buy all the necessary medicines and machines, and even go at once from north to the south, to these or those mineral waters, as the case may be.

Their science is such that every country surgeon complains that there is no possibility of attending to the working-people, who are so poor that they cannot afford sanitary accommodations, and that there are no hospitals, and that he cannot attend to the business alone, that he requires help and assistant-surgeons. What does this really mean?

It means this, — that the want of the necessaries of life is the chief cause of people's misfortunes, and as well the source of diseases as also of their spreading and incurability. And now science, under the banners of the division of labor, calls its champions to help the people. Science has settled satisfactorily about rich classes, and seeks how to cure those who can get everything necessary for the purpose, and it sends persons to cure in the same way those who have nothing to spare. But there are no means; and therefore they are to be raised from the people, who become ill, and catch diseases, and cannot be cured for want of means.

The advocates of the healing art for the people say that, up to the present time, this business has not been sufficiently developed.

Evidently it is not yet developed, because if, which God forbid! it were developed among our people, and, instead of two doctors and midwives and two assistant-surgeons in the district, there should be twenty sent, as they want, then there would soon be no one left to attend to. The scientific coöperation for the people must be quite a different one. And such coöperation, which ought to be, has not yet begun.

It will begin when a man of science, an engineer or a surgeon, will cease to consider as lawful that division of labor, or rather that taking away other men's labor, which now exists, and when he no longer considers that he has the right to take, I do not say hundreds of thousands, but even a moderate sum of one thousand or five hundred rubles as a compensation for his services; but when such a man comes to live among laboring people in the same condition and in the same way as they, then he will apply his information in mechanics, technics, hygiene, to the curing of working-people.

But now scientific men, who are fed at the expense of the working-man, have quite forgotten the conditions of the life of these men: they ignore (as they say) these conditions, and are quite seriously offended that their imaginary knowledge does not find application among the people.

The departments, as well of the healing art as the

mechanical, have not yet been touched: the questions how best to divide the time of labor, how and upon what it is best to feed, how best to dress, how to counteract dampness and cold, how best to wash, to suckle, and swaddle children, and so on, and all these applied to those conditions in which the working-people are, — all these questions have not yet been put.

The same applies to the activity of scientific teachers, — pedagogues. Science has arranged this business, too, in such a way that teaching according to science is possible only for those who are rich; and the teachers, like the engineers and surgeons, are involuntarily drawn toward money, and among us in Russia especially toward the government.

And this cannot be otherwise, because a school properly arranged (and the general rule is that the more scientifically a school is arranged, the more expensive it is), with convertible benches, globes, maps, libraries, and method-manuals for teachers and pupils, is just such a school for whose maintenance it is necessary to double the taxes of the people. So science wants to have it. The children are necessary for work, and the more so with the poorer people. The advocates of science say, Pedagogy is even now of use for the people; but let it be developed, and instead of twenty schools in a district, let there be a hundred, all of them scientifically arranged, and the people will support these schools. But then they will be still poorer, and will want the labor of their children still more urgently.

What is then to be done?

To this they reply, The government will establish schools, and will make education obligatory as it is in the rest of Europe. But the money will still have to be raised from the people, and labor will be still harder for them, and they will have less time to spare from their labor, and there will be then no obligatory education at all.

There is, again, only one escape, — for a teacher to live in the conditions of a working-man, and to teach for that compensation which will be freely offered him.

Such is the false tendency of science which deprives it of the possibility to fulfil its duty in serving the people. But this false tendency of our educated class is still more obvious in art-activity, which, for the sake of its very meaning, ought to be accessible to the people.

Science may point to its stupid excuse that science is acting for science, and that, when it will be fully developed, it will become accessible to the people; but art, if it is art indeed, ought to be accessible to all, especially to those for the sake of whom it is created. And our art strikingly denounces its factors in that they do not wish, and do not understand, and are not able to be of use to the people. A painter, in order to produce his great works, must have a large studio, in which at least forty joiners or bootmakers might work, who are now freezing or suffocating in wretched lodgings. But this is not all: he requires models, costumes, journeys from place to place. The Academy of Art has spent millions of rubles collected from the people for the encouragement of art; and the productions of this art are hung in palaces, and are neither intelligible to the people, nor wanted by them.

Musicians, in order to express their great ideas, must gather about two hundred men with white neckties or in costumes and spend hundreds of thousands of rubles to arrange operas. But this art-production would never appear to the people (even if they could afford to use it) as anything but perplexing or dull. The authors, writers, seem not to want any particular accommodations, studios, models, orchestras, and actors; but here also it turns out that an author, a writer, to say nothing of all the comforts of his dwelling and all the comforts of his life, in order to prepare his great works, wants traveling, palaces, cabinets, enjoyments of art, theaters, concerts, mineral waters, and so on. If he himself has not saved up enough money for this purpose, he is given a pension in order that he may compose better. And, again, these writings, which we value so highly, remain, for the people, rubbish, and are not at all necessary to them.

What if, according to the wish of men of science and

art, such producers of mental food should multiply, so that, in every village, it would be necessary to build a studio, provide an orchestra, and keep an author in the conditions which men of art consider indispensable to them? I dare say working-people would make a vow never to look at a picture, or listen to a symphony, or read poetry and novels, in order only not to be compelled to feed all these good-for-nothing parasites.

And why should not men of art serve the people? In every cottage there are holy images and pictures; each peasant, each woman of the people, sings; many have instruments of music; and all can relate stories, repeat poetry; and many of them read. How came it to pass that these two things were separated which were as much made for one another as a key for a lock, and how are they so separated that we cannot imagine how to reunite them?

Tell a painter to paint without a studio, models, costumes, and to draw penny pictures, he will say that this would be a denying of art as he understands it. Tell a musician to play on a harmonium, and to teach country-women to sing songs; tell a poet to throw aside writing poems and novels and satires, and to compose song-books for the people, and stories and tales which might be intelligible to ignorant persons, — they will say you are cracked.

But is it not being worse than cracked when men who have freed themselves from labor because they promised to provide mental food for those who have brought them up and are feeding and clothing them, afterward have so forgotten their promise that they have ceased to understand how to make food fit for the people? Yet this very forsaking of their promises they consider dignifies them. Such is the case everywhere, they say. Everywhere the case is very unreasonable, then; and it will be so while men, under the pretext of division of labor, promise to provide mental food for the people, but only swallow up the labor of the people. Men will serve the people with science and art, only when, living among and in the same way as do the people, putting forth no claims whatever, they offer to the people their scientific and artistic services, leaving it to the free will of the people to accept or refuse them.

CHAPTER XXXV

To say that the activities of the arts and sciences have coöperated in forwarding the progress of mankind, and by these activities to mean that which is now called by this name, is the same as to say that an awkward moving of the oars, hindering the progress of a boat going down the stream, is forwarding the progress of the boat; but it only hinders it. The so-called division of labor — that is, the violation of other men's labor which has become in our time a condition of the activity of men of art and science — has been, and still remains, the chief cause of the slowness of the progress of mankind.

The proof of it we have in the acknowledgment of all men of science and art that the acquisitions of art and science are not accessible to the working-classes because of a wrong distribution of wealth. And the incorrectness of this distribution does not diminish in proportion to the progress of art and science, but rather increases. And it is not astonishing that such is the case; because the incorrect distribution of wealth proceeds solely from the theory of the division of labor, preached by men of art and science for selfish purposes.

Science, defending the division of labor as an unchangeable law, sees that the distribution of wealth based upon the division of labor is incorrect and pernicious, and asserts that its activity, which recognizes the division of labor, will set all right again, and lead men to happiness.

It appears, then, that some men utilize the labor of others; but if they will only continue to do this for a long time, and on a still larger scale, then this incorrect distribution of wealth, that is, utilizing of other men's labor, will vanish.

Men are standing by an ever increasing spring of water, and are busy turning it aside from thirsty men, and then they assert that it is they who produce this water, and that soon there will be so much of it that everybody will have enough and to spare. And this water, which has been running unceasingly, and nourishing all mankind, is not only not the result of the activity of those men who, standing at the source of it, turn it aside, but this water runs and spreads itself in spite of the endeavors of those men to stop it from doing so.

There has always existed a true church, — in other words, men united by the highest truth accessible to them at a certain epoch, — but it has never been that church which gave herself out for such; and there have always been real art and science, but it was not that which calls itself now by these names.

Men who consider themselves to be the representatives of art and science in a given period of time, always imagine that they have been doing, and will continue to do, wonderful things, and that beyond them there has never been any art or science. Thus it seemed to the sophists, to the scholiasts, alchemists, cabalists, Talmudists, and to our own scientific science and to our artistic art.

CHAPTER XXXVI

"But science! art! You repudiate science, art; that is, you repudiate that by which mankind live."

I am always hearing this: people choose this way to put aside my arguments altogether without analyzing them. He repudiates science and art; he wishes to turn men back again to the savage state; why, then, should we listen to him, or argue with him?

But it is unjust. I not only do not repudiate science — human reasonable activity — and art, — the expression of this reasonable activity, — but it is only in the name of this reasonable activity, and its expression, that I say what I do, in order that mankind may avoid the savage state toward which they are rapidly moving, owing to the false teaching of our time.

Science and art are as necessary to men as food, drink, and clothes, — even still more necessary than these; but they become such, not because we decide that what we call science and art are necessary, but because they indeed are necessary to men. Now, if I should prepare hay for the bodily food of men, my idea that hay is the food for men would not make it to be so. I cannot say, Why do you not eat hay when it is your necessary food? Food is, indeed, necessary, but perhaps what I offer is not food at all.

This very thing has happened with our science and art. And to us it seems that when we add to a Greek word the termination *logy*, and call this science, it will be science indeed; and if we call an indecency, like the dancing of naked women, by the Greek word "chorography," and term it art, it will be art indeed.

But however much we may say this, the business which we are about, in counting up the insects, and chemically analyzing the contents of the Milky Way, in painting water-nymphs and historical pictures, in writing novels, and in composing symphonies, this, our business, will not become science or art until it is willingly accepted by those for whom it is being done.

And till now it has not been accepted. If only some men were allowed to prepare food, and all others were either forbidden to do it, or be rendered incapable of producing it, I dare say that the quality of the food would deteriorate. If these men who have the exclusive privilege of producing food were Russian peasants, then there would be no other food than black bread, kvas, potatoes, and flour, which they are fond of, and which is agreeable to them. The same would be the case with that highest human activity in art and science if their exclusive privilege were appropriated by one caste, with this difference only, that in bodily food there cannot be too great digressions from the natural; bread as well as onions, though unsavory food, is still eatable: but in mental food, there may be great digressions; and some men may for a long time feed upon an unnecessary, or even hurtful and poisonous, mental food; they themselves may slowly kill themselves with opium or with spirits, and this sort of food they may offer to the masses of the people.

This very thing has happened with us. And it has happened because men of art and science are in privileged conditions; because art and science in our world are not that mental activity of all mankind, without any exception, who separate their best powers for the service of art and science: but it is the activity of a small company of men having the monopoly of these occupations, and calling themselves men of art and science; and therefore they have perverted the very conceptions of art and science, and lost the sense of their own calling, and are merely occupied in amusing, and saving from burdensome dulness, a small company of parasites.

Since men have existed they have always had science, in the plainest and largest sense of the word. Science, as the sum of all human information, has always been in existence; and without it life is not conceivable, and there is no necessity whatever either to attack or defend it.

But the fact is this, that the region of this knowledge is so various, so much information of all kinds enters into it, from the information how to obtain iron up to the knowledge about the movements of the celestial bodies, that man would be lost among all this varied information if he had no clue which could help him to decide which of all these kinds of information is more, and which less, important.

And, therefore, the highest wisdom of men has always consisted in finding out the clue according to which must be arranged the information of men, and by which decided what kinds of information are more, and what are less, important. And this, which has directed all other knowledge, men have always called science in the strictest sense of the word. And such science has always been, up to the present time, in human societies which have left the savage state behind them. Since mankind has existed, in every nation teachers have appeared to form science in this strict sense, — the science about what it is most necessary for men to know. This science has always had for its object the inquiry as to what was the destiny, and therefore the true welfare, of each man and of all men. This science has served as a clue in determining the importance and the expression of all other sciences. The kinds of information and the art which coöperated with the science of man's destiny and welfare were considered highest in public opinion.

Such was the science of Confucius, Buddha, Moses, Socrates, Christ, Mohammed, — science such as it has been understood by all men except by our own circle of so-called educated people.

Such a science has not only always occupied the first place, but it is the one science which has determined the importance of other sciences. And this, not at all because so-called learned men of our time imagine that it is only deceitful priests and teachers of this science who have given it such an importance, but because, indeed, as every one can learn by his own inward experience, without the science of man's destiny and welfare there cannot be any determining of other values, or any choice of art and science for man. And, therefore, there cannot be any study of science, for there are *innumerable* quantities of subjects to which science may be applied. I italicize the word innumerable, as I use it in its exact value.

Without knowledge as to what constitutes the calling and welfare of all men, all other arts and sciences become, as is really the case at present with us, only an idle and pernicious amusement. Mankind have been living long, and they have never been living without a science relative to the calling and welfare of men: it is true that the science of the welfare of men to a superficial observation appears to be different with Buddhists, Brahmins, Hebrews, Christians, with the followers of Confucius and those of Laotse, though one need only reflect on these teachings in order to see their essential unity; where men have left the savage state behind them, we find this science; and now of a sudden it turns out that modern men have decided that this very science which has been till now the guide of all human information, is that which is in the way of everything.

Men build houses: one architect makes one estimate, another makes a second, and so on. The estimates are a little different, but they are separately correct; and every one sees that, if each estimate is fulfilled, the house will be erected. Such architects are Confucius, Buddha, Moses, Christ. And now some men come and assure us that the chief thing to come by is the absence of any estimate, and that men ought to build anyhow, according to eyesight. And this "anyhow" these men call the most exact science, as the Pope terms himself the "most holy."

Men deny every science, the most essential science of man's calling and welfare; and this denial of science they call science. Since men have existed, great intellects have always appeared, which, in the struggle with the demands of their reason and conscience, have put to themselves questions concerning the calling and welfare, not only of themselves individually, but of every man. What does that Power which created me require from me and from each man? And what am I to do in order to satisfy the craving ingrafted in me for a personal and common welfare?

They have asked themselves, I am a whole and a part of something unfathomable, infinite: what are to be my relations to other parts similar to me, — to men and to the whole?

And from the voice of conscience and from reason, and from considerations on what men have said who lived before, and from contemporaries who have asked themselves the same questions, these great teachers have deduced teachings, — plain, clear, intelligible to all men, and always such as could be put into practice.

The world is full of such men. All living men put to themselves the question, How am I to reconcile my own demands for personal life with conscience and reason, which demand the common good of all men? And out of this common travail are evolved slowly, but unceasingly, new forms of life, satisfying more and more the demands of reason and conscience.

And of a sudden a new caste of men appears, who say, All these are nonsense, and are to be left behind. This is the deductive way of thinking (though wherein lies the difference between the inductive and the deductive way of thinking, nobody ever has been able to understand), and this is also the method of the theological and metaphysical periods.

All that men have understood by inward experience, and have related to each other concerning the consciousness of the law of their own life (functional activity, in their cant phrase); all that from the beginning of the world has been done in this direction by the greatest intellects of mankind, — all these are trifles, having no weight whatever.

According to this new teaching, You are a cell of an organism, and the problem of your reasonable activity consists in trying to ascertain your functional activity. In order to ascertain this, you must make observations outside yourself.

The fact that you are a cell which thinks, suffers, speaks, and understands, and that for that very reason you can inquire of another similar speaking, suffering cell whether he or she suffers and rejoices in the same way as yourself, and that thus you may verify your own experience; and the fact that you may make use of what the speaking cells, who lived and suffered before you, wrote on the subject; and your knowledge that millions of cells, agreeing with what the past cells have written, confirm your own experience, that you yourself are a living cell, who always, by a direct inward experience, apprehend the correctness or incorrectness of your own functional activity, — all this means nothing, we are told: it is all a false and evil method.

The true scientific method is this: If you wish to learn in what consists your functional activity, what is your destiny and welfare, and what the destiny of mankind, and of the whole world, then first you must cease to listen to the voice and demands of your conscience and of your reason, which manifest themselves inwardly to you and to your fellow-men; you must leave off believing all the great teachers of humanity have said about their own conscience and reason, and you must consider all this to be nonsense, and begin at the beginning.

And in order to begin from the beginning, you have to observe through a microscope the movements of amœbæ and the cells of tapeworms; or, still easier, you must believe everything that people with the diploma of infallibility may tell you about them. And observing the movements of these amœbæ and cells, or reading what others have seen, you must ascribe to these cells your own human feelings and calculations as to what they desire, what are their tendencies, their reflections and calculations, their habits; and from these *observations* (in which each word contains some mistake of thought or of expression), according to analogy, you must deduce what is your own destiny, and what that of other cells similar to you.

In order to be able to understand yourself, you must study not merely the tapeworm which you see, but also microscopic animalcules which you cannot see, and the transformation from one set of beings into another, which neither you nor anybody else has ever seen, and which you certainly will never see.

The same holds good with art. Wherever a true science has existed, it has been expressed by art. Since men have existed they have always separated out of all their activities, from their varied information, the chief expression of science, the knowledge of man's destination and welfare; and art, in the strict sense of the word, has been the expression of this.

Since men have existed, there have always been persons particularly sensitive to the teaching of man's welfare and destiny, who have expressed in word, and upon psaltery and cymbals, their human struggle with deceit which led them aside from their true destiny, and their sufferings in this struggle, their hopes about the victory of good, their despair about the triumph of evil, and their raptures in expectation of coming welfare.

Since men have existed, the true art, that which has been valued by men most highly, had no other destiny than to be the expression of science on man's destiny and welfare.

Always down to the present time art has served the teaching of life (afterward called religion), and it has only been this art which men have valued so highly.

But contemporaneously with the fact that in the place of the science of man's destiny and welfare appeared the science of universal knowledge, since science lost its own sense and meaning, and the true science has been scornfully called religion, true art, as an important activity of men, has disappeared.

As long as the church existed, and taught man's calling and welfare, art served the church, and was true; but from the moment it left the church, and began to serve a science which served everything it met, art lost its meaning, and, notwithstanding its old-fashioned claims, and a stupid assertion that art serves merely art itself, and nothing else, it turned out to be a trade which procures luxuries for men, and unavoidably mixes itself with chorography, culinary art, hair-dressing, and cosmetics, the producers of which may call themselves artists with the same right as the poets, painters, and musicians of our day.

Looking back, we see that during thousands of years, from among thousands of millions of men who have lived, there came forth a few like Confucius, Buddha, Solon, Socrates, Solomon, Homer, Isaiah, David. Apparently true artist-producers of spiritual food appear seldom among men, notwithstanding the fact that they appear, not from one caste only, but from among all men; and it is not without cause that mankind have always so highly valued them. And now it turns out that we have no longer any need of all these former great factors of art and science.

Now, according to the law of the division of labor, it is possible to manufacture scientific and artistic factors almost mechanically; and we shall manufacture, in the space of ten years, more great men of art and science than have been born among all men from the beginning of the world. Nowadays there is a trade corporation of learned men and artists, and they prepare by an improved way all the mental food which is wanted by mankind. And they have prepared so much of it, that there need no longer be any remembrance of the old producers, not only of the very ancient, but of more recent ones, — all this, we are told, was the activity of the theological and metaphysical period: all had to be destroyed, and the true mental activity began some fifty years ago.

And in these fifty years we have manufactured so many great men that in a German university there are more of them than have been in the whole world, and of sciences we have manufactured a great number too; for one need only put to a Greek word the termination *logy*, and arrange the subject according to ready-made paragraphs, and the science is made: we have thus manufactured so many sciences that not only one man cannot know them all, but he cannot even remember all their names, — these names alone would fill a large dictionary; and every day new sciences come into existence.

In this respect we are like that Finnish teacher who taught the children of a landowner the Finnish language instead of the French. He taught very well; but there was one drawback, — that nobody, except himself, understood it.

But of this there is also an explanation: Men do not understand all the utility of the scientific science because they are still under the influence of the theological period of knowledge, that stupid period when all the people of the Hebrew race, as well as the Chinese and Indians and Greeks, understood everything spoken to them by their great teachers.

But whatever may be the cause, the fact is this, — that art and science have always existed among mankind; and when they really existed, then they were necessary and intelligible to all men.

We are busy about something which we call art and science, and it turns out that what we are busy about is neither necessary nor intelligible to men. And therefore, however fine the things we are about may be, we have no right to call them art and science.

CHAPTER XXXVII

But it is said to me, "You only give another narrower definition of art and science, which science does not agree with; but even this does not exclude them, and notwithstanding all you say, there still remain the scientific and art activities of men like Galileo, Bruno, Homer, Michael Angelo, Beethoven, Wagner, and other learned men and artists of lesser magnitude, who have devoted all their lives to art and science."

Usually this is said in the endeavor to establish a link connecting the activity of former learned men and artists with the modern ones, trying to forget that new principle of the division of labor by reason of which art and science are occupying now a privileged position.

First of all, it is not possible to establish any such connection between the former factors and the modern ones, as the holy life of the first Christian has nothing in common with the lives of popes: thus, the activity of men like Galileo, Shakespeare, Beethoven, has nothing in common with the activities of men like Tyndall, Hugo, and Wagner. As the Holy Fathers would have denied any connection with the Popes, so the ancient factors of science would have denied any relationship with the modern ones.

And secondly, owing to that importance which art and science ascribe to themselves, we have a very clear standard established by them by means of which we are able to determine whether they do or do not fulfil their destiny; and we therefore decide, not without proofs, but according to their own standard, whether that activity which calls itself art and science has, or has not, any right to call itself thus.

Though the Egyptians or Greek priests performed mysteries known to none but themselves, and said that these mysteries included all art and science, I could not, on the ground of the asserted utility of these to the people, ascertain the reality of their science, because this said science, according to their *ipse dixit*, was a supernatural one; but now we all have a very clear and plain standard, excluding everything supernatural; art and science promise to put forth the mental activity of mankind for the welfare of society or even of the whole of mankind. And therefore we have a right to call only such activity art and science which has this aim in view, and attains it. And therefore, however those learned men and artists may call themselves, who excogitate the theory of penal laws, of state laws, and of the laws of nations, who invent new guns and explosive substances, who compose obscene operas and operettas, or similarly obscene novels, we have no right to call such activity the activity of art and science, because this activity has not in view the welfare of society or of mankind, but on the contrary it is directed to the harm of men. Therefore none of these efforts are either art or science.

In like manner, however these learned men may call themselves who in their simplicity are occupied during all their lives with the investigations of the microscopical animalcule and of telescopical and spectral phenomena; or those artists who, after having carefully investigated the monuments of old times, are busy writing historical novels, making pictures, concocting symphonies and beautiful verses, — all these men, notwithstanding all their zeal, cannot be, according to the definition of their own science, called men of science and art; first, because their activity in science for the sake of science, and of art for art, has not in view man's welfare; and secondly, because we do not see any results of these activities for the welfare of society or mankind.

And the fact that sometimes something comes of their activities useful or agreeable for some men, as out of everything something useful and agreeable may result for some men, by no means gives us any right, according to their own scientific definition, to consider them to be men of art and science.

In like manner, however those men may call themselves who excogitate the application of electricity to lighting, heating, and motion; or who invent some new chemical combinations, producing dynamite or fine colors; men who correctly play Beethoven's symphonies; who act on the stage or paint portraits well, domestic pictures, landscapes, and other pictures; who compose interesting novels, the object of which is merely to amuse rich people, — the activity of these men, I say, cannot be called art and science, because this activity is not directed, like the activity of the brain in the organism, to the welfare of the whole, but is guided merely by personal gain, privileges, money, which one obtains for the inventing and producing of so-called art; and therefore this activity cannot possibly be separated from other covetous, personal activity, which adds agreeable things to life, like the activity of innkeepers, jockeys, milliners, and prostitutes, and so on, because the activity of the first, the second, and the last do not come under the definition of art and science, on the ground of the division of labor, which promises to serve for the welfare of all mankind.

The scientific definition of art and science is a correct one; but, unluckily, the activity of modern art and science does not come under it. Some produce directly hurtful things, others, useless things; and a third party invent trifles fit only for the use of rich people. They may all be very good persons, but they do not fulfil what they, according to their own definition, have taken upon themselves to fulfil; and therefore they have as little right to call themselves men of art and science as the modern clergy, who do not fulfil their duties, have the right to consider themselves the bearers and teachers of divine truth.

And it is not difficult to understand why the factors of modern art and science have not fulfilled, and cannot fulfil, their calling. They do not fulfil it, because they have converted their duty into a right. The scientific and art activities, in their true sense, are fruitful only when they ignore their rights and know only their duties. Mankind value this activity so highly only because it is a self-denying one.

If men are really called to serve others by *mental* labor, they will have to suffer in performing this labor, because it is only by sufferings that spiritual fruit is produced. Self-denying and suffering are the lot and portion of a thinker and an artist, because their object is the welfare of men. Men are wretched: they suffer and go to ruin. One cannot wait and lose one's time.

A thinker and an artist will never sit on the heights of Olympus, as we are apt to imagine: he must suffer in company with men in order to find salvation or consolation. He will suffer because he is constantly in anxiety and agitation: he might have found out and told what would give happiness to men, might have saved them from suffering; and he has neither found it out nor said it, and to-morrow it may be too late — he may die. And therefore suffering and self-sacrifice will always be the lot of the thinker and the artist.

Not that man will become a thinker and an artist who is brought up in an establishment where learned men and artists are created (but, in reality, they create only destroyers of art and science), and who obtains a diploma, and is well provided for, for life, but he who would gladly abstain from thinking, and expressing that which is ingrafted in his soul, but which he cannot overlook, being drawn to it by two irresistible powers, — his own inward impulse and the wants of men.

Thinkers and artists cannot be sleek, fat men, enjoying themselves, and self-conceited. Spiritual and mental activity, and their expression, are really necessary for others, and are the most difficult of men's callings, — a cross, as it is called in the Gospel.

And the only one certain characteristic of the presence of a calling is the self-denying, the sacrifice of one's self in order to manifest the power ingrafted in man for the benefit of others. To teach how many insects there are in the world, and observe the spots on the sun, to write novels and operas, can be done without suffering; but to teach men their welfare, which entirely consists in self-denial, and in serving others, and to express powerfully this teaching, cannot be done without self-denial.

The Church existed in her purity as long as her teachers endured patiently and suffered; but as soon as they became fat and sleek, their teaching activity was ended. "Formerly," say the people, "priests were of gold, and chalices of wood; now chalices are of gold, and priests of wood." It was not in vain that Christ died on a cross: it is not in vain that sacrifice and suffering conquer everything.

And as for our art and sciences, they are provided for: they have diplomas, and everybody is only thinking about how to provide still better for them; that is, to make it impossible for them to serve men. A true art and a true science have two unmistakable characteristics,—the first, an interior one, that a minister of art or science fulfils his calling, not for the sake of gain, but with self-denial; and the second, an exterior one, that his productions are intelligible to all men, whose welfare he is aiming at.

Whatever men may consider to be their destiny and welfare, science will be the teacher of this destiny and welfare, and art the expression of this teaching. The laws of Solon, of Confucius, are science; the teachings of Moses, of Christ, are science; the temples in Athens, the psalms of David, church worship, are art; but finding out the fourth dimension of matter, and tabulating chemical combinations, and so on, have never been, and never will be, science.

The place of true science is occupied, in our time, by theology and law; the place of true art is occupied by the church and state ceremonies, in which nobody believes, and which are not considered seriously by anybody: and that which with us is called art and science, is only the productions of idle minds and feelings which have in view to stimulate similarly idle minds and feelings, and which are unintelligible and dumb for the people, because they have not their welfare in view.

Since we have known the lives of men, we always and everywhere have found a ruling false doctrine, calling itself science, which does not show men the true meaning of life, but rather hides it from them.

So it was among the Egyptians, the Indians, the Chinese, and partially among the Greeks (sophists); and among the mystics, Gnostics, and cabalists; in the Middle Ages, in theology, scholasticism, alchemy; and so on down to our days. How fortunate indeed are we to be living in such a peculiar time, when that mental activity which calls itself science is not only free from errors, but, as we are assured, is in a state of peculiar progress! Does not this good fortune come from the fact that man cannot and will not see his own deformities? While of the sciences of theologians, and that of cabalists, nothing is left but empty words, why should we be so particularly fortunate?

The characteristics of our and of former times are quite similar: there is the same self-conceit and blind assurance that we only are on the true way, and that only with us true knowledge begins; there are the same expectations that we shall presently discover something very wonderful; and there is the same exposure of our error in the fact that all our wisdom remains with us, while the masses of the people do not understand it, and neither accept nor want it. Our position is a very difficult one, but why should we not look it in the face?

It is time to come to our senses, and to look more closely to ourselves. We are, indeed, nothing but scribes and Pharisees, who, sitting in Moses' seat, and having the key of the kingdom of God, do not enter themselves, and refuse entrance to others.

We, priests of art and science, are most wretched deceivers, who have much less right to our position than the most cunning and depraved priests ever had.

For our privileged position there is no excuse whatever: we have taken up this position by a kind of swindling, and we retain it by deceit. Pagan priests, the clergy, as well

Russian as Roman Catholic, however depraved they may have been, had rights to their position, because they profess to teach men about life and salvation. And we, who have cut the ground from under their feet, and proved to men that they were deceivers, we have taken their place, and not only do not teach men about life, we even acknowledge that there is no necessity for them to learn. We suck the blood of the people, and for this we teach our children Greek and Latin grammars, in order that they also may continue the same parasitic life which we are living.

We say, There have been castes, we will abolish them. But what means the fact that some men and their children work, and other men and their children do not work?

Bring a Hindu who does not know our language, and show him the Russian and the European lives of many generations, and he will recognize the existence of two important definite castes, of working-people and of non-working-people, as they are in existence in his own country. As in his country, so also among us, the right of not working is acquired through a peculiar initiation which we call art and science, and, generally, education.

This education it is, and the perversions of reason associated with it, that have brought us to this wonderful folly, whence it has come to pass that we do not see what is so plain and certain. We are eating up the lives of our brethren, and consider ourselves to be Christians, humane, educated, and quite righteous people.

CHAPTER XXXVIII

WHAT is to be done? What must we do?

This question, which includes the acknowledgment of the fact that our life is bad and unrighteous, and at the same time hints that there is no possibility of changing it, — this question I hear everywhere, and therefore I chose it for the title of my work.

I have described my own sufferings, my search, and the answer which I have found to this question.

I am a man, like all others; and if I distinguish myself from an average man of my own circle in anything, it is chiefly in the fact that I, more than this average man, have served and indulged the false teaching of our world, that I have been praised by the men of the prevalent school of teaching, and that therefore I must be more depraved, and have gone farther astray, than most of my fellows.

Therefore I think that the answer to this question which I have found for myself will do for all sincere persons who will put the same question to themselves. First of all, to the question, "What is to be done?" I answer that we must neither deceive other men nor ourselves; that we must not be afraid of the truth, whatever the result may be.

We all know what it is to deceive other men; and notwithstanding this we do deceive from morning to evening, — "Not at home," when I am in; "Very glad," when I am not at all glad; "Esteemed," when I do not esteem; "I have no money," when I have it, and so on.

We consider the deception of others, particularly a certain kind of deception, to be evil; but we are not afraid to deceive ourselves: but the worst direct lie to men, seeing its result, is nothing in comparison with that lie to ourselves according to which we shape our lives. Now, this very lie we must avoid if we wish to be able to answer the question, "*What is to be done?*"

And, indeed, how am I to answer the question as to what is to be done, when everything I do, all my life, is based upon a lie, and I carefully give out this lie for truth, to others and to myself? Not to lie in this sense means to be not afraid of truth; not to invent excuses, and not to accept excuses invented by others, in order to hide from one's self the deduction of reason and conscience; not to be afraid of contradicting all our environment, and of being left alone with reason and conscience; not to be afraid of that condition to which truth and conscience lead us; however dreadful it may be, it cannot be worse than that which is based upon deceit.

To avoid lying, for men in our privileged position of mental labor, means not to be afraid of learning. Perhaps we owe so much that we should never be able to pay it all; but, however much we may owe, we must make out our bill; however far we have gone astray, it is better to return than to continue straying.

Lying to our fellows is always disadvantageous. Every business is always more directly done, and more quickly too, by truth than by lies. Lying to other men makes the matter only more complicated, and retards the decision; but lying to one's self, which is given out to be the truth, entirely ruins the life of man.

If a man considers a wrong road to be a right one, then his every step only leads him farther from his aim; a man who has been walking for a long time on a wrong road may find out for himself, or be told by others, that his road is a wrong one; but if he, being afraid of the thought of how far he has gone astray, tries to assure himself that he may, by following this wrong way, still come across the right one, then he will certainly never find it. If a man becomes afraid of the truth, and, on seeing it, will not acknowledge it, but takes falsehood for truth, then this man will never learn what is to be done.

We, not only rich men, but men in a privileged position, so-called educated men, have gone so far astray that we require either a firm resolution or very great sufferings on our false way in order to come to our senses again, and to recognize the lie by which we live.

I became aware of the lie of our life, thanks to those sufferings to which my wrong road led me; and, having acknowledged the error of the way on which I was bent, I had the boldness to go, first in theory, then in reality, wherever my reason and conscience led me, without any deliberation as to whither they were tending.

And I was rewarded.

All the complex, disjointed, intricate, and meaningless phenomena of life surrounding me became, of a sudden, clear; and my position, formerly so strange and vile, among these phenomena became, of a sudden, natural and easy.

And in this new situation my activity has exactly determined itself, but it is quite a different activity from that which appeared possible to me before; it is a new activity, far more quiet, affectionate, and joyous. The very thing which frightened me before, now attracts me.

And therefore I think that every one who sincerely puts to himself the question, "What is to be done?" and in answering this question does not lie or deceive himself, but goes wherever his reason *and conscience* may lead him, that man has already answered the question.

If he will only avoid deceiving himself, he will find out what to do, where to go, and how to act. There is only one thing which may hinder him in finding an answer, — that is, a too high estimate of himself and his own position. So it was with me; and therefore the second answer to the question, "What is to be done?" resulting from the first, consisted for me in repenting, in the full meaning of this word, that is, entirely changing the estimate of my own position and activity: instead of considering such to be useful and of importance, we must come to acknowledge it to be harmful and trifling; instead of considering ourselves educated, we must get to see our ignorance; instead of imagining ourselves to be kind and moral, we must acknowledge that we are immoral and cruel; instead of our importance, we must see our own insignificance.

I say, that besides avoiding lying to myself, I had moreover to *repent*, because, though the one results from the other, the wrong idea about my great importance was so much a part of my own nature, that until I had sincerely repented, and had put aside that wrong estimate of myself which I had, I did not see the enormity of the lie of which I had been guilty.

It was only when I repented, — that is, left off considering myself to be a peculiar man, and began to consider myself to be like *all* other men, — it was then that my way became clear to me. Before this, I was not able to answer the question, "What is to be done?" because the very question itself was put incorrectly.

Before I repented, I had put the question thus: "What activity should I choose, I, the man with the education I have acquired? How can I compensate by this education and these talents for what I have been taking away from the people?"

This question was a false one, because it included a wrong idea as to my not being like other men, but a peculiar man, called to serve other men with those talents and that education which I had acquired in forty years.

I had put the question to myself, but in reality I had already answered it in advance by having determined beforehand the kind of activity agreeable to myself by which I was called upon to serve men. I really asked myself, "How have I, so fine a writer, one so very well informed, and with such talents, how can I utilize them for the benefit of mankind?"

But the question ought to have been put thus, as it would have to be put to a learned rabbi who had studied all the Talmud, and knew the exact number of the letters in the Holy Scripture, and all the subtleties of his science: "What have I to do, who, from unlucky circumstances, have lost my best years in study instead of accustoming myself to labor, in learning the French language, the piano, grammar, geography, law, poetry; in reading novels, romances, philosophical theories, and in performing military exercises? what have I to do, who have passed the best years of my life in idle occupations, depraving the soul? what have I to do, notwithstanding these unlucky conditions of the past, in order to requite those men, who, during all this time, have fed and clothed me, and who still continue to feed and to clothe me?"

If the question had been put thus, after I had repented, "What have I, so ruined a man, to do?" the answer would have been easy: First of all, I must try to get my living honestly, — that is, learn not to live upon the shoulders of others; and while learning this, and after I have learned it, to try on every occasion to be of use to men with my hands and with my feet, as well as with my brain and my heart, and with all of me that is wanted by men.

And therefore I say that for one of my own circle, besides avoiding lying to others and to ourselves, it is necessary moreover to repent, to lay aside that pride about our education, refinement, and talents, not considering ourselves to be benefactors of the people, advanced men, who are ready to share our useful acquirements with the people, but to acknowledge ourselves to be entirely guilty, ruined, good-for-nothing men, who desire to turn over a new leaf, and not to be benefactors of the people, but to cease to offend and to humiliate them. Very often good young people, who sympathize with the negative part of my writings, put to me the question, "What must I then do? What have I, who have finished my study in the university or in some other high establishment, — what have I to do in order to be useful?"

These young people ask the question; but in the depths of their souls they have already decided that that education which they have received is their great advantage, and that they wish to serve the people by this very advantage.

And therefore there is one thing which they do not do, — honestly and critically examine what they call their education, by asking themselves whether it is a good or a bad thing.

But if they do this, they will be unavoidably led to deny their education, and to begin to learn anew; and this is alone what is wanted. They never will be able to answer the question as to what there is to be done, because they put it wrongly. The question should be put thus: "How can I, a helpless, useless man, seeing now the misfortune of having lost my best years in studying the scientific Talmud, pernicious for soul and body, how can I rectify this mistake, and learn to serve men?" But the question is always put thus: "How can I, who have acquired so much fine information, how can I be useful to men with this my information?"

And, therefore, a man will never answer the question, "What is to be done?" until he leaves off deceiving himself, and repents. And repentance is not dreadful, even as truth is not dreadful, but it is equally beneficent and fruitful of good. We need only accept the whole truth and fully repent in order to understand that in life no one has any rights or privileges, and that there is no end of duties, and no limits to them, and that the first and unquestionable duty of a man is to take a part in the struggle with nature for his own life, and for the lives of other men. And this acknowledgment of men's duty forms the essence of the third answer to the question, "What is to be done?"

I have tried to avoid deceiving myself. I have endeavored to extirpate the remainders of the false estimate of the importance of my education and talents, and to repent; but before answering the question, *What is to be done?* stands a new difficulty.

There are so many things to be done that one requires to know what is to be done in particular. And the answer to this question has been given me by the sincere repentance of the evil in which I have been living.

What is to be done? What is there exactly to be done? everybody keeps asking; and I, too, kept asking this, while, under the influence of a high opinion of my own calling, I had not seen that my first and unquestionable business is to earn my living, clothing, heating, building, and so forth, and in doing this to serve others as well as myself, because, since the world has existed, the first and unquestionable duty of every man has been comprised in this.

In this one business, man receives, if he has already begun to take part in it, the full satisfaction of all the bodily and mental wants of his nature: to feed, clothe, take care of himself and of his family, will satisfy his bodily wants; to do the same for others, will satisfy his spiritual.

Every other activity of man is only lawful when these first have been satisfied. In whatever department a man thinks to be his calling, whether in governing the people, in protecting his countrymen, in officiating at divine services, in teaching, in inventing the means of increasing the delights of life, in discovering the laws of the universe, in incorporating eternal truths in artistic images, the very first and the most unquestionable duty of a reasonable man will always consist in taking part in the struggle with nature for preserving his own life and the lives of other men.

This duty will always rank first, because the most necessary thing for men is life: and therefore, in order to protect and to teach men, and to make their lives more agreeable, it is necessary to keep this very life; while by not taking part in the struggle, and by swallowing up the labor of others, lives are destroyed. And it is folly to endeavor to serve men by destroying their lives.

Man's duty to acquire in the struggle with nature the means of living will always be unquestionably the very first of all duties, because it is the law of life, the violation of which unavoidably brings with it a punishment by destroying the bodily or mental life of man. If a man, living alone, free himself from the duty of struggling with nature, he will at once be punished by his body perishing.

But if a man free himself from this duty by compelling other men to fulfil it for him, in ruining their lives, he will be at once punished by the destruction of his reasonable life, — that is, the life which has a reasonable sense in it.

I had been so perverted by my antecedents, and this first and unquestionable law of God or nature is so hidden in our present world, that the fulfilling of it had seemed to me strange, and I was afraid and ashamed of it, as if the fulfilment, and not the violation, of this eternal, unquestionable law were strange, unnatural, and shameful. At first it seemed to me that, in order to fulfil this law, some sort of accommodation was necessary, some established association of fellow-thinkers, the consent of the family, and life in the country (not in town): then I felt ashamed, as if I were putting myself forward in performing things so unusual to our life as bodily labor, and I did not know how to begin.

But I needed only to understand that this was not some exclusive activity, which I had to invent and to arrange, but that it was merely returning from a false condition in which I had been to a natural one, merely rectifying that lie in which I had been living, — I had only to acknowledge all this, in order that all the difficulties should vanish.

It was not at all necessary to arrange and accommodate anything, or to wait for the consent of other people, because everywhere, in whatever condition I was, there were men who fed, dressed, and warmed me as well as themselves; and everywhere, under all circumstances, I was able to do these for myself and for them, if I had sufficient time and strength.

Nor could I feel a false shame in performing matters unusual and strange to me, because, in not doing so, I already experienced, not a false, but a real, shame.

And having come to this acknowledgment, and to the practical deduction from it, I had been fully rewarded for not having been afraid of the deductions of reason, and for having gone whither they led me.

Having come to this practical conclusion, I was struck by the facility and simplicity of the solution of all those problems which had formerly seemed to me so difficult and complicated. To the question, "What have we to do?" I received a very plain answer: Do first what is necessary for yourself; arrange all you can do by yourself, — your tea-urn, stove, water, and clothes.

To the question, "Would not this seem strange to those who had been accustomed to do all this for me?" it appeared that it was strange only during a week, and after a week it seemed more strange for me to return to my former condition.

In answer to the question, "Is it necessary to organ

ize this physical labor, to establish a society in a village upon this basis?" it appeared that it was not at all necessary to do all this; that if the labor does not aim at rendering idleness possible, and at utilizing other men's labor, as is the case with men who save up money, but merely the satisfying of necessities, then such labor will naturally induce people to leave towns for the country, where this labor is most agreeable and productive.

There was also no need to establish a society, because a working-man will naturally associate with other working people. In answer to the question, "Would not this labor take up all my time, and would it not deprive me of the possibility of that mental activity which I am so fond of, and to which I have become accustomed, and which in moments of self-conceit I consider to be useful to others?" the answer will be quite an unexpected one. In proportion to bodily exercise the energy of my mental activity increased, having freed itself from all that was superfluous.

In fact, having spent eight hours in physical labor, — half a day, — which formerly I used to spend in endeavoring to struggle with dullness, there still remained for me eight hours, out of which in my circumstances I required five for mental labor; and if I, a very prolific writer, who had been doing nothing during forty years but writing, and who had written three hundred printed sheets, that if during these forty years I had been doing ordinary work along with working people, then, not taking into consideration winter evenings and holidays, if I had been reading and learning during the five hours a day, and written only on holidays two pages a day (and I have sometimes written sixteen pages a day), I should have written the same three hundred printed sheets in fourteen years.

A wonderful thing, perhaps, but a most simple arithmetical calculation which every boy of seven years of age may do, and which I had never done. Day and night have together twenty-four hours; we sleep eight hours; there remain sixteen hours. If any man labor mentally five hours a day, he will do a vast amount of business; what do we, then, do during the remaining eleven hours?

So it appears that physical labor not only does not exclude the possibility of mental activity, but improves and stimulates it.

In answer to the question whether this physical labor would deprive me of many innocent enjoyments proper to man, such as the enjoyment of art, the acquirement of knowledge, of social intercourse, and, generally, of the happiness of life, it was really quite the reverse: the more intense my physical labor was, the more it approached that labor which is considered the hardest, that is, agricultural labor, the more I acquired enjoyments, knowledge, and the closer and more affectionate was my intercourse with mankind, and the more happiness did I feel in life.

In answer to the question (which I hear so often from men who are not quite sincere), "What result can there be from such an awfully small drop in the sea? what is all my personal physical labor in comparison with the sea of labor which I swallow up?"

To this question I also received a very unexpected answer.

It appeared that as soon as I had made physical labor the ordinary condition of my life, then at once the greatest part of my false and expensive habits and wants which I had, while I had been physically idle, ceased of themselves, without any endeavor on my part. To say nothing of the habit of turning day into night, and *vice versa*, of my bedding, clothes, my conventional cleanliness, which all became impossible and embarrassing when I began to labor physically, both the quantity and the quality of my food was totally changed. Instead of the sweet, rich, delicate, complicated, and highly spiced food which I was formerly fond of, I now required and obtained plain food as the most agreeable, — sour cabbage soup, porridge, black bread, tea with a bit of sugar.

So that, to say nothing of the example of common working-men, who are satisfied with little, with whom I came into closer intercourse, my very wants themselves were gradually changed by my life of labor; so that my drop of physical labor, in proportion to my growing accustomed to this labor and acquiring the ways of it, became indeed more perceptible in the ocean of common labor; and in proportion as my labor grew more fruitful, my demands for other men's labor grew less and less, and my life naturally, without effort or privation, came nearer to that simple life of which I could not even have dreamed without fulfilling the law of labor.

It became apparent that my former most expensive demands — the demands of vanity and amusement — were the direct result of an idle life. With physical labor there was no room for vanity, and no need for amusement, because my time was agreeably occupied; and after weariness, simple rest while drinking tea, or reading a book, or conversing with the members of my family, was far more agreeable than the theater, playing at cards, concerts, or large parties.

In answer to the question, "Would not this unusual labor be hurtful to my health, which is necessary for me in order that I may serve men?" it appeared that, in spite of the positive assurance of eminent doctors that hard physical labor, especially at my age, might have the worst results (and that Swedish gymnastics, riding, and other expedients intended to supply the natural conditions of man, would be far better), the harder I worked, the stronger, sounder, more cheerful, and kinder I felt myself.

So that it became undoubtedly certain that just as all those inventions of the human mind, such as newspapers, theaters, concerts, parties, balls, cards, magazines, novels, are nothing else than means to sustain the mental life of men out of its natural condition of labor for others, in the same way all the hygienic and medical inventions of the human mind for the accommodation of food, drink, dwelling, ventilation, warming of rooms, clothes, medicines, mineral waters, gymnastics, electric and other cures, are all merely means to sustain the bodily life of man out of its natural conditions of labor; that all these are nothing else than an establishment hermetically closed, in which, by the means of chemical apparatus, the evaporation of water for the plants is arranged when you only need to open the window, and do that which is natural, not only to men, but to beasts too; in other words, having absorbed the food, and thus produced a charge of energy, to discharge it by muscular labor.

All the profound thoughts of hygiene and of the art of healing for the men of our circle are like the efforts of a mechanic, who, having stopped all the valves of an overheated engine, should invent something to prevent this engine from bursting.

When I had plainly understood all this, it became to me ridiculous, that I, through a long series of doubt, research, and much thinking, had arrived at this extraordinary truth, — that if man has eyes, they are to be seen through; ears to hear by; feet to walk with, and hands and back to work with; and that if man will not use these, his members, for what they are meant, then it will be worse for him. I came to this conclusion, that with us, privileged people, the same thing has happened which happened to the horses of a friend of mine: The steward, who was not fond of horses, and did not understand anything about them, having received from his master orders to prepare the best cobs for sale, chose the best out of the drove of horses, and put them into the stable; fed them upon oats; but being over-anxious, he trusted them to nobody, neither rode them himself, nor drove nor led them.

All of these horses became, of course, good for nothing.

The same has happened to us, with this difference, — that you cannot deceive horses, and in order not to let them out, they must be secured; and we are kept in unnatural and hurtful conditions by all sorts of temptations, which fasten and hold us as with chains.

We have arranged for ourselves a life which is against the moral and physical nature of man, and we use all the powers of our mind in order to assure men that this life is a real one. All that we call culture, — our science and arts for improving the delights of life, — all these are only meant to deceive man's natural acquirements: all that we call hygiene, and the art of healing, are endeavors to deceive the natural physical want of human nature.

But these deceits have their limit, and we are come to these limits. "If such be real human life, then it is better not to live at all," says the fashionable philosophy of Schopenhauer and Hartman. "If such be life, it is better for future generations, too, not to live," says the indulgent healing art, and invents means to destroy women's fecundity.

In the Bible the law to human beings is expressed thus: "In the sweat of thy face shalt thou eat bread," and "In sorrow thou shalt bring forth children."

The peasant Bondaref, who wrote an article about this, threw great light upon the wisdom of this sentence. During the whole of my life, two thinking men — Russians — have exercised a great moral influence over me: they have enriched my thoughts, and enlightened my contemplation of the world.

These men were neither poets, nor learned men, nor preachers: they were two remarkable men, both living peasants,— Sutaief and Bondaref. But "nous avons changé tout ça," as says one of Molière's personages, talking at random about the healing art, and saying that the liver is on the left side, "we have changed all that." Men need not work — all work will be done by machines; and women need not bring forth children. The healing art will teach different means of avoiding this, and there are already too many people in the world.

In the Krapivensky district,[1] there lives a ragged peasant who during the war was a purchaser of meat for a commissary of stores. Having become acquainted with this functionary, and having seen his comfortable life, he became mad, and now thinks that he, too, can live as gentlemen do, without working, being provided for by the Emperor.

[1] Count Tolstoï's village of Yasnaya Polyana is situated in this district. — Am. Ed.

This peasant now calls himself "the Most Serene Marshal Prince Blokhin, purveyor of war-stores of all kinds."

He says of himself that he has gone through all ranks, and for his services during the war he has to receive from the Emperor an unlimited bank-account, clothes, uniforms, horses, carriages, tea, servants, and all kinds of provision. When anybody asks him whether he would like to work a little, he always answers, "Thanks: the peasants will attend to all that." When we say to him that the peasants also may not be disposed to work, he answers, "Machines have been invented to ease the labor of peasants. They have no difficulty in their business." When we ask him what is he living for, he answers, "To pass away the time."

I always consider this man as a mirror. I see in him myself and all my class: to pass through all ranks in order to live, to pass away the time, and to receive an unlimited bank-account, while peasants attend to everything, and find it easy to do so, because of the invention of machines.

This is the very form of the foolish belief of men of our class. When we ask what have we particularly to do, we are in reality asking nothing, but only asserting — not so sincerely indeed as the Most Serene Marshal Prince Blokhin, who had passed through all ranks, and lost his mind — that we do not wish to do anything.

He who has come to his senses cannot ask this, because from one side all that he makes use of has been done, and is being done, by the hands of men: on the other side, as soon as a healthy man has got up and breakfasted, he feels the inclination to work, as well with his feet as with his hands and brain. In order to find work, he has only not to restrain himself from labor. Only he who considers labor to be a shame, like the lady who asked her guest not to trouble herself to open the door, but to wait till she called a servant to do it, only such persons can ask what is there to be done in particular.

The difficulty is not in inventing some work, — every one has enough to do for himself and for others, — but in losing this criminal view of life, that we eat and sleep for our own pleasure, and in appropriating that simple and correct view in which every working-person grows up, that man first of all is a machine which is charged with food, in order to earn his living, and that therefore it is shameful, difficult, and impossible to eat and not to work; that to eat and not to work is a most dangerous state, and as bad as incendiarism.

It is necessary merely to have this consciousness, and we shall find work will always be pleasant, and capable of satisfying all the wants of our soul and body.

I picture to myself the whole matter thus: Every man's day is divided by his meals into four parts, or four stages as it is called by the peasants: First, before breakfast; secondly, from breakfast to dinner; thirdly, from dinner to poldnik (a slight evening meal between dinner and supper); and fourthly, from poldnik to night. The activity of man to which he is drawn is also divided into four kinds: First, the activity of the muscles, the labor of the hands, feet, shoulders, back, — hard labor, by which one perspires; secondly, the activity of the fingers and wrists, the activity of skill and handicraft; thirdly, the activity of the intellect and imagination; fourthly, the activity of intercourse with other men.

And the goods which man makes use of may also be divided into four kinds: First, every man makes use of the productions of hard labor, — bread, cattle, buildings, wells, bridges, and so on; secondly, the productions of handicraft, — clothes, boots, hardware, and so on; thirdly, the productions of mental activity, — science, art; and fourthly, the intercourse with men, acquaintanceship, societies.

And I thought that it would be the best thing so to arrange the occupations of the day that one might be able to exercise all these four faculties, and to return all the four kinds of production of labor, which one makes use of; so that the four parts of the day were devoted, first, to hard labor; secondly, to mental labor; thirdly, to handicraft; fourthly, to the intercourse with men. It would be good if one could so arrange his labor; but if it is not possible to arrange thus, one thing is important, —to acknowledge the duty of laboring, the duty of making a good use of each part of the day.

I thought that it would be only then that the false division of labor would disappear which now rules our society, and a just division would be established which should not interfere with the happiness of mankind.

I, for instance, have all my life been busy with mental work. I had said to myself that I have thus divided the labor that my special work is writing; that is, mental labor: and all other works necessary for me I left to be done by other men, or rather compelled them to do it. But this arrangement, seemingly so convenient for mental labor, became most inconvenient, especially for mental labor. I have been writing all my life, have accommodated my food, sleep, amusements, with reference to this special labor, and besides this work I did nothing.

The results of which were, first, that I had been narrowing the circle of my observation and information, and often I had not any object to study, and therefore, having had to describe the life of men (the life of men is a continual problem of every mental activity), I felt my ignorance, and had to learn and to ask about such things, which every one not occupied with a special work knows; secondly, it happened that when I sat down to write, I often had no inward inclination to write, and nobody wanted my writing itself, that is, my thoughts, but people merely wanted my name for profits in the magazines.

I made great efforts to write what I could; sometimes I did not succeed at all; sometimes succeeded in writing something very bad, and I felt dissatisfied and dull. But now, since I have acknowledged the necessity of physical labor as well as hard labor, and also that of handicraft, it is all quite different: my time is occupied humbly, but certainly in a useful way, and pleasantly and instructively for me.

And therefore I, for the sake of my specialty, leave off this undoubtedly useful and pleasant occupation only when I feel an inward want, or see a direct demand for my literary work. And this has improved the quality, and therefore the usefulness and pleasantness, of my special labor.

So that it has happened that my occupation with those physical works, which are necessary for me as well as for every man, not only did not interfere with my special activity, but was a necessary condition of the utility, quality, and pleasantness of this activity.

A bird is so created that it is necessary for it to fly, to walk, to peck, to consider; and when it does all this, it is satisfied and happy; then it is a bird. Exactly so with a man when he walks, turns over heavy things, lifts them up, carries them, works with his fingers, eyes, ears, tongue, brain; then only is he satisfied, then only is he *a man.*

A man who has come to recognize his calling to labor will naturally be inclined to that change of labor which is proper for him for the satisfying of his outward and inward wants, and he will reverse this order only when he feels an irresistible impulse to some special labor, and other men will require from him this labor. The nature of labor is such that the satisfying of all men's wants requires that very alternation of different kinds of labor which renders labor easy and pleasant.

Only the erroneous idea that labor is a curse could lead men to the freeing themselves from some kinds of labor, that is, to the seizure of other men's labor which requires a forced occupation with a special labor from other men which is called nowadays the division of labor.

We have become so accustomed to our false conception of the arrangement of labor that it seems to us that for a bootmaker, a machinist, a writer, a musician, it would be better to be freed from the labor proper to man. Where there is no violence over other men's labor, nor a false belief in the pleasures of idleness, no man for the sake of his special labor will free himself from physical labor necessary for the satisfying of his wants, because special occupation is not a privilege, but a sacrifice of a man's inclination for the sake of his brethren.

A bootmaker in a village having torn himself from

his usual pleasant labor in the field, and having begun his labor of mending or making boots for his neighbors, deprives himself of a pleasant, useful labor in the field for the sake of others, only because he is fond of sewing, and knows that nobody will do it better than he does, and that people will be thankful to him.

But he cannot wish to deprive himself for all his life of the pleasant alternation of labor. The same with the starosta, the machinist, the writer, the learned man.

It is only to us, with our perverted ideas, that it seems, when the master sends his clerk to be a peasant, or government sentences one of its ministers to deportation, that they are punished, and have been dealt with hardly. But in reality they have had a great good done to them, — that is, they have exchanged their heavy special work for a pleasant alternation of labor.

In a natural society all is quite different. I know a commune where the people earn their living themselves. One of the members of this community was more educated than the rest; and they required him to deliver lectures, for which he had to prepare himself during the day, in order to be able to deliver them in the evening. He did it joyfully, feeling that he was useful to others, and that he could do it well. But he got tired of the exclusive mental labor, and his health suffered accordingly. The members of the community therefore pitied him, and asked him to come again and labor in the field.

For men who consider labor to be the essential thing and the joy of life, the ground, the basis, of it will always be the struggle with nature, — not only agricultural labor, but also that of handicraft, mental work, and intercourse with men.

The divergence from one or many of these kinds of labor, and specialties of labor, will be performed only when a man of special gifts, being fond of this work, and knowing that he performs it better than anybody else, will sacrifice his own advantage in order to fulfil the demands of others put directly to him.

Only with such a view of labor, and the natural division

of labor resulting from it, will the curse disappear which we in our imagination have put upon labor; and every labor will always be a joy, because man will do either an unquestionably useful, pleasant, and easy work, or will be conscious that he makes a sacrifice in performing a more difficult special labor for the good of others.

But the division of labor is, it is said, more advantageous. Advantageous for whom? Is it more advantageous to make as quickly as possible as many boots and cotton prints as possible? But who will make these boots and cotton prints? Men who from generation to generation have been making only pinheads? How, then, can it be more advantageous for people? If the question were to make as many cotton prints and pins as possible, it would be so; but the question is, how to make people happy?

The happiness of men consists in life. And life is in labor.

How, then, can the necessity of a painful, oppressing work be advantageous for men? If the question were only for the advantage of some men without any consideration of the welfare of all, then it would be most advantageous for some men to eat others.

The thing most advantageous for all men is that which I wish for myself, — the greatest welfare and the satisfying of all my wants, those of body as well as those of soul, of conscience, and of reason, which are ingrafted in me.

And now, for myself, I have found that for my welfare and for the satisfying of these wants, I need only to be cured of the folly in which I, as well as the Krapivensky madman, have lived, which consisted in the idea that gentlefolk need not work, and that all must be done for them by others, and that, producing nothing, I have to do only what is proper to man, — satisfy my own wants.

And having discovered this, I became persuaded that this labor for the satisfying of my own wants is divisible into various kinds of labor, each of which has its own charm, and is not only not a burden, but serves as rest after some other.

I have divided my labor into four parts parallel to the four parts of the laborer's day's work, which are divided by his meals; and thus I try to satisfy my wants.

These are, then, the answers to the question, "What is to be done?" which I have found for myself.

First, To avoid deceiving myself. However far I have gone astray from that road of life which my reason shows to me, I must not be afraid of the truth.

Secondly, To renounce my own righteousness, my own advantages, peculiarities, distinguishing me from others, and to confess the guilt of such.

Thirdly, To fulfil that eternal, unquestionable law of man, — by laboring with all my being to struggle with nature, to sustain my own life, and the lives of others.

CHAPTER XXXIX

I HAVE now finished, having said all that concerns myself; but I cannot restrain my desire to say that which concerns every one, and to verify by several considerations my own deductions.

I wish to explain why it is I think that a great many of my own class must arrive where I myself am, and I must also speak of what will result if even some few men arrive there; and in the first place, if only men of our circle, our caste, will seriously think the matter out themselves, the younger generation, who seek their own personal happiness, will become afraid of the ever increasing misery of lives which obviously lead them to ruin; scrupulous persons among us (if they would examine themselves more closely) will be terrified at the cruelty and unlawfulness of their own lives, and timid persons will be frightened at the danger of their mode of life.

The misery of our lives! However we, rich men, may try to mend and to support, with the assistance of our science and art, this our false life, it must become weaker every day, unhealthier, and more and more painful: with each year suicide, and the sin against the unborn babe, increase; with each year the new generations of our class grow weaker, with each year we more and more feel the increasing dullness of our lives.

It is obvious that on this road, with an increase of the comforts and delights of life, of cures, artificial teeth and hair, and so on, there can be no salvation.

This truth has become such a truism, that in newspapers advertisements are printed about stomach powder for rich people, under the title "Blessings of the poor," where they say that only poor people have a good digestion, and the rich need help, and among other things this powder. You cannot ameliorate this matter by any kind of amusements, comforts, powders, but only by turning over a new leaf.

Our lives are in contradiction to our consciences. However much we may try to justify to ourselves our treason against mankind, all our justification falls to pieces before evidence: around us, people are dying from overwork and want; and we destroy the food, clothes, labor of men merely in order to amuse ourselves. And therefore the conscience of a man of our circle, though he may have but a small remainder of it in his breast, cannot be stifled, and poisons all these comforts and charms of life which our suffering and perishing brethren procure for us. But not only does every scrupulous man feel this himself, but he must feel it more acutely at present, because the best part of art and science, that part in which there still remains a sense of its high calling, constantly reminds him of his cruelty, and the unlawfulness of his position.

The old secure justifications are all destroyed; and the new ephemeral justifications of the progress of science for science's sake, and art for art's sake, will not bear the light of plain common sense.

The conscience of men cannot be calmed by new ideas: it can be calmed only by turning over a new leaf, when there will no longer be any necessity for justification.

The danger to our lives! However much we may try to hide from ourselves the plain and most obvious danger of exhausting the patience of those men whom we oppress; however much we may try to counteract this danger by all sorts of deceit, violence, and flattery, — it is still growing with each day, with each hour, and it has long been threatening us; but now it is so ripe that we are scarcely able to hold our course in a vessel tossed by a roaring and overflowing sea, — a sea which will presently swallow us up in wrath.

The workman's revolution, with the terrors of destruction and murder, not only threatens us, but we have been already living upon its verge during the last thirty years, and it is only by various cunning devices that we have been postponing the crisis.

Such is the state in Europe; such is the state in Russia, because we have no safety-valves. The classes who oppress the people, with the exception of the Tsar, have no longer in the eyes of our people any justification; they all keep up their position merely by violence, cunning, and expediency; but the hatred toward us of the worst representatives of the people, and the contempt of us from the best, is increasing with every hour.

Among the Russian people during the last three or four years, a new word, full of significance, has been circulating: by this word, which I never heard before, people are swearing in the streets, and calling us parasites.

The hatred and contempt of the oppressed people are increasing, and the physical and moral strength of the richer classes are decreasing: the deceit which supports all this is wearing out, and the rich classes have nothing wherewith to comfort themselves. To return to the old order of things is impossible: one thing only remains for those who are not willing to change the course of their lives, and to turn over a new leaf, — to hope that, during their lives, they will fare well enough, after which the people may do as they like. So think the blind crowd of the rich; but the danger is ever increasing, and the awful catastrophe is coming nearer and nearer.

There are three reasons which prove to rich people the necessity of turning over a new leaf: First, the desire for their own personal welfare and that of their families, which is not secured by the way in which rich people are living; secondly, the inability to satisfy the voice of conscience, which is obviously impossible in the present condition of things; and thirdly, the threatening and constantly increasing danger to life, which cannot be met by any outward means. All these together ought to induce rich people to change their mode of life. This change alone would satisfy the desire of welfare and conscience, and would remove the danger. And there is but one means of making such change, — to leave off deceiving ourselves, to repent, and to acknowledge labor to be, not a curse, but the joyful business of life.

To this it is replied, "What will come from the fact of my physical labor during ten, eight, or five hours, which thousands of peasants would gladly do for the money which I have?"

The first good would be, that you will become livelier, healthier, sounder, kinder; and you will learn that real life from which you have been hiding yourself, or which was hidden from you.

The second good will be, that, if you have a conscience, it will not only not suffer as it suffers now looking at the labor of men, the importance of which we always, from our ignorance, either increase or diminish, but you will constantly experience a joyful acknowledgment that with each day you are more and more satisfying the demands of your conscience, and are leaving behind you that awful state in which so much evil is accumulated in our lives that we feel that we cannot possibly do any good in the world; you will experience the joy of free life, with the possibility of doing good to others; you will open for yourself a way into the regions of the world of morality which has hitherto been shut to you.

The third good will be this, that, instead of constant fear of revenge for your evil deeds, you will feel that you are saving others from this revenge, and are principally saving the oppressed from the cruel feeling of rancor and resentment.

But it is usually said that it would be ridiculous if we, men of our stamp, with deep philosophical, scientific, political, artistic, ecclesiastical, social questions before us, we state ministers, senators, academists, professors, artists, singers, we whose quarter-hours are valued so highly by men, should spend our time in doing — what? Cleaning our boots, washing our shirts, digging, planting potatoes, or feeding our chickens and cows, and so on, — in such business which not only our house-porter, our cook, but thousands of men besides who value our time, would be very glad to do for us.

But why do we dress, wash, and comb our hair ourselves? Why do we walk, hand chairs to ladies, to our guests, open and shut the door, help people into carriages, and perform hundreds of such actions which were formerly performed for us by our slaves?

Because we consider that such may be done by ourselves; that it is compatible with human dignity, that is, human duty. The same holds good with physical labor. Man's dignity, his sacred duty, is to use his hands, his feet, for that purpose for which they were given him, and not to be wasted by disuse, not that he may wash and clean them and use them only for the purpose of stuffing food and cigarettes into his mouth.

Such is the meaning of physical labor for every man in every society. But in our class, with the divergence from this law of nature came the misery of a whole circle of men; and for us, physical labor receives another meaning, — the meaning of a preaching and a propaganda which divert the terrible evil which threatens mankind.

To say that for an educated man physical labor is a useless occupation, is the same as to say, in the building of a temple, What importance can there be in putting each stone exactly in its place? Every great act is done under the conditions of imperceptibility, modesty, and simplicity. One can neither plow, nor feed cattle, nor think, during a great illumination, or thundering of guns, or while in uniform.

Illumination, the roar of cannon, music, uniforms,

cleanliness, brilliancy, which we usually connect with the idea of the importance of any act, are, on the contrary, tokens of the absence of importance in the same. Great, true deeds are always simple and modest. And such is also the greatest deed which is left to us to do, — the solution of those awful contradictions in which we are living. And the acts which solve those contradictions are those modest, imperceptible, seemingly ridiculous acts, such as helping ourselves by physical labor, and, if possible, helping others too: this is what we rich people have to do, if we understand the misery, wrong, and danger of the position in which we are living.

What will come out of the circumstance that I, and another, and a third, and a tenth man, do not despise physical labor, but consider it necessary for our happiness, for the calming of our consciences, and for our safety? This will come of it, — that one, two, three, ten men, coming into conflict with no one, without the violence either of the government or of revolution, will solve for themselves the problem which is before all the world, and which has appeared insolvable; and they will solve it in such a way that life will become for them a good thing: their consciences will be calm, and the evil which oppresses them will cease to be dreadful to them.

Another effect will be this: that other men, too, will see that the welfare, which they have been looking for everywhere, is quite close by them, that seemingly insolvable contradictions of conscience and the order of the world are solved in the easiest and pleasantest way, and that, instead of being afraid of men surrounding them, they must have intercourse with them, and love them.

The seemingly insolvable economical and social questions are like the problem of Krilof's casket. The casket opened of itself, without any difficulty: but it will not open until men do the very simplest and most natural thing, — that is, open it. The seemingly insolvable question is the old question of utilizing some men's labor by others: this question in our time has found its expression in property.

Formerly, other men's labor was used simply by violence, by slavery: in our time, it is being done by the means of property. In our time, property is the root of all evil and of the sufferings of men who possess it, or are without it, and of all the remorse of conscience of those who misuse it, and of the danger from the collision between those who have it and those who have it not.

Property is the root of all evil; and, at the same time, property is that toward which all the activity of our modern society is directed, and that which directs the activity of the world. States and governments intrigue, make wars, for the sake of property, for the possession of the banks of the Rhine, of land in Africa, China, the Balkan Peninsula. Bankers, merchants, manufacturers, landowners, labor, use cunning, torment themselves, torment others, for the sake of property; government functionaries, tradesmen, landlords, struggle, deceive, oppress, suffer, for the sake of property; courts of justice and police protect property; penal servitude, prisons, all the terrors of so-called punishments, — all is done for the sake of property.

Property is the root of all evil; and now all the world is busy with the distribution and protecting of wealth.

What, then, is property? Men are accustomed to think that property is something really belonging to man, and for this reason they have called it property. We speak indiscriminately of our own house and our own land. But this is obviously an error and a superstition. We know, and if we do not it is easy to perceive, that property is only the means of utilizing other men's labor. And another's labor can by no means belong to me.

Man has been always calling his own that which is subject to his own will and joined with his own consciousness. As soon as man calls his own something which is not his body, but which he should like to be subject to his will as his body is, then he makes a mistake, and gets disappointment, suffering, and compels other people to suffer as well. Man calls his wife his own, — his children, his slaves, his belongings, his own too; but the reality always shows him his error, and he must either get rid of this superstition, or suffer and make others suffer.

Now we, having nominally renounced the possessing of slaves, owing to money (and to its exactment by the government), claim our right also to money; that is, to the labor of other men.

But as to our claiming our wives as our property, or our sons, our slaves, our horses, — this is pure fiction contradicted by reality, and which only makes those suffer who believe in it; because a wife or a son will never be so subject to my will as my body is; therefore my own body will always remain the only thing I can call my true property; so also money, — property will never be real property, but only a deception and a source of suffering, and it is only my own body which will be my property, that which always obeys me, and is connected with my consciousness.

It is only to us, who are so accustomed to call other things than our body our own, that such a wild superstition may appear useful for us, and be without evil results; but we have only to reflect upon the nature of the matter in order to see how this, like every other superstition, brings with it only dreadful consequences.

Let us take the most simple example. I consider myself my own, and another man like myself I consider my own, too. I must understand how to cook my dinner: if I were free from the superstition of considering another man as my property, I should have been taught this art as well as every other necessary to my real property (that is, my body); but now I have it taught to my imaginary property, and the result is that my cook does not obey me, does not wish to humor me, and even runs away from me, or dies, and I remain with an unsatisfied want, and have lost the habit of learning, and recognize that I have spent as much time in cares about this cook as I should have spent in learning the art of cooking myself.

The same is the case with the property of buildings, clothes, wares; with the property of the land; with the property of money. Every imaginary property calls forth in me a non-corresponding want which cannot always be gratified, and deprives me of the possibility of acquiring for my true and sure property — my own body — that information, that skill, those habits, improvements, which I might have acquired.

The result is always that I have spent (without gain to myself, — to my true property) strength, sometimes my whole life, on that which never has been and never could be my property.

I provide myself with an imaginary "private" library, a "private" picture-gallery, "private" apartments, clothes; acquire my "own" money in order to purchase with it everything I want, and the matter stands thus, — that I, being busy about this imaginary property, as if it were real, leave quite out of sight that which is my true property, upon which I may really labor, and which really may serve me, and which always remains in my power.

Words have always a definite meaning until we purposely give them a false signification.

What does property mean?

Property means that which is given to me alone, which belongs to me alone, exclusively; that with which I may always do everything I like, which nobody can take away from me, which remains mine to the end of my life, and that I ought to use in order to increase and to improve it. Such property for every man is only himself.

And it is in this very sense that imaginary property is understood, that very property for the sake of which (in order to make it impossible for this imaginary property to become a real one) all the sufferings of this world exist, — wars, executions, judgments, prisons, luxury, depravity, murders, and the ruin of mankind.

What, then, will come out of the circumstance that

ten men plow, hew wood, make boots, not from want, but from the acknowledgment that man needs work, and that the more he works, the better it will be for him?

This will come out of it: that ten men, or even one single man, in thought and in deed, will show men that this fearful evil from which they are suffering is not the law of their destiny, nor the will of God, nor any historical necessity, but a superstition; not at all a strong or overpowering one, but weak and null, in which it is only necessary to leave off believing, as in idols, in order to get rid of it, and to destroy it as a frail cobweb is swept away.

Men who begin to work in order to fulfil the pleasant law of their lives, who work for the fulfilment of the law of labor, will free themselves from the superstition of property which is so full of misery, and then all these worldly establishments which exist in order to protect this imaginary property outside of one's own body will become not only unnecessary for them but burdensome; and it will become plain to all that these institutions are not necessary, but pernicious, imaginary, and false conditions of life.

For a man who considers labor not a curse, but a joy, property outside his own body — that is, the right or possibility of utilizing other men's labor — will be not only useless, but an impediment. If I am fond of cooking my dinner, and accustomed to do it, then the fact that another man will do it for me will deprive me of my usual business, and will not satisfy me as well as I have satisfied myself; besides, the acquirement of an imaginary property will not be necessary for such a man: a man who considers labor to be his very life fills up with it all his life and therefore requires less and less the labor of others — in other words, property in order to fill up his unoccupied time and to embellish his life.

If the life of a man is occupied by labor, he does not require many rooms, much furniture, various fine clothes; he does not require expensive food, carriages, amusements. But particularly a man who considers labor to be the business and the joy of his life will not seek to ease his own labor by utilizing that of others.

A man who considers life to consist in labor, in proportion as he acquires more skill, craft, and endurance, will aim at having more and more work to do, which should occupy all his time. For such a man, who sees the object of his life in labor, and not in the results of this labor for the acquirement of property, there cannot be even a question about the instruments of labor. Though such a man will always choose the most productive instrument of labor, he will have the same satisfaction in working with the most unproductive.

If he has a steam-plow, he will plow with it; if he has not such, he will plow with a horse-plow; if he has not this, he will plow with the plain Russian sokha; if he has not even this, he will use a spade: and under any circumstances, he will attain his aim; that is, will pass his life in a labor useful to man, and therefore he will have fullest satisfaction; and the position of such a man, according to exterior and interior circumstances, will be happier than the condition of a man who gives his life away to acquire property.

According to exterior circumstances, he will never want, because men, seeing that he does not mind work, will always try to make his labor most productive to them, as they arrange a mill by running water; and in order that his labor may be more productive, they will provide for his material existence, which they will never do for men who aim at acquiring property.

And the providing for material wants is all that a man requires. According to interior conditions, such a man will be always happier than he who seeks for property, because the latter will never receive what he is aiming at, and the former always in proportion to his strength: even the weak, old, dying (according to the proverb, with a Kored in his hands), will receive full satisfaction, and the love and sympathy of men.

One of the consequences of this will be that some odd, half-insane persons will plow, make boots, and so on, instead of smoking, playing cards, and riding about, carrying with them, from one place to another, their dullness during the ten hours which every man of letters has at his command.

Another result will be that those silly people will demonstrate, in deed, that that imaginary property for the sake of which men suffer, torment themselves and others, is not necessary for happiness, and even impedes it, and is only a superstition; and that true property is only one's own head, hands, feet; and that in order to utilize this true property usefully and joyfully, it is necessary to get rid of the false idea of property outside one's own body, on which we waste the best powers of our life.

Another result will be that these men will show that, when a man leaves off believing in imaginary property, then only will he make real use of his true property, — his own body, which will yield him fruit an hundred-fold, and such happiness of which we have no idea as yet; and he will be a useful, strong, kind man, who will everywhere stand on his own feet, will always be a brother to everybody, will be intelligible to all, desired by all, and dear to all.

And men, looking at one, at ten, such silly men will understand what they have all to do in order to undo that dreadful knot in which they have all been tied by the superstition respecting property, in order to get rid of the miserable condition from which they are groaning now, and from which they do not know how to free themselves.

But what can a man do in a crowd who do not agree with him? There is no reasoning which could more obviously demonstrate the unrighteousness of those who employ it as does this. The boatmen are dragging vessels against the stream. Is it possible that there could be found such a stupid boatman who would refuse to do his part in dragging because he alone cannot drag the boat up against the stream? He who, besides his rights of animal life, — to eat and to sleep, — acknowledges any human duty, knows very well wherein such duty consists: just in the same way as a boatman knows that he has only to get into his breast-collar, and to walk in the given direction, to find out what he has to do and how to do it.

And so with the boatmen, and with all men who do any labor in common, so with the labor of all mankind; each man need only keep on his breast-collar, and go in the given direction. And for this purpose one and the same reason is given to all men, that this direction may always be the same.

And that this direction *is* given to us is obvious and certain from the lives of those who surround us, as well as in the conscience of every man, and in all the previous expressions of human wisdom; so that only he who does not want work may say that he does not see it.

What will, then, come out of this?

This: that first one man, then another, will drag; looking at them, a third will join; and so one by one the best men will join, until the business will be set a-going, and will move as of itself, inducing those also to join who do not yet understand why and wherefore it is being done.

First, to the number of men who conscientiously work in order to fulfil the law of God, will be added those who will accept half conscientiously and half upon faith; then to these a still greater number of men, only upon the faith in the foremost men; and lastly the majority of people: and then it will come to pass that men will cease to ruin themselves, and will find out happiness.

This will happen soon when men of our circle, and after them all the great majority of working-people, will no longer consider it shameful to clean sewers, but will consider it shameful to fill them up in order that other men, *our brethren*, may carry their contents away; they will not consider it shameful to go visiting in common boots, but they will consider it shameful to walk in goloshes by barefooted people; they will not think it shameful not to know French, or about the last novel, but they will consider it shameful to eat bread, and not to know how it is prepared; they will not consider it shameful not to have a starched shirt or a clean dress, but that it is shameful to wear a clean coat as a token of one's idleness; they will not consider it shameful to have dirty hands, but not to have callouses on their hands.

Within my memory, still more striking changes have taken place. I remember that at table, behind each chair, a servant stood with a plate. Men made visits accompanied by two footmen. A Cossack boy and a girl stood in a room to give people their pipes, and to clean them, and so on. Now this seems to us strange and remarkable. But is it not equally strange that a young man or woman, or even an elderly man, in order to visit a friend, should order his horses to be harnessed, and that well-fed horses are only kept for this purpose? Is it not as strange that one man lives in five rooms, or that a women spends tens, hundreds, thousands of rubles for her dress when she only needs some flax and wool in order to spin dresses for herself and clothes for her husband and children?

Is it not strange that men live doing nothing, riding to and fro, smoking and playing, and that a battalion of people are busy feeding and warming them?

Is it not strange that old people quite gravely talk and write in newspapers about theaters, music, and other insane people drive to look at musicians or actors?

Is it not strange that tens of thousands of boys and girls are brought up so as to make them unfit for every work (they return home from school, and their two books are carried for them by a servant)?

There will soon come a time, and it is already drawing near, when it will be shameful to dine on five courses served by footmen, and cooked by any but the masters themselves; it will be shameful not only to ride thoroughbreds or in a coach when one has feet to walk on; to wear on week-days such dress, shoes, gloves, in which it is impossible to work; it will be shameful to play on a piano which costs one hundred and fifty pounds, or even ten pounds, while others work for one; to feed dogs upon milk and white bread, and to burn lamps and candles without working by their light; to heat stoves in which the meal is not cooked. Then it would be impossible to think about giving openly not merely one pound, but six pence, for a place in a concert or in a theater. All this will be when the law of labor becomes public opinion.

CHAPTER XL

As it is said in the Bible, there is a law given unto man and woman, — to man, the law of labor; to woman, the law of child-bearing. Although with our science, "*nous avons changé tout ça*," the law of man as well as of woman remains as immutable as the liver in its place; and the breach of it is as inevitably punished by death. The only difference is that, for man, the breach of law is punished by death in such a near future that it can almost be called present; but for woman, the breach of law is punished in a more distant future.

A general breach, by all men, of the law, destroys men immediately; the breach by women destroys the men of the following generation. The evasion of the law by a few men and women does not destroy the human race, but deprives the offender of rational human nature.

The breach of this law by men began years ago in the classes which could use violence with others; and, spreading on its way, it has reached our day, and has now attained madness, the ideal contained in a breach of the law, the ideal expressed by Prince Blokhin, and shared by Renan and the whole educated world; work will be done by machines, and men will be bundles of nerves enjoying themselves.

There has been scarcely any breach of the law by women. It has only manifested itself in prostitution, and in private cases of crime in destroying progeny. Women of the wealthy classes have fulfilled their law, while men did not fulfil theirs; and therefore women have grown stronger, and have continued to govern, and will govern, men, who have deviated from their law;

and who, consequently, have lost their reason. It is generally said that women (the women of Paris, especially those who are childless) have become so bewitching, using all the means of civilization, that they have mastered man by their charms.

This is not only wrong, but it is just the reverse of the truth. It is not the childless woman who has mastered man, but it is the mother, the one who has fulfilled her duty, while man has not fulfilled his.

As to the woman who artificially remains childless, and bewitches man by her shoulders and curls, she is not a woman, mastering man, but a woman corrupted by him, reduced to his level, to the corrupted man, and who, as well as he, has deviated from her duty, and who, as well as he, has lost every reasonable sense of life.

This mistake produces also the astounding nonsense which is called "woman's rights." The formula of these rights is as follows: —

"You men," says woman, "have deviated from your law of true labor, and want us to carry the load of ours. No: if so, we also, as well as you, will make a pretense of labor, as you do in banks, ministries, universities, and academies; we wish, as well as you, by the pretense of division of work, to profit by other people's work, and to live only to satisfy our lust." They say so, and in deed show that they can make that pretense of labor, not at all worse, but even better, than men do it.

The so-called question of woman's rights arose, and only could arise, among men who had deviated from the law of real labor. One has only to return to it, and that question must cease to exist. A woman who has her own particular, inevitable labor will never claim the right of sharing man's labor, — in mines, or in plowing fields. She claims a share only in the sham labor of the wealthy classes.

The woman of our class was stronger than man, and is now still stronger, not through her charms, not through her skill in performing the same pharisaic similitude of work as man, but because she has not stepped outside of the law; because she has borne that true labor with danger of life, with uttermost effort; true labor, from which the man of the wealthy classes has freed himself.

But within my memory has begun also the deviation from the law by woman, — that is to say, her fall; and within my memory, it has proceeded farther and farther. A woman who has lost the law believes that her power consists in the charms of her witchery, or in her skill at a pharisaic pretense of intellectual labor. But children hinder the one and the other. Therefore, with the help of science, within my memory it has come to pass that among the wealthy classes, scores of means of destroying progeny have appeared. And behold, — women, mothers, some of them of the wealthy classes, who held their power in their hands, let it slip away, only to place themselves on a level with women of the street. The evil has spread far, and spreads farther every day, and will soon grasp all the women of the wealthy classes; and then they will become even with men, and together with them will lose every reasonable sense of life. But there is yet time.

If only women would understand their worth, their power, and would use them for the work of salvation of their husbands, brothers, and children! the salvation of all men!

Women, mothers of the wealthy classes, the salvation of men of our world from the evils from which it suffers, is in your hands!

Not those women who are occupied by their figures, bustles, head-dresses, and their charms for men, and who, contrary to their will, by oversight and with despair, bear children, and then give their children to wet-nurses; nor yet those who go to different lectures, and talk of psychometrical centers and differentiation, and who also try to free themselves from bearing children in order not to hinder their folly, which they call development, — but those women and mothers who, having the power of freeing themselves from child-bearing, hold strictly and consciously to that eternal, immutable law, knowing that the weight and labor of that submission is the aim of their life. These women and mothers of our wealthy classes are those in whose hands, more than in any others, lies the salvation of the men of our sphere in life, from the calamities which oppress them.

You women and mothers who submit consciously to the law of God, you are the only ones who, in our miserable, mutilated world, which has lost all semblance of humanity, you are the only ones who know the whole true meaning of life according to the law of God; and you are the only ones who, by your example, can show men the happiness of that submission to God's law, of which they rob themselves.

You are the only ones who know the joy and happiness which takes possession of one's whole being; the bliss which is the share of every man who does not deviate from God's law. You know the joy of love to your husband, — a joy never ending, never destroyed, like all other joys, but forming the beginning of another new joy, — love to your child. You are the only ones, when you are simple and submissive to God's law, who know, not the farcical pretense of labor, which men of your world call labor, but that true labor which is imposed by God upon men, and know the rewards for it, — the bliss which it gives.

You know it when, after the joys of love, you expect, with emotion, fear, and hope, the torturing state of pregnancy, which makes you ill for nine months, and brings you to the brink of death and to unbearable sufferings and pains; you know the conditions of true labor, when with joy you expect the approach and increase of the most dreadful sufferings, after which comes the bliss, known to you only.

You know it when, directly after those sufferings, without rest, without interruption, you undertake another series of labors and sufferings, — those of nursing; for the sake of which you subjugate to your feeling, and renounce, the strongest human necessity, — that of sleep, which, according to the saying, is sweeter than father and mother. And for months and years you do not sleep two nights running, and often you do not sleep whole nights; walking alone to and fro, rocking in your wearied arms an ailing baby, whose sufferings tear your heart. And when you do all this, unapproved and unseen by anybody, not expecting any praise or reward for it; when you do this, not as a great deed, but as the laborer of the gospel parable, who came from the field, considering that you are only doing your duty, — you know then what is false, fictitious labor, — for human fame; and what is true labor, — the fulfilment of God's will, the indication of which you feel in your heart. You know, if you are a true mother, that not only nobody has seen and praised your labor, considering that it is only what ought to be, but even those for whom you toiled are not only ungrateful to you, but often torment and reproach you. And with the next child you do the same, — again you suffer, again you bear unseen, terrible toil, and again you do not expect any reward from anybody, and feel the same satisfaction.

If you are such, you will not say, after two or after twenty children, that you have borne children enough; as a fifty-year-old workman will not say that he has worked enough, when he still eats and sleeps, and his muscles demand work. If you are such, you will not cast the trouble of nursing and care on a strange mother, any more than a workman will give the work which he has begun, and nearly finished, to another man, because in that work you put your life, and because, the more you have of that work, the fuller and happier is your life.

But when you are like this, — and there are yet such women, happily for men, — the same law of fulfilment of God's will, by which you guide your own life, you will apply also to the life of your husband, of your children, and of men near to you. If you are such, and if you know by experience that only self-denied, unseen, unrewarded labor with danger of life, and uttermost effort for the life of others, is that mission of man which gives satisfaction, you will claim the same from others, you will encourage your husband to do the same labor, you will value and appreciate the worth of men by this same labor, and for it you will prepare your children.

Only that mother who looks on child-bearing as a disagreeable accident, and upon the pleasures of love, comfort, education, sociability, as the sense of life, will bring up her children so that they shall have as many pleasures, and enjoy them as much as possible; will feed them luxuriously, dress them smartly, will artificially divert them, and will teach them, not that which will make them capable of self-sacrificing man's and woman's labor with danger of life and uttermost effort, but that which will deliver them from that labor. Only such a woman, who has lost the sense of her life, will sympathize with that false, sham man's labor, by means of which her husband, freeing himself from man's duty, has the possibility of profiting, together with her, by the labor of others. Only such a woman will choose a similar husband for her daughter, and value men, not by what they are in themselves, but by what is attached to them, — position, money, the art of profiting by the labor of others.

A true mother, who really knows God's law, will prepare her children for the fulfilment of it. For such a mother to see her child overfed, delicate, overdressed, will be a suffering, because all this she knows will hinder it in the fulfilment of God's law experienced by herself. Such a woman will not teach that which will give her son or daughter the possibility of delivering themselves from labor, but that which will help them to bear the labor of life.

She will not want to ask what to teach her children, or for what to prepare them, knowing what it is and in what consists the mission of men, and consequently knowing what to teach her children, and for what to prepare them. Such a woman will not only discourage her husband from false, sham labor, the only aim of which is to profit by other people's work, but will view with disgust and dread an activity that will serve as a double temptation for her children. Such a woman will not choose her daughter's husband according to the whiteness of his hands, and the refinement of his manners, but, knowing thoroughly what is labor and what deceit, will always and everywhere, beginning with her husband, respect and appreciate men, will claim from them true labor with waste and danger of life, and will scorn that false, sham labor which has for its aim the delivering of one's self from true labor.

Such a mother *will bring forth and nurse her children herself*, and, above all things else, will feed and provide for them, will work for them, wash and teach them, will sleep and talk with them, because she makes that her life-work. Only such a mother will not seek for her children external security through her husband's money, or her children's diplomas, but she will exercise in them the same capacity of self-sacrificing fulfilment of God's will which she knows in herself, the capacity for bearing labor with waste and danger of life, because she knows that only in that lie the security and welfare of life. Such a mother will not have to ask others what is her duty: she will know everything beforehand, and will fear nothing.

If there can be doubts for a man or for a childless woman about the way to fulfil God's will, for a mother that way is firmly and clearly drawn; and if she fulfils it humbly, with a simple heart, standing on the highest point of good, which it is only given to a human being to attain, she becomes the guiding-star for all men, tending to the same good. Only a mother before her death can say to Him who sent her into this world, and to Him whom she has served by bearing and bringing up children, beloved by her more than herself, — only she can peacefully say, after having served Him in her appointed service: —

"'Now lettest Thou thy servant depart in peace.'"

And this is that highest perfection, to which, as to the highest good, men aspire.

Such women, who fulfil their mission, are those who reign over reigning men; those who prepare new generations of men, and form public opinion: and therefore in the hands of these women lies the highest power of men's salvation from the existing and threatening evils of our time.

Yes, women, mothers, in your hands, more than in those of any others, lies the salvation of the world!

NOTE TO CHAPTER XL

THE vocation of every man and woman is to serve other people. With this general proposition, I think all who are not immoral people will agree. The difference between men and women in the fulfilment of that vocation, is only in the means by which they attain it; that is to say, by which they serve men.

Man serves others by physical work, — procuring food; by intellectual work, — studying the laws of nature in order to master it; and by social work, — instituting forms of life, and establishing mutual relations between people.

The means of serving others are various for men. The whole activity of mankind, with the exception of bearing children and rearing them, is open for his service to men. A woman, in addition to the possibility of serving men by all the means open to man, by the construction of her body is called, and is inevitably attracted, to serve others by that which alone is excepted from the domain of the service of man.

The service of mankind is divided into two parts, — one, the augmentation of the welfare of mankind; the other, the continuation of the race. Men are called chiefly to the first, as they are deprived of the possibility of fulfilling the second. Women are called exclusively to the second, as they only are fitted for it. This difference one should not, one cannot, forget or destroy; and it would be sinful to do so. From this difference proceed the duties of each, — duties not invented by men, but which are in the nature of things. From the same difference proceeds the estimation of virtue and vice for woman and man, — the estimation which has existed in every century, which exists now, and which will never cease to exist while in men reason exists.

It always has been, and it always will be, the case that a man who spends a great part of his life in the various physical and mental labors which are natural to him, and a woman who spends a great part of her life in the labor of bearing, nursing, and rearing children, which is her exclusive prerogative, will equally feel that they are doing their duty, and will equally rise in the esteem and love of other people, because they both fulfil that which is appointed to them by their nature.

The vocation of man is broader and more varied, the vocation of woman more uniform and narrower, but more profound; and therefore it has always been, and always will be, the case that man, having hundreds of duties, will be neither a bad nor a pernicious man, even when he has been false to one or ten out of them, if he fulfils the greater part of his vocation; while woman, as she has a smaller number of duties, if she is false to one of them, instantly falls lower than a man who has been false to ten out of his hundreds of duties. Such has always been the general opinion, and such it will always remain, — because such is the substance of the matter.

A man, in order to fulfil God's will, must serve Him in the domain of physical work, thought, and morality: in all these ways he can fulfil his vocation. Woman's service to God consists chiefly and almost exclusively in bearing children (because no one except herself can render it). Only by means of work is man called to serve God and his fellow-men: only by means of her children is a woman called to serve them.

And therefore, love to her own children which is inborn in woman, that exclusive love against which it is quite vain to strive by reasoning, will always be, and ought to be, natural to a woman and a mother. That love to a child in its infancy is not egotism, but it is the love of a workman for the work which he is doing while it is in his hands. Take away that love for the object of one's work and the work becomes impossible. While I am making a boot, I love it above everything. If I did not love it, I could not work at it. If anybody spoils it for me, I am in despair; but I only love it thus while I am working at it. When it is completed, there remains an attachment, a preference, which is weak and illegitimate.

It is the same with a mother. A man is called to serve others by multifarious labors, and he loves those labors while he is accomplishing them. A woman is called to serve others by her children, and she cannot help loving those children of hers while she is rearing them to the age of three, seven, or ten years.

In the general vocation of serving God and others, man and woman are entirely equal, notwithstanding the difference of the form of that service. The equality consists in the equal importance of one service and of the other, — that the one is impossible without the other, that the one depends upon the other, and that for efficient service, as well for man as for woman, the knowledge of truth is equally necessary.

Without this knowledge, the activity of man and woman becomes, not useful, but pernicious for mankind. Man is called to fulfil his multifarious labor; but his labor is only useful, and his physical, mental, and social labor is only fruitful, when it is fulfilled in the name of truth and the welfare of others.

A man can occupy himself as zealously as he will to increase his pleasures by vain reasoning and with social activity for his own adtantage: his labor will not be fruitful. It will only be so when it is directed toward lessening the suffering of others from want and ignorance, and from false social organization.

The same with woman's vocation: her bearing, nursing, and bringing up children will only be useful to mankind when she not only gives birth to children for her own pleasure, but when she prepares future servants of mankind; when the education of those children is done in the name of truth and for the welfare of others, — that is to say, when she will educate her children in such a manner that they shall be the very best men possible, and the very best laborers for others.

The ideal woman, in my opinion, is the one who, appropriating the highest view of life of the time in which she lives, yet gives herself to her feminine mission, which is irresistibly placed in her, — that of bringing forth, nursing, and educating the greatest possible number of children, fitted to work for people according to the view which she has of life.

But in order to appropriate the highest view of life, I think there is no need of visiting lectures: all that she requires is to read the Gospel, and not to shut her eyes, ears, and, most of all, her heart.

Well, and if you ask what those are to do who have no children, who are not married, or are widows, I answer that those will do well to share man's multifarious labor. But one cannot help being sorry that such a precious tool as woman is, should be bereft of the possibility of fulfilling the great vocation which it is proper to her alone to fulfil.

Especially as every woman, when she has finished bearing children, if she has strength left, will have the time to occupy herself with that help in man's labor. Woman's help in that labor is very precious; but it will always be a pity to see a young woman fit for child-bearing, and occupied by man's labor.

To see such a woman is the same as to see precious vegetable soil covered with stones for a place of parade or for a walking-ground. Still more a pity, because this earth could only produce bread, and a woman could produce that for which there cannot be any equivalent, higher than which there is nothing — man. And only she is able to do this.

LIFE

"Man is only a reed, the feeblest in nature; but he is a thinking reed. It is not necessary that the whole universe should rise in arms to crush him. A vapor, a drop of water, suffices to kill him. But if the entire universe were to crush him, man would still be more noble than that which slays him, because he knows that he is dying; and of the advantage which the universe possesses over him the universe knows nothing. Thus all our dignity consists in thought. It is that upon which we must take our stand, not upon space and duration. Let us, then, labor to think well; that is the principle of morals." — PASCAL.

"Two things fill my spirit with ever fresh and increasing wonder and awe, the oftener and the more steadfastly my thoughts occupy themselves therewith, — the starry heavens above me and the moral law within me. . . . The first begins from the place which I occupy in the outer world of sense, and extends the connection in which I stand to invisible space beyond the eye of man, with worlds on worlds, systems on systems, to their periodical movements in endless time, their beginning and continuance. The second begins with my unseen self, my personality, and places me in a world which has true eternity, but which is perceptible only to the understanding, and with which I am conscious of being, not, as in the former case, accidental, but in universal and indispensable connection." — KANT ("Critique of Pure Reason," Conclusion).

"A new commandment I give unto you, that ye love one another." — GOSPEL OF JOHN, xiii. 34.

INTRODUCTION

LET us picture to ourselves a man whose only means of livelihood is a mill. This man is the son and grandson of a miller, and knows thoroughly, by tradition, how to deal with every part of the mill so that it shall grind well. This man, though ignorant of mechanics, adjusts all the parts of the mill to the best of his ability, so that the product may be profitable and good, and that men may live and eat.

But it has chanced that this man has begun to reflect upon the construction of the mill, to hear some confused statements about its mechanism, and he has begun to observe what part is turned by what other part.

And, from the fly-wheel to the grindstone, from the grindstone to the mill-race, from the mill-race to the wheel, from the wheel to the gate, the dam, and the water, he has come clearly to comprehend that the whole matter lies in the dam and the river. And the man has rejoiced so greatly in this discovery of his, that instead of scrutinizing, as heretofore, the quality of the flour which comes forth, instead of raising and lowering the millstones, of shoeing them, of tightening and slackening the belt, he has begun to study the river. And his mill has been thrown entirely out of gear. People have begun to tell the miller that he is not behaving rightly. He has disputed, and continued to reason about the river. And he has worked so much, so very much, over this, he has disputed so much and so hotly with those who have proved to him the falsity of his premises, that he has, at last, become convinced that the river is the mill itself.

To every proof of the falsity of his course of reasoning such a miller will reply: "No mill grinds without water. Consequently, in order to know the mill, it is requisite to know how to admit the water, to know the force of its current and whence it is derived; hence, in order to know the mill, it is necessary to know the river."

The miller cannot be logically controverted in his line of argument. The only means of dispelling his illusion lies in showing him that, in every course of reasoning, the reasoning itself is not so important as the place occupied by the reasoning, *i.e.* that, in order to meditate fruitfully, it is indispensable to know upon what to meditate first, and what afterward; to demonstrate to him that sensible activity is distinguished from senseless activity only in this, — that sensible activity disposes its meditations in the order of their importance, deciding which reasoning must come first, second, third, tenth, and so on. But senseless activity consists in reasoning without order. It must be demonstrated to him that the order of this arrangement is not accidental, but that it depends upon the object for which the reasoning is conducted.

The object of all courses of reasoning determines the order in which the separate trains of thought must be arranged in order to be understood.

And reasoning not bound together by a common aim of all the arguments is foolish, no matter how logical it may be.

The aim of the miller consists in producing good flour, and this aim, if he will keep it in view, will determine for him the most unquestionable regularity and order of sequence for his reasoning about the millstones, the wheel, the dam, and the river.

But without this relation to the aim of his reasoning, the miller's arguments, no matter how fine and logical they may be, will be inherently irregular and, what is the principal consideration, vain; they will be like the reasoning of Kifa Mokeevitch,[1] when he argued as to what should be the thickness of the shell of an elephant's egg, if elephants were produced from the egg, like birds.

[1] An incoherent reasoner, introduced in Part Second of Gogol's "Dead Souls." — TRANS.

And such in my opinion are the arguments of our contemporary science about life.

Life is the mill which man desires to investigate. The mill is necessary to grind well; life is necessary only in order that it may be good. And this branch of investigation man cannot abandon for a single moment with impunity. If he does abandon it, his deliberations infallibly lose their place, and become like the reasoning of Mokeevitch as to how much powder would be required to break the shell of elephants' eggs.

Man studies life only in order that it may become better. In this manner have those men studied life who have advanced humanity in the path of knowledge. But, by the side of these true teachers and benefactors of humanity, there always have existed, and there exist now, reasoners who have abandoned the aim of reasoning, and who, in its stead, investigate the question as to the origin of life, — as to why the mill turns. Some assert that it is by reason of the water; others, that it is in consequence of the arrangement. The dispute waxes hot, and the subject of discussion moves farther and farther away, and is completely replaced by utterly foreign topics.

There is an ancient jest regarding the dispute of a Jew and a Christian. The story runs that the Christian, replying to the confused subtleties of the Jew, slapped the latter on his bald pate with his palm, so that it cracked, and put the question: "Did the crack come from the pate or the palm?" And the dispute about faith was replaced by a fresh and insoluble problem.

Something of the same sort has been in progress since the most ancient times, side by side with men's true wisdom, and in connection with the question about life.

Discussions are known to have arisen in the most ancient times as to the origin of life? whether from an immaterial beginning, or from the combination of various materials? And these discussions have continued down to the present day, so that no end to them can be foreseen, because the aim of all discussion has been abandoned, and life is reasoned upon apart from its aim, and by the word life — life itself is not understood, but that from which it proceeds, or that which accompanies it.

Now, not only in scientific books, but even in conversation, when life is mentioned, the discussion is not about what we all know, — about life; about life of which I am conscious by those sufferings which I fear and which I hate, and by those joys and pleasures which I desire; but of something which came into existence, perhaps, through the play of chance according to some physical laws, and, perhaps, because it possesses in itself some secret cause.

Now the word "life" is ascribed to something contestable, which does not contain within itself the chief signs of life: the consciousness of suffering and of enjoyment, and of aspirations toward goodness.

"La vie est l'ensemble des fonctions, qui resiste à la mort. La vie est l'ensemble des phénomènes, qui se succédent pendant un temps limité dans un être organisé." Life is the sum total of the functions which resist death. Life is the sum total of the phenomena which follow each other in the course of a limited time in an organic being.

Setting aside the inaccuracy, the tautology, with which these definitions are filled, the substance of them all is identical, namely, — that which all men in common understand incontestably by the word "life" is not defined by them, but some processes or other which are accompanied by life and other phenomena.

Under the majority of these definitions comes the activity of the crystal in process of formation; under some comes the activity of fermentation, decomposition; and under all comes the life of each separate cell in my body, for which there nothing exists — neither good nor evil. Some of the processes that take place in the crystal, in the protoplasm, in the germ of the protoplasm, in the cells of my body and of other bodies, are called by a word which is indissolubly connected in me with the consciousness of an aspiration toward my welfare.

Arguments upon some of the conditions of life, as life itself, are precisely the same as the argument about the river, as about the mill. These arguments are, possibly, very necessary for some purpose or other. But they do not touch the subject which they intend to discuss. And, therefore, all deductions as to life drawn from such arguments cannot fail to be false.

The word "life" is very short and very clear, and every one understands what it signifies, and we are bound always to employ it in that sense which is comprehensible to every one. Surely this word is comprehensible to every one, not because it is very accurately defined by other words and ideas, but, on the contrary, because this word expresses a fundamental conception, from which are deduced many, if not all, other conceptions, and therefore, in order to draw deductions from this conception, we are bound, first of all, to accept that conception in its central signification which is undisputed by every one. And precisely this, it seems to me, has been neglected by the contending parties in connection with the conception of life. It has come to pass that the fundamental conception of life, taken at first, not in its central significance, in consequence of disputes about it, and departing ever more and more from its fundamental meaning, accepted by every one, has finally lost the thought upon which it is based, and has received another meaning, which does not correspond to it. This has come to pass, that the very center from which the figure was drawn has been deserted and transferred to another point. Men dispute over the question, whether life lies in the cell or in the protoplasm, or, still lower, in inorganic matter.

But, before disputing, we should ask ourselves, have we a right to attribute the conception of life to a cell?

We say, for instance, that there is life in the cell, that the cell is the living being. But the fundamental conception of human life and the conception of life which is contained in the cell are two conceptions which are not only utterly different, but which cannot be united. One conception excludes the other. I discover that the whole of my body, without exception, consists of cells. These cells, I am informed, possess the same sort of life as myself, and are precisely such living beings as myself; but I acknowledge that I am alive only because I am conscious that I, with all the cells which constitute me, am one living, indivisible being. But I am informed that the whole of me, without exception, is composed of living cells. To whom am I to attribute the property of life, to the cells or to myself? If I admit that the cells have life, then from the idea of life I must obtain the chief indication of my life, the consciousness that I am a single, living being; but if I do not admit that I have life as an independent being, then it is evident that I can by no means attribute that property to the cells of which my body is composed, and of whose consciousness I know nothing.

Either I am alive, and there are portions of me which are not alive, called cells, or there exists an assemblage of living cells, and my consciousness of life is not life, but merely an illusion.

For we do not say that there is in the cells anything that we call *bryzn*, but we say that there is "life" (Zhizn). We say "life" because by this word we understand, not some indefinite *x*, but a thoroughly well-defined dimension, which we all call by the same name, and know only through ourselves as the consciousness of ourselves with our own unit of body, indivisible from ourselves,—and hence such a conception is inapplicable to those cells of which my body is composed.

In whatever investigations or observations a man engages, he is bound, in stating his observations, by every word to mean that which every one indisputably understands alike, and not some conception or other which is necessary to him, but wholly incompatible with its fundamental conception comprehensible to all.

If the word "life" can be used so that it designates, indifferently, both the property of an object as a whole, and entirely different properties of all its component parts, as is done in the case of the cell and the animal composed of cells, then other words may also be employed in the same way. We may say, for example, that, as all thoughts are composed of words, and all words are composed of letters, and letters are made up of lines, the drawing of lines is the same as the exposition of thoughts, and that, therefore, lines may be called thoughts.

The most ordinary phenomenon in the scientific world is to hear and to read discussions upon the origin of *life* from the play of physical, mechanical powers.

But it is doubtful if the majority of the scientific people hold to this — I find it difficult to express it — opinion which is not an opinion, this paradox which is not a paradox, but rather a jest or a riddle.

It asserts that life proceeds from the play of physical and mechanical forces, of those physical forces which we have named physical and mechanical merely in contradistinction to the conception of life.

It is evident that the word "life," improperly applied to conceptions which are foreign to it, departing farther and farther from its fundamental signification, has abandoned its center to such a degree that life is already assumed to be where, according to our conceptions, life cannot exist. The assumption is equivalent to asserting that there exists a circle or sphere whose center lies outside of its periphery.

In fact, life, which I cannot imagine as otherwise than as a striving from evil toward good, proceeds from those regions where I can discern neither good nor evil. It is evident that the center of the conception of life has been entirely shifted. Moreover, following up the investigations into that something called life, I even see that these investigations touch hardly any of the conceptions with which I am acquainted. I perceive an entire series of new conceptions, and of words which possess their conventional meaning in the scientific jargon, but which have nothing in common with existing conceptions.

The conception of life which is familiar to me is not understood as every one understands it, and the conceptions deduced from it do not accord with the usual conceptions, but present themselves as new, conventional conceptions, having received manufactured names to correspond.

The human language is becoming more and more supplanted in scientific investigations, and instead of language, the means of expression of existing objects and ideas, a scientific volapük reigns, distinguished from the real volapük only in this, that the real volapük calls existing objects and conceptions by universal words, but the scientific volapük calls, by words which do not exist, conceptions which do not exist.

The sole means of mental communication between men is language, and, in order that this communication may be possible, it is necessary so to employ language that every word shall infallibly evoke, in every one, corresponding and accurate conceptions. But if it be possible to use language at random, and by that language to understand whatever occurs to us, it is better not to speak, but to indicate everything by signs.

I admit that to settle the laws of the world from the deductions of the mind alone, without experience or observation, is a false and unscientific course — that is to say, it cannot afford true knowledge; but will it not be still worse to study the phenomena of the world by experiments and observations, and at the same time be guided in these experiments and observations by conceptions which are not fundamental and common to all men, but conventional, and to describe the results of these experiments in words to which a varying significance can be attached? The best apothecary's shop is productive of the greatest injury if the labels are pasted on the bottles not according to their contents, but to suit the convenience of the apothecary.

But men say to me: "Science does not set itself the task of examining all the combinations of life (including within it, will, the desire for good, and the spiritual world); it makes only an abstract from the ideas of life of those phenomena which are subject to its experimental investigations.

This would be very good and lawful. But we know that this is not at all the case in the representations of the scientific men of our times. If, first of all, the conception of life were admitted in its central significance, in that in which every one understands it, it would afterward be clearly settled that science, having made from this conception an abstraction of all its sides, except of the one subject to external observation, looks upon the phenomena from that side only for which it has its own peculiar methods of investigation, it would all be very well, and it would be quite another thing; then the place which science would have occupied, and the results to which we should have arrived on the foundation of science, would have been entirely different. That which is must be said, and we must not conceal that which we all know. Do we not know that the majority of experimental scientific investigators are fully convinced that they are studying, not one side only of life, but all life?

Astronomy, mechanics, physics, chemistry, and all the other sciences, together and separately, work over the side of life appertaining to each without coming to any results as to life in general. Only during the period of their savagery, that is to say, of their indistinctness, their ill-defined state, did some of these sciences endeavor from their own point of view to grasp all the phenomena of life, and became confused, through inventing for themselves new conceptions and new words. Thus it was with astronomy when it was astrology, thus it was with chemistry when it was alchemy. The same thing now takes place with that experimental science of evolution which, surveying one side or several sides of life, brings forward a claim to the study of all life.

Men with such a false view of science by no means wish to admit that only a few sides of life are subject to their investigation, but they affirm that all life, with all its phenomena, will be studied by them, by the path of external experiment. "If," say they, "*psychics*" (they are fond of this indefinite word of their volapük) "are still unknown to us, they will yet be known to us. By following up one side or several sides of the phenomena of life, we shall learn to know all sides. That is to say, in other words, that, if we gaze very long and earnestly upon an object from one side, we shall see the object from all sides, and even from its interior."

Amazing as is this strange doctrine,—explicable only by the fanaticism of superstition,—it does exist, and, like every whimsical, fanatical doctrine, it produces its destructive effect, directing the activity of human thought in a false and frivolous path. Conscientious toilers perish, having consecrated their lives to the study of an almost utterly worthless thing. The material forces of people perish from being turned in a direction which is useless. The young generations perish, being directed to the same idle activity as Kifa Mokeevitch, erected into the rank of the highest service to humanity.

It is generally said: Science studies life from all sides. And here lies the point, that every subject has as many sides as there are radii in a sphere, that is to say, they are innumerable, and it is impossible to study from all sides; but one must know from which side it is most important and necessary, and from which it is less important and less useful. As it is impossible to approach an object from all sides at once, so it is impossible to study the phenomena of life from all sides and at once. And, willy-nilly, an order of succession is established. And herein lies the gist of the matter. But this order of succession is furnished only by an understanding of life.

Only a right understanding of life imparts the proper significance and direction to science in general, and to each science in particular, regulating them according to the importance of their significance in connection with life. But if the understanding of life is not such as is implanted within all of us, then science itself will be erroneous.

Not what we call science determines life, but our conception of life determines what should be acknowledged as science. And therefore, in order that science may be science, the question must first be settled as to what is and what is not science, and to this end our idea of life must be elucidated.

I will express the whole of my thought frankly; we all know the fundamental dogma of faith of this false experimental science.

Matter and its energy exist! Energy moves; mechanical movement is converted into molecular; molecular movement is expressed by heat, electricity, nervous, and brain movement. And all the phenomena of life, without exception, present themselves as relations of energy. Everything is thus beautiful, simple, clear, and, chief of all, convenient. So that, if there is nothing of all that which we so much desire, and which so simplifies our life, then all this must be invented in some manner or other.

And here is the whole of my audacious thought: the chief portion of the energy, zeal, and activity of experimental science is founded on the desire to invent everything that is necessary for the firm establishment of so comfortable a representation.

In all the activity of this science we behold, not so much a desire to investigate the phenomena of life, as the one ever present anxiety to prove the veracity of its fundamental tenet. That force is wasted on experiments to explain the origin of organic from inorganic and psychical activity from the processes of organism. The organic does not pass into the inorganic: let us seek at the bottom of the sea, we shall find a bit of stuff which we will call the kernel, a monera.

And it is not there; we shall believe that it is to be found, — the more so as the whole infinity of centuries stands at our service, into which we can thrust everything that ought to be in our creed, — but which is not there in reality.

It is the same with the transition from organic to psychical activity. It does not yet exist. But we believe that it will exist, and we bend all the powers of our intelligence to prove the possibility of this at least.

Disputes as to that which does not concern life, namely, as to whence life proceeds — whether it is animism or vitalism, or, again, the idea of some special force — have concealed from men the principal question of life — that question without which the conception of life loses its coherence, and have gradually led scientific men — those who should guide others — into the position of a man who walks along, and even hastens his steps, but who has forgotten precisely whither he is going.

But perhaps I am deliberately endeavoring not to see the vast results afforded by science in its present course? But, surely, no results can correct a false course? Let us concede the impossible, — that all that contemporary science desires to know of life, and of which it asserts (though it does not believe this itself) — that all this will be revealed; let us concede that all has been revealed, that all is as clear as day. It is clear how organic material arises from inorganic through adaptations; it is clear how physical energy is converted into feeling, will, thought, and that all this is known, not only to students in the gymnasiums, but to village schoolboys.

I am aware that such and such thoughts and feelings proceed from such and such movements. Well, and what then? Can I or can I not direct these movements, in order to arouse in myself such and such thoughts? The question as to how I must awaken thoughts and feelings in myself and in others remains not only unsettled, but even untouched.

I know that scientific men do not trouble themselves to answer this question. The solution of this problem seems to them very simple, as the solution of a difficult problem always seems to a man who does not understand it. The answer to the question, how to regulate our life when it is in our power, seems very easy to men of science. They say: Regulate it so that people may satisfy their wants; science provides means, in the first place, for the proper determination of wants, and, in the second, means to produce so easily and in such abundance that all wants can be easily satisfied, and then people will be happy.

But if we inquire what they call needs, and where lie the limits of needs, they simply reply: "Science — that is what science is for — to portion them out into physical, mental, æsthetic, even moral, and plainly to define what needs are legitimate and in what measure they are illegitimate. It will define this in course of time." But if they are asked how one must guide one's self in the decision as to the legitimacy and illegitimacy of needs, they reply boldly: "By the study of the needs." But the word *need* has only two meanings: either a condition of existence, and the conditions of existence of every object are innumerable in quantity, and hence all the conditions cannot be studied; or the need of happiness for human beings can be known and determined only by consciousness, and is therefore even less susceptible of investigation by contemporary science.

There is an institution, a corporation, an assembly of some sort, either of people or of minds, which is infallible, and which is called science. It will determine all this in course of time.

Is it not evident that all this settlement of the question is merely a paraphrase of the kingdom of the Messiah, in which the part of the Messiah is played by science, and that, for the sake of having the explanation explain anything, it is necessary to believe in the dogmas of science as indisputably as the Hebrews believe in the Messiah, which is what the orthodox scientists do, with this difference only, that the orthodox Jew, representing to himself the Messiah as the envoy of God, can believe that all that the Messiah will establish by his power will be excellent, but the orthodox believer in science cannot, from the nature of things, believe that by means of the external investigation of needs the chief and only question concerning life can be decided?

CHAPTER I

THE FUNDAMENTAL CONTRADICTION OF HUMAN LIFE

EVERY man lives only for his own good, for his personal welfare. If man feels no desire for happiness, he is not even conscious that he is alive. Man cannot imagine life without the desire for happiness. To live is, for every man, the same thing as to desire and to attain happiness; to desire and to attain happiness is synonymous with living. Man is conscious of life only in himself, only in his own personality, and hence, at first, man imagines that the happiness which he desires for himself personally is happiness, and nothing more.

At first, it seems to him that he and he alone really lives.

The life of other beings seems to him not in the least like his own. He imagines it as merely the semblance of life. Man only observes the life of other beings, and learns from observation only that they are alive. Man knows about the life of other beings when he is willing to think of them, but he *knows* of his own, he cannot for a single moment cease to *know* that he lives, and hence to every man his own life only appears real life. The life of other beings about him seems to him to be merely one of the conditions of his own existence. If he does not desire evil to others, it is only because the sight of the sufferings of others interferes with his happiness. If he desires good to others, it is not at all the same as for himself — it is not in order that the person to whom he wishes good may be well placed, but only in order that the happiness of other beings may augment the happiness of his own life. Only that happiness in this life is important and necessary to a man which he feels to be his own, *i.e.* his own individual happiness.

And behold, in striving for the attainment of this, his own individual happiness, man perceives that his happiness depends upon other beings. And upon watching and observing these other beings, man sees that all of them, both men and even animals, possess precisely the same conception of life as he himself. Each one of these beings, precisely like himself, is conscious only of his own life and his own happiness, considers his own life alone of importance and real, and the life of all other beings only as a means to his individual happiness. Man sees that every living being, precisely like himself, must be ready, for the sake of his petty happiness, to deprive all other beings of greater happiness and even of life.

And, having comprehended this, man involuntarily makes this calculation; that if this is so, — and he knows that it is indubitably so, — then, not one being or not half a score of beings only, but all the innumerable beings in the world, for the attainment, each of his own object, are ready every moment to annihilate him, — that man for whom alone life exists. And, having apprehended this, man sees that his personal happiness, in which alone he understands life, is not only not to be easily won by him, but that it will assuredly be taken from him.

The longer a man lives, the more firmly is this conviction confirmed by experience, and the man perceives that the life of the world in which he shares, composed of individualities bound together, desirous of exterminating and devouring each other, not only cannot be a happiness for him, but will, assuredly, be a great evil.

But this is not all: if the man is placed in such favorable conditions that he can successfully contend with other personalities, fearing nothing for his own, both experience and reason speedily show him that even those semblances of happiness which he wrests from life, in the form of enjoyment for his own personality, do not constitute happiness, and are but specimens of happiness as it were, vouchsafed him merely in order that he may be the more vividly conscious of the suffering which is always bound up with enjoyment.

The longer man lives, the more plainly does he see that weariness, satiety, toils, and sufferings become ever greater and greater, and enjoyments ever less and less.

But this is not all: on beginning to become conscious of a decline of strength, and of ill-health, and gazing upon ill-health, age, and the death of others, he perceives this also in addition, that even his existence, in which alone he recognizes real, full life, is approaching weakness, old age, and death, with every hour, with every movement; that his life, besides being subject to thousands of chances of annihilation from other beings warring with him, and from ever increasing sufferings, is, in virtue of its very nature, nothing else than an incessant approach to death, to that condition in which, together with the life of the individual, will, assuredly, be annihilated every possibility of any personal happiness. The man perceives that he, his own personality, — that in which alone he feels life, does nothing but struggle with those with whom it is impossible to struggle — with the whole world; that he is in search of enjoyments which give only the semblances of happiness, and which always terminate in sufferings, and he wishes to hold back life, which it is impossible to hold back. The man perceives that he himself, his own personality, that for which, alone, he desires life and happiness, can have neither life nor happiness. And that which he desires to have — life and happiness — is possessed only by those beings who are strangers to him, whom he does not feel, and cannot feel, and of whose existence he cannot know and does not wish to know.

That which for him is the most important of all, and which alone is necessary to him, that which — as it seems to him — alone possesses life in reality, his personality, that which will perish, will become bones and worms, is not he; but that which is unnecessary for him, unimportant to him, which he does not feel to be alive, all that world of ever changing and struggling beings, that is to say, real life, will remain, and will exist forever

So that the sole life which is felt by man, and which evokes all this activity, proves to be something deceptive and impossible; but the inward life, which he does not love, which he does not feel, of which he is ignorant, is the one real life.

That of which he is not conscious, — that alone possesses those qualities of which he would fain be the sole possessor. And this is not that which presents itself to a man in the evil moments of his gloomy moods, this is not a representation which it is possible for him not to have, but it is, on the contrary, such a palpable, indubitable truth, that if this thought once occurs to man, or if others explain it to him, he can never again free himself from it, he can never more force it out of his consciousness.

CHAPTER II

THE SOLE AIM OF LIFE

The contradiction of life has been admitted by mankind from the most ancient times. The enlighteners of mankind expounded to men the definition of life, solving the problem of this inward contradiction, but the Scribes and Pharisees conceal it from the people.

THE sole aim of life, as it first presents itself to man, is the happiness of himself as an individual, but individual happiness there cannot be; if there were anything resembling individual happiness in life, then that life in which alone happiness can exist, the life of the individual, is borne irresistibly, by every movement, by every breath, toward suffering, toward evil, toward death, toward annihilation.

And this is so self-evident and so plain that every thinking man, old or young, learned or unlearned, will see it.

This argument is so simple and natural that it presents itself to every reasoning man, and has been known to mankind ever since the most ancient times.

"The life of man as an individual, striving only toward

his own happiness, amid an endless number of similar individuals, engaged in annihilating each other and in annihilating themselves, is evil and absurdity, and real life cannot be like that." This is what man has been saying to himself from the most ancient times down to the present day, and this inward inconsistency of the life of man was expressed with remarkable force and clearness by the Indian, and the Chinese, and the Egyptian, and the Greek, and the Jewish sages; and from the most ancient times the mind of man has been directed to the study of such a happiness for man as should not be canceled by the contest of beings among themselves, by suffering, and by death. In the increasingly better solution of this indubitable, unavoidable happiness for man inviolable by contest, by sufferings, and by death, lies the whole progress of mankind during the period of our acquaintance with its life.

From the most ancient times, and among the most widely varying peoples, the great teachers of mankind have revealed to men more and more the clear definitions of life, solving its inward contradictions, and have pointed out the true happiness and true life which is proper to men.

And, since the position of all men in the world is identical, since the contradiction of his strivings after his personal happiness, and the consciousness of its impossibility is identical for every man, all the definitions of true happiness, and therefore of true life, revealed to men by the grandest minds of humanity, are identical in their nature.

"Life is the diffusion of that light which, for the happiness of men, descended upon them from heaven," said Confucius, six hundred years before Christ.

"Life is the peregrination and the perfection of souls, which attain to greater and ever greater happiness," said the Brahmins of the same day.

"Life is the abnegation of self, with the purpose of attaining blessed Nirvana," said Buddha, a contemporary of Confucius.

"Life is the path of peacefulness and lowliness, for

the attainment of happiness," said Lao-dzi, also a contemporary of Confucius.

"Life is that which God breathed into man's nostrils, in order that he, by fulfilling his law, might receive happiness," says the Hebrew sage, Moses.

"Life is submission to the reason, which gives happiness to man," said the Stoics.

"Life is love toward God and our neighbor, which gives happiness to man," said Christ, summing up in his definition all those which had preceded it.

Such are the definitions of life, which, thousands of years before our day, pointing out to men real and indestructible happiness in the place of the false and impossible happiness of the individual, solve the contradictions of human life and impart to it a reasonable sense.

It is possible not to agree with these definitions of life, it is possible to assume that these definitions can be expressed more accurately and more clearly; but it is impossible not to see that these definitions are such that the acknowledgment of them, since it does away with the inconsistencies of life, and replaces the aspiration for the unattainable happiness of the individual, by another aspiration, — for a happiness indestructible by suffering and death, imparts to life a reasonable sense. It is impossible not to see this also, that these definitions, while theoretically correct, are also confirmed by the experience of life, and that millions and millions of men, who have accepted and who do accept such definitions of life, have, in fact, proved, and do prove, the possibility of replacing the aspiration toward individual welfare by an aspiration toward another happiness, of a sort which is not to be destroyed by suffering and death.

But, in addition to those men who have understood and who do understand the definitions of life, revealed to men by the great enlighteners of humanity, and who live by them, there always have been and there are now an immense number of people who, during a certain period of their life, and sometimes their whole life long, have led and do lead a purely animal existence, being not only ignorant of those definitions which serve to solve the contradictions of human life, but not even perceiving that contradiction of it which they solve. And there always have been and there now exist among those people, men who, in consequence of their exclusively external position, regard themselves as called upon to guide mankind, and who, without themselves comprehending the meaning of human life, have taught and do teach other people life, which they themselves do not understand; to the effect that human life is nothing but individual existence.

Such false teachers have existed in all ages, and exist in our day also. Some confess in words the teachings of those enlighteners of mankind, in whose traditions they have been brought up, but not comprehending their rational meaning, they convert these teachings into supernatural revelations as to the past and future life of men, and require only the fulfilment of ceremonial forms.

This is the doctrine of the Pharisees in the very broadest sense, *i.e.* of the men who teach that a life preposterous in itself can be amended by faith in a future life, obtained by the fulfilment of external forms.

Others, who do not acknowledge the possibility of any other life than the visible one, reject all marvels and everything supernatural, and boldly affirm that the life of man is nothing but his animal existence from his birth to his death. This is the doctrine of the Scribes — of men who teach that there is nothing preposterous in the life of man, any more than in that of animals.

And both the former and the latter false prophets, in spite of the fact that the teaching of both is founded upon the same coarse lack of understanding of the fundamental inconsistency of human life, have always been at enmity with each other, and are still at enmity. Both these doctrines reign in our world, and, contending with each other, they fill the world with their dissensions — by those same dissensions concealing from men those definitions of life which reveal the path to the true happiness of men, and which were given to men thousands of years ago.

The Pharisees, not comprehending this definition of life, which was given to men by those teachers in whose traditions they were brought up, replace it with their false interpretations of a future life, and, in addition to this, strive to conceal from men the definition of life of other enlighteners of humanity, by presenting the latter to their disciples in the coarsest and harshest aspect, assuming that, by so doing, they will uphold the absolute authority of that doctrine upon which they found their interpretation.[1]

And the Scribes, not even suspecting in the teachings of the Pharisees those rational grounds from which they took their rise, flatly reject all doctrines concerning a future life, and boldly affirm that all these doctrines have no foundation whatever, but are merely remnants of the coarse customs of ignorance, and that the forward movement of mankind consists in not putting any questions whatever to one's self concerning life which overleap the bounds of the animal existence of man.

CHAPTER III

THE ERROR OF THE SCRIBES

AND, marvelous to relate! the fact that all the teachings of the great minds of mankind so startled men by their grandeur that the rude populace attributed to them, for the most part, a supernatural character, and accepted their authors as demigods, — the very fact which serves as the chief indication of the importance of these doctrines, — that very fact serves the Scribes, so they think, as their best proof of the incorrectness and antiquated character of these doctrines.

The fact that the insignificant teachings of Aristotle, Bacon, Comte, and others have remained, and will al-

[1] The unity of the rational idea of the definition of life by other enlighteners of mankind does not present itself to them as the best proof of the truth of their teaching, since it injures faith in the senseless, false interpretations with which they replace the substance of doctrine.

ways remain, the property of a small number of their readers and admirers, and on account of their falsity, never could influence the masses, and hence were never subjected to superstitious distortions and excrescences, — this mark of their insignificance is recognized as a proof of their truth. But the teachings of the Brahmins, of Buddha, of Zoroaster, Lao-dzi, Confucius, Isaiah, and Christ are accounted superstitious and erroneous, merely because these teachings have effected a change in the lives of millions.

The fact that millions of men have lived, and do still live, according to these superstitions, because even in their mutilated form they furnish men with answers to questions about true happiness; the fact that these doctrines not only are shared by, but serve as a foundation for the thoughts of the best men of all ages, and that the theories professed by the Scribes alone are shared only by themselves, are always contested, and sometimes do not live ten years, and are forgotten as quickly as they were evolved, — does not disturb them in the least.

On no point does that false direction of learning followed by contemporary society express itself with such clearness as on the place which is held in this society by the doctrines of those great teachers of life by which mankind has lived and developed, and by which it still lives and develops itself. It is affirmed in the calendars, in the department of statistical information, that the creeds now professed by the inhabitants of this globe number one thousand. Among the list of these creeds are reckoned Buddhism, Brahmanism, Confucianism, Laodism, and Christianity. There are a thousand creeds, and the people of our day believe this implicitly. There are a thousand creeds, they are all nonsense — why study them? And the men of our time consider it a disgrace if they do not know the latest apothegms of wisdom of Spencer, Helmholtz, and others; but of Brahma, Buddha, Confucius, Mentizus, Lao-dzi, Epictetus, and Isaiah they sometimes know the names, and sometimes they do not even know that much. It never enters their heads that the creeds professed in our day number not one thousand, but three, in all: the Chinese, the Indian, and the European-Christian (with its offshoot, Mahometanism), and that the books pertaining to these faiths can be purchased for five rubles, and read through in two weeks, and that in these books, by which all mankind has lived and now lives, with the exception of seven per cent, almost unknown to us, is contained all human wisdom, all that has made mankind what it is.

But not only is the populace ignorant of these teachings, the learned men are not acquainted with them, unless it is their specialty; philosophers by profession do not not consider it necessary to glance into these books. And why, indeed, study those men who have solved the inconsistency of his life admitted by the sensible man, and have defined true happiness and the life of men?

The Scribes, not understanding this contradiction or inconsistency which constitutes the beginning of rational life, boldly assert that there is no contradiction, because they do not perceive it, and that the life of man is merely his animal existence.

Those who do see, understand and define that which they see before them — the blind man fumbles before him with a cane, and asserts that nothing exists except that which the touch of his cane reveals to him.

CHAPTER IV

THE TEACHING OF THE SCRIBES, UNDER THE CONCEPTION OF THE WHOLE LIFE OF MAN, PRESENTS THE VISIBLE PHENOMENA OF HIS ANIMAL EXISTENCE, AND FROM THEM DRAWS DEDUCTIONS AS TO THE AIM OF HIS LIFE

"Life is what takes place in a living being from the time of his birth to his death. A man, a dog, a horse, is born; each one has his special body; and this special body of his lives and then dies; the body decomposes, passes into other beings, but will never be the former being again. Life was, and life came to an end; the heart beats, the lungs breathe, the body does not decompose,—which means that the man, the horse, the dog, is alive; the heart has ceased to beat, breathing has come to an end, the body has begun to decompose,—which means that it is dead, and that there is no life. Life is that process which goes on in the body of man, as well as in that of the animal, in the interval of time between birth and death. What can be clearer?"

Thus have the very rudest people, who have hardly emerged from animal existence, always looked upon life, and thus do they look upon it now. And lo! in our day, the teaching of the Scribes, entitling itself science, professes this same coarse, primitive presentation of life as the only true one. Making use of all those instruments of inward knowledge which mankind has acquired, this false teaching is systematically desirous of leading man back into that gloom of ignorance from which he has been striving to escape for so many thousand years.

"We cannot define life in our consciousness," says this doctrine. "We go astray when we observe it in ourselves. That conception of happiness, the aspiration toward which in our consciousness constitutes our life, is a deceitful illusion, and life cannot be understood in that consciousness. In order to understand life, it is only necessary to observe its manifestations as movements of matter. Only from these observations, and the laws deduced from them, can we discover the law of life itself, and the law of the life of man."[1]

The science of physics talks of the laws and relations of forces, without putting to itself any questions as to what force is, and without endeavoring to explain the nature of force. The science of chemistry speaks of the relations of matter, without questioning what matter is, and without seeking to define its nature; the science of biology deals with the forms of life, putting to itself no questions as to what life is, and not seeking to define its nature. And force and matter and life are accepted

[1] Real science, knowing its proper place and hence its object, modest and hence powerful, never has said and never says this.

as real sciences, not as subjects for study, but adopted as axioms from other realms of learning, as bases of operation upon which is constructed the edifice of every separate science. Thus does real science regard the subject, and this science cannot have any injurious influence upon the masses, inclining them to ignorance. But not thus does the false, philosophizing science look upon the subject. "We will study matter and force and life; and, if we study them, we can know them," say they, not reflecting that they are not studying matter, force, and life, but merely their relations and their forms.

And behold, false science, having placed under the conception of the whole life of man its visible portion which is known to him through his consciousness, — the animal existence, — begins to study these apparent phenomena at first in the animal man, then in animals in general, then in plants, then in matter, constantly asserting, in the meanwhile, that they are studying not a few phenomena, but life itself. Their observations are so complicated, so varied, so confused, so much time and strength have been wasted upon them, that men gradually forget the original error of admitting a portion of the subject as the whole subject, and finally become fully convinced that the study of the visible properties of matter, plants, and animals is study of life itself, of that life which is known to man only through his consciousness.

What takes place is somewhat similar to that which happens when a person is showing something in the dark, and is desirous of upholding that mistake under which the spectators are laboring.

"Look nowhere," says the exhibitor, "except in the direction where the reflections appear, and, most of all, do not look at the object itself; for there is no object, but only its reflection."

This is the very thing which the false science of the Scribes of our day does, conniving with the rude throng, looking upon life without its chief definition, without its aspiration toward happiness, which is discovered only in the consciousness of man.[1] Proceeding directly from the definition of life, independent of the aspiration toward happiness, false science observes the objects of human beings, and, finding in them aims foreign to man, forces them upon him.

The aim of human beings, as presented by these external observations, is the preservation of one's individuality, the preservation of one's species, the production of others similar to one, and the struggle for existence; and this same fancied aim of life is also thrust on man.

False science, having adopted as a base of operation an antiquated presentation of life, in which that contradiction of human life which constitutes its chief property is not visible, — this fictitious science in its most extreme deductions arrives at that point which the coarse majority of mankind requires, — at the admission of the possibility of the happiness of individual life alone, at the admission for humanity of the happiness of the animal existence alone.

False science goes much farther even than the demands of the coarse herd for whom it wishes to find an explanation, — it arrives at the assertion that it rejects the rational consciousness of man from its first flash, it arrives at the deduction that the life of man, like that of every animal, consists in the struggle for the existence of individuality, race, and species.[2]

CHAPTER V

THE FALSE DOCTRINES OF THE SCRIBES AND PHARISEES GIVE NEITHER EXPLANATIONS OF THE MEANING OF REAL LIFE, NOR GUIDANCE THEREIN; THE INERTIA OF LIFE, WHICH HAS NO RATIONAL EXPLANATION, APPEARS AS THE SOLE GUIDE OF LIFE

"It is useless to define life; every one knows it, so let us live!" say, in their error, the men who are upheld

[1] See appendix at the end of the book, on "The false definition of life."
[2] See second appendix.

by false teachings. And, not knowing what life and its happiness are, it seems to them that they live, as it may seem to a man who is being borne along by the waves without exercising any control of his course, that he is sailing to the place where he should go, and where he wishes to go.

A child is born in want or in luxury, and he receives the training of the Pharisees or of the Scribes. For the child, for the young man, there exists as yet no contradiction in life nor problems concerning it, and therefore neither the explanations of the Pharisees nor the explanations of the Scribes are necessary to him, and they cannot govern his life. He learns simply from the example of the people who live around him, and this is equally the example of the Scribes and Pharisees; and both the former and the latter live only for personal happiness, and this is what they teach him.

If his parents are poor, he learns from them that the aim of life is the acquisition of as much bread and money as possible, and as little work as possible, so that his animal person may be as comfortable as possible.

If he has been born in luxury, he learns that the aim of life is wealth and honors, so that he may pass his time in the merriest and most agreeable manner possible.

All the knowledge acquired by the poor man is of use to him only for the purpose of improving the comfortable condition of his own person. All the attainments in science and art acquired by the rich man are of use to him only for the combating of ennui, and passing the time pleasantly. The longer both of them live, the more and more strongly do they imbibe the prevailing views of men of the world. They marry, have families, and their thirst for the acquisition of animal welfare of life is augmented by the justificatory excuse of their families; the struggle with others grows fiercer, and the inertia of the custom of life arranges itself solely with a view to the welfare of the individual.

And if there occurs to either the rich or the poor man a doubt as to the reasonableness of such a life, if to either there presents itself the question, "What is the reason for this objectless struggle for my existence, which my children will continue? or why this delusive pursuit of enjoyments, which end in suffering for me and for my children?" then there is hardly any likelihood that he will learn those definitions of life which were given long ago to mankind by its great teachers, who thousands of years before him found themselves in the same situation. The teachings of the Scribes and Pharisees so thickly veil them that he rarely succeeds in seeing them.

The Pharisees alone, to the question, "To what purpose this miserable life?" make reply: "Life is miserable, and always has been so, and must always be so; the happiness of life consists not in its present, but in the past, before life was, and in the future, after life is ended."

Brahmin, and Buddhist, and Lao-dziist, and Jewish, and Christian Pharisees always say one and the same thing. The present life is evil, and the explanation of this evil lies in the past, in the phenomenon of the world and of man; but the correction of the existing evil lies in the future, beyond the grave. All that man can do for the acquisition of happiness, not in this but in a future life, is — to believe in that teaching which we impart to you — to fulfil the ceremonial forms which we prescribe.

And the doubter, perceiving in the life of all men who are living for their own happiness, and in the life of the very Pharisees who live only for the same thing, the falsity of this explanation, and not penetrating the meaning of their reply, flatly refuses to believe them, and betakes himself to the Scribes.

"All teachings about any other life whatsoever than this which we see in the animal is the fruit of ignorance," say the Scribes. "All your doubts as to the reasonableness of your life are empty fancies. The life of worlds, of the earth, of man, of animals, of plants, have their laws, and we are investigating them, we are studying the origin of worlds, and of man, of animals and plants, and of all matter; we are also investigating what awaits the worlds when the sun shall cool, and so forth, and what has been and what will be with man, and with every animal and plant. We can show and prove that all has been and will be as we say; besides this, our investigations will contribute to the amelioration of mankind. But of your life and your aspirations toward happiness, we can tell you nothing more than what you already know without us: you are alive, so live as best you can."

And the doubter, having received no reply to his question from these either, remains as he was before, without any guidance whatever in life, except the impulses of his own personality.

Some of the doubters, according to the reasoning of Pascal, having said to themselves: "What if all the things with which the Pharisees frighten us for non-fulfilment of their prescribed forms should be true?" and so fulfil *in their leisure time* all the dictates of the Pharisees (there can be no loss, and there is a possibility that the profit may be great), while others, agreeing with the Scribes, flatly reject any other life and all religious forms, and say to themselves: "Not I alone, but all the rest, have lived and do live thus, — let what will be, be." And this discrepancy confers no superiority on either the one set or the other; and both the former and the latter remain without any explanation whatever of the meaning of their present life.

But it is necessary to live.

Human life is a series of actions from the time a man rises until he goes to bed; every day, of actions which are possible to him, man must incessantly make his choice out of hundreds of those which he will perform. Neither the teaching of the Pharisees, which explains the mysteries of the heavenly life, nor the teaching of the Scribes, which investigates the origin of worlds and of man, and draws conclusions concerning their future fate, furnishes that guidance for actions. But without guidance in the choice of his action a man cannot live. And so the man submits, perforce, not to reason, but to that external guidance of life which has always existed, and does exist in every community of men.

This guidance has no rational explanation, but it directs the vast majority of the actions of all men. This guidance is the habit of life of communities of men, ruling all the more powerfully over men in proportion as men have less comprehension of the meaning of their life. This guidance cannot be accurately defined, because it is composed of facts and actions, the most varied as to place and time. It is: lights upon the boards of their ancestors for the Chinese; pilgrimages to certain places for the Mahometan; a certain amount of prayer words for the Indian; it consists of fidelity to his flag, and honor to his uniform, for the warrior; the duel for the man of the world; blood-vengeance for the mountaineer; it means certain sorts of food on specified days, a particular mode of education for one's children; it means visits, a certain decoration of one's dwelling, specified manners of celebrating funerals, births, and deaths. It is an interminable number of facts and actions, filling the whole of life. It is what is called propriety, custom, and, most frequently of all, duty, and even sacred duty.

And it is to this guidance that the majority of mankind submit themselves, in spite of the explanations of life furnished by the Scribes and Pharisees. Man beholds everywhere about him, from his very childhood, men accomplishing those deeds with complete conviction and outward solemnity, and possessing no rational explanation of his life, and the man not only begins to do the same things, but even attempts to ascribe a rational meaning to these deeds. He wishes to believe that the people who do these things possess an explanation as to why, and to what end they do what they do. And he begins to be convinced that these deeds have a rational meaning, if not wholly known to him, yet known to these persons at least.

But the majority of the rest of mankind, not being possessed, any more than himself, of a rational explanation of life, find themselves in precisely the same situation as himself. They, also, do these things only because others, who, as it seems to them, have an explanation of these deeds, demand the same from them. And thus, involuntarily deceiving each other, people become ever more and more accustomed, not only to do these things without possessing a rational explanation, but they become accustomed to ascribing to these deeds some mysterious meaning incomprehensible even to themselves. And the less they understand the meaning of what they do, the more doubtful to themselves these acts become, the more importance do they attach to them, and with all the greater solemnity do they fulfil them. And the rich man and the poor man do that which others do round about them, and they call these acts their duty, their sacred duty, reassuring themselves by the thought that what has been done so long by so many people, and is so highly prized by them, cannot but be the real business of life. And men live on to hoar old age, to death, striving to believe that if they themselves do not know why they live, others do know this — the very people who know precisely as little about it as those who depend upon them.

New people come into existence, are born, grow up, and, looking upon this whirlpool of existence called life, — in which old, gray, respected men, surrounded by the reverence of the people, assert that this senseless commotion is life, and that there is no other, — go away after being jostled at its doors. Such a man, who has never beheld an assembly of men, having seen a crowding, lively, noisy throng at the entrance, and having decided that this is the assembly itself, after having been elbowed at the door, goes home with aching ribs and under the full conviction that he has been in the assembly.

We pierce mountains, we fly round the world; electricity, microscopes, telephones, wars, parliaments, philanthropy, the struggle of parties, universities, learned societies, museums, — is this life?

The whole of men's complicated, seething activity, with their trafficking, their wars, their roads of communication, their science and their arts, is, for the most part, only the thronging of the unintelligent crowd about the doorway of life.

CHAPTER VI

DIVISION OF CONSCIOUSNESS IN THE MEN OF OUR WORLD

"But verily, verily, I say unto you, the time is at hand, and is even now come, when the dead shall hear the voice of the Son of God, and, hearing, shall be made alive." And this time will come.

However much a man may have assured himself, and however much others may have assured him of this,— that life can only be happy and rational beyond the grave, or that only personal life can be happy and rational, — man cannot believe it. Man cherishes in the depths of his soul an ineffaceable demand that his life shall be happy and have a rational meaning; but a life having before it no other aim than the life beyond the grave, or an impossible bliss of personality, is evil and nonsense.

"Live for the future life?" says the man to himself: "but if this life, the only specimen of life with which I am acquainted, — my present life, — must be irrational, then it not only does not confirm in my mind the possibility of another, a rational life, but, on the contrary, it convinces me that life is, in its very substance, irrational, and that there can be no other life than an irrational one.

"Live for myself? But my individual life is evil and senseless. Live for my family? For my society? For my country or even mankind? But if my individual life is miserable and senseless, then the life of every other human individual is miserable and senseless also; and therefore an endless quantity of senseless and irrational persons, collected together, will not form even one happy and rational life. Live for myself, not knowing why, doing that which others do? But, surely, I am aware that others know no more than I why they do what they do."

The time will come when a rational consciousness will outgrow the false doctrines, and man will come to a halt in the midst of life, and demand explanations.[1]

Only the rare man, who has no connection with people of other modes of life, and only the man who is constantly engaged in an intense struggle with nature for the support of his bodily existence, can believe that the fulfilment of those senseless acts which he calls his duty can be the peculiar duty of his life.

The time is coming, and is already come, when that delusion which sets forth the renunciation — in words — of this life, for the sake of preparing for one's self one in the future, and the admission of the mere individual animal existence alone as life, and so-called duty as the business of life, — when that delusion will become clear to the majority of men, and only those forced by necessity, and dulled by a vicious career, will be able to exist without being conscious of the senselessness and poverty of their existence.

More and more frequent will be men's awakening to a rational sense; they will in their graves return to life, and the fundamental contradiction of human life will, in spite of all men's efforts to hide it from themselves, present itself before the majority of men with terrible power and distinctness.

"All my life consists of a desire for happiness for myself," says the man to himself, on awakening, "but my reason tells me that this happiness cannot exist for me, and that, whatever I may do, whatever I may attain to, all will end in one and the same thing, — in sufferings and death, in annihilation. I desire happiness, I desire life, I desire a rational sense, but in myself and in all who surround me there is evil, death, and incoherence. How am I to exist? How am I to live? What am I to do?" and there is no reply.

The man looks about him, and seeks an answer to his question, and finds it not. He finds around him doc-

[1] See third appendix at the end of the book.

trines that answer questions which he has never put to himself; but there is no answer in the world surrounding him to the question which he does put to himself. There is one anxiety for men who do, without themselves knowing why, the things which others do, when they themselves know not why.

All live as though unconscious of the wretchedness of their position and the senselessness of their activity. "Either *they* are irrational or *I* am," says the awakened man to himself. "But all cannot be irrational, so it must be that the irrational one is myself. But no — the rational *I* which says this to me cannot be irrational. Let it stand alone against all the world, but I cannot do otherwise than trust it."

And the man recognizes himself as alone in all the world, with all the terrible questions which rend his soul.

But it is necessary to live.

One *I*, his individuality, bids him live.

But another *I*, his reason, says, "It is impossible to live."

The man is conscious that he has been parted in twain. And this partition rends his soul like torture.

And the cause of this partition and of his suffering seems to him to be his reason.

Reason, the loftiest of man's faculties, which is indispensable to his life, which gives to him, naked and helpless amid the powers of nature which destroy him, both means of existence and means of enjoyment, — this faculty poisons his existence. In all the world which surrounds him, among living beings, the faculties peculiar to these beings are necessary to them all in common, and constitute their happiness. Plants, insects, animals, submitting to the law of their being, live a blissful, joyous, tranquil life.

But behold, in man, this loftiest faculty of his nature produces in him such a torturing condition of things that often — with ever increasing frequency of late days — man cuts the Gordian knot of his life, and kills himself simply for the sake of escaping from the torturing in ward contradictions produced by intelligent consciousness which, in our day, has been carried to the last degree of tension.

CHAPTER VII

THE PARTITION OF CONSCIOUSNESS ARISES FROM THE BLENDING OF THE LIFE OF THE ANIMAL WITH THE LIFE OF MAN

It seems to man that the partition of rational consciousness which has awakened within him shatters his life in fragments, and brings it to a standstill, only because he recognizes as his life that which has not been, is not, and could not be his life.

Having been reared and having grown up in the false doctrines of our world, which have confirmed in him the conviction that his life is nothing else than his individual existence, which began with his birth, it seems to man that he lived when he was a boy, a baby; then it seems to him that he has lived, without a break, when he was a youth and when he had reached full manhood. He has lived a very long time, as it seems to him, and during all that time has never ceased to live, and lo, all at once, he has reached a point where it has become indubitably clear to him that it is impossible for him to continue to live as he has lived before, and that his life has stopped and been shattered.

False teaching has confirmed him in the idea that his life is the period of time from birth to death; and, looking at the visible life of animals, he has confounded the idea of apparent life with his consciousness, and has become quite convinced that this life which he can see is his life.

The intelligent consciousness which has awakened within him, having advanced such demands as are not to be satisfied by the animal life, shows him the error of his conception of life; but the false teaching which has eaten into him prevents his confessing his error; he cannot reject his conception of life as an animal existence, and it seems to him that his life has come to a standstill through the awakening of intelligent consciousness. But that which he calls his life, his existence since his birth, has never even existed; his idea that he has been living all the time from his birth to the present moment is an illusion of consciousness, similar to the illusion of the senses in the visions of sleep; up to the time of his awakening he had no visions, they have all formed at the moment of his awakening. Before the awakening of his intelligent consciousness, there was no life of any sort; his conception of his past life was formed at the awakening of his intelligent consciousness.

A man has lived like an animal during the period of his childhood, and has known nothing of life. If the man had lived only ten months, he would never have known anything about his own existence or any one else's; he would have known just as little of life as though he had died in his mother's womb. And not only can the baby not know, but the unintelligent grown-up men and the utter idiot cannot know, that they live, and that other human beings live. And therefore they have no human life.

Man's life begins only with the appearance of rational consciousness,—of that which reveals to man simultaneously his life in the present and the past, and the life of other individuals, and all that flows inevitably from the relations of these individuals, sufferings and death,—of that same thing which calls forth in him the renunciation of personal happiness in life, and the inconsistency which, as it seems to him, brings his life to a standstill.

Man tries to define his life by dates, as he defines an existence outside himself which he sees, and all of a sudden a life awakens in him which does not correspond with the date of his birth in the flesh, and he does not wish to believe that that which is not defined by a date can be life. But seek as a man may in time that point which he can consider as the beginning of his rational life, he will never find it.[1]

[1] Nothing is more common than to hear discussions as to the birth and development of man's life, and of life in general, in time. It seems to

He will never find in his reminiscences, that point, that beginning of rational consciousness. He imagines that rational consciousness has always existed in him. But if he does find something which bears a resemblance to the beginning of this consciousness, he does not, by any means, find it in his birth in the flesh, but in a realm which has nothing in common with that birth in the flesh. He recognizes his rational origin not as at all the same as his birth in the flesh seems to him. When questioning himself as to his rational consciousness a man never thinks that he, as a rational being, was the son of his father and mother and the grandson of his grandfathers and grandmothers, who were born in such and such a year; but he always recognizes himself, not as a son, but as joined in one with the consciousness of other reasoning beings, the most remote from him in point of time and place, who have sometimes lived a thousand years before him, and at the other end of the world. In his rational consciousness man does not even perceive his origin at all, but he recognizes his union, independent of time and space, with other rational consciousnesses, so that they enter into him and he enters into them. And this rational consciousness, awakened in man, seems to bring to a halt that semblance of life which the error of men regards as life: to people in error it seems that their life stops just when it has first been aroused.

people who reason thus that they stand on the very firm ground of reality, but, nevertheless, there is nothing more fantastic than discussions of the development of life in time. These discussions resemble the actions of a man who should undertake to measure a line, and who should not place a mark at the one point which he knows, on which he stands, but should take imaginary points on an endless line, at various and indefinite distances from himself, and from them should measure the distance to himself. Is not this the very thing that men do when they discuss the origin and development of life in man? In fact, where can we take on that endless line which represents development — from the past in the life of man, — that arbitrary point, from which it is possible to begin the fantastic history of the development of this life? In the birth or generation of the child or of his parents, or still further back, in the original animal, and protoplasm, in the first bit that broke away from the sun? Surely, all these discussions will be the most arbitrary fantasies — a measuring without measures.

CHAPTER VIII

THERE IS NO DIVISION AND CONTRADICTION, IT ONLY SO APPEARS THROUGH FALSE DOCTRINE

ONLY the false doctrine of human life, as the existence of an animal from birth to death, in which men are reared and abide, produces that torturing condition of division into which men enter on the discovery in them of their rational consciousness.

To a man who finds himself laboring under this error, it seems as though the life within him were being rent in twain.

Man knows that his life is a unit, but he feels that it consists of two parts. A man, when he crooks two fingers, and rolls a little ball between them, knows that there is but one ball, but he feels as though there were two balls. Something of the same sort occurs with the man who has acquired a false idea of life.

A false direction has been imparted to the mind of man. He has been taught to recognize as life his one fleshly, individual existence, which cannot be life.

With the same false conception of life as he imagines it, he has looked upon life and has beheld two lives,—the one which he has imagined to himself, and the one which actually exists.

To such a man it seems as though the renunciation by his rational consciousness of the happiness of individual existence, and the demand for a different happiness, is something sickly and unnatural.

But, for man as a rational being, the renunciation of the possibility of personal happiness and life is the inevitable consequence of the conditions of individual life, and a property of the rational consciousness connected with it. The renunciation of personal happiness and life is, for a rational being, as natural a property of his life as flying on its wings, instead of running on its feet, is for a bird. If the feathered fowl runs on its legs, it does not prove that it is not its nature to fly. If we see around us men with unawakened consciousness, who consider that their life lies in their happiness as individuals, this does not prove that man is incapable of living a rational life. The awakening of man to the true life which is peculiar to him takes place in our society with such a painful effort, merely because the false teaching of the world strives to convince men that the phantom of life is life itself, and that the appearance of true life is the violation of it.

With the people of our society who enter into true life, something of the same sort happens as would take place with a maiden from whom the nature of woman had been concealed. On feeling the symptoms of sexual maturity, such a maiden would take a condition which summons her to the future family life, for an unhealthy and unnatural condition, and be driven to despair.

The self-same despair is felt by the men of our society at the first symptoms of awakening to the real life of man.

The man in whom rational consciousness has awakened, but who, at the same time, understands his life only as an individual, finds himself in that position of torture in which an animal would find itself, which, having acknowledged its life as the movement of matter, should not have recognized its law of individuality, but should have merely seen its life in subjection to laws of matter that would go on even without its efforts. Such an animal would experience a painful inward contradiction and division. By submitting itself to the one law of matter, it would see that its life consists in lying still and breathing, but its individuality would have required something else from it; food for itself, a continuation of its species,—and then it would seem to the animal that it suffered division and contradiction. "Life," it would say to itself, "consists in submitting to the laws of gravity, *i.e.* in not moving, in lying still, and in submitting to the chemical processes which go on in the body, and lo, I am doing that, but I must move, and procure myself food, and seek a male or a female." The animal would suffer, and would perceive in this condition a painful inconsistency and division.

The same thing takes place with a man who has been taught to recognize the lower law of his life, the animal individuality, as the law of his life. The highest law of life, the law of his rational consciousness, demands from him another; and the life surrounding him on all sides, and false doctrines, retain him in a deceptive consciousness, and he feels contradiction and division.

But as the animal, in order that it may cease to suffer, must confess as its law not the lower law of matter, but the law of its individuality, and, by fulfilling it, profit by the laws of matter for the satisfaction of its aims as an individual, exactly so is it only requisite for a man to recognize his life not in the lower law of individuality, but in the higher law, which includes the first law, — in the law revealed to him in his rational sense, — and the inconsistency is annihilated, and he, as an individual, will be free to submit himself to his rational consciousness, and it will serve him.

CHAPTER IX

THE BIRTH OF TRUE LIFE IN MAN

By observing the times, by watching the appearance of life in the human being, we see that true life is preserved in man as it is preserved in the seed; and that a time comes when this life makes its appearance. The appearance of true life consists in the animal personality inclining man to his own happiness, while his rational sense shows him the impossibility of personal happiness, and points him to another happiness. Man looks at this happiness, which is pointed out to him in the distance, is incapable of seeing it, at first does not believe in this happiness, and turns back to personal happiness; but the rational consciousness, which thus indistinctly indicates his happiness to him, so indubitably and convincingly demonstrates the impossibility of individual happiness that man once more renounces individual happiness and takes another look at this new happiness which has been pointed out to him. No rational happiness is visible, but individual happiness is so indubitably destroyed that it is impossible to continue individual existence; and in the man there begins to form a new relation of his animal to his rational consciousness. The man begins to be born into the true life of mankind.

Something of the same sort takes place which takes place in the material world at every birth. The child is born not because it desires to be born, because it is better for it to be born, and because it knows that it is good to be born, but because it is ready, and can no longer continue its previous existence; it must yield itself to a new life, not so much because the new life calls it, as because the possibility of the former existence has been annihilated.

Rational consciousness imperceptibly springing up in his person grows to such a point that life in individuality becomes impossible.

What takes place is precisely what takes place at the birth of everything. The same annihilation of the germ of the previous form of life, and the appearance of a new shoot; the same apparent strife of the preceding form, decomposing the germ, and the increase in size of the shoot, — and the same nourishment of the shoot at the expense of the decomposing germ. The difference for us between the birth of the rational consciousness and the fleshly birth visible to us consists in this, — that, while in the fleshly birth we see, in time and space, from what and how, when and what is born from the embryo, we know that the seed is the fruit, that from the seed, under certain well-known conditions, a plant will proceed, that there will be a flower upon it, and then fruit, of the same sort as the seed (the entire cycle of life is accomplished before our very eyes), — we do not perceive the growth of the rational consciousness in time, and we do not see its cycle. We do not see all the growth of the rational consciousness, and its cycle, because we are ourselves accomplishing it; our life is nothing else than the birth of this being, invisible to us, which is brought forth within us, and hence we can in no wise see it.

We cannot see the birth of this new being, of this new relation of the rational consciousness to the animal, just as the seed cannot see the growth of its stalk. When the rational consciousness emerges from its concealed condition, and reveals itself to us, it seems to us that we experience a contradiction. But there is no contradiction whatever, as there is none in the sprouting seed. In the sprouting seed we perceive only that the life, which formerly resided only within the covering of the seed, has now passed into its shoot. Precisely the same in man, on the awakening of the rational consciousness there is no contradiction whatever, there is only the birth of a new being, of a new relationship of the rational consciousness to the animal.

If a man exists without knowing that other individuals live, without knowing that pleasures do not satisfy him, that he will die, — he does not even know that *he* lives, and there is no contradiction in him.

But if a man has perceived that other individuals are the same as himself, that sufferings menace him, that his existence is a slow death, he will no longer place his life in that decomposing individuality, but he must inevitably place it in that new life which is opening before him. And again there is no contradiction, as there is no contradiction in the seed which sends forth a shoot and then dies.

CHAPTER X

REASON IS THAT LAW ACKNOWLEDGED BY MAN ACCORDING TO WHICH HIS LIFE MUST BE ACCOMPLISHED

THE true life of man, revealed in the relation of his rational consciousness to his animal individuality, begins only when renunciation of individual happiness begins. But what is this rational sense? It only begins when the renunciation of the happiness of the animal personality begins. But the renunciation of the happiness of the animal individuality only begins when the rational consciousness is aroused.

But what is this rational consciousness? The gospel of John begins by saying that the Word, *Logos* (sense, wisdom, word), is the beginning, and that in it is all and from it comes all; and that therefore reason is that which determines all the rest, and which cannot be determined by anything else.

Reason cannot be determined, and we are not called upon to determine it, because we all of us not only know it, but because reason is the only thing that we do know. Communicating one with another, we are convinced beforehand, more than of anything else, of the identical obligation for all of us of this common reason. We are convinced that reason is the only foundation which unites all of us living beings together in one. We know reason most firmly and earliest of all, so all that we know in the world we know only because that which we know is consonant with the laws of that reason which is indubitably known to us. We know reason, and it is impossible for us not to know it. It is impossible, because reason is that law by which reasoning beings — men — must inevitably live. Reason is for man that law in accordance with which his life is perfected, such a law as is that law for the animal in accordance with which it feeds and reproduces itself, as is that law for the plant in accordance with which grows and blossoms the grass or the tree, as is that law for the heavenly bodies in accordance with which the earth and the stars move. And the law which we know in ourselves as the law of our life is that law in accordance with which are accomplished all the external phenomena of the world; only with this difference, — that we know this difference, that we know this law in ourselves, as that which *we* ourselves must fulfil, and in external phenomena as that which is fulfilled, in accordance with that law, without our participation. All that we know about the world is only what we see accomplished outside of us, in the heavenly bodies, in animals, in plants, in all the world, subject to reason.

In the outer world we see this subjection to the law of reason; but in ourselves we know this law as that which we are bound to fulfil.

The common error in regard to life consists in this, — that the subjection of our animal body to the law, not accomplished by us, but only seen by us, is taken for human life; while this law of our animal body, with which our rational consciousness is bound up, is accomplished in our animal bodies as unconsciously to ourselves as it is accomplished in a tree, a crystal, a heavenly body.

But the law of our life — the subservience of our animal body to our reason — is the law which we nowhere see, because it has not yet been accomplished, but is accomplished by us in our life. In the fulfilment of this law, in the subjection of our animal part to the law of reason for the attainment of happiness, consists our life. By not understanding that the happiness of our life consists in the subjection of our animal individuality to the law of reason, and taking happiness and the existence of our animal individuality for our whole life, and rejecting the work of life which has been appointed for us, we deprive ourselves of our true happiness and our true life; in place of it we set up that existence which we can see, of our animal activity, which operates independently of us, and which cannot, therefore, be our life.

CHAPTER XI

THE FALSE DIRECTION OF LEARNING

THE error of supposing that the law accomplished in our animal persons, and visible to us, is the law of our life, is an ancient one, into which men have always fallen, and into which they still fall. This error, concealing from men the chief subject of their knowledge, the subjection of the animal individual to reason for the attainment of the happiness of life, sets in its place a study of the existence of men independent of the happiness of life.

Instead of making a study of that law to which, for the attainment of his happiness, the animal individuality of man must be subjected, and, as soon as this law is learned, studying, with it as a foundation, all the other phenomena of the world, this false knowledge directs its efforts only to the study of happiness, and of the existence of the animal individuality of man, without any relation to the chief subject of knowledge, — the subjection of this animal individuality of man to the law of reason for the attainment of the happiness of true life.

False knowledge directs its efforts to the study of happiness alone, and, not having in view the chief object of knowledge, directs its efforts to the study of the animal existence of past and contemporary people, and to the study of the conditions of existence of man in general, as an animal. It seems to it that from this study there may be derived also a guide for the happiness of human life.

False knowledge reasons thus: "Men exist and have existed before us. Let us see how they have existed, what changes have come about in their existence through time and situation, in what direction these changes point. From these historical alterations in their existence we shall discover the law of their life."

Not having in view the principal aim of learning, the study of that rational law to which the personality of man must submit itself for his happiness, the so-called learned men of this category, by the very aim which they set themselves for their study, pronounce the condemnation on the futility of their study.

In point of fact: if the existence of men alters only in consequence of the general laws of their animal existence, then the study of those laws, to which it is thus subjected, is utterly useless and vain. Whether men know or do not know about the law of change in their existence, this law is accomplished, exactly as the change is accomplished in the life of moles and beavers, in consequence of those conditions in which they find them selves.

But if it is possible for man to know that law of reason to which his life must be subservient, then it is evident that he can nowhere procure the knowledge of that law of reason, except where it is revealed to him: in his rational consciousness. And therefore, however much men may have studied the subject of how men have *existed* as animals, they will never learn concerning the existence of man anything which would not have taken place of itself in men without the acquirement of that knowledge; and no matter how much they have studied the animal existence of man, they will never learn the law to which, for the sake of his life's happiness, the animal existence of man must be subjected.

This is one category of the vain reasonings of men upon life, called historical and political science.

Another category of reasonings, widely disseminated in our day, in which the only object of knowledge is utterly lost sight of, is as follows: —

"Looking upon man as an object of knowledge," say the wise men, "we see that he is nourished, grows, reproduces his species, becomes old and dies, exactly like any other animal; but some phenomena (psychical, as they are designated) prevent accuracy of observation, present too great complications, and hence, in order the better to understand man, we will first examine his life in simpler phenomena, similar to those which we see in animals and plants, which lack this psychical activity.

"With this aim, we will investigate the life of animals and plants in general. But, on investigating animals and plants, we see that in all of them there reveal themselves still more simple laws of matter, which are common to them all. And as the laws of the animal are simpler than the laws of the life of man, and the laws of the plant simpler still, investigation must be based upon the simplest — upon the laws of matter. We see that what takes place in the plant and the animal is precisely what takes place in the man," say they, "and hence we conclude that everything which takes place in man we can explain to ourselves from what takes place in the very simplest dead matter that is visible to us, and open to our investigations, the more so as all the peculiarities of the activity of man are found in constant dependence upon powers which act in matter. Every change of the matter constituting the body of man alters and infringes upon his whole activity." And hence, they conclude, the laws of matter are the cause of man's activity. But the idea that there is in man something which we do not see in animals or in plants, or in dead matter, and that this something is the only subject of knowledge, without which every other is useless, does not disturb them.

It does not enter their heads that, if the change of matter in the body of man infringes upon his activity, —this merely proves that the change of matter is one of the causes which affects the activity of man, but not that the movement of matter is one of the causes of man's activity being interfered with, nor in the least that the movement of matter is the cause of his activity. Exactly as the injury done by the removal of earth from under the root of a plant proves that the earth may or may not be everywhere, but not that the plant is merely the product of the earth. And they study in man that which takes place also in dead matter, and in the plant, and in animals, assuming that an explanation of the laws, and the phenomena accompanying the life of man, can elucidate for them the life of man itself.

In order to understand the life of man, that is to say, that law to which, for the happiness of man, his animal person must be subservient, men examine either historical existence, but not the life of man, or the subservience, not acknowledged by man but only seen by him, of the animal and the plant, and of matter, to various laws; *i.e.* they do the same thing that men would do if they studied the situation of objects unknown to them, for the sake of finding that unknown goal which must be followed.

It is perfectly true that the knowledge of the phenomenon, visible to us, of the existence of man in history, may be instructive for us; and that the study of the laws of the animal individuality of man and of other animals may be equally instructive for us, as well as the study of those laws to which matter is subject. The study of all this is important for man, since it shows him, as in a mirror, that which is infallibly accomplished in his life; but it is evident that the knowledge of that which is already in process of accomplishment and visible to us, however full it may be, cannot furnish us with the chief knowledge, which is necessary to us, the knowledge of that law to which, for our happiness, our animal individuality must be subservient. The knowledge of the laws that are accomplished is instructive for us, but only when we acknowledge that law of reason to which our animal personality must be subservient, but not when that law is not recognized at all.

However well the tree may have studied (if it could but study) all those chemical and physical phenomena which take place in it, it can by no means, from these observations and from this knowledge, deduce for itself the necessity of collecting sap and of distributing it for the growth of the bole, the leaf, the flower, and the fruit.

Precisely this is the case with man; however well he may know the law which guides his animal personality, and the laws which control matter, — these laws will afford him not the slightest guidance as to how he is to proceed with the bit of bread which is in his hands: whether he is to give it to his wife, to a stranger, to a dog, or to eat it himself; to defend this bit of bread, or to give it to the person who shall ask him for it. But a man's life consists solely of the decision of these and similar questions.

The study of laws which guide the existence of animals, plants, and matter is not only useful but indispensable for the elucidation of the law of the life of man, but only when that study has as its chief aim the subject of man's knowledge: the elucidation of the law of reason.

But on the assumption that the life of man is merely his animal existence, and that the happiness indicated by rational consciousness is impossible, and that the law of reason is but a vision, — such study becomes not only vain but deadly, since it conceals from man the sole object of knowledge, and maintains him in the error that, by following up the reflection of the object, he can know the object also. Such study is similar to that which a man should make by attentively studying all the changes and movements of the shadow of the living being, assuming that the cause of the movement of the living being lies in the changes and movements of its shadow.

CHAPTER XII

THE CAUSE OF FALSE KNOWLEDGE IS THE FALSE PERSPECTIVE IN WHICH OBJECTS PRESENT THEMSELVES

"TRUE knowledge consists in knowing that we know that which we know, and that we do not know that which we do not know," said Confucius.

But false knowledge consists in thinking that we know that which we do not know. And it is impossible to give a more accurate definition of that false knowledge which reigns among us. It is assumed by the false knowledge of our day that we know that which we cannot know, and that we do not know that which alone we can know. It seems to a man possessed of false knowledge that he knows everything which presents itself to him in space and time, and that he does not know that which is known to him through his rational consciousness.

To such a man it seems that happiness in general, and his happiness in particular, is the most unfathomable of subjects for him. His reason and his rational consciousness seem to him as almost equally unfathomable subjects. A little more comprehensible subject appears to be himself as an animal; still more comprehensible appear to him animals and plants, and more comprehensible still seems dead, endlessly diffused matter.

Something of the same sort takes place with man's vision. A man always unconsciously directs his sight chiefly on the objects which are more distant, and which therefore seem to him the most simple in color and outline; on the sky, the horizon, the far-off meadows, the forest. These objects present themselves to him as better defined and more simple in proportion as they are more distant, and, *vice versa*, the nearer the object, the more complicated is it in outline and color.

If man did not know how to compute the distance of objects, he would not, as he looked, arrange objects in perspective, but would acknowledge the great simplicity and definiteness of outline and color, their greater degree of visibility; and to such a man the interminable sky would appear the simplest and most visible, and then as less visible objects would the more complicated outlines of the horizon appear to him, and still less visible would appear to him his own hands, moving before his face, and light would appear to him the most invisible of all.

Is it not the same with the false knowledge of man? What is indubitably known to him — his rational consciousness — seems to him to be beyond comprehension, while that which is, indubitably, unattainable for him — boundless and eternal matter — seems to him to be within the scope of knowledge, because on account of its distance from him it seems simple to him.

But it is precisely the reverse. First of all, and most indubitably of all, every man can know and does know the happiness toward which he is striving; then, as indubitably, he knows the reason which points out to him that happiness, — he already knows that his animal part is subject to that reason, and he already sees, though he does not know, all the other phenomena which present themselves to him in space and time.

Only to the man with a false idea of life does it seem that he knows objects better in proportion as they are more clearly defined by time and space; in point of fact, we know fully only that which is defined neither by time nor by space: happiness and the law of reason. But we know external objects the less in proportion as our consciousness has less share in the knowledge, in consequence of which an object is defined only by its place in time and space. And hence, the more exceptionally an object is defined by time and space, the less comprehensible is it to man.

The true knowledge of man ends with the knowledge of his individuality—of the animal part. A man knows his animal part, which seeks happiness and is subject to the law of reason, quite apart from the knowledge of that which is not his individuality. He actually knows himself in this animal; and knows himself, not because he is something appertaining to time and space (on the contrary, he never can know himself as a phenomenon appertaining to time and space), but because he is something which must, for its own happiness, be subservient to the law of reason.' He knows himself in this animal as something independent of time and space.

When he questions himself as to his place in time and space, it seems to him, first of all, that he stands in the middle of time, which is endless on both sides of him, and that he is the center of a sphere, whose surface is everywhere and nowhere. And this self of his, exempt from time and space, man actually knows, and with this, his "*ego*," ends his actual knowledge. All that is contained outside of this, his "*ego*," man does not know, and he can only observe and define it in an external and conventional manner.

Having departed, for a time, from the knowledge of himself as a rational center, striving toward happiness, *i.e.* as a being independent of time and space, man can, for a time, conditionally admit that he is part of the visible world appearing in time and space. Regarding himself thus, in time and space, in connection with other beings, man combines his true inward knowledge of himself with external observations on himself, and receives of himself a conception of a man in general similar to all other men; through this conventional knowledge of himself man conceives of other men, also, a certain external idea, but he does not know them.

The impossibility, for man, of true knowledge of men, proceeds also from the fact that of such men he sees, not one, but hundreds, thousands, and he knows that there have existed and that there will exist men whom he has never seen and whom he never will see.

Beyond men, still farther removed from himself, man beholds, in time and space, animals differing from men and from each other. These creatures would be utterly incomprehensible to him if he were not possessed of a knowledge of man in general; but, having this knowledge, and deducing from his conception of man his rational consciousness, he receives some idea concerning animals also; but this idea is for him less like knowledge than his idea of men in general. He beholds a vast quantity of the most varied animals, and the greater their numbers, the less possible, apparently, is any knowledge of them for him.

Farther removed from himself he beholds plants; and the diffusion of these phenomena in the world is even greater, and knowledge of them is still more impossible for him.

Still farther from him, beyond animals and plants, in space and time, man beholds living bodies, and forms of matter which are but little or not at all distinguishable from each other. Matter he understands least of all. The knowledge of the forms of matter is already quite indifferent to him, and he not only does not know it, but he only imagines it to himself, the more so as matter already presents itself to him, in space and time, as endless.

CHAPTER XIII

THE RECOGNIZABILITY OF OBJECTS IS AUGMENTED, NOT BECAUSE OF THEIR MANIFESTATION IN SPACE AND TIME, BUT BECAUSE OF THE UNITY OF THE LAW WHERETO WE AND THOSE SUBJECTS WHICH WE STUDY ARE SUBSERVIENT

WHAT can be more clear than the words: the dog is sick; the calf is affectionate; he loves me; the bird rejoices; the horse is afraid; a good man; a vicious animal? And all these most important and comprehensible words are not defined by space and time; on the contrary, the more incomprehensible to us the law to which a phenomenon is subservient, the more accurately is the phenomenon defined by time and space. Who will say that he understands that law of gravity in accordance with which the movements of the earth, moon, and sun take place? Yet an eclipse of the sun is determined in the most accurate manner by space and time.

We know fully only our life, our aspiration for happiness, and the reason which points us to that happiness. The knowledge which stands next to it in point of sureness is the knowledge of our animal personality, striving toward happiness and subservient to the law of reason. In the knowledge of our animal personality there already appear conditions of time and space, visible, palpable, observable, but not accessible to our understanding. After this, in point of sureness of knowledge, is the knowledge of animal personalities, similar to ourselves, in which we recognize an aspiration toward happiness, as well as a rational consciousness, in common with ourselves. In so far as the life of these personalities approaches the laws of our life, of aspiration toward happiness, and submission to the law of reason, to that extent do we know them; in so far as it reveals itself under conditions of time and space, to that extent we do not know them. Thus, more than in any other way, do we know men.

The next thing in point of surety of knowledge is our knowledge of animals, in which we see a personality striving toward welfare, like our own,—though now we hardly recognize a semblance of our rational consciousness,— and with which we cannot communicate through that rational consciousness.

After animals, we behold plants, in which we with difficulty recognize a personality similar to our own, aspiring to happiness. These beings present themselves to us chiefly in phenomena of time and space, and are hence still less accessible to our knowledge.

We know them only because in them we behold a personality, similar to our animal personality, which, equally with ours, aspires to happiness, and matter which subjects itself to the law of reason under the conditions of time and space.

Still less accessible to our knowledge are impersonal, material objects; in them we no longer find semblances of our personality, we perceive no striving at all after happiness, but we behold merely the phenomena of time and space, of the laws of reason, to which they are subject.

The genuineness of our knowledge does not depend upon the accessibility to observation of objects in time and space, but contrariwise; the more accessible to observation the phenomena of the object in time and place, the less comprehensive is it to us.

Our knowledge of the world flows from the consciousness of our striving after happiness, and of the necessity, for the attainment of this happiness, of the subjection of our animal part to reason. If we know the life of the animal, it is only because we behold in the animal a striving toward happiness, and the necessity of subjection to the law of reason, which is represented in it by the law of organism.

If we know matter, we know it only because, in spite of the fact that its happiness is incomprehensible to us, we nevertheless behold in it the same phenomenon as in ourselves — the necessity of subjection to the law of reason, which rules it.

We cannot know ourselves from the laws which rule animals, but we can know animals only by that law which we know in ourselves. And so much the less can we know ourselves from the laws of our life transferred to the phenomena of matter.

All that man knows of the external world he knows only because he knows himself and in himself finds three different relations to the world: one relation of his rational consciousness, another relation of his animal, and a third relation of the matter which enters into his animal body. He knows in himself these three different relations, and therefore all that he sees in the world is always disposed before him in a perspective of three planes, separate from each other: (1) rational beings; (2) animals; and (3) lifeless matter.

A man always sees these three categories in the world, because he contains within himself these three subjects of knowledge. He knows himself: (1) as a rational consciousness, subjecting the animal part; (2) as an animal, subject to the rational consciousness; (3) as matter, subject to the animal part.

Not from a knowledge of the laws of matter, as they think of it, can we learn the law of organisms, and not from the laws of organism can we know ourselves as a rational creation, but *vice versa*. First of all, we may and we must know ourselves, *i.e.* that law of reason to which, for our own happiness, our personality must be subject, and only then can we and must we know also the law of our animal personality, and of other personalities like it, and, at a still greater distance from us, the laws of matter.

We need to know and we do know only ourselves. The animal world is for us a reflection of what we know in ourselves. The material world is, as it were, a reflection of a reflection.

The laws of matter seem peculiarly clear to us, only because they are uniform for us: and they are uniform for us because they are especially far removed from the law of our life as we recognize it.

The laws of organisms seem to us simpler than the

law of our life, also on account of their distance from us. But in them we merely observe laws, but we do not know them, as we know the law of our rational consciousness, which we must fulfil.

We know neither the one being nor the other, but we merely see, we observe outside of ourselves. Only the law of our rational consciousness do we know indubitably, because it is necessary to our happiness — because we live by this consciousness; but we do not see it because we do not possess that highest point from which we might be able to observe it.

Only, if there were higher beings subjecting our rational consciousness as our rational consciousness subjects itself to our animal personality, and as our animal personality (our organism) subjects matter to itself — these higher beings might behold our rational life as we behold our animal existence and the existence of matter.

Human life presents itself as indissolubly bound up with two modes of existence, which it includes within itself: the existence of animals and plants (of organisms), and the existence of matter.

Man himself makes his real life, and lives it; but in the two modes of existence bound up with his life, man cannot take part. Body and matter, of which he consists, exist of themselves.

These forms of existence present themselves to man as preceding lives lived through, included in his life, as reminiscences of former lives.

In the real life of man, these two forms of existence furnish him with implements and materials for his work, but not the work itself.

It is useful for a man to study thoroughly both the materials and the implements of his work. The better he knows them, the better condition will he be in to work. The study of these forms of existence included within his life, of his animal and the material constituting the animal, shows man, as though in a reflection, the universal law of all existence — submission to the law of reason, and thereby confirms, as to his conviction, the necessity of subjecting his animal to its laws; but man cannot and must not confound the material and implements of his work with the work itself.

However much a man may have studied the visible, palpable life, observed by him in himself and in others, the life which is fulfilled without any effort of his, this life will always remain a mystery to him; he will never understand a life of which he is unconscious, and by observations upon this mysterious life, which is always hiding from him in the infinity of space and time, he will be in no wise enlightened as to his real life, which is revealed to him in his consciousness, and which consists in the subservience of his animal personality, quite peculiar from all and well known to himself, to the law of reason, quite peculiar and well known to himself, for the attainment of his happiness, entirely independent and well known to himself.

CHAPTER XIV

THE TRUE LIFE OF MAN IS NOT THAT WHICH TAKES PLACE IN SPACE AND TIME

MAN knows life in himself as an aspiration toward happiness, to be attained by the submission of his animal personality to the law of reason.

He does not and cannot know any other life of man. For the man recognizes the animal as living only when the matter constituting it is subject, not only to its laws, but to the higher law of organism.

There is in a certain conjunction of matter submission to the higher law of organism; we recognize life in this conjunction of matter; no, this submission has not begun or ended; and that does not yet exist, which distinguishes this matter from all other matter, in which act only mechanical, physical, and chemical laws, — and we do not recognize in it the life of the animal.

In precisely the same manner, we recognize people like ourselves, or even ourselves, as living only when our animal personality, in addition to submission to the law of organism, is subservient to the higher law of our rational consciousness.

As soon as there is none of this submission of the personality to the law of reason, as soon as the law of personality alone acts in man, subjecting to itself the matter which constitutes it, we do not know and we do not see human life either in others or in ourselves, as we do not see the life of the animal in matter, which is subject only to its own laws.

However powerful and rapid may be a man's movements in delirium, in madness, in agony, in intoxication, in a burst of passion even, we do not recognize a man as alive, we do not bear ourselves toward him as to a living man, and we recognize in him only the possibility of life. But however weak and motionless a man may be, if we see that his animal personality is subservient to his reason, we recognize him as living, and bear ourselves toward him as such.

We cannot understand man's life otherwise than as the subjection of the animal personality to the law of reason.

This life reveals itself in space and time, but is not defined by the conditions of space and time, but only according to the degree of subjection of the animal personality to the reason. Defining life by conditions of space and time is precisely the same as defining the height of an object by its length and breadth.

The movement upward of an object which is also moving on a plane surface will furnish an accurate simile of the relationship of the true life of man to the life of the animal personality, or of the true life to the life of time and space. The movement of the object upward does not depend upon its movement on a plane surface, and can be neither augmented nor diminished thereby. It is the same with the definition of the life of man. True life always reveals itself in personality, and does not depend upon and cannot be either augmented or diminished by this, that, or the other existence of personality.

The conditions of time and space, in which the

animal personality of man finds itself, cannot wield influence over the true life, which consists of the submission of the animal personality to the rational consciousness.

It is beyond the power of man, who desires to live, to annihilate or to arrest the movement of his existence in time and space; but his true life is the attainment of happiness by submission to reason, independently of those visible movements of time and space. It is only in this increasing attainment of happiness, through submission to reason, that what constitutes the life of man consists. There is none of this augmentation in submission, and man's life proceeds in the two visible directions of time and space, and is one existence.

There is this upward movement, this greater and greater submission to reason, — and between two powers and one a relationship is established; and more or less movement takes place in accordance with the rising existence of man in the realm of life.

The powers of time and space are definite, final, incompatible with the conception of life, but the power of aspiration toward good through submission to reason is a power rising on high, the very power of life, for which there are no bounds of time or space.

Man imagines that his life comes to a standstill and is divided, but these hindrances and hesitations are only an illusion of the consciousness (similar to the illusions of the external senses). Obstacles and hesitations there are not and there cannot be in real life: they only seem such to us because of our false view of life. Man begins to live with real life, *i.e.* he rises to a certain height above the animal life, and from this height he sees the shadowy nature of his animal existence, which infallibly ends in death; he sees that his existence on a plane surface is encompassed on all sides by precipices, and, recognizing the fact that this ascent on high is life itself, he is terrified by that which he has beheld from the height.

Instead of recognizing the power of his life which has raised him on high, and instead of going in the direction revealed to him, he takes fright at what has been laid open before him from the heights, deliberately descends, and lies as low as possible, in order not to see the abysses yawning around him. But the force of rational consciousness raises him once more, again he sees, again he takes fright, and again he falls to earth in order to avoid seeing. And this goes on until he finally recognizes the fact that, in order to save himself from terror before the movement of a pernicious life, he must understand that his movement on a plane surface — his existence in time and space — is not his life, but that his life consists only in the movement upward, that in the submission of his animal personality to the law of reason lies the only possibility of life and happiness. He must understand that he has wings which raise him above the abyss; that, were it not for those wings, he never would have mounted on high, and would not have beheld the abyss. He must believe in his wings, and soar whither they bear him.

It is only from this lack of faith that proceed those phenomena which seem strange to him at first, of the fluctuation of true life, of its arrests, and the division of consciousness.

Only to the man who understands his life in its animal existence, defined by time and space, does it appear that the rational consciousness has revealed itself at times in the animal creature. And, looking thus upon the revelation in himself of rational consciousness, man asks himself when and under what conditions his rational consciousness revealed itself in him? But, scrutinize his past as carefully as he will, man will never discover those times of revelation of the rational consciousness: it will always seem to him either that it has never existed, or that it has always existed. If it appears to him that there have been gaps in rational consciousness, it is only because he does not recognize the life of rational consciousness as life. Comprehending his life only as an animal existence, determined by conditions of time and space, man tries to measure the awakening and activity of rational consciousness by the same measure: he asks himself, "When, for how long a time, under what conditions, did I find myself in possession of rational consciousness?"

But the intervals between the awakenings of rational life exist only for the man who understands his life as the life of an animal personality. But for the man who understands his life as consisting in the activity of the rational consciousness — there can exist none of these intervals.

Rational life exists. It alone does exist. Intervals of time of one minute or of fifty thousand years are indistinguishable by it, because for it time does not exist.

The true life of man, from which he forms for himself an idea of every other life, is the aspiration toward happiness, attainable by the subjection of his personality to the law of reason. Neither reason nor the degree of his submission to it are determined by either time or space. The true life of mankind arises outside of space and time.

CHAPTER XV

THE RENUNCIATION OF HAPPINESS OF THE ANIMAL PERSONALITY IS THE LAW OF MAN'S LIFE

LIFE is a striving toward happiness.[1] A striving toward happiness is life. Thus all men have understood, do understand, and always will understand life. And hence the life of man is an aspiration toward the happiness of man, and an aspiration toward the happiness of man is human life. The common herd, unthinking men, understand the happiness of man to lie in the happiness of his animal part.

False science, excluding the conception of happiness from the definition of life, understands life in its animal existence, and hence it sees the happiness of life only in animal happiness, and agrees with the error of the masses.

[1] *Blago*, good, happiness, welfare.

In both cases, the error arises from confounding the personalities, the individualities, as science calls them, with rational consciousness. Rational consciousness includes in itself individuality. But individuality does not always include in itself rational consciousness. Individuality is a property of the animal, and of man as well as of the animal. Rational consciousness is the property of man alone.

The animal may live for his own body only — nothing prevents his living thus; he satisfies his individual and unconsciously plays his part, and does not know that he is an individual; but reasoning man cannot live for his own body alone. He cannot live thus because he knows that he is an individual, and therefore knows that other beings are individualities also, as well as himself, and he knows all that must result from the relations of these individualities.

If man aspired only to the happiness of his individuality, if he loved only himself, — his own individuality, — he would not know that other beings love themselves also, any more than animals know this; but if man knows that he is a personality, striving toward the same thing as all the personalities surrounding him, he can no longer strive for that happiness which evidently is evil for his rational consciousness, and his life can no longer consist in striving for his individual happiness.

It merely seems to man, at times, that his aspiration toward happiness has, for its object, the satisfaction of the demands of the animal personality. This delusion arises from the fact that man takes that which he sees proceeding in his animal part for the object of the activity of his rational consciousness. What results is something in the nature of what would take place if a man were to govern himself, in a waking state, by what he had seen in dreams.

And if this delusion is upheld by false teachings, there results in man a confounding of his personality with his rational consciousness.

But his rational consciousness always shows man that

the satisfaction of the demands of his animal personality cannot constitute his happiness, and hence his life, and therefore it draws him irresistibly toward that happiness, hence toward the life which is proper to him, and it does not become confused with his animal personality.

It is generally thought and said that renunciation of the happiness of personality is a deed worthy of a man. Renunciation of the happiness of personality is not a merit, is not an exploit, but an indispensable condition of the life of man. At the same time that a man recognizes himself as an individual, separated from all the world, he also recognizes other individuals separated from all the world, and their mutual connection, and the transparency of the happiness of his personality, and the sole actuality of happiness to be only of such a sort as may be satisfied by his rational consciousness.

In the case of an animal, activity which does not have for its object its individual welfare, but is directly opposed to that welfare, is renunciation of life; but in the case of man, it is precisely the reverse. The activity of man, directed solely to the attainment of individual happiness, is a complete renunciation of the life of man.

For the animal, who has no rational consciousness to demonstrate to him the poverty and limited character of his existence, personal happiness, and the reproduction of its species therefrom resulting, constitute the highest aim of life. But for man, personality is merely that step in existence from which the true happiness of his life, which is not synonymous with the happiness of his personality, is revealed to him.

The consciousness of individuality is not life for man, but that boundary from which his life, consisting in ever greater and greater attainment to the happiness which is proper to him, and which does not depend upon the welfare of his animal part, begins.

According to the prevalent conception of life, human life is the fragment of time from the birth to the death of his animal part. But this is not human life; this is merely the existence of man as an animal personality. But human life is something which only reveals itself in the animal existence, just as organic life is something which only reveals itself in the existence of matter.

First of all, the apparent objects of man's personality present themselves to him as the objects of his life. These objects are visible, and hence they seem to be comprehensible.

But the aims pointed out to him by his rational consciousness seem incomprehensible, because they are invisible to him. And man, at first, finds it terrible to repulse the visible and yield himself to the invisible.

To a man perverted by the false teachings of the world, the demands of the animal which fulfil themselves, and which are visible both in himself and in others, seem simple and clear, but the new, invisible requirements of rational consciousness present themselves as conflicting; the satisfaction of them, which is not accomplished by themselves, but which a man must himself attend to, seem, in some way, complicated and indistinct. It is painful and alarming to renounce the visible idea of life and yield one's self to its invisible consciousness, as it would be painful and alarming to a child to be born, were he able to feel his birth — but there is nothing to be done when it is evident that the visible idea leads to death, while the invisible consciousness alone gives life.

CHAPTER XVI

THE ANIMAL PERSONALITY IS THE INSTRUMENT OF LIFE

Surely no arguments can conceal from man this patent and indubitable truth, that his personal existence is something which is constantly perishing, hasting on to death, and that there can be, therefore, no life in his animal personality.

Man cannot avoid seeing that the existence of his personality from birth and childhood to old age and death is nothing else than a constant waste and diminution of this animal personality, ending in inevitable death; and hence, the consciousness of one's life in personality, including in itself a desire for enlargement and indestructibility of personality, cannot be otherwise than uninterrupted contradiction, and suffering cannot be otherwise than evil, while the only sense of his life lies in its aspiration toward happiness.

In whatever the genuine happiness of man consists, renunciation of the happiness of his animal person is inevitable for him.

Renunciation of the happiness of the animal personality is the law of man's life. If it is not accomplished freely, expressing itself in submission to rational consciousness, then it is accomplished violently in every man at the fleshly death of his animal, when, in consequence of the burden of suffering, he desires but one thing: to escape from the torturing consciousness of a perishing personality, and to pass into another form of existence.

Entrance into life, and the life of man, is similar to that which takes place with the horse whom his master leads forth from the stable and harnesses. It seems to the horse, on emerging from the stable and beholding the light, and scenting liberty, that in that liberty is life; but he is harnessed, and driven off. He feels a weight behind him, and if he thinks that his life consists in running at liberty, he begins to kick, falls down, and sometimes kills himself. But if he does not kick he has but two alternatives left to him: either he will go his way and drag his load, and discover that the burden is not heavy, and trotting not a torment, but a joy; or else he will kick himself free, and then his master will lead him to the treadmill, and will fasten him by his halter, the wheel will begin to turn beneath him, and he will walk in the dark, in one place, suffering; but his strength will not be wasted; he will perform his unwilling labor, and the law will be fulfilled in him. The only difference will lie in this: that the first work will be joyful, but the second compulsory and painful.

"But to what purpose this personality, whose happiness I am bound to renounce, in order to receive life?" say men, who accept their animal existence as life.

"But for what purpose is this consciousness of individuality, which is opposed to the revelation of his true life, given to man?"

This question may be answered by a similar question which might be put by the animal, striving toward his aims, the preservation of his life and species.

"Why," it might ask, "this matter and its laws, mechanical, physical, chemical, and others, with which I must contend in order to attain my ends? If my calling," the animal would say, "be the accomplishment of animal life, then why all these obstacles, which must be overcome?"

It is clear to us that all matter and its laws, with which the animal contends, and which it subjugates to itself for the accomplishment of its animal existence, are not obstacles, but means for the attainment of its ends. Only by working over matter, and by means of its laws, does the animal live. It is precisely the same in the life of man. His animal personality, in which man finds himself, and which he is called upon to subject to his rational consciousness, is no obstacle, but a means whereby he attains the aim of his happiness; his animal personality, is, for man, that instrument with which he works. Animal personality is, for man, the spade given to a rational being in order that he may dig with it, and, as he digs, dull and sharpen it, and wear it out, but not in order that he may polish it up and lay it away. This talent is given to him to increase, and not to hoard. "And whoso saveth his life shall lose it. And he that loseth his life for my sake, shall find it."

In these words it is declared that we must not save but lose, and lose unceasingly; and that only by renouncing what is destined to perish, our animal personality, shall we acquire our true life, which will not and cannot perish. It is declared that our true life begins only when we cease to count as life that which was not and could not be our life, — our animal existence. It is declared that he who will save the spade which he has for the preparation of his food, to sustain his life, — that he, having saved his spade, shall lose both his food and his life.

CHAPTER XVII

BIRTH IN THE SPIRIT

"Ye must be born anew," said Christ. It is not that any one has commanded man to be born, but that man is inevitably led to it. In order to see life, he must be born again into that existence through rational consciousness.

Rational consciousness is bestowed upon man in order that he may place life in that happiness which is revealed to him by his rational consciousness. He who has placed his life in that happiness has life; but he who does not place his life therein, but in his animal personality, thereby deprives himself of life. In this consists the definition of life given by Christ.

Men who accept as life their aspiration toward happiness hear these words, and not only do not admit them, but do not understand and cannot understand them. These words seem to them to mean nothing, or very little, as designating some sentimental and mystical mood, which has been let loose upon them. They cannot understand the significance of these words, which furnish the explanation of a condition that is inaccessible to them, just as a dry seed which has not sprouted could not understand the condition of a moist and already growing seed. For the dry seeds, that sun which shines in its rays upon the seed which is being born into life is only an insignificant accident,—something large and warm and light; but for the sprouting seed it is the cause of birth unto life. Just the same, for those people who have not yet attained to the inward inconsistency of the animal personality and rational consciousness, the light of the sun of reason is only an insignificant accident, only sentimental, mystical words. The sun leads to life only those in whom life has already been engendered.

No one has ever learned how, why, when, and where it is engendered; either in men or in animals and plants

Of its origin in man, Christ has said that no one knows or can know it. And, in fact, what can a man know about the manner in which life is engendered within him? Life is the light of men, the beginning of all things; how can man know when it is engendered? That is engendered and perishes for man which does not live, that which is revealed in space and time. But true life *is*, and therefore it cannot either begin or perish.

CHAPTER XVIII

THE DEMANDS OF RATIONAL CONSCIOUSNESS

YES, rational consciousness indubitably, incontrovertibly says to man that, with the constitution of the world which he sees from his personality, he, his personality, can have no happiness. His life is a desire for happiness for himself, for himself in particular, and he sees that this happiness is impossible. But, strange to say, in spite of the fact that he undoubtedly perceives that this happiness is impossible for him, he still lives in the one desire for this impossible happiness — happiness for himself alone.

A man with an awakened (just awakened) rational consciousness, which has not yet, however, subjected to itself his animal personality, if he does not kill himself, lives only for the purpose of realizing that impossible happiness; the man lives and acts only in order that happiness may be his alone, in order that all people, and even all creatures, should live and work to the end that his welfare alone may be provided for, that he may enjoy himself, that for him there may be no suffering and no death.

It is astonishing: in spite of the fact that his experience and observation of life, the life of all about him, and his reason, indubitably point out to each man the inaccessibility of this, show him that it is impossible to make other living beings cease to love themselves, and love him alone; in spite of this, the life of each man consists only in this, — by means of wealth, power, honor, glory, flattery, deceit, in some manner or other, to compel other beings to live, not for themselves, but for him alone; to force all beings to love, not themselves, but him alone.

Men have done and do everything that they can for this object, and at the same time they see that they are attempting the impossible. "My life is a striving after happiness," says man to himself. "Happiness is possible for me only when all shall love me more than themselves, and all creatures love only themselves — hence all that I do to make them love me is useless. It is useless, and I can do nothing more."

Centuries pass; men learn the distance from the planets, determine their weight, learn the structure of the sun and stars, but the question as to how to reconcile the demands of personal happiness with the life of the world, which excludes the possibility of that happiness, remains for the majority of men as insoluble a problem as it was for men five thousand years ago.

Rational consciousness says to every man: "Yes, thou must have happiness, but only on condition that all will love thee more than themselves." And the same rational consciousness demonstrates to men that this cannot be, because they all love themselves alone. And therefore the only happiness which is opened to men by rational consciousness is closed to him again by it.

Centuries pass, and the puzzle as to the happiness of man's life still remains for the majority of men insoluble. But the problem has been solved long ago. And it always seems astonishing to all who have learned the solution of the riddle that they have not themselves solved it, — it seems as though they had known it long ago and had merely forgotten it, so simply and voluntarily does the solution of that riddle, which seemed so difficult amid the false teachings of our world, offer itself.

Dost thou wish that all should live for thee, that all should love thee better than themselves? There is only one condition in which thy desire can be fulfilled, — namely, that all creatures should live for the good of others, and should love others better than themselves.

Then only canst thou and all creatures be loved by all, and then only canst thou, among their number, receive that happiness which thou desirest. But if happiness be possible for thee only when all creatures love others better than themselves, then thou, a living creature, must love other creatures more than thyself.

Only under these conditions are the happiness and the life of man possible, and only under these conditions will that be annihilated which has poisoned the life of man, — will the strife of beings, the torment of suffering, and the fear of death be annihilated.

What, in fact, has constituted the impossibility of the happiness of personal existence? In the first place, the strife among themselves of beings in search of their personal happiness. In the second, the delusion of enjoyment which leads to waste of life, to satiety, to suffering, and, in the third, — death. But it is worth while to admit mentally that man may replace the striving for his own personal happiness by a striving for the happiness of other beings, in order that the impossibility of happiness may be annihilated, and that happiness may present itself as attainable to man. Looking upon the world from his idea of life, as a striving after personal happiness, man has beheld in the world a senseless conflict of beings engaged in destroying each other. But it is only requisite that man should recognize the fact that his life lies in a striving after the good of others, in order to see the world in quite a different light; to behold, side by side with chance phenomena of the strife of beings, a constant, mutual service of each other by these beings, — a service without which the existence of the world is inconceivable.

All that is necessary is to admit this, and all previous senseless activity, directed toward the unattainable happiness of the individual, will be replaced by another activity, in conformity with the law of the world and directed to the attainment of the greatest possible happiness for one's self and the whole world.

Another cause of the poverty of personal life, and of the impossibility of happiness for man, has been the deceitfulness of personal enjoyments, which waste life, and lead to satiety and sufferings. A man need only admit that his life consists in a striving after the good of others, and the delusive thirst for enjoyments will cease; and the vain, painful activity, directed to the filling of the bottomless cask of animal personality, will be replaced by an activity engaged in maintaining the life of other beings, which is indispensable for his happiness, and the torture of personal suffering, which annihilates the activity of life, will be replaced by a feeling of sympathy for others, infallibly evoking fruitful activity which is also the most joyful.

A third cause of the poverty of personal life has been the fear of death. Man has but to admit that his life does not consist in the happiness of his animal personality, but in the happiness of other beings, and the bugbear of death vanishes forever from before his eyes. For the fear of death arises only from the fear of losing the happiness of life with its death in the flesh. But if a man could place his happiness in the happiness of other beings, *i.e.* if he would love them more than himself, then death would not represent to him that discontinuance of happiness and life, such as it does represent to a man who lives only for himself. Death to the man who should live only for others could not seem to be a cessation of happiness and of life, because the happiness and the life of other beings is not only not interrupted with the life of a man who serves them, but is frequently augmented and heightened by the sacrifice of his life.

"But that is not life," replies the troubled and erring consciousness of man. "That renunciation of life is suicide." — "I know nothing about that," replies rational consciousness; "I know that such is the life of man, and that there is no other, and that there can be no other. I know more than that. I know that such a life is life and happiness both for a man and for all the world. I know that, according to my former view of the world, my life and the life of every living being was an evil and without sense; but according to this view, it appears as the realization of that law of reason which is placed in man.

"I know that the greatest happiness of the life of every being, which is capable of being infinitely enhanced, can be attained only through this law of the service of each to all, and, hence, of all to each."

"But if this can exist as an imaginary law, it cannot exist as an actual law," replies the perturbed and erring consciousness of man. "Others do not now love me more than themselves, and therefore I cannot love them more than myself, and deprive myself of enjoyment, and subject myself to suffering, for their sakes. I have nothing to do with the law of reason; I desire enjoyment for myself, and freedom from suffering. But a strife is now in progress between creatures, and if I do not struggle also, the others will crush me. It makes no difference to me by what road in imagination the greatest success for all is attained — all I need at present is my own actual greatest happiness," says false consciousness.

"I know nothing about that," replies rational consciousness. "I only know that what thou callest enjoyment will only become happiness for thee when thou shalt not thyself take, but when others shall give of theirs to thee, and thy enjoyments will become superfluous and sufferings, as they now are, only when thou shalt seize them for thyself. Only then, also, shalt thou free thyself from actual suffering, when others shall release thee from them, and not thou, thyself — as now, when, through fear of imaginary sufferings, thou deprivest thyself of life itself.

"I know that an individual life, a life where it is indispensable that all should love me alone, and that I shall love only myself, and in which I shall receive as much enjoyment as possible, and free myself from suffering and death, is the greatest and most incessant suffering. The more I love myself and strive with others, the more will others hate me, and the more viciously will they struggle with me; the more I hedge myself in from suffering, the more torturing will it be come, and the more I guard myself against death, the more terrible will it become.

"I know that, whatever a man may do, he will attain to no happiness until he lives in harmony with the law of his life. But the law of his life is not contest but, on the contrary, the mutual service of individuals to each other."

"But I know life only in my own person. It is impossible for me to place my life in the happiness of other persons."

"I know nothing about that," replies rational consciousness; "I only know that my life and the life of the world, which has hitherto seemed to me malicious nonsense, now appear to me as one rational whole, alive and striving toward the same happiness, through submission to one and the same law of reason, which I know in myself."

"But this is impossible to me," says erring consciousness, and at the same time there is not a man who would not have done this impossible thing, who would not have placed in this impossibility the best happiness of his life.

"It is impossible to place one's happiness in the happiness of other beings;" yet there is no man who has not known a condition in which the happiness of beings outside himself has become his happiness.

"It is impossible to place one's happiness in labors and sufferings for others;" but a man need only yield to that feeling of compassion, and personal pleasures lose their sense for him, and the force of his life is transferred into toils and sufferings for the happiness of others, and these sufferings and toils become happiness for him.

"It is impossible to sacrifice one's life for the happiness of others;" but a man need only recognize this feeling, and death is not only no longer visible and terrible to him, but it appears as the highest bliss to which he can attain.

A reasoning man cannot fail to see that if we mentally admit the possibility of replacing the striving for his own happiness, with a striving for the happiness of other beings, his life will become rational and happy, instead of senseless and poverty-stricken as before.

He cannot fail, also, to see that, by admitting the same conception of life in other people and beings, the life of the whole world, in place of the incoherence and harshness which were formerly apparent, will become the most rational, elevated happiness which man can desire, and that in place of its former incoherence and aimlessness, it will acquire for him a rational meaning; to such a man the aim of life appears as the infinite enlightenment and union of beings in the world, toward which life leads, and in which men first, and afterward all other creatures, submitting themselves ever more and more to the light of reason, will understand (what is at present granted to man alone to understand) that the happiness of life is to be attained, not by the striving of each being toward his own personal happiness, but by a united striving of each creature for the good of all the rest.

But this is not all: admitting the mere possibility of a change of aspiration toward one's own personal happiness, into an aspiration for the good of other beings, man cannot fail to perceive, also, that precisely this gradual, ever increasing renunciation of his individuality, and transference of the object of his activity from himself to other beings, constitutes the whole movement in advance of mankind, and of those living beings which stand nearest to man.

Man cannot but see in history that the movement of life in general lies not in the growth and augmentation of strife of beings among themselves, but, on the contrary, in the diminution of disagreement and in the mitigation of the strife; that the movement of life consists only in this, that the world, through submission to the law of reason, passes from enmity and discord ever more toward concord and unity.

Having admitted this, man cannot but see that those who have been in the habit of devouring each other cease to devour each other; that those who have been in the habit of slaying prisoners and their children cease to slay them; that warriors who have taken pride in murder are ceasing to take pride in it; that people who have been in the habit of killing animals are beginning to tame them, and to kill them less; they are beginning to subsist on the eggs and milk of animals, instead of upon their bodies; that they are beginning to restrain their destructiveness, even in the world of plants.

Man perceives that the best representatives of mankind condemn researches for gratification, exhort men to abstinence, and that the very best men, who are lauded by posterity, present examples of the sacrifice of their own existences for the good of others. Man perceives that that which he has only admitted at the demand of reason is the very thing which actually takes place in the world, and is confirmed by the past life of mankind.

But this is not all: more powerfully and convincingly than through either reason or history, and from quite a different source, as it were, does the aspiration of man's heart reveal itself to him, impelling him to immediate happiness; to that very activity which his reason has pointed out to him, and which is expressed in his heart by love.

CHAPTER XIX

THE DEMAND OF THE INDIVIDUALITY APPEARS INCOMPATIBLE WITH THE DEMAND OF RATIONAL CONSCIOUSNESS

Reason and judgment and history and his inward feeling, — all, it would appear, should convince a man of the justice of this conception of life; but to the man educated in the doctrines of the world it appears, nevertheless, as though the satisfaction of the demands of his rational consciousness and of his feeling could not be the law of his life.

"Not contend with others for one's personal happiness, not seek enjoyment, not ward off suffering, and not fear death! But that is impossible, that is equivalent to renouncing the whole of life! And how am I to renounce my individuality, when I feel the demands of my individual self, and when I know, by my reason, the legitimacy of these demands?" say the cultivated men of our world, with full conviction.

And here is a noteworthy phenomenon. Laboring men, simple men, who exercise their judgment but little, hardly ever defend the demands of individuality, and always feel in themselves demands opposed to the demands of individuality; but an almost complete denial of the demands of rational consciousness and, chief of all, a refutation of the legality of those demands and a defense of the rights of the individual, are to be met with only among wealthy, refined people with cultivated judgment.

The cultivated, enervated, idle man will always prove that individuality has its inalienable rights. But the hungry man will not demonstrate that a man must eat: he knows that every one knows that, and that it is impossible either to prove or to controvert it; he will only eat.

This arises from the fact that the simple, so-called uncultivated man, having toiled all his life with his body, has not perverted his judgment, but has preserved it in all its purity and force.

But the man who has thought all his life, not only of insignificant, trivial objects, but even of such things as it is unnatural for a man to think of, has perverted his mind; his mind is no longer untrammeled. His mind is occupied with matter which is foreign to it, with a consideration of the requirements of its individuality,—with the development, the augmentation, of them, and with devising means to gratify them.

"But I am conscious of the demands of my individuality, and therefore those demands are legitimate," say so-called men of culture, brought up in the doctrine of the world.

And it is impossible for them not to feel the demands

of their personality. The whole life of these people is directed toward the imaginary satisfaction of the happiness of the individual. But this happiness of the individual seems to them to lie in the gratification of wants. And they call all those conditions of the existence of the individual upon which they have bent their minds, wants. But the wants recognized — those upon which the mind is bent — always grow to unlimited dimensions in consequence of this recognition. But the satisfaction of these wants veils from them the wants of their real life.

Social science, so-called, places at the foundation of its investigations the doctrine of the requirements of man, forgetful of the circumstance, very inconvenient for this doctrine, that no man has any wants at all, like the man who commits suicide or the man who is dying with hunger, or that they are literally innumerable.

There are as many requirements for the existence of the animal man as there are sides to that existence, and these sides are as numerous as the radii in a sphere. Need of food, of drink, of breathing, of the exercise of all the muscles and nerves; need of labor, of rest, of pleasure, of family life; need of science, of art, of religion, of their diversity. Wants, in all these connections, of the child, the youth, the man, the old man, the young girl, the woman, the aged crone, the wants of the Chinese, the Parisian, the Russian, the Laplander. Wants corresponding to the customs of the race, and to maladies. ....

One might go on enumerating them to the end of his days without enumerating all which constitute the wants of the individual existence of man. All the conditions of existence may be wants, and the conditions of existence are innumerable.

Only those conditions which are recognized are called wants. But recognized conditions, as soon as they are recognized, lose their true meaning, and acquire that always exaggerated meaning which is given to them by the mind directed upon them, and which veils from it its true life.

What are called needs, *i.e.* the conditions of man's animal existence, may be compared with countless little balls which are capable of being inflated, of which some body or other should have been formed. All the little spheres are equal to each other, and have their own places, and are not impeded in any way. As long as they are not inflated, all their wants are equal, and have room, and they do not feel painful until they are recognized. But all that is necessary is to begin to inflate one sphere, and it will occupy more space than all the rest, it will crowd the rest, and be crowded itself. It is the same with wants: all that is required is to direct the rational consciousness upon one of them, and this recognized want takes possession of the whole life and makes the man's whole being suffer.

CHAPTER XX

WHAT IS REQUIRED IS, NOT RENUNCIATION OF INDIVIDUALITY, BUT ITS SUBJECTION TO RATIONAL CONSCIOUSNESS

YES, the assertion that man does not feel the wants of his rational consciousness, but feels only the wants of his individual part, is nothing else than an assertion that our animal desires, to the satisfaction of which we have devoted all our mind, rule us, and have hidden from us our true life as men. The weeds of our thickly grown vices have stifled the germs of true life.

And how can it be otherwise in our world, when it has been frankly admitted and is admitted, by those who consider themselves teachers of others, that the highest perfection of the isolated man is the development on all sides of the refined wants of his personality, that the happiness of the masses lies in this, that they should have many wants, and that they should be able to satisfy them, that the happiness of men consists in gratifying their wants.

How can men reared in such a doctrine do otherwise

than affirm that they do not feel the demands of rational consciousness, but feel only the wants of the individual? And how are they to feel the wants of reason when their entire mind, without reservation, has gone to the increase of their carnal desires? and how are they to renounce the demands of their desires when these desires have swallowed up their whole life?

"The renunciation of individuality is impossible," these people generally say, endeavoring intentionally to turn the question, and placing, instead of an idea of the subjection of the individuality to the law of reason, the idea of the renunciation of it.

"It is unnatural," they say, "and therefore impossible." But no one is talking about renouncing individuality. Individuality is, to the rational man, the same that breath, the circulation of blood, is to the animal. How is the animal personality to renounce the circulation of its blood? It is impossible to discuss this. Equally impossible is it to talk to the rational man about renouncing individuality. Individuality is, for the reasoning man, as indispensable a condition of his life as the circulation of the blood is a condition of the existence of his animal individuality.

Individuality, as an animal individuality, cannot present and does not present any demands. These demands are presented by a falsely directed mind; a mind directed, not to a guidance of life, not to its enlightenment, but to the inflation of the carnal desires of individuality.

The demands of the animal are always satisfied. Man cannot say, "What shall I eat?" or "Wherewithal shall I be clothed?" All these wants are guaranteed to man, as to the animal and the bird, if he lives a rational life. And, in fact, what thinking man can believe that he could diminish the wretchedness of his position by the guarantee of his individuality?

The wretchedness of man's existence arises, not from the fact that he is an individual, but from the fact that he recognizes the existence of his individuality as life and happiness. Only then do contradiction, division, and the suffering of man make their appearance.

The sufferings of the man begin only when he employs the force of his mind in the strengthening and augmentation to an unlimited extent of the growing demands of his individual, for the sake of concealing from himself the demands of reason.

It is neither possible nor necessary to renounce individuality, any more than in the case of all those conditions under which man exists; but he neither can nor must admit these conditions as life itself. He may and ought to make use of the given conditions of life, but it is impossible to look, and he must not look, upon these conditions as upon the aim of life. It is not necessary to renounce individuality, but to renounce the happiness of the individual, to cease to recognize individuality as life: this is what man must do in order to return to unity, and in order that that happiness, the striving toward which constitutes his life, may be attainable to him.

From the most ancient times the doctrine that the recognition of one's life in personality is the annihilation of life, and that renunciation of the happiness of personality is the only road to the attainment of life, has been preached by the great teachers of mankind.

"Yes, but what is this? This is Buddhism?" say the people of our day, as a rule, in reply to this. "This is Nirvana, this is standing on a pillar." And when they have said this, it seems to the people of our day that they have overthrown in the most successful manner what all know very well, and what it is impossible to conceal from any one: that individual life is poverty-stricken and can have no sense.

"This is Buddhism, Nirvana," they say; and it seems to them that with these words they have overthrown all that has been and is confessed by milliards of people, and what each of us, in the depths of his soul, knows very well, — namely, that life for the aims of the individual is pernicious and senseless, and that if there is any escape from this perniciousness and senselessness, that escape indubitably leads through the renunciation of the happiness for the individual.

The fact that the larger half of mankind has understood and does understand life thus, the fact that the grandest minds have understood life in the same manner, the fact that it is impossible to understand it otherwise, does not trouble them in the least. They are so firmly convinced that all the questions of life, if not settled in the most satisfactory manner, are set aside by the telephone, operettas, bacteriology, electric lighting, and so on, that the idea of renouncing their individual life appears to them only as an echo from ancient ignorance.

But, in the meanwhile, the unhappy men do not suspect that the very roughest Hindu, who stands for years upon one leg, in the name only of renunciation of individual happiness for Nirvana, is, without any comparison, a more living man than they, the men of our contemporary European society, who have turned to beasts, who fly all over the world on railways, and exhibit to the whole world, by the electric light, their brutish condition.

That Hindu has understood that in the life of individuality and the life of reason there is a contradiction, and he is solving it according to his light; but the men of our cultivated world have not only not comprehended this contradiction, but do not even believe that it exists. The proposition that the life of man is not the existence of the individuality of man, won by the spiritual toil of all mankind prolonged through thousands of years — this proposition has become for the man (not for the animal) not only as indubitable and unalterable a truth as the revolution of the earth or the laws of gravity, but even more indubitable and unalterable than these. Every thinking man, learned or ignorant, child or old man, understands and knows this; it is concealed only from the savage men of Africa and Australia, and from well-to-do people in our European towns and capitals who have become savage.

This truth has become the property of mankind, and if mankind does not retrograde in its illegitimate branches of learning, mechanics, algebra, astronomy, still less can it retrograde in the fundamental and chief learning of the definition of its life. It is impossible to forget and erase from the consciousness of man that which he has gathered from his life of many thousand years — the solution of vanity and senselessness, and the wretchedness of individual life. The attempts to resuscitate the savage, antediluvian view of life as an individual existence, with which the so-called science of our European world is engaged, only exhibit more visibly the growth of rational consciousness in mankind, and demonstrate clearly how mankind has already outgrown its childish garments. And the philosophical theories of self-annihilation, and the practice of suicide, which is growing to fearful proportions, prove the impossibility of a return of mankind to the degrees of consciousness already lived through.

Life, as an individual existence, has been outlived by mankind; and it is impossible to return to it, and to forget that the individual existence of man has no sense is impossible. Whatever we may write or say or discover, to whatever point we may perfect our personal life, the renunciation of possible happiness for the individual remains an incontrovertible truth for every thinking man of our times.

"But, nevertheless, it does revolve."

The point does not lie in overthrowing the proposition of Galileo and Copernicus, and in devising new Ptolemaic circles, — they are no longer to be devised; but the point lies in proceeding further, in drawing the most extreme conclusions from this proposition, which has already passed into the general knowledge of mankind. The same with the proposition relating to the impossibility of personal happiness, enounced by the Brahmins, and by Buddha, and Lao-dzi, and Solomon, and the Stoics, and by all the true thinkers of mankind. We must not conceal from ourselves this proposition, and get around it in every way, but boldly and clearly confess it, and draw from it the most extreme deductions.

CHAPTER XXI

THE FEELING OF LOVE IS A PHENOMENON OF THE INDIVIDUAL ACTIVITY BROUGHT INTO SUBJECTION TO RATIONAL CONSCIOUSNESS

It is impossible for a rational being to live for the aims of individuality. It is impossible because all roads are prohibited to it; all aims to which the animal individuality of man is drawn are plainly unattainable. Rational consciousness points out other aims, and these aims are not only attainable, but give full satisfaction to the rational consciousness of man; at first, however, under the influence of the false teaching of the world, it seems to man that these aims are opposed to his individuality.

Try as a man may, who has been reared in our world with cultivated, exaggerated desires of the individual, to acknowledge himself as an "I" in his reason, he will not feel in this "I" the aspiration toward life which he feels in his animal person. The "I" of the reason contemplates life, as it were, but does not itself live, and has no aspirations toward life; but the animal "I" must suffer, and therefore but one thing remains, — to free itself from life.

Thus, in bad faith, do the negative philosophers of our times (Schopenhauer, Hartmann) settle the question — philosophers who deny life and who yet remain in it, instead of availing themselves of the possibility of quitting it. And thus, in good faith, do suicides decide this question by quitting a life which offers them nothing but evil. Suicide presents to them the only escape from the incoherence of the human life of our times.

The argument of pessimistic philosophy and of the most commonplace suicides is as follows: there is an animal *ego* in which there is an inclination for life. This *ego* and its inclination cannot be gratified. There is another *ego*, of the reason, in which there is no inclination for life, which only critically surveys all the false joy of life, and the passion of the animal *ego*, and rejects all of it.

If I yield myself to the former, I see that I live senselessly, and that I am on my way to misery, plunging ever deeper and deeper in it. If I yield myself to the latter, to the rational *ego*, there remains within me no inclination for life. I see that to live for that which alone it pleases me to live, for my personal happiness, is awkward and impossible. It would be possible to live for rational consciousness, but there is no object in it, and I do not wish it. Serve that origin from which I proceeded — God? Why? God — if he exists — will find other servitors without me. But why should I?

It is possible to look on at all this game of life until it becomes tiresome. And when it does become tiresome, I can leave it — I can kill myself. And that is what I am doing.

This is the contradictory representation of life which mankind had reached before Solomon's day, before Buddha's, and to which the false teachers of our times wish to lead it back.

The demands of the individual are pushed to the most extreme limits of senselessness. The reason, on awakening, rejects them. But the demands of the individual have grown to such proportions, have so encumbered man's consciousness, that it seems to him that reason rejects the whole of life. It seems to him that if he eradicates from his consciousness of life all that his reason rejects, nothing will remain. He does not yet perceive what will remain. The remnant, that remnant in which is life, seems nothing to him.

"But the light shineth in darkness and the darkness comprehendeth it not."

The teaching of the truth recognizes this dilemma — either a senseless existence or a renunciation of it — and "it solves it."

The doctrine which has always been called the doctrine of happiness — the doctrine of the truth — has pointed out to people that, instead of the deceptive happiness which they seek for their animal personality, they always possess, here and now, an inalienable and actual happiness which is always attainable by them, not that which they may receive somewhere and at some time.

This happiness is not merely something deduced from reasoning, it is not that something or other which must be sought somewhere, it is not that happiness promised somewhere and at some time, but is that very happiness which is familiar to man, and toward which every unperverted human soul is drawn.

All men know from the earliest years of their childhood that, in addition to the happiness of the animal personality, there is still another and better happiness of life, which is not only independent of the gratification of the carnal desires of the animal personality, but which, on the contrary, becomes all the greater in proportion to the renunciation of the happiness of the animal personality.

This feeling, which solves all the contradictions of human life, and gives the greatest possible happiness to man, these men know. This feeling is *love*.

Life is the activity of the animal personality, subjected to the law of reason. Reason is that law to which, for its own happiness, the animal personality of man must be rendered subservient. Love is the only reasonable activity of mankind.

The animal personality inclines to happiness; reason demonstrates to man the delusiveness of personal happiness, and leaves but one path. Activity along this pathway is love.

The animal personality of man demands happiness; rational consciousness shows man the misery of all beings who contend with each other, demonstrates to him that there can be no happiness for his animal individuality, shows him that the only happiness possible to him is one in which there shall be no contest with other beings, no cessation of happiness, no satiety; in which there shall be no phantom and fear of death.

And lo, like a key made for this one lock alone, man finds in his own soul a feeling which gives him that very happiness which his reason indicates to him as the only possible one. And this feeling not only solves the former contradictions of life, but finds in these very contradictions, as it were, a possibility of manifesting itself.

Animal individualities desire to employ for their ends the individuality of man. But the feeling of love inclines him to give his existence for the good of other beings.

The animal individuality suffers. And this suffering and its alleviation constitute the chief activity of love. The animal individuality, in striving after happiness, strives with every breath toward the greatest evil — toward death, the phantom of which has destroyed every bliss of the individual.

But the feeling of love not only annihilates this fear, but inclines man to the extremest sacrifice of his fleshly existence for the happiness of others.

CHAPTER XXII

THE MANIFESTATION OF THE FEELING OF LOVE IS IMPOSSIBLE FOR MEN WHO DO NOT UNDERSTAND THE MEANING OF THEIR LIFE

EVERY man knows that in the feeling of love there is something peculiar, capable of solving all the contradictions of life, and of giving man that full happiness in the striving for which his life consists.

"But this feeling comes rarely, continues for but a brief time, and its consequences are still worse than suffering," say men who do not understand life.

To these men, love does not present itself as the sole legitimate manifestation of life which it represents to the rational consciousness, but merely as one among thousands of the varied accidents which occur in life; it presents itself as one of those thousands of varied moods in which man finds himself in the course of his existence: there are times when a man parades as a dandy, there are times when he is attracted by science or art, there are times when he is inclined to service, to ambition, to acquisition; there are times when he loves some one. The mood of love presents itself to men who do not understand life, not as the essence of human life, but as an accidental frame of mind, — and hence as independent of their will, like all the others to which man is subject in the course of his life. It is often possible even to read and to hear arguments to the effect that love is something irregular, which disturbs the regular current of life, — a torturing state of mind. Something like what it must seem to the owl when the sun rises.

It is true that even these people feel that there is in the state of love something peculiar and more important than in all other frames of mind. But, not understanding life, these people cannot understand love, and the condition of love seems to them as lamentable and as deceptive as all other conditions.

"Love? — But whom? It is not worth while to love for a time; and to love forever is impossible."

These words accurately express the confused knowledge of people that in love there is salvation from the misery of life, and the only thing resembling true happiness, and, at the same time, a confession that, for people who do not understand life, love cannot be an anchor of safety. There is no one to love, and all love passes away. And, therefore, love can be happiness only when there is some one to love, and when it is some one whom it would be possible to love eternally. And, as there is nothing of the kind, there is no salvation in love, and love is as much of a delusion and suffering as everything else.

And thus, and not in any other way, can people understand love, who have learned and who themselves teach that life is nothing else than an animal existence.

For such people, life does not even correspond to that conception which we all involuntarily connect with the word love. It is not a beneficial activity, giving happiness to the one who loves, and to the person loved. It very frequently happens that love, in the estimation of people who recognize life in the animal person, is the same feeling in consequence of which one mother, for the welfare of her child, will deprive another hungry child of its mother's milk, and suffer with anxiety for the success of the nursing; that feeling which makes the father, to his own torture, take the last bit of bread from starving men in order to provide for his children; it is the feeling through which he who loves a woman suffers from this love, and causes her to suffer, seducing her, or killing both himself and her out of jealousy; that feeling through which it even happens that a man violates a woman out of love; it is that feeling through which men belonging to one association injure other associations for the sake of upholding their own fellows; it is that feeling which makes a man torment himself over his favorite occupations, and by these same occupations cause grief and suffering to the people about him; it is the feeling which renders a man unable to endure an insult to his beloved fatherland, strews the plain with dead and wounded, his own countrymen and others.

But even this is not all: the activity of love, for people who recognize life as lying in the happiness of the animal individuality, presents such difficulties that its manifestations become not only painful, but often impossible. "Love must not be discussed," is what is generally said by the people who do not understand life; "but one must yield to that direct feeling of preference, of passion, for people, which one experiences—and this is genuine love."

They are right in saying that love must not be argued about, that every argument about love destroys love. But the point lies in this, — that only those people can refrain from discussing love who have already applied their reason to the understanding of life, and who have renounced the happiness of individual life; but those people who have not attained to a comprehension of life, and who exist for the animal personality, cannot do otherwise than discuss it. It is indispensable that they should discuss it, in order to be able to give themselves over to that feeling which they call love. Every

degree; people or our fatherland? our fatherland or our friends? our friends or our own wife? our wife or our father? our father or our children? our children or ourselves? (In order to be in a condition to serve others when this is necessary.)

For all these are the demands of love, and all are so interwoven with each other that the satisfaction of the demands of some deprives a man of the possibility of satisfying the demands of the others. If I admit that it is possible not to clothe a shivering child because my children will be in want, some day, of the garment which is asked of me, then I need not yield to other demands of love in the name of my future children.

It is precisely the same in relation to love for one's country, for chosen occupations, and for all men. If a man can deny the demands of the very smallest present love, in the name of the very greatest love in the future, is it not clear that such a man, even if he desire this with all his heart, will never be in a condition to weigh in what measure he can refuse the demands of the present in the name of the future, and therefore, not being competent to decide this question, he will always choose that manifestation of love which is agreeable to him, *i.e.* he will act, not in the name of his love, but in the name of his individuality. If a man decides that it is better for him to refrain from the demands of the smallest present love in the name of a future and different manifestation of a greater love, then he deceives either himself or others, and loves no one but himself alone.

There is no love in the future. Love is only activity in the present. And the man who manifests no love in the present has no love.

The same thing also comes to pass in the conception of life, in those people who have no life. If men were animals without reason they would exist like animals, and would not discuss life; and their animal existence would be legitimate and happy. It is the same with love; if men were animals without reason, they would love those whom they do love; their wolf-cubs, their flock; and they would not know that they love their wolf-cubs or their flock, and they would not know that other wolves love their cubs, and other flocks their comrades in the flock, and their love would be that love and that life which are possible on that plane of consciousness upon which they find themselves.

But men are reasoning beings, and they cannot help perceiving that others cherish the same love for their own, and that therefore these feelings of love must come in conflict and produce something not favorable, but quite opposed to the conception of love.

But if men employ their reason in justifying and strengthening that animal and ill-disposed sentiment which they call love, communicating to that sentiment monstrous proportions, then that sentiment becomes not only the reverse of good, but it makes of man — a truth long since established — the most malign and terrible of animals. That takes place which is described in the Gospels: "If the light that is in thee be darkness, how great is that darkness!" If there were nothing in man except love for himself and his children, there would not be even ninety-nine hundredths of the evil that now exists among men. Ninety-nine per cent of the evil among men springs from that false feeling which they, lauding it, call love, and which is as much like love as the life of the animal is like the life of man.

What people who do not understand life call love is only the familiar preference of some conditions of their personal happiness to others. When a man who does not understand life says that he loves his wife or his child or his friend, he merely says that the presence in his life of his wife or his child or his friend heightens the happiness of his individual life.

These preferences bear the same relation to love that existence bears to life. And as existence is called life by the people who do not know what life is, so the preference of some conditions of personal existence to others is called love by the same people.

These feelings — preferences for certain beings, as for example, for one's children, or even for certain occupations, for science, for instance, or for art, — we also call love; but such feelings of preference, infinitely varied, constitute the whole complication of the visible, tangible, animal life of men, and cannot be called love, because they have not the chief mark of love, — activity, which has for its aim and end, happiness.

The violence of manifestation of these preferences only demonstrates the energy of the animal personality. The violence of preference of some people over others, inaccurately called love, is merely the stock upon which true love, and even its fruits, may be grafted. But as the stock is not the apple tree and does not yield fruit, or gives only bitter fruit, instead of sweet, so passion is not love, and does no good to people, or produces still greater evil. And therefore the much vaunted love for wife and children, as well as for friends, brings the greatest evil to the world, not to mention love for science, for art, for one's country, which is nothing else than a preference, for the time being, of certain conditions of the animal life over others.

CHAPTER XXIII

TRUE LOVE IS THE RESULT OF THE RENUNCIATION OF THE HAPPINESS OF THE PERSONALITY

TRUE love, then, becomes possible, only on the renunciation of happiness for the animal personality.

The possibility of true love begins only when a man has comprehended that there is no happiness for his animal personality. Only then wlll all the sap of his life pass into the one ennobling shoot of genuine love, which has already grown stout with all the powers of the trunk of the wild sapling of the animal person. And the doctrine of Christ is the graft for this love, as He Himself said. He said that He, His love, was the one branch which could bring forth fruit, and that every branch which bringeth not forth fruit is cut off.

Only he who has not only understood, but has also

by his life confessed that he who loves his soul loses it, and that he who hates his soul in this world preserves it to life everlasting, — only he understands genuine love.

"And he who loveth father or mother more than Me is unworthy of Me. And he that loveth son or daughter more than Me is unworthy of Me. If ye love them that love you; that is not love; but love your enemies, love them that hate you."

It is not by love for father, or son, or wife, or friends, or good and amiable people, as it is generally thought, that men renounce their individuality, but only as a result of the recognition of the vain existence of the individual, a recognition of the impossibility of its happiness, and therefore as a result of the renunciation of individual life, that man becomes acquainted with real love, and can really love father, son, wife, children, and friends.

Love is the preference of other beings to one's self, to one's animal personality.

The neglect of the nearest interests of the individual for the attainment of distant aims of the same individual, as is the case with what is generally called love, which has not grown to self-sacrifice, is merely the preference of some beings over others, for one's own individual happiness. True love, before it becomes an active sentiment, must be a certain condition. The beginning of love, its root, is not a burst of feeling, clouding the reason, as is generally imagined, but is that most rational, luminous, and therefore tranquil and joyous state, peculiar to children and to reasonable people.

That state is a state of affection toward all people, which is inherent in children, but which in grown persons arises only on renunciation, and increases only with the degree of renunciation of the happiness of the individuality. How often are we forced to hear the words: "It is all the same to me, I need nothing," and in connection with these words to see an unloving mien toward men. But let every man try, at least once, at a moment when he is ill-disposed toward people, to say to himself honestly and from his soul, "It is all the same to me, I need nothing," and, only for a time, to desire nothing for himself, and every man will learn, through this simple, inward experiment, how instantaneously, in proportion to the honesty of his renunciation, all malevolence will disappear, and how, afterward, affection toward all people will gush from his heart, sealed up to that time.

Love is, in truth, a preference of other beings to one's self — surely that is the way we all understand love, and it is impossible to understand it otherwise. The amount of love is the amount of the fraction whose numerator, my partiality, my sympathy for others, is not in my power; but the denominator, my love for myself, can be augmented or diminished by me, to infinity, in proportion to the significance which I attribute to my animal personality. But the judgment of our world concerning love, concerning its grades, is a judgment as to the size of the fraction according to the numerator alone, without regard to the denominator.

Real love always has as its foundation renunciation of individual happiness, and the affection toward all men which arises therefrom. Only upon this universal affection can spring up genuine love for certain people, — one's own relatives or strangers. And such love alone gives the true bliss of life, and solves the apparent contradictions of the animal and the rational consciousness.

Love which has not for its foundation renunciation of individuality, and, as a consequence, affection for all people, is merely the life of the animal, and is subject to the same miseries as, and to even greater miseries and to still greater folly than, life without this fictitious love. The feeling of partiality called love not only does not remove the conflict of existences, does not free an individual from the pursuit of enjoyments, and does not save from death, but merely darkens life still more, embitters the strife, augments the thirst for pleasures for one's self and others, and increases the terror of death for one's self and others.

The man who places his life in the existence of the animal individuality cannot love, because love must seem to him an activity directly opposed to his life. The life of such a man is only in the happiness of his animal existence; but love demands, first of all, the sacrifice of that happiness. Even if a man who does not understand life should sincerely wish to give himself up to the activity of love, he will not be in a condition to do this, until he understands life, and changes his whole relation to it. The man who sets his life in the happiness of his animal person, who increases, during the whole course of his life, the means of his animal happiness, by acquiring wealth and hoarding it, will make others serve his animal happiness, and will distribute that happiness among those individuals who have been most useful to him for the happiness of his personality. But how is he to give up his life, when his life is supported, not by himself, but by other people? And still more difficult will it be for him to choose to which of the persons whom he prefers he shall give the happiness which he has accumulated, and whom he shall serve.

In order to be in a position to give up his life, he must first give away that superfluity which he takes from others for the happiness of his own life; and more than that, he must accomplish the impossible: decide which of the people he is to serve with his life.

Before he will be in a condition to love, that is, to do good, sacrificing himself, he must cease to hate, that is, to do evil, and he must cease to prefer some people to others for the happiness of his personality.

Only for the man who does not acknowledge happiness in individual life, and who does not, therefore, trouble himself about that false happiness and about that affection toward all men proper to man, which is set free in him, is the activity of love, which always satisfies him and others, possible.

The happiness of the life of such a man in love is like the happiness of the plant in the light; and hence, as the plant which is not in the least covered cannot inquire, and does not inquire, in what direction it is to grow and whether the light is good, whether it must not wait for some other and better light, but takes the only light that exists in the world, and stretches toward it, — thus the man who has renounced individual happiness does not argue about what he must give up of that which he has taken from other people, and to what beloved beings, and whether there is not some better love than the one which makes the demand, but gives himself, his being, to the love which is accessible to him, and which lies before him. Only such love gives full satisfaction to the reasoning nature of man.

CHAPTER XXIV

LOVE IS LOVE ONLY WHEN IT IS THE SACRIFICE OF SELF

AND there is no other love than this, that a man should lay down his life for his friend. Love is love only when it is the sacrifice of one's self. Only when a man gives to another, not merely his time and his strength, but when he spends his body for the beloved object, gives up his life for him, — only this do we all acknowledge as love; and only in such love do we all find happiness, the reward of love. And only in virtue of the fact that there is such love toward men, only in this, does the world stand. A mother who nurses her child gives herself directly, her body, for the nourishment of the children, who, were it not for this, would not be alive. And this is love. Exactly in the same manner does every laborer for the good of others give his body for the nourishment of another, when he exhausts his body with toil, and brings himself nearer to death. And such love is possible only for the man between whom and the possibility of sacrifice of himself and other beings whom he loves there stands no limit to sacrifice. The mother who gives her child to a nurse cannot love it; a man who acquires and hoards his money cannot love.

"If any man say that he is in the light, and hateth his brother, he is still in darkness. If any man love his brother, that man abideth in the light and there is no deceit in him. But he that hateth his brother dwelleth in darkness, and walketh in darkness, and knoweth not whither he goeth, because darkness hath blinded his eyes. .... Let us love not in word or with the tongue, but in deed and truth. And hereby do we know that we are of the truth, and our hearts are set at rest. .... Love attaineth such perfection in us that we have boldness in the day of judgment, because we so walk in the world even as He walked. There is no fear in love, but perfect love casteth out fear, for in fear there is torment. He that feareth is not made perfect in love."

Only such love gives true life to men.

"Thou shalt love the Lord thy God with all thy heart and all thy soul and all thy mind. This is the first and great commandment." And the second is like unto it: "Thou shalt love thy neighbor as thyself," said the lawyer to Christ. And to this Jesus replied: "Thou hast said rightly, so do," — *i.e.* love God and thy neighbor — and *thou shalt live.*

True love is life itself. "We know that we have passed from death to life, because we love the brethren," says a disciple of Christ. "He that loveth not his brother abideth in death." Only he is alive who loves.

Love, according to the doctrine of Christ, is life itself, but not a senseless, suffering, and perishing life, but a blessed and endless life. And we all know this. Love is not a deduction of the mind, it is not the result of certain activity; but it is itself the joyful activity of the life which encompasses us on all sides, and which we all know in ourselves from the first memories of our childhood to the time when the false teaching of the world veils it in our soul and deprives us of the possibility of testing it.

But love is not a partiality for that which enhances the temporal happiness of man's personality, like love toward selected individuals or objects, but that striving toward the good of that which is within man, which will remain in man after the renunciation of the happiness of the animal individuality.

Who among living people does not know that blissful sensation, — even if but once experienced, and most frequently of all in the earliest childhood, before the soul is yet choked up with all that lie which stifles the life in us, — that blessed feeling of emotion, during which one desires to love everybody, both those near to him, his father, and mother, and brothers, and wicked people, and his enemies, and his dog, and his horse, and a blade of grass; he desires one thing, — that it should be well with everybody, that all should be happy; and still more he desires that he himself may act so that it may be well with all, that he may give himself and his whole life to making others comfortable and happy. And this, and this alone, is that love in which lies the life of man.

This love, in which alone is life, manifests itself in the soul of man as a hardly perceptible, tender shoot, in the midst of the coarse shoots of weeds resembling it, of the various carnal desires of man which we call love. At first, it seems to men, and to the man himself, that this shoot is the one from which must grow that tree in which the birds shall shelter themselves, — and that all the other shoots are the same.

At first, men even prefer the weeds which grow faster, and the only shoot of life is stifled and languishes; but what is even worse is that which most frequently happens: men have heard that among the number of these shoots there is one which is genuine, life-giving, called love, and, trampling it down, they begin to rear another shoot from the weeds, calling it love.

But, what is still worse, men seize the shoot with rough hands and cry: "Here it is, we have found it; now we know it, let us train it up; love, love! the most elevated sentiment; here it is!" and men begin to transplant it, to correct it, and they grasp it, and tread it under foot, until the shoot dies before it has flowered, and these same men or others say: "All this is nonsense, folly, sentimentality."

The shoot of love, when it appears, is tender, it does not bear handling; it is powerful only when it has attained its growth. All that men do to it is but the worse for it. It needs but one thing, — that men should not hide from it the sun of reason, which alone will promote its growth.

CHAPTER XXV

MEN'S EFFORTS, DIRECTED TO THE IMPOSSIBLE AMELIORATION OF THEIR EXISTENCE, DEPRIVE THEM OF THE POSSIBILITY OF THE ONE TRUE LIFE

ONLY the knowledge of the visionary and delusive character of the animal existence, and the setting free within him of the one true life of love, confers happiness upon man. And what steps do men take for the attainment of this happiness? Men, whose existence consists in the gradual annihilation of personality, and in the approach of that personality to inevitable death, and who cannot fail to be aware of this, strive in every way, during the whole period of their existence, to establish that perishing existence, to gratify its desires, and thereby to deprive themselves of the possibility of the only happiness in life — love.

The activity of men who do not understand life is directed, during the entire period of its existence, to a conflict for their own existence, to the acquisition of enjoyments, to emancipating themselves from suffering, and to putting away from them inevitable death.

But the increase of enjoyment increases the strain of the conflict, the sensitiveness to suffering, and brings death nearer. In order to hide from himself the approach of death, there is but one means: still further to augment pleasure. But the augmentation of pleasures reaches its limits, pleasure cannot be further increased, it passes into suffering, and remains only in the form of sensitiveness to suffering and terror before death, which is approaching ever nearer and nearer in the midst of suffering alone. And a vicious circle makes its appearance: one is the cause of the other and one augments the other. The chief horror in the life of people who do not understand life lies in the fact that what they regard as pleasures (all pleasures of a rich life), being of such a nature that they cannot be shared equally among all men, must be taken from others, must be obtained by force, by evil, by annihilating the possibility of that kindly inclination toward people from which springs love. So that pleasure is always directly opposed to love, and the stronger it is, the more opposed is it. So that, the stronger, the more intense the activity for the attainment of pleasure, the more impossible becomes the only happiness accessible to man — love.

Life is understood, not as it is recognized by the rational consciousness — as an invisible but undoubted submission at every moment of one's animal nature to the law of reason, setting free the affection toward all people which is proper to man, and the activity of love which flows from it, but only as an existence in the flesh during a certain period of time under settled conditions arranged by us, which exclude the possibility of kindliness to all men.

To people of the doctrine of the world, who bend their minds to the organization of fixed conditions of existence, it seems that the augmentation of the happiness of life proceeds from the best external arrangement of one's existence. But the best external arrangement depends upon the exercise of greater violence over men, which is directly opposed to love. So that the better their organization, the less possibility of love, the less possibility of life, is there left to them.

Having applied their reason, not to understanding that identical happiness for all men of the animal existence is equal to a cipher, men have recognized this cipher as a quantity which can be augmented or diminished, and in this supposititious augmentation and diminution of the cipher they use all the reason which remains unapplied in them.

Men do not perceive that nothing, however much it may be multiplied, remains the same to every other person a cipher; they do not perceive that the existence of the animal personality of every man is equally wretched, and cannot be rendered happy by any external conditions. Men do not wish to see that no one existence, in the flesh, can be happier than any other, that this is as much a law as that whereby the water on the surface of a lake can nowhere rise higher than the general level. Men who have perverted their understanding do not see this, and apply themselves to this impossible work, and in this elevation of the water in various places above the level of the lake — after the manner of what is done by children bathing, who call it "brewing beer" — passes the whole of their existence.

It seems to them that the lives of men are more or less happy and good; the existence of a poor laborer or of a sickly man, they say, is evil, unhappy; the existence of a rich or a healthy man is good and happy; and they bend all the strength of their minds to escaping an evil, unhappy, poor, and sickly existence, and in constructing for themselves a good, rich, healthy, and happy one.

They work out for generations the processes for organizing and maintaining these various and happiest of lives, and hand down the programmes of these fancied better lives, as they call their animal existence, to their descendants. Men vie with each other in endeavoring to maintain as well as possible that happy *life* which they have inherited from the organization of their parents, or to organize for themselves a new and still happier *life*. It seems to men that, by maintaining the order of existence which they have inherited, or by establishing a new one which is better, as they imagine, they are accomplishing something.

And thus upholding each other in this delusion, men often become so sincerely convinced that this senseless beating of the water, the absurdity of which is evident to themselves, constitutes life — they become so convinced of this, that they turn away with scorn from the summons to true life, which they hear incessantly: both in the teaching of the truth, and the examples of life presented by people who are alive, and in their own suppressed hearts, in which, even to the end, the voice of reason and of love is never stifled.

A wonderful thing takes place. Men, vast numbers of men, who possess the possibility of a life of love and reason, find themselves in the position of those sheep who are being dragged out of a burning house, while they, imagining that people want to fling them into the fire, exert all their strength to contend with those who are trying to save them.

Through fear of death, men do not wish to escape from it; through fear of suffering, men torture themselves, and deprive themselves of the only happiness and life that are possible for them.

CHAPTER XXVI

THE FEAR OF DEATH IS ONLY A CONFESSION OF THE UNSOLVED CONTRADICTION OF LIFE

"There is no death," the voice of truth says to men. "I am the Resurrection and the Life; he that believeth in Me, though he were dead, yet shall he live. And every one that liveth and believeth in Me shall never die. Believest thou this?"

"There is no death," say all the great teachers of the world; and the same say millions of men who understand life, and bear witness to it with their lives. And every living man feels the same thing in his soul, at the moment when his consciousness clears up. But men who do not understand life cannot do otherwise than fear death. They see it, and believe in it.

"How is there no death?" cry these people in wrath and indignation. "This is sophistry! Death is before us; it has mowed down millions, and it will mow us down as well. And you may say as much as you please that it does not exist, it will remain all the same. Yonder it is!"

And they see that of which they speak, as a man mentally afflicted sees the vision which terrifies him. He cannot handle the vision, it has never touched him; of its intentions he knows nothing; but he is afraid, and he suffers from this imaginary vision, which is deprived of the possibility of life. And it is the same with death. Man does not know his death, and never can know it; it has never yet touched him; of its intentions he knows nothing. Then what is it that he fears?

"It has never yet seized me, but it will seize me, that I surely know — it will seize me and annihilate me. And that is terrible," say men who do not understand life.

If men with false ideas of life could reason calmly, and think accurately, on the basis of that conception which they have of life, they would be forced to the conclusion that in what is produced in my fleshly existence by the change which I see proceeding, incessantly, in all beings, and which I call death, there is nothing disagreeable or terrible.

I shall die. What is there terrible about that? How many different changes have taken place, and are now in progress, in my fleshly existence, and I have not feared them? Why should I fear this change which has not yet come, and in which there is not only nothing repulsive to my reason and experience, but which is so comprehensible, so familiar, and so natural for me, that during the whole course of my life I have formed fancies, I still form them, in which the death, both of animals and of people, has been accepted by me as a necessary and often an agreeable condition of life. What is there terrible about it?

For there are but two strictly logical views of life: one false — that by which life is understood as those seeming phenomena which take place in my body from my birth to my death; and another, the true one — by which life is understood as that invisible consciousness of it which I bear within myself. One view is false, the other is true; but both are logical, and men may hold either the one or the other; but in neither the one nor the other is the fear of death possible.

The first false view, which understands life as the visible phenomena in the body from birth to death, is as old as the world itself. This is not, as many think, a view of life which has been worked out by the materialistic science and philosophy of our day; the science and philosophy of our times have only carried this view to its extreme limits, by which it becomes more visible than hitherto how little this view corresponds to the fundamental demands of human life; but this is the ancient and primitive view of men who stood upon the lower steps of culture. It is expressed among the Chinese, among the Greeks, and among the Hebrews, in the Book of Job, and in the sentence: "Dust thou art, and to dust shalt thou return."

This view, in its present expression, runs as follows: Life is the fortuitous play of forces in matter, manifesting itself in space and time. And what we call our consciousness is not life, but a certain delusion of the feelings, which makes it appear that life lies in this consciousness. Consciousness is the spark which flashes up from matter under certain conditions of the latter. This spark flashes up, burns, again grows feeble, and finally goes out. This spark, that is to say, consciousness, experienced by matter in the course of a certain time, between two endless spaces of time, is nothing. And in spite of the fact that consciousness sees and passes judgment on itself and on all the infinite world, and beholds all the play of chance of this world, — and *chief of all*, in the contradistinction to something that is not accidental, calls this play accidental, — this consciousness itself is only the product of dead matter, a specter, appearing and disappearing without any trace or reason. All is the product of matter, infinitely varied; and what is called life is only a certain condition of dead matter.

Such is one view of life. This view is utterly false. According to this view, the rational consciousness of man is merely an accident, accompanying a certain condition of matter; and therefore, what we, in our consciousness, call life, is a phantom. What is dead alone exists. What we call life is the play of death. With such a view of life, death should not only not be terrible, but life ought to be terrible, as something unnatural and senseless, as it is among the Buddhists, and the new pessimists, Schopenhauer and Hartmann.

The other view of life is as follows. Life is only that which I recognize in myself. But I am always conscious of my life, not as I have been or as I shall be (thus I meditate upon my life), but I am conscious of my life thus — that I am — that I never begin anywhere, that I shall never end anywhere. No comprehension of time and space is connected with my consciousness of life. My life is manifested in time, in space, but this is merely its manifestation. But the life itself of which I am conscious makes itself perceptible to me outside of time and space; so that, according to this view, it appears, on the contrary, not that the consciousness of life is a phantom, but all that which is dependent upon space and is visionary in time.

And, therefore, a curtailment of the bodily existence, so far as connected with time and space, has nothing wretched about it, according to this view, and can neither shorten nor destroy my true life. And, according to this view, death does not exist.

There could be no fear of death according to either view of life, if men held strictly to either the one or the other.

Neither as an animal nor as a rational being can man fear death. As the animal has no consciousness of life, it does not see death; but the rational being, having a consciousness of life, cannot see in the death of the animal anything except a natural and never ending movement of matter. But if man fears, what he fears is not death, which he does not know, but life, which alone he does know, and his animal and rational existence. That feeling which is expressed in men by the fear of death is only the consciousness of the inward contradiction of life; just as the fear of ghosts is merely a consciousness of a sickly mental condition.

"I shall cease to be; I shall die; all that which I value in life will die," says one voice to a man.

"I am," says another voice; "and I cannot die, and I ought not to die. I ought not to die, and I am dying."

Not in death, but in this contradiction lies the cause of that terror which seizes upon a man at the thought of death of the flesh: the fear of death lies not in the fact that man dreads the curtailment of his animal existence, but in the fact that it seems to him that that will die which cannot and must not die. The thought of future death is only a transference to the future of the death which takes place in the present. The specter which presents itself of a future death of the flesh is not an awakening of the thought of death, but, on the contrary, an awakening of the thought of the life which a man should have and which he has not.

This feeling is similar to that which a man would experience on awaking to life in his grave, under ground. "There is life, but I am in death; and this is it — death!" He imagines that what is and must be will be annihilated. And the mind of man mourns and grows afraid. The best proof of the fact that the fear of death is not the fear of death, but of false life, is this, that men frequently kill themselves from the fear of death.

Men are not terrified by the thought of the death of the flesh because they are afraid that their life will end with it, but because the death of the flesh plainly demonstrates to them the necessity of a true life, which they do not possess. And this is why people who do not understand life are so disinclined to think of death. To think of death is exactly the same with them as to confess that they are not living as their rational consciousness demands.

People who fear death, fear it because it represents emptiness and darkness to them; but they behold emptiness and darkness because they do not see life.

CHAPTER XXVII

THE DEATH OF THE FLESH ANNIHILATES THE BODY WHICH BELONGS TO SPACE AND THE CONSCIOUSNESS WHICH BELONGS TO TIME, BUT IT CANNOT ANNIHILATE THAT WHICH CONSTITUTES THE FOUNDATION OF LIFE: THE SPECIAL RELATION OF EVERY CREATURE TO THE WORLD

BUT if men who do not see life would only approach nearer to the phantoms which alarm them, and would examine them, they would perceive that for them also they are only phantoms, and not realities.

The fear of death always proceeds, in these people, from the fear of losing, at their death in the flesh, their special *ego*, which, they feel, constitutes their life. I shall die, my body will molder and destroy my *ego*. But my *ego* is that which has lived in my body so many years.

Men prize this *ego* of theirs; and, assuming that this *ego* corresponds with their fleshly life, they draw the deduction that it must be annihilated with the destruction of their fleshly life.

This is a very common deduction, and it rarely enters any one's head to doubt it, yet, nevertheless, this deduction is entirely arbitrary. Men — both those who consider themselves materialists, and those who regard themselves as spiritualists — have become so habituated to the notion that their *ego* is the consciousness of their body, which has lived so many years, that it never enters their heads to verify the authenticity of such a conviction.

I have lived fifty-nine years, and during the whole of that time I have been conscious of myself in my body, and this consciousness of myself has, as it seems to me, been my life. But, as a matter of fact, it only seems so to me. I have lived neither fifty-nine years, nor fifty-nine thousand years, nor fifty-nine seconds. Neither my body nor the length of its existence in any way determines the life of my *ego.* If I, at every moment of my life, ask myself in my own consciousness, "What am I?" I reply: "Something thinking and feeling," *i.e.* bearing itself to the world in its own entirely peculiar fashion.

Only this *ego* do I recognize as my *ego*, and nothing more. As to when and where I was born, when and where I began to think and to feel as I now think and feel, I know absolutely nothing. My consciousness merely says to me: "I am; I am with that relation of mine to the world in which I find myself at the present moment."

Of my birth, my childhood, of many periods of youth, of middle age, of times not very far past, I often remember nothing at all. But if I do recall anything, or if I am reminded of something in my past, then I remember it — and remember it almost exactly as those things which are told me about others.

On what foundation, therefore, do I assert that, during the whole course of my existence, I have been but *one ego?* My body, assuredly, never has been and is not one: my body has always been, and is ceaselessly wasting substance — through something immaterial and invisible, that recognizes this which flows through it as its body. My whole body has been changed scores of times; nothing has been left of the old: muscles and inward parts, and bones, and brain, — all have undergone a change.

My body is one only because there is something immaterial which acknowledges this changing body as one and its own. This immaterial something is that which we call consciousness: it alone holds the whole body together, and recognizes it as one and its own. Without this knowledge of myself as separate from everything else, I should know nothing of my own or of any other life. And therefore, on first thinking the matter over, it appears that the foundation of all — consciousness — must be constant. But this also is incorrect; and consciousness is not constant. During our whole life, and even now, there is repeated that phenomenon of sleep, which seems to us very simple because we all sleep every day, but which is decidedly incomprehensible, if we admit, what it is impossible not to admit, that consciousness is often entirely suspended during sleep.

Every twenty-four hours, during the period of profound slumber, consciousness is entirely suspended, and is afterward resumed. But, in the meantime, this same consciousness is the only basis upon which the whole body is held together, and recognized as its own. It would seem as though, on the suspension of consciousness, the body should fall apart, and lose its independent existence; but this does not happen either in natural or artificial sleep.

But not only is the consciousness which binds the whole body together periodically interrupted, without the body falling apart, — this consciousness, in addition, changes like the body. As there is nothing in common with my body of ten years ago and my present body, — as it is not one and the same body, so there has not been one consciousness in me. My consciousness as a child three years of age, and my present consciousness, are as different as is the matter of my body now from what it was thirty years ago. Consciousness is not a unit, and there is a series of successive states of consciousness which might be subdivided to infinity.

So even that consciousness which holds the whole body together, and recognizes it as its own, is not a unit, but something which is suspended and which undergoes change. Consciousness, a single consciousness of one's self, as we generally imagine it, does not exist in man, just as there is not one body. There is in man neither one and the same body nor one of that thing which sets apart this body from every other — there is no consciousness which is constantly the same, throughout the whole life of a man, but there is only a series of successive states of consciousness, in some manner united — and, nevertheless, man feels himself to be himself.

Our body is not one, and that which recognizes this changing body to be one and ours is not continuous in point of time, but is merely a series of changing states of consciousness, and we have already lost both our body and our consciousness many times; we lose our body constantly, and we lose our consciousness every day, when we fall asleep; and every day and hour we feel in ourselves the alteration of this consciousness, and we do not fear it in the least.

Hence, if there is any such thing as our *ego*, which we are afraid of losing at death, then that *ego* cannot reside in the body which we call ours, nor in that consciousness which we call ours for a certain time, but in some other, whole series of successive states of consciousness united into one.

What is this something which binds in one all the states of consciousness which succeed each other in point of time? What is my same radical and peculiar *ego*, which is not composed of the substance of my body and of the series of states of consciousness which proceed in it, but that fundamental *ego* upon which as upon a cord are strung, one after the other, the various consciousnesses which follow each other in point of time? The question seems very profound and wise, but there is not a child who would not know how to answer it, and who would not utter the response twenty times a day.

"But *I* love this and I don't love that."

These words are very simple, but in them lies the solution of the question as to the peculiar *I* which binds all consciousness in one. It is that *I* which loves this thing and does not love that. Why one loves this and does not love that, no one knows, and, at the same time, it is this very thing which constitutes the foundation of life for every man, and it is this which binds in one all the states of consciousness, varying in point of time, of every individual man.

The external world acts upon all men alike, but the impressions of men, even when under the very same conditions, differ infinitely, both in the number received and in their capacity for being infinitely subdivided, and in their strength. From these impressions is formed the series of successive states of consciousness of every man. But all these successive consciousnesses are connected only because, even in the present, some impressions act, and others do not act, upon his consciousness. But certain impressions act or fail to act upon a man only because he loves this more or less, and does not love that.

Only in consquence of this greater or lesser degree of love is a certain series of some judgments, and not of others, formed. So that only in the property of loving one more or less, and not loving the other, lies that peculiar and fundamental *ego* of man, in which all the scattered and fragmentary senses are united. And this property, although it is developed in our life, is borne by us, all ready prepared, into this life, from some past invisible and unknown to us.

This peculiar property of men, of loving one thing in a greater or less degree and not loving another, is usually called character. And by this word the peculiar qualities of each individual man, which have taken form in consequence of certain conditions of place and time, are often understood. But this is an error.

The fundamental quality of man, of loving one thing more or less and not loving another, does not proceed from conditions of time and space, but, on the contrary, conditions of time and place act or do not act upon a man only because man, on his entrance into the world, already has a very well-defined property of loving one and not loving another. Only from this cause does it happen that men, born and reared in identical conditions of time and space, often present the sharpest contrast in their internal *ego*.

That which unites in one all the scattered states of consciousness, which, in their turn, bind our body in one, is a very definite thing, although independent of conditions of time and place, and is brought into the world by us from the realm of the spaceless and the timeless: it is that *something* which lies in my well-known exceptional relations to the world, and is my genuine and acting *ego*. I understand myself as that fundamental quality; and other men, if I know them, I know only as some peculiar relations to the world. On entering into serious spiritual communion with men, none of us, surely, is guided by their external marks, but each of us seeks to penetrate into their nature; that is, to understand what is their relation to the world, what they love, and in what degree, and what they do not love.

Every separate being, — a horse, a dog, or a cow, if I know them, and have any spiritual relations with them, I know, not by their external marks, but by that peculiar relation to the world in which each one of them stands — by the fact that each one of them loves and does not love, and in what degree each loves and does not love. If I know the special and various races of animals, then, strictly speaking, I know them, not so much by their external marks, as because each one of them — the lion, the fish, the spider — presents a general peculiar relation to the world. All lions, as a rule, love one thing, and all fish another, and all spiders a third; only because they love differently are they distinguished in my imagination as different living creatures.

But what I do not yet distinguish in each of these creatures, his special relation to the world, does not prove that it has not existed, but only that the peculiar relation to the world which constitutes the life of a single individual spider is remote from that relation to the world in which I find myself, and that therefore I have not yet understood him as Silvio Pellico understood his individual spider.

The basis of all I know about myself, and about all the world, is that peculiar relation to the world in which I find myself, and in consequence of which I see other beings, who are in their own peculiar relations to the world. But my special relation to the world has not been settled in this life, and did not begin with this body, nor with the series of consciousnesses which have followed each other in point of time.

And, therefore, my body, bound in one by my temporal senses, may be annihilated, and even my temporal existence may be annihilated, but that which cannot be annihilated is my peculiar relation to the world, which constitutes my peculiar *ego*, from which has been created for me all that is. It cannot be annihilated, because it alone has existence. If it did not exist, I should not know the series of my consecutive states of consciousness, I should not know my body, I should not know my own life or any other. And, therefore, the annihilation of the body and the senses cannot serve as a sign of the annihilation of myself and judgment, cannot serve as a sign of the destruction of my peculiar relations to the world, which neither began nor arose in this life.

CHAPTER XXVIII

THE FEAR OF DEATH ARISES FROM THE FACT THAT MEN ACCEPT AS LIFE ONE SMALL PORTION OF IT LIMITED BY THEIR OWN FALSE IDEA

We are afraid of losing, at the death of the flesh, our special *ego*, uniting the body and a series of conscious states, which manifest themselves temporally, into one; but, nevertheless, this, my peculiar *ego*, did not begin with my birth, and, therefore, the suspension of a certain temporary consciousness cannot annihilate that which unites in one all temporal states of consciousness.

The death of the flesh actually does destroy that which holds the body together, — the consciousness of temporal life. But this happens with us invariably, and every day when we fall asleep. The question lies here: does the death of the flesh destroy that which unites all the consecutive states of consciousness into one, that is to say, my special relation to the world? In order to verify this, it is necessary first to demonstrate that this special relation to the world, which unites in one all succeeding states of consciousness, was born with my birth in the flesh, and that it will, therefore, die with it. But this is not so.

Reasoning upon the foundation of my consciousness,

I see that what binds all my states of consciousness into one is a certain susceptibility toward one thing, and a coldness toward another, in consequence of which one remains, while the other disappears in me, the degree of my love for good and of my hatred for evil, — that is, my peculiar relation to the world, which constitutes me, my special *me*, is not the result of any external cause, but is the fundamental cause of all the other phenomena of my life.

Reasoning upon the foundation of observation, it seems to me at first that the causes of peculiarity in my *ego* are to be found in the peculiarities of my parents, and in the conditions which have influenced them and me; but, on proceeding further in this path of reasoning, I cannot fail to perceive that if my special *ego* lies in the peculiarities of my parents, and the conditions which have affected them, then it lies also in the peculiarities of all my ancestors, and in the conditions of their existence, so that my special *ego* has been produced outside the limits of all space, and outside of all time; that is, that it is the very thing which I recognize it to be.

In this, and only in this timeless and spaceless foundation of my special relation to the world, uniting all the states of consciousness within my memory, and all those states which preceded memory, of my life (as Plato puts it, and as we all feel it in our lives), in this foundation, in my special relation to the world, is there that special *ego*, as to which we fear that it will be annihilated at the death of the flesh.

But it is merely necessary to understand that what unites all states of consciousness in one, that what constitutes the special *ego* of a man, is to be found independent of time, that it always has been and is, and that what can suspend itself is only a series of states of consciousness, within a given time, — in order to make it clear that the destruction of the last state of consciousness in point of time, at the death of the flesh, can as little destroy man's true *ego* as his daily slumber. For no man ever feared to fall asleep, although in sleep precisely the same thing takes place as at death, namely, a temporary suspension of consciousness. But not a single man is afraid of going to sleep, although the suspension of consciousness is precisely the same as in death, — not because he has reasoned it out that he has gone to sleep and waked again, and that therefore he will wake again (this reasoning is inaccurate: he might wake a thousand times and not waken on the thousand and first); — no one ever goes through this reasoning, and this reasoning could not reassure him; but the man knows that his real *ego* lives independent of time, and that therefore the suspensions of his consciousness which manifest themselves in time cannot destroy his life.

If a man were to fall asleep, as in the fairy tales, for a thousand years, he would go to sleep as tranquilly as for two hours. For consciousness, which is not temporary, but of true life, a break of a million years and of eight hours are all the same, because, for such a life, time does not exist.

The body is annihilated, the consciousness of to-day is annihilated.

But it is surely time for man to become accustomed to the changes of his body, and to the replacement of temporary states of consciousness by others. For these changes began as long ago as man can remember himself, and have proceeded uninterruptedly. Man does not fear the change in his body, and not only is he not terrified, but he often desires to hasten these changes, he desires to grow up, to become a man, to recover health. The person has been a red piece of flesh, and all his consciousness has consisted in the demands of the stomach; now he is a bearded, sensible man, or a woman loving her grown-up children! ....

For there is nothing similar either in body or mind, and man has not been terrified by these changes which have brought him to his present condition, but he has only welcomed them. What is there terrible about the impending change? Annihilation? Why, that in which all these changes are effected — a special relation to the world — that in which consists the consciousness of the true life, did not begin with the birth of the body, but independently of the body and independently of time. Then how can any change connected with time and space destroy that which is not connected with it? A man fixes his eyes upon a small, insignificant bit of his life, does not wish to see all of it, and trembles lest this tiny fragment which is dear to him should be lost. This recalls the anecdote of the madman who imagined that he was made of glass, and who, when he was thrown down, said, "Smash!" and immediately died. In order that a man may have life, he must take the whole of it, and not that small scrap of it which reveals itself in time and space. To him that taketh the whole of life there shall be added, but from him that taketh a portion of it shall be taken away even that which he hath.

CHAPTER XXIX

LIFE IS A RELATION TO THE WORLD. THE MOVEMENT OF LIFE IS THE ESTABLISHMENT OF A NEW, A HIGHER, RELATION, AND THEREFORE DEATH IS THE ENTRANCE UPON A NEW RELATION

We cannot understand life otherwise than as a certain relation to the world: thus do we understand life in ourselves, and thus do we understand it in other beings.

But we understand life in ourselves not only as a relation to the world once existing, but as the establishment of a new relation to the world through greater and ever greater subjection of the animal personality to the reason, and the appearance of a greater degree of love. The inevitable destruction of fleshly existence, which we see in ourselves, proves to us that the relation in which we stand to the world is not permanent, but that we are compelled to establish another. The establishment of this new relation, *i.e.* the movement of life, also destroys the conception of death. The idea of death presents itself only to the man who has not recognized his life as lying in the establishment of a rational relation to the world, and its manifestation in ever increasing love, and who has remained in this relation, *i.e.* in that degree of love to one thing and dislike to another, with which he entered upon existence.

Life is an unceasing movement, but by remaining in the same relation to the world, by remaining in the same degree of love, with which he entered life, he feels its cessation, and death presents itself to him.

And death is visible and terrible to such a man only. The whole existence of such a man is one constant death. Death is visible and terrible to him, not only in the future, but in the present, at all manifestations of the diminution of animal life, from youth to old age; because the movement of existence from childhood to manhood only seems like a temporary augmentation of strength, while it is, in reality, merely a hardening of the limbs, a decrease of flexibility, of vitality, which never ceases from birth to death. Such a man beholds death constantly before him, and cannot save himself from it by any means whatever. The situation of such a man becomes worse and worse with every day and hour, and nothing can improve it. His special relation to the world, love to one and lack of love for another, seems to such a man only one of the conditions of his existence; and the only business of life, the establishment of a new relation to the world, the increase of love, appears to him as a useless matter. His whole life is passed in the impossible effort to escape from the inevitable diminution of life, the hardening and weakening of it through old age and death.

But it is not thus for the man who understands life. Such a man knows that he brought his peculiar relation to the world into his present life, his love for one and his dislike for the other, from his past, which is concealed from him. He knows that this love of his to one and dislike to another, which has been brought into his existence by himself, is the very essence of his life; that this is not an accidental property of his life, but that this alone possesses the movement of life — and he places his life in this movement alone, in the augmentation of love.

Looking at his past in this life, he perceives, from the series of the conscious states which he understands, that his relation to the world has changed, that his submission to the law of reason has increased, and that the strength and scope of his love have constantly grown — giving him ever more and more happiness, independent of and sometimes directly contrary to it in proportion to the decrease of the personal existence.

Such a man, having received his life from a past that is invisible to him, and recognizing its constant and unbroken growth, transfers it also to the unseen future, not only calmly, but also joyfully.

It is said: sickness, old age, infirmity, relapse into childhood, are annihilation of the consciousness and of the life of man.

For what sort of man?

I imagine to myself, according to tradition, John the Divine fallen into childishness from old age. According to tradition, he merely said: "Brethren, love one another." The old man of a hundred years, who can hardly move, mumbles, with tearful eyes, ever the same words: "Love one another." In such a man the animal existence hardly flickers — it is all devoured by new relations to the world, by a new existence which has not yet succeeded in establishing itself in the fleshly man.

For a man who understands life as lying in that in which it really does lie, to speak of the decrease of his life in sickness and old age, and to grieve over this, is the same as though a man, on approaching the light, were to bewail the decrease in his darkness in proportion to the nearness of his approach to the light. And to believe in the destruction of one's life because the body is destroyed is the same as believing that the destruction of the shadow of an object, after that object has stepped into the full light, is a sure sign of the destruction of the body itself. Such conclusions could be drawn only by a man who has gazed so long upon the shadow alone that he has at last come to imagine that it is the object itself.

But for the man who knows himself, not by his reflection in an existence defined by time and space, but by his growth in a loving relation toward the world, the destruction of the shadow of the conditions of time and space is merely the token of a greater degree of light. The man who, understanding his life as that certain special relation to the world with which he entered into existence, and which has grown in his life by the augmentation of love, believes in his annihilation, is on a level with the man who, being acquainted with the external and visible laws of the world, believes that his mother found him under a cabbage-leaf, and that his body will suddenly fly off somewhere so that nothing will remain of it.

CHAPTER XXX

THE LIFE OF DEAD MEN IS NOT ENDED IN THIS WORLD

But even more plain does the superstition about death become, I will not say when looked at from another side, but according to the very constitution of life as we know it. My friend, my brother, has lived precisely like myself, and he has now ceased to live like me. His life has been his consciousness, and it has been passed under the conditions of his bodily existence; that is to say, there is no place or time for the manifestation of his consciousness, and he does not exist for me. My brother has been, I have had relations with him, but now he is not, and I shall never know where he is.

"All bonds between him and us are broken. He does not exist for us, and, in like manner, we shall not exist for those who remain behind. What is this if not death?" So speak the people who do not understand life.

These people see, in a visible suspension of external communication, an indubitable proof of actual death.

But on no occasion does the visionary character of the conception of death more clearly and more visibly disappear than on the suspension of the fleshly existence of people who are near to us. My brother is dead; what has happened? That has happened which is accessible to my observations in time and space; the manifestation of his relation to the world has disappeared from before my eyes, and nothing has been left behind.

"Nothing has been left behind," — thus would speak a chrysalis, a cocoon, which had not yet released the butterfly, on seeing that the cocoon lying beside it has been left empty. But the cocoon might say this if it could think and speak, because, on losing its neighbor, it would, in reality, no longer feel it in any way. It is not thus with man. My brother has died; his cocoon, it is true, has been left empty. I do not see him in the form in which I have hitherto seen him, but his disappearance from my vision has not destroyed my relations to him. I retain, as the expression goes, a remembrance of him.

A remembrance remains, — not a remembrance of his hands, his face, his eyes, but a remembrance of his spiritual form.

What is this remembrance? such a simple and comprehensible word as it seems! The forms of crystals and animals disappear, — no remembrance of them remains among crystals and animals. But I retain a remembrance of my friend and brother. And this remembrance is all the more vivid in proportion as the life of my friend and brother was more in conformity with the law of reason, and in proportion as it revealed itself more greatly in love.

This recollection is not merely a representation, but this recollection is something of a sort which acts on me, and acts precisely as the life of my brother did during the period of his earthly existence. This memory is that same invisible, immaterial atmosphere of his which encompassed his life and acted upon me and upon others during his earthly existence, exactly as it acts upon me after his death. This remembrance demands of me now, after his death, the same that it demanded of me during his lifetime.

And this is not all; this recollection has become more obligatory for me since his death than it was during his life. That force of life which resided in my brother has not only not vanished nor suffered diminution, but has not even remained the same; it has increased, and acts more powerfully upon me than before.

The force of his life after his death in the flesh has the same action as before his death, or an even more powerful one, and acts like every truly living thing.

On what grounds can I, feeling in myself that power of life, precisely what it was during the existence in the flesh of this brother, *i.e.* as his relation to the world, which has elucidated to me my relation to the world, assert that my dead brother has no longer life? I can say that he has quitted that lower relation to the world in which he stood as an animal, and in which I still find myself,—and that is all; I can say that I do not see the new center of relation to the world in which he now stands; but I cannot deny his life, because I am conscious of its power upon me. I have gazed in the reflecting surface upon the way in which a man holds me; the reflecting surface has grown dim. I no longer see how he holds me, but I feel in all my being that he still holds me as before, and hence that he exists.

But this is not all; this life of my dead brother, which is invisible to me, not only acts upon me, but enters into me. His special, living *ego*, his relation to the world, becomes my relation to the world. In the establishment of his relation to the world, he elevates me, as it were, to that step to which he has himself risen, and that succeeding step to which he has already ascended, vanishing from my vision, but drawing me with him, becomes clearer to me, to my special, living *ego*. Thus I am conscious for myself of the life of that brother who has fallen asleep in the death of the flesh, and, therefore, I cannot doubt it. But by observing the action in the world of this life which has disappeared from my sight, I am still more indubitably convinced of the reality of this life which has passed beyond the reach of my eyes. The man is dead, but his relation to the world continues to act upon men, and not even as during life, but in a vast number of times more powerfully, and this action is heightened, and grows like every living thing, in proportion to its wisdom and love, never ceasing, and knowing no suspension.

Christ died a very long time ago, and His existence in the flesh was brief, and we have a clear idea of His person in the flesh; but the power of His wisely loving life, His relation to the world, and no one else's, acts to the present day upon millions, who receive His relation to the world into themselves, and live accordingly. What is it that acts? What is it that was formerly bound up with the existence of Christ in the flesh, and which constitutes the continuation and the growth of this same life of His? We say that it is not the life of Christ, but its results. And, having uttered these words, utterly destitute of meaning, it seems to us that we have said something clearer and more definite than that this power is the living Christ Himself.

But this is exactly the way in which ants might talk who are clustered about an acorn that has grown up and become an oak; the acorn has sprung up and become an oak, and it tears up the soil with its roots, drops branches, leaves, and fresh acorns; it screens from the light, the rain, completely changes everything that formerly grew around it. "This is not the life of the acorn," say the ants, "but the results of its life, which came to an end when we dragged off the acorn and threw it into a hole."

My brother died yesterday, or a thousand years ago, and the same force of his life which acted during his existence in the flesh continues to act still more powerfully on me and on hundreds, thousands, millions of people, in spite of the fact that the center of the power of his temporary existence in the flesh, which was visible to me, has disappeared from my sight.

What does this mean?

I have seen the light of grass burning before me.

This grass has been extinguished, but the light has only increased; I do not see the cause of this light, I do not know what is burning, but I may infer that the same fire which consumed the grass is now consuming the distant forest, or something else which I cannot see.

But the light is such that I not only see it now, but it alone guides me and gives me life. I live by this light. How can I deny it?

I may think that the power of this life has now another center, invisible to me. But deny it I cannot, because I feel it. I live and move in it. What this center, what this life is in itself, I cannot know — I can guess, if I like guessing, and if I am not afraid of becoming entangled. But if I am in search of a rational comprehension of life, I content myself with the clear and indubitable, and I do not wish to spoil the clear and indubitable by combining with it obscure and arbitrary surmises. It is enough for me to know that all that by which I live has been formed from the life of those who have lived before me, and of men who have died long since, and that, hence, every man who fulfils the law of life, submitting his animal personality to reason, and manifesting the power of love, has lived and does live in other people after the disappearance of his corporeal existence, — in order that the clumsy and alarming superstition of death should never again torment me.

We can also observe this in people who have left behind them a force which continues to act, because these people, having submitted their personality to reason and yielded up their lives to love, could never doubt, and have not doubted, the possibility of the annihilation of life.

In the life of such people we can also find the grounds of their faith in life everlasting; and then penetrating into our own life we can find these grounds in ourselves Christ said that He would live after the disappearance of the semblance of life. He said this because already, during the period of His corporeal existence, he had entered upon that true life which cannot end. Already, during the time of his corporeal existence, he lived in the rays of the light from that other center of life, to which he was going, and during his lifetime he saw how the rays of that light illuminated the people about him. The same thing is seen by every man who renounces his personality and lives a rational, loving life.

However contracted may have been the sphere of man's activity, — whether he be Christ or Socrates, a good, obscure, self-sacrificing old man, a youth, a woman, — if he lives, renouncing his personality, for the happiness of others, he already enters here, in this life, upon that new relation to the world which is the business of this life for all men.

The man who has placed his life in subjection to the law of reason, and the manifestation of love, already beholds in this life, on one side, the rays of light from that new center of life toward which he is traveling, and, on the other, the action which this light, passing through him, produces upon those about him. And this gives him an unwavering faith in the impossibility of the decrease of life, in its immortality and in the eternal augmentation of life. It is impossible to receive faith from any one, it is impossible to convince one's self of immortality. In order to have faith in immortality it is necessary that the latter should exist; and in order that the latter should exist, it is necessary to understand one's life in that in which it is immortal. Only he can believe in a future life who has performed his work of life, who has established in that life that new relation to the world which does not, as yet, find a place in the world.

CHAPTER XXXI

THE SUPERSTITION OF DEATH ARISES FROM THIS, THAT MAN CONFOUNDS HIS DIFFERENT RELATIONS TO THE WORLD

YES, if we look upon life in its true significance, it becomes difficult even to understand by what the terrible superstition of death is supported.

Thus, if you examine that which has frightened you in the dark as a phantom, you can never again, by any means, revive that visionary fear.

The fear of losing that which alone is, arises only from the fact that life appears to man not only in the relation of his mental consciousness to the world, which is known to him, but invisible, peculiar to him, but also in two relations which are unknown, though visible to him: that of his animal consciousness and that of his body to the world. All that exists presents itself to man: (1) as the relation of his rational consciousness to the world; (2) as the relation of his animal consciousness to the world; and (3) as the relation of the matter of his body to the world. Not understanding that the relation of his rational consciousness to the world is his sole life, man imagines his life as still lying in the relation of his animal consciousness to the world, and he is afraid of losing his special relation of rational consciousness to the world, when in his personality the former relations of his animal person and of the matter which constitutes him, to the world, shall have been destroyed.

To such a man it appears that he proceeds from the movement of matter passing to the stage of a personal animal consciousness. It seems to him that this animal consciousness passes into rational consciousness, and that afterward this rational consciousness grows weak, passes back again into the animal, and that the animal finally weakens and passes into the dead matter from which it was derived.

But the relation of his rational consciousness to the

world seems to him, from this point of view, something accidental, unnecessary, perishable. From this point of view it seems to him that the relation of his animal consciousness to the world cannot perish — that his animal will be continued in his species; that the relation of matter to the world cannot be annihilated in any way, and is eternal; but that the most precious thing — his rational consciousness — is not only not eternal, but is merely a gleam of something unnecessary and superfluous.

And man feels that this cannot be. And therein lies the fear of death. In order to save themselves from this fear, some men try to convince themselves that their animal consciousness is their rational consciousness, and that the immortality of the animal man, that is to say, of his race, satisfies the demand for the immortality of the rational consciousness, which they bear within them. Others try to convince themselves that a life which has never previously existed, which suddenly reveals itself in corporeal form, and vanishes in it, will rise again in the flesh and live. But belief in either is impossible for men who do not recognize life as residing in the relation of the rational sense to the world. It is evident to them that the continuation of the human race does not satisfy the ever recurring demand for the immortality of one's individual *ego;* and the idea of a life which begins again includes in itself an idea of a suspension of life, and if life never existed formerly, has not always existed, then it cannot exist afterward.

For both classes of men, the earthly life is a wave. From dead matter a person is developed, from the person a rational consciousness, the crest of the wave; having risen to their height, the waves, rational consciousness and individuality, fall back in the same place from which they started, and are annihilated. Human life is the visible life for both classes. Man has grown up and matured and died, and after death there can be nothing for him, — that which is after him and from him remains; neither posterity nor its deeds can satisfy him. He pities *himself,* he fears the cessation of *his* life.

That this life of his, which has begun here on earth in his body, and which has here come to an end — that this life will revive again of itself he cannot believe.

Man knows that if he has not existed before, and if he has made his appearance from nothing, and has died, that he, his special person, will never exist longer, and that it cannot exist. Man recognizes the fact that he will not die only when he has recognized the fact that he has never been born, that he always has existed, does exist, and always will exist. Man will believe in his immortality only when he comprehends that his life is not a wave, but is that eternal movement which in this life reveals itself only as a wave.

It seems to me that I shall die, and my life will come to an end, and this thought tortures and frightens me because I am sorry for myself. And what will die? For what do I feel compassion? What am I from the ordinary point of view? First of all, I am flesh. What then? Am I afraid for that, am I sorry for that? It seems not: my body, matter, can never be lost anywhere, not a single particle of it. Hence, this part of me is secure; there is nothing to fear for this part. All will be preserved in its entirety.

But no, people say, that is not what I pity. I pity Lyeff Nikolaevitch, Ivan Semyonitch. But no one is any longer what he was twenty years ago, and every day he is a different person. How then do I pity myself? No, they say, that is not it; I do not pity that. I pity my consciousness, my *ego*.

But this consciousness of yours has not always been one, but it has been several; it was one thing a year ago, it was something still more different ten years ago, and utterly different still earlier. As far back as you can remember, it has kept on changing; does your present consciousness please you so greatly that you are so sorry to lose it?

If it had always been the same in you, then one could understand this; but it has done nothing but change. You do not see and cannot find its beginning, and, all of a sudden, you desire that there shall be no end to it, that this consciousness now existing in you shall exist forever. You have been moving on ever since you can remember. You came into this life you yourself know not how, but you know that you came as that special *ego* which you are, and then moved on and on until you have reached the half-way point, and, all of a sudden, you do not exactly rejoice or fear, but you have begun to resist, and you do not wish to stir from the spot, because you do not see what there is ahead. But neither did you see the place from which you came; but you came, nevertheless: you have entered at the entrance gate, and you do not wish to go out through the gate of exit.

Your whole life has been a progress through corporeal existence; you have advanced, you have hastened your pace, and all at once you have been seized with pity because that very thing is being accomplished which you have yourself done incessantly. The great change in your position at the death of your body is terrible to you, but the same great change took place with you at your birth, and not only did nothing bad come of it for you, but, on the contrary, so good a thing came of it that you do not wish to part with it.

What can frighten you? You say that you are sorry for yourself, with your present feelings and thoughts, with such views of the world, with your present relations to the world.

You are afraid of losing your present relation to the world. What relation is it? In what does it consist?

If it consists in your eating thus, drinking, reproducing your race, building a dwelling, dressing yourself, bearing yourself this way or that to other people and animals, then this is the relation of every man, as a reasoning animal, to life, and this relation cannot disappear; such have been, and are, and will be millions, and their posterity will be preserved as indubitably as every particle of matter. The instinct for the preservation of their race is inherent in all animals with such force, and therefore in so durable a manner, that there is no occasion to fear for it. If you are an animal, there is nothing for you to fear; and if you are matter, you are still surer of your immortality.

But if you are afraid of losing that which is not animal, you fear to lose your special rational relation to the world — that with which you entered upon this existence: but you know that this did not have its source at your birth; it exists independently of the animal, which is born, and therefore cannot be dependent upon its death.

CHAPTER XXXII

THE VISIBLE LIFE IS A PART OF THE ENDLESS MOVEMENT OF LIFE

My earthly life and the lives of all other men present themselves to me thus: —

I and every living man find ourselves in this world with a certain, well-defined relation to the world, with a certain degree of love. It seems to us at first that our life begins with this relation of ours to the world, but observation of ourselves and others shows us that this relation to the world, and the degree of love of each one of us, did not begin with this life, but were brought into life by us from a past that is concealed from us by our birth in the flesh; moreover, we see that the whole course of our life here is nothing but a never ceasing augmentation, strengthening of our love, which will never come to an end, but will only be veiled from our eyes by the death of the flesh.

Our visible life appears to me like a section of a cone, the apex and base of which are concealed from my mental vision. The narrowest portion of the cone represents my relation to the world, from which I first recognize myself; the widest part is that higher relation to life to which I have now attained. The beginning of this cone, its apex, is concealed from me in time by my birth; the continuation of the cone is hidden from me, both by my corporeal existence and by my death in the flesh. I see neither the apex of the cone, nor its base; but I recognize its nature without any doubt from that part of it in which my visible life, as it comes within my recollection, passes. It seems to me at first that this section of a cone is the whole of my life; but in proportion to the movement of my true life, I see on one hand that what constitutes the foundation of my life lies behind it, outside of its bounds; according to the measure of my life I feel more clearly and vividly my bond with my past which is visible to me.

On the other hand, I see how this foundation rests upon my future, which is invisible to me. I feel more clearly and vividly my bond with the future, and I come to the conclusion that the life which is visible to me, my earthly life, is but a small portion of my whole life, from both its ends — before birth and after death — undoubtedly existing, but concealed from my present knowl edge. And therefore the cessation of the visibility of life, after the death of the flesh, as well as its invisibility before my birth, does not deprive me of the indubitable knowledge of its existence before birth and after death. I enter life with certain ready-prepared qualities of love for the world outside of me; my corporeal existence, short or long, passes in the augmentation of this love, which I brought into life, and hence I conclude, without any doubt, that I lived before my birth, and that I shall live not only after the present moment, in which I now find myself as I meditate, but after every other moment of time, either before or after my corporeal death, as well.

Looking outside of myself at the corporeal beginnings and endings of the existence of other people (even of beings in general), I perceive that one life seems longer, another shorter; one makes its appearance earlier, and continues to be visible to me for a longer time; another makes its appearance later, and is concealed from me again very quickly; but I see in all the revelation of one and the same law, for every true life, — an increase of love, — like the broadening out of the rays of life.

Sooner or later the curtain falls, concealing from me the temporary course of the life of men, but the life of all men is one and the same, and, like every life, it has no beginning and no end. And the fact that a man has lived for a longer or a shorter time in the conditions of this existence which are visible to me cannot present any difference in his true life.

The fact that one man has taken longer to pass across the field which is open to my vision, or that another has passed quickly across it, can by no means cause me to ascribe more reality to the life of the first, or less to the second. I know beyond a doubt that if I have seen a man pass my window, whether fast or slowly, it makes no difference, — I know beyond a doubt that the man existed before the time when I saw him, and that he will continue to exist even when he has disappeared from my sight.

But why do some pass quickly, and others slowly? Why does the old man, dried up and morally hardened, incapable, according to our view, of fulfilling the law of life — the increase in love — live on, while a child, a young man, a maiden, a man in the full strength of his spiritual work, dies, passes beyond the bounds of this fleshly life, when, according to our ideas of the matter, he has only just begun to establish in himself a correct relation to life?

The deaths of Pascal and Gogol are comprehensible; but how about Chenier, Lermontoff, and thousands of other men, who, as it seems to us, had but just begun their inner labor, which might have been, as it seems, completed here?

But this only seems so to us. None of us knows anything about the foundations of life which are brought into the world by another, and about that movement of life which has taken place in him; about those obstacles to the movement of life which exist in that being; and, chief of all of those other conditions of life, possible, but unseen by us, in which, in another existence, the life of that man may be placed.

It seems to us, as we look at the blacksmith's work,

that the horseshoe is completely ready, — that it needs only a couple of blows, — but he breaks it and throws it into the fire again, knowing that it is not thoroughly smelted. We cannot know whether the work of the true life is being accomplished in a man or not. We only know this so far as we ourselves are concerned. It seems to us that a man dies when it is not necessary, but this cannot be so. A man dies only when it is indispensable for his welfare, just as a man grows up and attains to manhood only when that is necessary for his welfare.

And in fact, if by life we mean life and not its semblance, if true life is the foundation of everything, its foundation may depend upon what it produces: — the cause cannot depend upon or proceed from the result, — the course of true life cannot be destroyed by a change in its manifestation. The movement, begun but not completed, of the life of man toward that world, cannot be suspended because he has an abscess, or because bacteria attack him, or because some one shoots him with a pistol.

A man dies only because the happiness of his true life cannot be enhanced, in this world, and not because his lungs pain him, or because he has a cancer, or because a bomb has been thrown at him. It generally appears to us that to live a life in the flesh is natural, and that it is not natural to perish by fire, water, cold, lightning, sickness, a pistol, a bomb; — but it is only necessary to reflect seriously, looking from one side upon the life of men, in order to perceive that, on the contrary, it is quite unnatural for a man to live a corporeal life in the midst of these deadly conditions, in the midst of the wide-spread and, for the most part, deadly and innumerable bacteria. It is natural for him to perish.

And therefore the corporeal existence, in the midst of all these destructive conditions, is, on the contrary, something of the most unnatural sort, in a material sense. If we are alive, it is not in the least because we take care of ourselves, but because we are doing the business of life. The business of life comes to a close, and nothing can arrest any longer the never ceasing destruction of the animal life of man, — this destruction is accomplished, and one of the most intimate causes which always accompany the life of man, the death of the flesh, seems to us its exclusive cause.

Our true life exists; we know it alone; from it alone we know the animal life, and therefore, if its semblance be subjected to immutable laws, then why should not that which this semblance performs be subject to laws also?

But we are troubled because we do not see the causes and effects of our true life as we see causes and effects in external manifestations: we do not know why one person enters life with such and such properties of his *ego*, and another person with others; why the life of one is broken off, and another continues. We ask ourselves: what, before my existence, were the causes of my being born such as I am? And what will be the result after my death, of my living thus or in some other way? And we complain because we receive no answers to these questions.

But to complain because I cannot now understand much that happened before my life, and that will take place after my death, is the same as complaining because I cannot see what is beyond the limits of my vision.

For if I saw what is beyond the limits of my vision, I should not see what is within its bounds. But for the happiness of my animal, it is more necessary that I should see all that is round about me.

And it is the same with the mind, by means of which I know. If I were able to see what is beyond the range of my intellect, I should not see what is within its range. But for the happiness of my true life, it is more necessary that I should know all that to which I must submit *then* and *now* my animal personality, in order to attain the happiness of life. And my mind reveals this to me, reveals to me in this life that sole path along which I do not perceive a cessation of my happiness.

It demonstrates to me indubitably that this life did not begin with birth, but was and is always; but that happiness always exists, — demonstrates to me that the happiness of this life grows and increases here, attaining to such an extent that it cannot be contained, and only then does it pass beyond those conditions which restrict its augmentation, and pass into another existence.

Reason sets a man upon that sole path of life which, like a cone-shaped, widening tunnel, inclosed in the center on all sides by its close walls, opens to him afar off the indubitable immortality of life and its happiness.

CHAPTER XXXIII

THE INEXPLICABILITY OF THE SUFFERINGS OF THE EARTHLY EXISTENCE PROVES TO MAN, MORE CONVINCINGLY THAN ANYTHING ELSE, THAT HIS LIFE IS NOT A LIFE OF PERSONALITY, WHICH BEGAN AT HIS BIRTH AND WHICH ENDS AT HIS DEATH

But even if a man could not help fearing death, or thinking of it, the sufferings alone — fearful, aimless, utterly unjustifiable, never to be averted sufferings — to which he is subject, would be sufficient to destroy every rational idea ascribed to life.

I am engaged in a work for others which is undoubtedly good, and all of a sudden I am seized with an illness, which interrupts my undertaking and exhausts and tortures me, without any sense or reason. A screw has grown rusty on the rails, and it must needs be that on that very day when it flies out, in the very train and carriage, a good woman should be traveling,—a mother,— and it must needs be that her children should be crushed before her very eyes. In an earthquake, precisely that spot sinks on which stands Lisbon or Vyerny, and perfectly innocent people plunge headlong, alive, into the earth, and die in terrible agony. What sense is there in this? Why did this happen to these people, and why thousands of other senseless, frightful cases of suffering, which astound men?

Argumentative explanations make nothing clear. Argumentative explanations of all such phenomena always dodge the actual question, and only prove the more conclusively its insolubility. I have fallen ill because such and such microbes or other have flown to me; or the children were crushed before their mother's eyes in the train because the dampness had acted in such and such a way on the iron; or Vyerny sank because of the existence of certain geological laws. But the real question is why just these particular people were subjected to such terrible sufferings, and how I am to avoid such accidents or sufferings?

To this there is no answer. Reflection, on the contrary, plainly demonstrates to me that there are no laws according to which one man is subject, but another man is not subject to these accidents, that there is and can be none; that there is an incalculable quantity of such accidents, and therefore that whatever I do, my life is liable every second to all the innumerable chances of the most terrible suffering.

For if people drew only those deductions which inevitably follow from their view of the world, people who understand their life as a personal existence would not remain alive for a minute. Assuredly, not a single laborer would live under a master who, on hiring the laborer, should stipulate for the right, on every occasion when he should see fit, to roast the laborer alive on a slow fire, or to flay him alive, or to pull out his sinews, and in general to commit all those horrors which he perpetrates upon his laborers, in the presence of the man hiring himself, without cause or explanation.

If people really did understand life thoroughly, as they say that they do, not one of them would remain alive in this world, from pure fear of all those torturing and utterly inexplicable sufferings which they see around them, and into which they might fall at any second.

But men, in spite of the fact that they are all acquainted with various easy ways of killing themselves, of escaping from this life filled with such harsh and inconceivable sufferings, — men live on; they complain, they weep over the sufferings, and go on living.

It is impossible to say that this arises from the fact that there is more pleasure than suffering in this life, because, in the first place, not only simple reflection, but also philosophical investigations, demonstrate that all earthly life is a series of sufferings, which are far from being redeemed by its enjoyments; in the second place, we know, both from ourselves and from others, that people in positions which present nothing but a series of increasing sufferings, without any possibility of alleviation except by death itself, do not, nevertheless, kill themselves, but cling to life.

There is but one explanation of this strange contradiction: men all know, in the depths of their own soul, that all sorts of sufferings are always necessary, indispensable to the happiness of their lives, and they only go on living foreseeing them or submitting to them. But they rebel against suffering because, with their false view of life, which demands happiness only for their personality, the interference with that happiness, which does not lead to evident happiness, must appear as something inconceivable, and therefore disturbing.

And people take fright in the face of suffering, they are amazed at it, as though at some utterly unexpected and incomprehensible thing. But, at the same time, every man is reared on sufferings, his whole life is a series of sufferings undergone by him and imposed by him on other beings, and it would seem as though it were time for him to have become accustomed to suffering, and not to quail before it, and not to ask himself why and to what end his sufferings. Every man, if he will but reflect, will see that all his enjoyments are purchased by the sufferings of other beings, that all his sufferings are indispensable for his own enjoyment; that without suffering there is no enjoyment; that suffering and enjoyment are two contrary states, one being evoked by the other, and each indispensable to the other.

Then what mean the questions, "Why?" — "To

what end is suffering?" which the reasoning man puts to himself? Why does a man, who knows that suffering is bound up with enjoyment, ask himself, "Why?" — "To what end is suffering?" while he does not ask himself, "Why?" — "To what end are enjoyments?"

The whole life of the animal, and of man as an animal, is an unbroken chain of sufferings. The whole activity of the animal, and of man as an animal, is called forth only by suffering. Suffering is a painful sensation which calls forth activity, that banishes this painful sensation and calls forth a state of pleasure. And the life of the animal, and of man as an animal, is not only not suspended by suffering, but is perfected only by suffering. Suffering, therefore, is that which moves life, and hence it is what it should be; then what does man ask about when he asks: "Why and to what end is suffering?"

The animal does not ask this.

When the perch, in consequence of hunger, torments the dace, when the spider tortures the fly, the wolf the sheep, they know that they are doing what must be, and that they are accomplishing the very thing which must be fulfilled; and therefore when the perch and the spider and the wolf fall into the same torments from those stronger than they, they know, as they flee and resist and wrench themselves away, that they are doing what must be done, and therefore there cannot be the slightest doubt in them that what is happening to them is precisely that which must be so.

But a man, occupied only with the healing of his legs when they have been torn off on the battle-field, upon which he has torn off the legs of others, or occupied only in passing his time as comfortably as possible in his solitary cell in jail, after having directly or indirectly consigned others to that place, or a man who cares only for fighting himself free and fleeing from the wolves, who are rending him, after having himself slain thousands of animals and eaten them, — a man cannot regard what happens to him as what must be, because, in submitting to these sufferings, he did not do all that he should have done, and therefore it seems to him that something is happening to him which should not be.

But what should a man do, who has been torn by wolves, except flee and fight free from them? — That which it is proper for a man as a rational being to do; confess the sin which has caused suffering, repent of it, and confess the truth.

The animal suffers only in the present, and therefore the activity called forth by the suffering of the animal direct upon itself in the present fully satisfies it. But man suffers not only in the present, but he suffers also in the past, and in the future, and therefore the activity called forth by the sufferings of man, if concentrated only upon the present of the animal man, cannot satisfy him. Only activity directed to the cause as well, and to the results of suffering, both upon the past and upon the future, satisfies the suffering man.

The animal is locked in and tears himself from his cage, or his foot is sore and he licks the spot that pains him, or he devours another and rids himself of him. The law of his life is broken from without, and he concentrates his activity upon restoring it, and he fulfils that which must be. But a man — I myself or some one closely connected with me — is in prison; or I lose my legs, or some one nearly related to me loses his legs in battle, or wolves rend me: the activity devoted to flight from prison, to the healing of my legs, to fighting myself free from wolves, does not satisfy me, because confinement in prison, pain in my leg, and the being torn by wolves, constitute only a very small portion of my suffering.

I perceive the cause of my suffering in the past, in my errors and in the errors of other people, and if my activity is not directed to the cause of the suffering, to the errors, and if I do not try to free myself from it, I do not do that which should be done; and therefore suffering presents itself to me in a way in which it should not, and not only in fact but in imagination does it grow to frightful proportions, which exclude all possibility of life.

The cause of suffering for the animal is the violation of the law of animal life; this violation makes itself known by a consciousness of pain, and the activity called forth by the violation of the law is directed to the removal of the pain; the cause of pain for rational consciousness is the violation of the law of life of rational consciousness; this violation reveals itself in a consciousness of error, of sin, and the activity called forth by the violation of the law is directed to the removal of the error — the sin. And as the suffering of the animal calls forth activity directed to pain, and this activity deprives suffering of its torture, so the sufferings of a rational being call forth activity directed to error, and this activity frees suffering from its torture.

The questions, "Why?" and, "To what purpose?" which make their way into the soul of man, at the experience or the imagination of suffering, only show that man has not recognized that activity which should be called forth in him by suffering, and which frees suffering from its torture. And in fact, for the man who recognizes his life as lying in his animal existence, there can be none of that activity which frees from suffering, and the less so in proportion as he already understands his life.

When a man, who recognizes personal existence as his life, finds the cause of his personal suffering in his personal errors, he understands that he has fallen ill because he has eaten something injurious, or that he has been beaten because he himself went out to fight, or that he is hungry and naked because he would not work, — he knows that he suffers because he has done that which he should not have done, and in order that he may do so no more, and that, directing his activity to the extinction of error, he does not rebel against suffering, but bears it lightly, and often joyously.

But when such a man is attacked by suffering exceeding the bounds of the bond of suffering and error which are visible to him — as when he suffers from causes which have always existed in his own personal activity, or when the results of his suffering can be in no way advantageous either to himself or to any other person, — it seems to him that he is overtaken by that which should not be, and he asks himself: Why? to what purpose? and, finding no object upon which to direct his activity, he rebels against suffering, and his suffering is converted into terrible torture. But the greater part of man's suffering is always such that its causes or its consequences — sometimes the one, and sometimes the other — are concealed from him in space and time: hereditary diseases, unhappy accidents, bad harvests, collisions, conflagrations, earthquakes, and so on, which end in death.

The explanation that this is necessary in order to furnish a lesson for the people of the future, that they must not yield to those passions which are reflected in the diseases of their descendants, or that they must build trains better, or handle fire with more caution, — all these explanations give me no answer at all. I cannot admit that the significance of my life lies in the illustration of the oversights of other people; my life is my life, with my aspirations for happiness, and not an illustration for other lives. And these explanations are fit only for the purpose of discussion, and do not alleviate that fear in the presence of the senselessness of the sufferings which threaten me, and which exclude all possibility of life.

But even if it were possible to understand in any way that, while causing other people to suffer through my errors, I by my sufferings bear the consequences of other people's errors; if it were possible also to understand even remotely that every suffering is a punishment for an error which must be rectified by men in this life, there still remains a long series of sufferings which are in no way explicable.

Wolves rend a man who is alone in the forest, a man is drowned, frozen, or burned up, or simply falls ill alone and dies, and no one ever knows how he suffered, and there are thousands of such cases. Of what use can this be to any one?

For the man who understands his life as an animal

existence, there is not, and there cannot be, any explana tion, because, for such a man, the connection between suffering and error lies only in the manifestations which are visible to him, and this connection is utterly lost from his mental vision in the sufferings which precede death.

A man has two alternatives of choice: either, not recognizing the connection between the sufferings which he has experienced in his life, to continue to endure the greater part of his sufferings as tortures, utterly devoid of reason: or to admit that my errors and the deeds committed in consequence of them — that my sins, whatever they may be — are the cause of my sufferings, and that my sufferings are a release and redemption for my sins, and the sins of other people, whatever may be their nature.

Only these two attitudes toward suffering are possible: one, according to which suffering is that which should not exist, because I do not perceive its external significance; and the other that it is just what it should be, because I know its inward significance for my true life. The first proceeds from the recognition of the happiness of my separate, individual life as happiness. The second proceeds from the recognition as happiness of the happiness of my whole past and future life, in its unbroken connection with the happiness of other men and creatures.

According to the first view there is no explanation for sufferings, and they call forth no other activity than a constantly increasing despair and bitterness, which are not to be alleviated. According to the second, suffering evokes that same activity which constitutes the movement of true life, — a consciousness of sin, a release from error, and submission to the law of reason.

If it is not man's reason, then it is the torture of suffering which forces him, willingly or unwillingly, to confess that his life is not contained in his personality, that his personality is only the visible part of his whole life, that the external bond between cause and effect, visible to him in his personality, does not coincide with that internal bond of cause and effect which is always known to man through his rational consciousness.

The connection between error and suffering, visible to the animal only under conditions of time and space, is always clear to a man, outside of those conditions in his consciousness. Suffering of any sort, man always recognizes as the result of his sin, whatever it may have been, and repentance for his sins as a release from suffering and the attainment of happiness.

A man's whole life, from the early days of his childhood, consists in this alone: in the acknowledgment, through suffering, of sin, and in the freeing himself from error. I know that I came into this life with a certain knowledge of the truth, and that the greater have been my errors the greater have been my sufferings and the sufferings of others, — that the more I have freed myself from error, the less have been my sufferings, and the more happiness have I attained. And, therefore, I know that the greater the knowledge of the truth which I carry out of this world, and which is given me by my sufferings, even by my last sufferings which precede death, the greater is the happiness that I attain.

The torture of suffering is experienced only by the man who, having separated himself from the life of the world, and not perceiving those sins of his by which he brought his sufferings into the world, regards himself as innocent, and who, therefore, rebels against all those sufferings which he endures for the sins of the world.

And, strange to say, that very thing which is clear to the reason, mentally, is confirmed by the sole and true activity of life, by love. Reason says that a man who confesses the connection of his sins and his sufferings with the sins and sufferings of the world, frees himself from the torture of suffering; love indeed confirms this.

The half of every man's life is passed in sufferings, which he not only does not recognize as torture, and which he does not perceive, but which he regards as his happiness only because they are borne as the results of error, and as a means of alleviating the sufferings of beloved individuals. So that the less love there is, the more is man subjected to the anguish of suffering; the more love there is, the less acuteness of suffering is there; but a thoroughly rational life, whose entire activity is manifested only in love, excludes the possibility of all suffering. The anguish of suffering is only that pain which men experience on their attempt to break that chain of love to their ancestors, to their descendants, to their contemporaries, which unites the life of a man with the life of the world.

CHAPTER XXXIV

BODILY SUFFERINGS CONSTITUTE AN INDISPENSABLE CONDITION OF THE LIFE AND HAPPINESS OF MEN

"BUT, nevertheless, it is painful, it is corporeally painful. Why this pain?" men ask.

"Because this is not only necessary for us, but because we cannot live without its being painful to us," that man would answer us who has caused our pain, and has rendered it as little painful as possible, and has made as much happiness out of this "pain" as possible.

For who does not know that the very first sensation in us of pain is the first and principal means both of preserving our bodies, and of prolonging our animal life? Bodily pain protects the animal personality. And while pain serves as a protection to the personality, as is the case with the child, pain cannot be that frightful torture, such as we know pain to be, at the times when we are in the full strength of our rational consciousness and resist pain, seeing in it that which it should not be.

Pain in the animal and the child is very well defined and small in size, never attaining that degree of anguish which it reaches in beings endowed with rational consciousness. In the case of the child, we see that he sometimes cries as pitifully from the bite of a flea as from the pain which destroys the internal organs.

And the pain of a being which does not reason leaves no traces whatever in the memory. Let any man endeavor to recall his childish sufferings from pain, and he will see that he not only does not remember these, but that he is incapable of even reconstructing them in his imagination. Our impression at the sight of the suffering of children and animals is our suffering more than theirs. The external expression of suffering in unreasoning beings is immeasurably greater than the suffering itself, and hence it evokes our sympathy in a far greater degree, as can be observed in diseases of the brain, in fevers, in typhus, in all cases of death agony.

At those periods when the rational consciousness has not yet been awakened, and pain serves only as a protection to the person, it is not acute; but in those periods when there is in a man a possibility of rational consciousness, it is the means of subjugating the animal personality to the reason, and in proportion to the awakening of that consciousness does it become less and less torturing.

In reality, only when we find ourselves the complete master of our rational consciousness can we talk of sufferings, because only with this condition does life begin, and those conditions of it which we call suffering. And in this condition the sensation of pain can increase to the greatest and shrink to the most insignificant dimensions. Who, in fact, does not know, without studying physiology, that there is a limit to sensibility, that, when pain exceeds a certain point, sensibility either comes to an end in a swoon, insensibility, a fever, or that death supervenes? Hence the augmentation of pain is a very accurately defined quantity, which cannot exceed certain bounds. But the sensation of pain can be infinitely augmented by our relations to it, and in the same way it can be decreased to infinite minuteness.

We all know how a man can, by submitting to pain, by acknowledging it as what must be, reduce it to insensibility, to a sensation of joy, even, in undergoing it.

Not to mention the martyrs, not to mention Huss, who sang in the fire at the stake — simple men, merely out of a desire to exhibit their courage, endure without a cry or a quiver what are considered the most torturing of operations. There are bounds to the augmentation of pain, but to the diminution of sensation under it there is no limit.

The anguish of pain is really frightful for people who consider their lives as consisting in the existence of the flesh. And how can it fail to be terrible to them when the force of reason bestowed upon man for the annihilation of acute suffering is directed only to its augmentation?

As Plato has a myth relating how God first fixed the period of man's existence at seventy years, but afterward, on perceiving that men were the worse for it, altered it to what it now is, that is to say, arranged it so that men do not know the hour of their death, — just so surely would reason have decided upon the present state of things, the myth narrating how men were first created without sensation of pain, but that afterward it was arranged as it is for their happiness.

If the gods had created men without the feeling of pain, men would very soon have begun to beg for it; women lacking the pains of childbirth would have brought forth children under conditions where but few of them would have remained alive; children and young people would have thoroughly spoiled their whole bodies, and grown people would never have known either the errors of those who had lived before them, and of people now living, nor, what is the most important of all, their own errors, — they would not have known what they must do in this life, they would have had no rational object of existence, they could never have reconciled themselves to the idea of impending death in the flesh, and they would have had no love.

For a man who understands life as a submission of his personality to the law of reason, pain is not only not an evil, but is an indispensable condition both of his animal and of his rational life. Were there no pain, this animal personality would have no indication when it had trangressed its laws; if rational consciousness suffered no pain, man would not know the truth, would not know his own law.

"But you are talking," people retort to this, "about your personal sufferings, but how can you deny the sufferings of others? The sight of these sufferings constitutes the most acute suffering," say people not in full sincerity.

The suffering of others? But the sufferings of others — what you call sufferings — have not ceased, and will not cease. The whole world of men and animals suffers, and has never ceased to suffer. Is it possible that we have learned this only to-day? Wounds, mutilations, cold, diseases, every sort of heart-rending accident, and, chief of all, the pains of birth, without which no one of us made his appearance in this world — surely all these are indispensable conditions of existence. Surely this is the very thing the alleviation of which, the assistance of which, forms the substance of the rational life of men — the very thing upon which the true activity of life is directed.

An understanding of the sufferings of personality and of men's errors, and activity directed toward their diminution, constitutes the whole business of human life. That is just why I am a man, — an individual,— in order that I may understand the sufferings of other individuals, and that is why I am a rational consciousness, in order that in the sufferings of every other separate individual I may see the general cause of suffering — error — and may eradicate it in myself and in others. How can the material of his work be a cause of suffering to the workman? It is the same as though a plowman were to say that unplowed soil was his suffering.

Unplowed land can be a source of suffering only for him who would like to see the field plowed, but who does not consider it the business of his life to plow it.

Activity directed to the immediate loving service of the suffering and to the diminution of the general cause of suffering — error — is the only joyful labor which lies before a man, and gives him that inalienable happiness in which his life consists.

There is, for a man, but one suffering, and it is that

suffering which makes a man, voluntarily or otherwise, give himself up to that life in which there is for him the only happiness.

This suffering is the consciousness of the contradiction between my own sinfulness and all the world, and not only the possibility, but the obligation, of realizing, not by some one or other, but in my own person, the whole truth in my own life and in that of all the world.

It is impossible to alleviate this suffering, either by sharing the sins of the world, or by perceiving one's own sin, or yet by ceasing to believe not only in the possibility, but also in the duty of any one else, but in my own, to realize all truth in my life and in the life of the world. The first only augments my sufferings, the second deprives me of the force of life. Only the consciousness and activity of true life alleviate this suffering, by annihilating the disproportion between individual life and its aim, as acknowledged by man.

Voluntarily or otherwise, man must acknowledge that his life does not hedge in his person from birth to death, and that the object recognized by him is an object that can be attained, and that, in his striving toward it, in the acknowledgment of his greater and greater sinfulness, and in the greater and greater realization of all the truth in his life, and in the life of the world, consists, has consisted, and always will consist, the business of his life, which is inseparable from the life of the whole world.

If rational consciousness does not drive a man, voluntarily or involuntarily, to the only true path of life on which there are no obstacles, no evil, but only an indestructible, ever growing, never beginning, never ending happiness, then the suffering which flows from error as to the sense of his life will so drive him.

CONCLUSION

The life of man is a striving after happiness, and what he strives for — that is given to him.

Evil in the form of death and suffering is visible to man only when he takes the law of his corporeal, animal existence from the law of his life. Only when he, being a man, descends to the level of the animal, does he see death and suffering. Death and suffering breathe sighs upon him from all quarters, like bugbears, and drive him upon the one path of human life which is open to him, subservient to his law of reason, and expressing itself in love. Death and suffering are only crimes committed by man against his law of life. For a man who lives according to his law, there is no death and no suffering.

"Come unto Me, all ye that labor and are heavy laden, and I will give you rest.

"Take My yoke upon you, and learn of Me; for I am meek and lowly in heart, and ye shall find rest unto your souls.

"For My yoke is easy, and My burden is light." (Matt. xi.)

The life of man is a striving toward good; what he strives for — that is given to him; since life cannot be death, and good cannot be evil.

APPENDIX I

People generally say: "We study life, not from the consciousness of our own life, in general, but outside of ourselves." But this is the same as saying: "We look at an object, not with our eyes, in general, but outside of ourselves."

We behold the objects outside of ourselves because we see them in our eyes, and we know life outside of ourselves only because we know it in ourselves. And we see objects only as we see them in our eyes, and we define life outside of ourselves only as we know it in ourselves. But we know life in ourselves as a striving after happiness. And therefore, without a definition of life as a striving after happiness, it is impossible, not only to observe, but even to see, life.

The first and principal act of our consciousness as living beings consists in our including many different objects in our conception of one living being, and this living being we exclude from every other.

We learn that a man on horseback is not a number of beings, and is not one being, not because we observe all the parts constituting the man and the horse, but because neither in the head, nor in the legs, nor in the other parts of the man and the horse do we see that separate striving after happiness which we know in ourselves. And we know that the man and the horse are not one being, but two beings, because we know in them two separate aspirations toward good, while in ourselves we know only one.

Only from this do we know that there is life in the combination of horse and rider, because there is life in a drove of horses, that there is life in birds, in insects, in trees, in the grass. But if we did not know that the horse and the man each desired his own happiness, that each horse in the drove desired this separately, that such happiness is desired by every bird, beetle, insect, tree, and blade of grass, we should not perceive separateness in the being, and, not perceiving separateness, we could never have understood any living being; and a regiment of cavalry, and a flock, and birds, and insects, and plants, — all would be like the waves in the sea, and all the world would melt together for us into one indistinguishable movement, in which we could not by any possibility find the secret of life.

If I know that the horse and the dog and the tick that lives upon him are living beings, and if I can observe them, it is only because the horse and the dog and the tick have each their separate aims, — the aim of each being his own happiness. I know this because I know myself as an individual striving after the same happiness.

In this striving after happiness also lies the foundation of every knowledge of life. Without a confession that this striving after good, which man feels within himself, is life, and an image of all life, no study of life is possible, and no observation of life is practicable. And hence, observation begins when life is already known, and no observation upon the manifestations of life can (as it appears to scientific man) define life itself.

Men do not recognize the definitions of life in the striving toward happiness which they find in their consciousness, but they recognize the possibility of the knowledge of this striving in the tick, and on the foundation of that supposititious knowledge, founded upon nothing at all, of this happiness toward which the tick is striving, they make observations and draw deductions even as to the very existence of life.

My every conception as to external life is founded upon the knowledge of my striving toward happiness. And therefore, only through having recognized in what my happiness and my life consist, I shall be in a condition to recognize in what consist the happiness and life of other beings. But the happiness and life of other beings I cannot in any way know without having recognized my own.

Observations upon other beings, striving toward their aims which are unknown to me, constituting semblances of that happiness the striving after which I know in myself, not only can explain nothing to me, but can certainly hide from me my true knowledge of life.

For, to study life in other beings, without having a definition of one's own life is the same as describing a surrounding district without having got its center. Only after having fixed upon an immovable point as a center can the region be described. But, whatever figures we may draw, without a center there will be no surrounding district.

APPENDIX II

FALSE science, studying the manifestations which accompany life, and assuming to study life itself, by this assumption distorts the idea of life: and hence, the longer it studies the manifestations of that which it calls life, the further it gets from the idea of life, which it wishes to study.

At first mammals are studied, then the other creatures, vertebrates, fishes, plants, corals, cells, microscopic organisms, and the matter is carried to such a point that the distinction between living and non-living, between the bounds of organic and of non-organic, between the bounds of one organism and another, are lost.

It is carried to such a point that what cannot be observed seems to be the most important subject of investigation and observation. The secret of life and the explanation of everything seems to lie in comma-shaped and other bacilli, which are not visible, but which are rather assumed, which are discovered to-day and forgotten to-morrow. The explanation of everything is assumed in those beings which are contained in microscopic beings, and in those which are also contained even in these, and so forth, to infinity, as though infinite activity of the little is not the same as infinite activity of the great.

The mystery will be revealed when all the infinity of the little shall have been investigated to the end, that is to say, never. And men do not see this — the idea that the question will attain solution in the infinitely small is an indubitable proof that the question is wrongly stated. And this, the last stage of folly, — that which clearly demonstrates the utter loss of sense in the investigation, — this stage is regarded as a triumph of science; the last degree of blindness appears the highest degree of vision. Men have come to their wits' end, and have thereby clearly proved to themselves the falsity of that path along which they have been journeying; and there are no limits to their rapture. If we can only increase the power of the microscope a little more, we shall understand the conversion of the inorganic into the organic, and of the organic into the psychic, and the whole mystery of life will be laid open to us.

Men who study shadows instead of objects have entirely forgotten the object which they were studying, and, plunging deeper and deeper into the shadows, they have reached utter darkness, and rejoice because the shadow is dense.

The meaning of life is revealed in the consciousness of man as a striving after happiness. The elucidation of this happiness, the more complete definition of it, constitutes the chief aim and work of the life of all mankind, and because this labor is difficult, that is to say, not a plaything, but toil, men come to the conclusion that the definition of this happiness cannot be found in that place where it is situated, that is to say, in the rational consciousness of man, and that, therefore, it is necessary to seek it everywhere, — except where it is indicated.

This is something of the sort that a man would do who had been given an accurate list of all that he required, and who, not knowing how to read it, should fling aside the list, and inquire of every one whom he met whether they did not know what he needed; for men seek everywhere, except in the consciousness of man itself, for the definition of life, which is inscribed in the soul of man in ineffaceable letters, in his aspiration for happiness. This is all the more strange because all mankind, in the persons of its wisest representatives, beginning with the Greek saying which runs, "Know thyself," has announced it, and continues to announce it, in precisely the opposite sense. All religious teachings are nothing else than definitions of life, than strivings toward that active happiness which is accessible to man, and which cannot lead astray.

APPENDIX III

Ever more and more clearly does the voice of reason become audible to man ; ever more and more frequently does man lend an ear to this voice; and the time will come, and has already come, when this voice has grown stronger than the voice summoning to personal happiness and to delusive duty.

On the one hand, it becomes ever clearer that the life of personality, with its enticements, cannot be happiness; on the other hand, that the payment of every debt prescribed by men is only a deceit, which deprives man of the possibility of settling the sole debt of man, — to that rational and honorable origin from which he proceeds. That old delusion which demands a belief in that which has no rational explanation has already been worn out, and it is impossible to return to it.

Formerly, men said: "Do not think, but believe in the duty which we prescribe. Reason will deceive you; faith alone will disclose to you the true happiness of life." And man tried to believe, and did believe; but his relations to men proved to him that other men believe in something entirely different, and assert that this other something gives greater happiness to man. The decision of the question has become inevitable, as to which faith — out of many — is the more true; but reason alone can decide this.

Man always learns all things through his reason, and not through faith. It might be possible to deceive by affirming that he learns all things through faith, and not through reason; but as soon as man knows two faiths, and sees men confessing another faith, just as he does his own, he is placed under the inevitable necessity of deciding the matter by his reason. A Buddhist, on becoming acquainted with Mahometanism, if he remains a Buddhist, will remain a Buddhist by faith no longer, but by reason. As soon as another faith has been presented to him, and the question as to whether he is to reject his own faith, or the one offered him, — that question is inevitably settled by the reason. And if, on becoming acquainted with Mahometanism, he has remained a Buddhist, his former blind faith in Buddha is now infallibly founded on a basis of reason.

Attempts in our day to instil spiritual matters into man by faith, while ignoring his reason, are precisely the same as attempts to feed a man and ignore his mouth.

Men's intercourse with each other has proved to them that they all have a common foundation of knowledge, and men can never more return to their former errors; and the time is coming, and is even now come, when the dead shall hear the voice of the Son of God, and, hearing, shall be made alive.

It is impossible to drown that voice, because that voice is not the single voice of any one person, but the voice of all the rational consciousness of mankind, which is expressed in every separate man, and in the best men of mankind, and now already in the majority of men.

www.ingramcontent.com/pod-product-compliance
Lightning Source LLC
Chambersburg PA
CBHW020943310726
48980CB00001B/35
* 9 7 8 1 4 3 4 4 9 4 2 6 9 *